What People Are Saying about the Left Behind Series

"This is the most successful Christian-fiction series ever."
—Publishers Weekly

"Tim LaHaye and Jerry B. Jenkins . . . are doing for Christian fiction what John Grisham did for courtroom thrillers."
—TIME

"The authors' style continues to be thoroughly captivating and keeps the reader glued to the book, wondering what will happen next. And it leaves the reader hungry for more."
—Christian Retailing

"Combines Tom Clancy–like suspense with touches of romance, high-tech flash and Biblical references."
—The New York Times

"It's not your mama's Christian fiction anymore."
—The Dallas Morning News

"Wildly popular—and highly controversial."
—USA Today

"Bible teacher LaHaye and master storyteller Jenkins have created a believable story of what could happen after the Rapture. They present the gospel clearly without being preachy, the characters have depth, and the plot keeps the reader turning pages."
—Moody Magazine

"Christian thriller. Prophecy-based fiction. Juiced-up morality tale. Call it what you like, the Left Behind series . . . now has a label its creators could never have predicted: blockbuster success."
—Entertainment Weekly

APOCALYPSE CRUCIBLE

BASED ON THE BEST-SELLING
LEFT BEHIND® SERIES

BEST-SELLING AUTHOR
MEL ODOM

TYNDALE HOUSE PUBLISHERS, INC.
WHEATON, ILLINOIS

Visit Tyndale's exciting Web site at www.tyndale.com

Discover the latest about the Left Behind series at www.leftbehind.com

Author photo by Michael Patrick Brown

Written and developed in association with Tekno Books, Green Bay, Wisconsin.

Designed by Dean H. Renninger

Edited by James Cain

Published in association with the literary agency of Alive Communications, Inc. 7680 Goddard Street, Suite 200, Colorado Springs, CO 80920.

Published in association with the literary agency of Sterling Lord Literistic, New York, NY.

Library of Congress Cataloging-in-Publication Data

Odom, Mel.
    Apocalypse crucible / Mel Odom.
        p. cm. — (Apocalypse series)
    ISBN 0-8423-8776-5 (sc)
    1. Rapture (Christian eschatology)—Fiction. 2. End of the world—Fiction. I. Title.
    PS3565.D53A855 2004
    813'.54—dc22   2004000464

Printed in the United States of America

07   06   05   04
5   4   3   2   1

"Incoming!"

First Sergeant Samuel Adams "Goose" Gander heard the cry from the spotter/sniper teams he had set up along the nearby rooftops. As the warning was repeated over the radio communications system his team used, he gathered his thoughts, feeling the adrenaline slam through his system.

"All right, Rangers," Goose barked over the ear/throat headset he wore, "stand sharp."

"Standing sharp, First Sergeant," one of the nearby soldiers responded. Others chimed in, letting Goose know they had heard him. Despite the constant threat they had been under for days, all of the men stood tall and solid. They were men Goose had trained, men he had placed on special assignment, and men he had promised to die with if that should become necessary.

Goose stood behind the barricade of cars and farm equipment the Rangers had set up at the edge of the city when they had arrived in Sanliurfa two days ago. The soldiers had barely escaped an avalanche of Syrian troops—Soviet-made tanks, a horde of infantrymen, and squadrons of jet fighters.

Since then, United States military personnel as well as the remaining local citizenry had added to the barricade, using abandoned vehicles and everything else that came to hand. The military teams and the locals fighting for their homes stayed busy filling sandbags and shoring up the defenses. Sandbags filled the cracks and crevices, made machine-gun nests, and reinforced primary buildings used for defense and tactical information. For the time being, all roads south out of Sanliurfa were closed.

The Syrians were coming. Everyone knew it. Their arrival was only a matter of time. Apparently, that time was fast approaching.

Goose closed down the manpower and equipment lists he'd been reviewing on his PDA and tucked the device inside a protected pocket on his belt at his back. The low-lit LCD screen had temporarily robbed him of his full night vision, but he had to check it. A sergeant should always know where his men and materials were, and where they were needed. The PDA made that task almost doable.

He ran a practiced eye down the line of soldiers who stood at battlefield positions along the barricade. Like him, they wore the battle-dress uniforms they had worn for days. All of the BDUs showed hard use in the form of rips and tatters covered by a layer of the ever-present dirt and grit that shifted across the sun-blasted lands. Every man in the field had been under fire during the last three days.

They'd had neither the time nor supplies to allow them the luxury of rest or fresh clothing. Thankfully, they'd had plenty of socks, and Goose had seen to it that each man changed socks frequently. A foot soldier was only as good as his feet. An infantry that couldn't march was no help to an army seeking survival and was often a burden.

Goose took pride in the way his men stood at their posts despite their hardships. His unit was undermanned, underequipped, and too far away from reinforcements that wouldn't have been sacrificed on Sanliurfa anyway. Sanliurfa, the City of Prophets, was a stopgap, a strategic position that would be given up at a dear price when the time came. The American forces planned to give the outlying troops a window of opportunity, a chance to put together a counteroffensive against the Turkish juggernaut rolling up out of the south. Despite the knowledge that they were already paying a hefty blood price for something they could never hold, Goose's Rangers stood tall and proud and vigilant.

Holding his M-4A1 assault rifle in his right hand, his finger resting on the trigger guard and not on the trigger, as his father had trained him even before he'd first put on the uniform of a United States fighting man seventeen years ago, Goose trotted down the barricade line.

His left knee ached as he moved. He'd sustained the original injury years ago in a war with Iraq. The military doctors had put everything back together as best they could, declaring him fit for duty. Then, only three days ago, he'd reinjured his knee, just before the Syrian army's unprovoked attack against the Turkish army forced 3rd Battalion's 75th to retreat from the Turkish-Syrian border. During that engagement, in what Goose believed to be a completely unrelated happening, a large percentage of the world's population had disappeared without explanation.

During the last two days in Sanliurfa, he and his men had gleaned from the sporadic news coverage that the world at large was as confused about the disappearances as his troops had been when it happened. Goose, of course, had developed his own theories about what had happened. But, according to the media, several possible explanations were being advanced for the mysterious disappearances that left empty clothing in piles where men and women and children had been.

Children.

The thought of all the missing children brought a sharp pang to Goose's heart. His five-year-old son, Christopher, had been one of the children who had disappeared without a trace. So far, although the facts hadn't been confirmed, it seemed that every young child on the face of the planet had vanished.

Goose hadn't been able to say good-bye to Chris. He hadn't even known until many hours later that he had lost his young son. He could only trust that Chris was in good hands—*is in God's hands*, he desperately reminded himself—because he struggled to believe the boy was in those hands. Everything had happened so suddenly.

"Eagle One," Goose called over the headset. "This is Phoenix Leader."

"Go, Leader. You have Eagle One." The reply was crisp and confident. Eagle One was Terry Mitchell, a career man with ten years service under his belt and one of the best spotter/snipers Goose had ever worked with.

"Where away, Eagle One?"

"South-southwest."

Goose reached the end of the barricade section that sealed off the street. The barricade stretched twenty blocks, backed by everything the Rangers could cobble together for defense. Heavy cavalry in the form of M1 Abrams tanks and Bradley M2 and M3 armored personnel carriers backed the barricaded sections in strategic locations. Supporting the tanks and APCs, scattered jeeps, Humvees, and Ranger Special Operations Vehicles (RSOVs) operated as couriers for ammo and stood ready to offer quick transportation for wounded. Several of their vehicles had been lost during the Syrian border attack, and his men had appropriated anything that was running for their defense of the city.

"What do you see?" Goose started up the metal fire escape that zigzagged up the outside of the three-story apartment building that stood as the cornerstone of the barricade.

"A line of vehicles. Tanks, APCs."

"ID?"

"Confirmed, Leader. Syrian. They're flying colors and proud of them."

"Any sign of aerial support?"

"Negative, Leader."

Goose pounded up the fire escape. Despite the cortisone shots he'd been given for the pain and inflammation, he felt the weakness in his knee. The pain had dulled to bearable, but his movements felt mushy and a little uncertain. So far the limb had held beneath him. He forced himself to go on, reaching the second-floor landing and hauling himself around to continue up. "How many vehicles?"

"Thirty or forty. Maybe more. Hard to say with all the dust they're stirring up. Daybreak's an hour away. Probably get a better look then."

Unless they're in the middle of us by that time, Goose couldn't help thinking. Despite the coolness that usually came with the fading sun in the evenings, perspiration beaded on his forehead and ran down into his eyes. He knew he was running a slight fever from the inflammation in his knee. The fever, like the pain, was familiar. He often felt it when he was pushing himself too far, too fast.

But that was the pace that dealing with the Syrians required. During the last two days, the Syrian army and air force had harried them mercilessly, probing and exploring the strength of the U.S. forces' hold on the city. The battalion's primary assignment from the Joint Chiefs was to hold the line against the Syrians in Sanliurfa while the cities of Ankara and Diyarbakir resupplied and got reinforcements.

Goose switched the headset to another frequency. As first sergeant, his personal com unit came with auxiliary channels that he used to communicate with other divisions of the Ranger companies. "Control, this is Phoenix Leader."

"Go, Leader," Captain Cal Remington's smooth voice answered immediately. If he'd just been shaken from slumber, his words showed no trace of it.

"We've got movement." Goose was currently the second-ranking officer among the companies since the first lieutenant had been killed in the border clash. Remington had chosen not to fill that post and kept Goose in his present position of sovereign command after him. Goose had more years experience as a soldier than any other man in the unit—most of those years with Remington, first as a co-staff sergeant and later as first sergeant after Remington completed Officer Candidate School.

"That's what I heard. I'm on my way there. Be with you in two."

"Yes, sir," Goose replied. Only slightly winded from running full tilt up three flights of switchback stairs in full gear, he reached the rooftop landing and stayed low. He switched back to the battlefield channel. "Eagle One, this is Phoenix Leader."

"Go, Leader."

"I'm at your twenty."

"Come ahead, Leader. Heard you coming up the fire escape. Eagle Three confirmed your ID before you reached the first landing."

The thought that a sniper, even one his Rangers, had placed him in rifle crosshairs—even for the few seconds necessary to identify him—made Goose uneasy. Friendly fire wasn't, and all too often it was initiated by fatigued troops stressed to the breaking point from living in fear.

The U.S. Rangers—accompanied by remnants of the Turkish Land Forces and the United Nations Peacekeeping teams that had survived the brutal attack along the border—had lived under those conditions since they'd retreated to Sanliurfa. The Turkish army, under Captain Tariq Mkchian, and the U.N. Peacekeeping teams, led by Colonel John Stone, backed the Rangers' efforts. Those troops hadn't fared any better than Goose's own. During the last few days, Captain Remington had proven to the two commanders that the Rangers were far better suited to the urban brawl that the Syrian army was forcing upon them than their own units. It had been a long, arduous fight, Goose knew, but Remington was a man who had consistently proven he could get his way.

During the last two days, scouting units had tagged and made contact with Syrian scouts pushing into the area. With the world in chaos from all the disappearances, the Syrian government had chosen to take as much land as possible before the world returned to some semblance of the status quo.

Goose kept his head low as he hauled himself up onto the rooftop. He glanced automatically to the north, east, and west.

For the most part, Sanliurfa was dark. With the blessing of the Turkish army, Captain Remington had imposed a dusk-to-dawn curfew on the city in an effort to control the looting. So far, because Sanliurfa was going to be offered as a sacrificial lamb to the invading Syrians while defenses in Ankara and Diyarbakir to the northeast and northwest were shored up and hardened, no one in the Turkish government had seen fit to tell the United States fighting men that they couldn't die in their places.

Pockets of soft golden light marked civilians gathered around lanterns or campfires. Looters moved among them, too, a reminder that primitive impulses lurked just below the surface of most people. The fear and uncertainty those people had experienced had brought those old instincts to the forefront.

The Syrian air force had made an unexpected raid the night before that had resulted in a number of casualties. Goose could make out the darker cavities in the city where that strike had compounded the destruction of the SCUD missile strikes that had hammered Sanliurfa in the opening minutes of the undeclared war. The Syrian fighters last night had mainly targeted Sanliurfa Airport, finishing off what the SCUD attacks had started. The enemy pilots had also targeted homes and businesses, areas where the U.S. forces had gathered to relax or sleep while off duty. A third of the city lay in ruins.

Syrian snipers had kept the perimeter guards busy as well, killing nineteen more soldiers and wounding forty-three. The Rangers and marine snipers had confirmed twenty-two kills among the Syrian snipers themselves, but no one took any solace in that. Compared to U.S. casualties and the two hundred and twelve confirmed civilian lives lost to bombs, the Syrians had come out on top during that attack. Goose was pretty sure their body counts were reasonably accurate, despite the carnage from the initial air strikes. Search-and-rescue teams could tell the difference between the newly dead and the early kills because the bodies were fresh as opposed to those that had lain there decomposing since the first attack. The wounded that night numbered over eight hundred, most of those also civilian.

Before the Syrian attack, two hundred and eighty thousand people had lived in Sanliurfa. With the addition of the Ataturk Baraji Dam, named one of the Seven Wonders of the Modern World, as part of the Southeastern Anatolia Project, the city had grown by leaps and bounds. Wealth and privilege had flowed into Sanliurfa, and it was no surprise that the Syrians wanted to capture the city and create a psychological advantage in their undeclared war.

Turning his attention to the south-southeast, Goose took his 10x50 binoculars from the front pack attached to his Load Carrying

Equipment harness. He dialed in the magnification, moving the binoculars slowly to where the Syrian advance stood out against the dark horizon. They stirred up gray-brown dust clouds as they traveled. There was no mistaking the blocky lines of the Soviet-made tanks and APCs.

"Do you think this is it?" Mitchell asked. He hunkered down beside Goose and kept one hand clamped over the pencil mike of his headset so his voice wouldn't be broadcast over the com. "Do you think they're going to try to rout us tonight?"

"Not in the dark." Goose put confidence in his voice. That was part of his job as first sergeant, to make the troops believe there was never a situation he hadn't seen, never an enemy he couldn't outguess. "On a hit-and-git mission, darkness is their friend. But trying to take over an urban area filled with hostiles—they'll want the light of day."

"So what's up with this?"

"Pressure," Goose responded. "Just knocking on the door and letting us know they're still out there. This is designed to keep the kettle primed and boiling hot. They can put a few men in the field and keep this whole city awake at night."

"Still means they'll be coming soon."

"Affirmative," Goose said. Keeping the confidence of the troops also meant never lying to them.

"How far do you think they'll push it tonight?"

"As far as they can." Goose surveyed the approaching vehicles. They weren't coming with any speed, and maybe that was a good thing.

Lowering the binoculars, he glanced at the Chase-Durer Combat Command Automatic Chronograph he'd gotten as a Father's Day gift from Megan and the kids. He needed a watch in the field, and though the timepiece was an expensive one, Megan had insisted on giving it to him, telling him that she knew he took care of his gear. She also knew that he would never check the time without thinking of her and Joey and Chris.

"They're stopping," Mitchell said.

Goose glanced back up and saw that the advancing line of military armor had indeed stopped. "Spotter teams," he called over the headset.

When the spotter teams acknowledged, Goose said, "Eyes on the skies. In case this is a feint for another aerial attack."

The spotter/sniper teams affirmed the order.

"Phoenix Leader."

Goose recognized Remington's voice at once. "Go, Control. You have Leader."

"Tach Two, Leader."

"Affirmative, Control. Oracle, this is Phoenix Leader."

Oracle was the com designation for Second Lieutenant Dan Knoffler, who was next in line for command of the company after Goose. Knoffler was currently sequestered in another part of the city, ready to take over at a moment's notice if Remington and Goose were both injured or knocked out of the com loop.

Knoffler also managed the constant flow of vehicles drafted into medical service to transport civilian and military wounded to Ankara. Planes and helicopters were used only in cases of extreme emergency.

"Go, Phoenix Leader," Knoffler radioed back. He was in his mid-twenties, innocent in a lot of ways, but a dedicated warrior all the same. He'd missed the latest Iraqi war, and this action in Turkey was the first actual combat he'd seen. If he lived through the coming firefights, Goose knew the young lieutenant would grow into a command.

"You're monitoring?" Goose asked.

"Affirmative. Oracle has the sit-rep."

"Oracle has the ball," Goose said, letting Knoffler know he was going to be overseeing the city defenses for the time being.

"Affirmative. Oracle has the ball."

Goose switched channels. He stared across the harsh terrain at the line of vehicles hunched like predatory beasts in the distance. "I'm here, Captain." He stepped away from Mitchell so even his side of the conversation would remain private.

"I'm looking at Syrian heavy cavalry, Goose," Remington said.

"Yes, sir."

"Tell me why."

"Don't know, sir."

Remington was silent for a moment. "C'mon, Goose; you and I have been around the block a time or two. We've tramped through some wars in our time. What does your gut tell you?"

"The Syrians didn't show up just to remind us they're out there."

"They could have," Remington said. For years—while they'd been privates together, then corporals, and later, sergeants—they had always played the devil's advocate for each other. If one of them came up with an exercise or a combat plan, the other did his level best to tear it to shreds, looking for weaknesses. They'd always been a good team.

We just don't always agree on things, Goose reminded himself. Corporal Dean Hardin was a good case in point. Goose put that sore point away.

"No, sir," Goose said. "I don't think that's the answer."

"Then what?"

Goose looked at the line of vehicles in the distance. Even though he didn't know for sure where Remington was, he felt certain the man was watching the Syrian cav with the same anticipation he was. "They're here to make a statement, sir."

"Being out there on the horizon isn't enough?"

"No, sir," Goose answered, "not hardly. After that attack last night, they should have been content to leave us alone for a while. The local people we're trading with, sir, we know they're trading with the Syrians, too. Those traders give the Syrians information just as they give us information."

That was why traders were met at the gates and not allowed to run unsupervised throughout the city. Trading for supplies was acceptable, but allowing them access to information about the city's defenses to sell to the Syrians was out of the question. Even so, Sanliurfa was huge. Policing the whole area while managing ongoing rescue and salvage operations was impossible.

"Think maybe we should put a bird in the air, Goose?" Remington asked.

The support aircraft from the marine wing that had arrived from the 26th Marine Expeditionary Unit—Special Operations Capable MEU(SOC) out in the Mediterranean Sea had AH-1W Cobra attack helicopters in their ranks. The Whiskey Cobra was a piece of serious hardware. After seeing the marines and the Cobras in action, Goose had a healthy respect for the pilots and their machines.

"We'd be risking the helo," Goose said. "And the pilot and gunner."

"Every military action is an investment of risk," Remington countered. "Whether you advance, fall back, or wait, you're at risk."

"Yes, sir."

"So, if they're a ticking clock, everything in me wants to spring the trap."

"Yes, sir," Goose replied. "One thing my daddy always taught me about hunting in the swamps down in Waycross, Georgia, Captain: A patient hunter makes fewer mistakes than a man breaking brush just because he's a little antsy."

"Do you think I'm antsy, First Sergeant?" Remington's tone was abrupt. Despite the friendship and the working relationship they had, Goose knew there was also a certain friction between them.

Goose had chosen not to follow Remington into OCS despite Remington's best arguments in favor of the move. Having served his country for seventeen years as a noncommissioned officer—a non-com—Goose remained happy to finish out his twenty as the same. A commission meant dealing more with paper and less with people. Goose preferred the people.

"No, sir," Goose answered. "I feel the same way. It's hard to pass up a snake hole without cutting a branch and shoving it down that hole to find out if the snake is home. But the way we're set up here, sir? We're prepared to skin the snake if it was to come to us. We are not prepared to go after it."

After a brief hesitation, Remington said, "Maybe we're not ready now, but we will be."

"Yes, sir." An uncomfortable silence passed for a few minutes. Goose stood on the rooftop with his binocs to his eyes. The gentle wind out of the south brought the thin scent of possible rain and a constant barrage of dust. Nearly every meal and Meal-Ready-to-Eat Goose had eaten since arriving in Sanliurfa tasted of dust. But even the prepacked MREs had been welcome.

"Still no sat-com relays in the area?" Goose asked.

"No," Remington answered.

Only a few days before, the new Romanian president, Nicolae Carpathia, had donated use of his satellite systems to aid the United States military teams in their assessment and eventual evacuation of the border. Yesterday, Carpathia had withdrawn that support. He had decided to go speak to the United Nations to focus the world's attention on staying together on the issue of the mysterious disappearances. Syria had protested the U.S. military's use of Carpathia's satellites, saying the United States was there only to protect their own interests. According to Remington, who had somehow managed to get the Romanian president's ear, Carpathia had reluctantly agreed and withdrawn the use of the satellites.

The United States–supplied sat-relay system in place now proved barely adequate to allow communications between the U.S. forces scattered around Turkey and USS *Wasp* in the Mediterranean Sea. Captain Mark Falkirk commanded *Wasp*, the lead ship in the seven-vessel Amphibious Readiness Group. At the time of the Syrian attack, the 26th MEU(SOC) had been assigned to a 180-float in the Med.

Now Falkirk and his ships were being used as staging areas to prepare for the coming battles in Turkey if Syria didn't stand down.

A flat tone buzzed in Goose's headset. Knoffler was calling for attention. "Cap," Goose said.

"Got it," Remington replied. "Go."

Goose flipped the radio back to the primary channel.

"Go, Oracle," Remington said. "You've got Control."

Goose didn't say anything. With the Ranger captain logging on, Knoffler would know that the first sergeant was there as well.

"We've got movement, Control," Knoffler said.

"Where?" Remington asked.

Goose raked the terrain with the binocs. Gray movement slid forward from the morass of shifting dust that hovered around the Syrian cav units.

"East end," Knoffler announced.

"Got it," Remington said. "One vehicle?"

"Affirmative, Control."

"Affirmative," Goose added. "Sweep perimeter checkpoints. By the numbers."

In quick succession, the perimeter checkpoint duty officers confirmed the reported sighting of one vehicle en route to Sanliurfa. All the checkpoints on the northern side of the city confirmed there was no questionable activity.

Tension filled Goose. He always got that way before combat. Then, when the first round was fired or the first move was executed, everything inside him became unstuck and he could move again. He said a brief prayer, asking God for His help during the course of the night, praying that his men and the people they defended would get through the encounter unscathed.

Three days ago, during the retreat from the border, a pass had become impassable for a short time. While the Syrians closed in at full speed, Corporal Joseph Baker had united the men in reciting the Twenty-third Psalm. Baker had declared his faith in God, offering salvation to the men trapped on that mountain.

And in the moment before the Syrians had opened fire into the trapped military, an earthquake had split the mountain and brushed the enemy army away. The 75th had lived, and Baker had stepped into his calling among the Rangers. Whenever he wasn't on duty or helping with the wounded, Baker was witnessing to and counseling men who reached out to a faith they had never known or had somehow forgotten about.

Goose counted himself among those who had forgotten their faith in God. Wes Gander, Goose's father, had taught Sunday school in the little Baptist church they'd attended in Waycross. Goose had always been there, but he hadn't always been attentive. Now he found himself wishing he'd listened better to the lessons his father had taught.

Peering through the binocs, Goose watched the vehicle approach, picking up speed. It was an American cargo truck. A charred and tattered remnant of the flag of the United States hung from a fiberglass pole in the back. Several of the Turkish, U.N., and U.S. vehicles had been abandoned at the border because there hadn't been enough gasoline salvaged to remove them all. Many of them had been left behind, booby-trapped. This one appeared to be finding its way to them despite its fate at the border.

"Eagle One," Goose called out, knowing from experience that Remington would want him to handle moment-to-moment operations to free up the captain to see the overall picture.

"Go, Leader," Mitchell replied.

"Can you ID the driver?" Goose said. The sniper had a telescopic lens on his M-24 bolt-action sniper rifle.

"Looking, Leader."

Goose felt cold inside. Although they'd searched diligently, he knew there was every possibility they had left some wounded behind. There were over two hundred men on Turkish, U.N., Ranger, and marine MIA lists. *The Syrians wouldn't bring prisoners here just to release them.* But maybe the man was an advance scout, one who was there to convince them that the Syrians had hostages.

"One man in the cab," Mitchell said a moment later. "He's wearing one of our uniforms."

"Anyone else?" Goose asked.

"Negative."

The other spotter/sniper teams quickly confirmed the information.

Goose put the binocs away. He knelt beside the retaining wall on the rooftop and unlimbered the M-4A1. The assault rifle had telescopic sights, but they didn't have the range of the binocs. Keeping the scope on target was also problematic.

The FIRM—Floating Integrated Rail Mount—system allowed a rifleman to mount a number of optical and sighting devices. The AN/PVS-4 night-vision scope limned the world and everything in it with a green glow.

Leaning forward slightly, bracing to take the recoil of the shot if it came to that, Goose focused on the cargo truck's driver. The uniform the man wore was that of a Ranger. His face, however, remained in shadows.

"Checkpoint Nineteen," Goose called as he tracked the cargo truck's progress. "This is Phoenix Leader."

"Go, Phoenix Leader. Checkpoint Nineteen reads you loud and clear."

"Get a loud-hailer, Nineteen," Goose instructed. "Warn that truck off."

The response was immediate. "Leader, that truck could have some of our guys in it."

"Get it done, Nineteen," Goose ordered, putting steel in his voice. "If those are our people in that truck, they'll be there when we get ready to bring them in."

A moment later, the mechanical basso thunder of the checkpoint commander's voice rang out over the dark city. "Stop the vehicle! Stop the vehicle *now!*"

But the cargo truck didn't stop. In fact, the vehicle gained speed, headed directly for the barricade two blocks over.

"Sniper teams," Goose said, "bring the truck down. Leave the driver intact." Before his words died away, shots roared from the Marine Corps' .50-caliber Barrett sniper rifles as they joined the thunder of the Ranger M-24s firing on the truck.

Bullets struck sparks from the cargo truck's metal hide. The canvas over the ribbed back end flapped loose, revealing huge tears. One of the tires went flat and the truck jerked to the right.

The driver immediately corrected the truck's direction. He drove straight for the barricaded area. The truck's transmission groaned like a dying beast and the vehicle gained speed. The flat tire skidded over the rough ground and threw off chunks of rubber.

"He's not stopping!" Goose called, watching the action through the M-4A1's starlight scope. "Bring down the driver! Bring down the driver!" It was a hard decision, and it had to be made on the fly.

The truck remained on a collision course with the barricade. A split second later, the driver opened the truck door and bailed from the bucking vehicle. He hit the ground in a flurry of flying dirt. Before he'd abandoned the vehicle, the driver had evidently locked the steering wheel into position. The truck drifted a little off the approach, but remained pretty much on target.

Even as the snipers and some of the Rangers stationed along the barricade kept up a withering rate of fire, the cargo truck made contact with the heap of abandoned cars and farm equipment. The resulting explosion blew the barricade apart. Cars, tractors, sandbags, and rocks skidded and flew backward and up into the air. The cargo truck became a mass of explosions. Yellow and red flames roiled in the air, and clouds of smoke filled the immediate vicinity.

Goose went deaf with the sudden, horrific cannonade of detonations. Even two blocks away, he was blown from his kneeling position by the concussive wave. Before he could get to his feet, a smoldering corpse landed on the rooftop near him.

Then dead men rained from the sky.

Highway 111
West of Marbury, Alabama
Local Time 2118 Hours

Cold darkness swirled around navy chaplain Delroy Harte as he trudged west. He felt a constant itch between his shoulder blades. He couldn't get past the thought that something was following him, or that the thing had been following him since Washington, D.C.

Some thing. The thought stirred acid in the chaplain's stomach and made him feel queasy. Memory of the demonic being that had confronted him and nearly killed him two days ago remained as fresh as the cuts and bruises on his body from the fight he'd had with it.

As he walked, he tried to resist the impulse to look over his shoulder, because he'd done it countless times in the last few hours and seen nothing. Finally, he looked back anyway. This time, too, he scanned the long length of highway and saw absolutely nothing that he didn't expect to see. Despite the fact that the driving rain that had pounded Delroy for the last hour had abated somewhat and the drumming thunder sounded more distant, lightning still lashed the sky, the clouds still rumbled, and drizzling precipitation created a silver fog that dimmed the edges of his vision. Alabama's stormy season in early March brought rain and lightning and managed to keep a hint of winter's cold breath in the roaring winds that scoured the land.

Delroy couldn't see far because of the curtain of rain. But even though he saw nothing out of the ordinary, his nagging feeling of being followed persisted. If the *thing* from Washington, D.C., still followed him, the creature remained just beyond his line of sight. His imagination told him the thing was out there, waiting, watching, choosing its moment to strike.

Like a predator, Delroy couldn't help thinking, and he knew the assessment was dead on the money. The thing had come hunting for him in Washington, and it would have killed him if he hadn't fought it off.

Despite the long military rain slicker he wore, Delroy was drenched and chilled to the bone. His back and legs ached from hiking for miles over the past few hours. At six feet six inches tall, built broad and muscular, he had a long stride. The military had taught him how to use that stride, and his efforts ate up the distance. For the last thirty-one plus years, he'd served the United States Navy as a chaplain. He was supposed to be a role model, someone who put his faith in God and prayed for the men who put their lives on the line every day they pulled on the uniform. He had seen action all around the world, in places he had never heard of while growing up in Marbury, places he would never forget.

As a navy chaplain, Delroy could have retired at twenty-five years, or again at thirty. At twenty-five years in, he could have simply pulled the pin and known that he'd done his service by his country. In fact, he'd put in a lot more years than most. But even when his wife, Glenda, had asked him to consider taking retirement, he hadn't been able to step down from his post. Although he hadn't known why then, he now knew that he still felt the need to do his duty by his God.

And maybe because he felt the need to recover his own faith, the faith he had lost while he'd been drowning in his own pain and confusion as he ministered to his men.

Then Delroy's only son, Lance Corporal Terrence David Harte, had died in action in the Middle East. Later, at thirty years in, Delroy still didn't retire because he hadn't known what to do with himself. He couldn't imagine going home. He would have been adrift without his mission. He would have gone mad with missing his son every day. Delroy had never allowed God to quiet the pain that filled him after the loss. Delroy's grief over his son's death filled the intervening years—or emptied them. That pain had estranged him from his wife—whom he'd cherished—and from the rest of their family. He hadn't been home to see any of them in years.

Well, he was headed home now.

Hurt and despairing and confused, Delroy Harte was finally coming home. He knew he should have returned to USS *Wasp* and joined in the efforts to resupply the struggling marines and Rangers holding

Sanliurfa against the coming Syrian invasion. But once he realized what had happened all around the world, that the Rapture had taken away a huge portion of the world's population, he hadn't been able to go back to his ship. More was at stake now than Turkey. The world hung on the brink of disaster, and millions of lives—and souls— would be lost over the next seven years.

Delroy knew his own efforts to help would be insignificant in the face of the global chaos that had resulted from the Rapture. The people who had been left behind needed a man who believed in God. Delroy was not yet that man. He had questions and needed answers. He hoped God would forgive him for not being strong enough to simply believe. No, he wasn't the man the troops needed, and he had to face the possibility that he never would be again.

Delroy gazed through the darkness ahead of him. His unabated and unbearable grief had taken him far from Marbury, where he had been born and raised, where his father had preached and ministered to a small but dedicated Baptist flock. They had needed a firm and generous hand to keep them aware of the Lord.

Delroy was afraid of what he would find in Marbury. He hoped that it would be nothing at all. He prayed silently, but he knew the words that tumbled through his mind were noise to fill the empty silence in his head. For the last five years, he'd served his ships with the same kind of dazed sincerity, giving lip service to something he couldn't believe in after losing Terrence.

Guilt for those failures nearly overwhelmed him. During the last five years, there had been a number of soldiers, sailors, and marines who'd deserved better counsel than he had given them. And they had deserved better prayers, too. He should have retired, but he hadn't been able to. Still, he was being honest with himself right now: Only doubt and fear drove him on through this rainy night, not belief.

Highway 111 rose slightly again. Although Delroy couldn't discern the rise in the darkness, he felt the extra effort necessary to keep going burn through his back and calves. If he hadn't been so fatigued, he might never have felt the slightly increased strain from climbing the incline. In the beginning, he had hoped that some kind of public transit still existed in the area.

He wasn't dressed for an all-night hike, although he had made preparations for a short trek. He wore black slacks and a black turtleneck under the olive drab rain slicker marked with bright yellow stripes. All-terrain, weatherproof hiking boots covered his feet and provided an amazing amount of comfort even after the long distance he'd covered since leaving U.S. Highway 231. He carried a backpack that contained a couple changes of clothes as well as his uniform, high-energy bars, and bottled water. He knew he didn't look like a common hitchhiker.

He breathed out, clearing his lungs in a great gray gust that rolled away from him in the chill of the night, then gripped the backpack's straps to change their positions on his shoulders. The straps were cutting into his flesh, and he was so tired he hadn't noticed until his arms had started going numb. He thought about Marbury, lying only a few miles ahead of him, and tried not to let the ghosts of the life he'd led there in happier years haunt him.

Thunder cannonaded again, racing up to him like a beast breaking the cover of the wooded land to his right. He broke his stride, darting away and half turning toward the trees and brush with his hands lifted defensively before him.

He heard only the wind and the rain. Nothing lunged for his throat. He stopped to take a few breaths. It was unsettling that it was stranger to him that nothing was there than it would have been if something had come for him.

Getting tired, Delroy. You need rest. The flesh is getting weak, and—Lord, help me—your spirit gave up on you a long time back. For a moment, he considered hunkering down under one of the trees at the roadside and taking his chances that the rain wouldn't pick up again or that lightning wouldn't strike the tree.

But the fire in his belly, the knotted ball of worry and doubt and fear that churned there, wouldn't leave him. Marbury and the horrible truth that lay there pulled him on. He turned his face toward the rain and started walking again. After standing just that short time, his boots felt leaden.

The low drone of a motor ate into the sound of the drizzling rain hissing like acid across the highway pavement. Delroy didn't know how long the noise had been there before he became aware of it.

Even as he recognized the chugging as the sound of an approaching vehicle, dim yellow lights chopped through the rain and the night around him. The wet pavement turned silver in front of him, becoming a two-dimensional surface that seemed fragile. His shadow stretched black and long across it, a scarecrow caricature of a man.

Hope lifted Delroy's spirits as he turned to face the vehicle coming slowly down the highway, but the feeling ebbed away almost as soon as it appeared. Fear lingered inside him that the thing he was certain followed him could be driving the vehicle. At times, the thing had chosen to resemble a human being, which it *definitely* was not.

Anxious, Delroy stepped from the roadside, retreating to the trees that he had feared only a moment ago. Since he'd left U.S. 231, no vehicles had traveled Highway 111 in either direction. He couldn't help but be suspicious of the one that closed in on him now.

The vehicle turned out to be an ancient Chevy pickup—early fifties, Delroy guessed—with blistered paint and a sticking valve that gave the engine a distinct clatter. Ruby beams glowed from the taillights as the pickup slowed to a halt in front of Delroy.

Wooden sideboards lined the truck bed, scarred from heavy use. Yard equipment—shovels, hoes, and rakes—stood in a neat row along the starboard side, held securely by clamps. A flicker of lightning revealed the white hand-lettering against the dark green paint of the passenger-side door. LUTHER'S YARD WORK. Smaller lettering below declared BY THE JOB OR BY THE HOUR.

Weak amber console light shimmered over the ancient black man seated behind the large steering wheel. He looked small and starved, clad in bib overalls. A ragged straw hat festooned with fishing lures covered his head.

The old man stared at Delroy through the window, then leaned across the seat and cranked the glass down. Lightning flared again, showing the pink of the man's tongue and the rheumy yellow of his eyes.

"Boy," the old man said in a hoarse voice, "you plan on standing out in that there rain all night? Why, I reckon that'd be a foolish thing for a growed man to do."

"Sir?" Delroy was taken aback. Decades had passed since someone had addressed him as *boy*.

The old man crossed his wrists on the steering wheel and leaned forward. He shook his head sorrowfully. "Ain't nobody never teach you when to come in outta the rain? That was one of the first things my momma done went and taught me."

"Aye, sir," Delroy responded out of respect to the man's age.

"Come ahead on then," the old man said. "You're gonna catch your death standin' around out there in all that cold and wet."

"Aye, sir." Still a little numb with surprise, Delroy shrugged out of his backpack and approached the pickup. The saturated ground of the small incline gave way as he walked toward the road's shoulder.

The pickup's wipers moved back and forth across the windshield like an arthritic metronome. The rubber blades pushed water over Delroy.

He stood in the open doorway of the truck and tried to kick the mud from his boots. He didn't want to drag any more problems than he had to into the cab. The grime, at least, he could try to wipe off. John Lee Hooker blasted through one of his defiant, upbeat tunes on the dashboard radio, his voice seasoned by whiskey and a knowledge of heartbreak.

"Step up on in here, boy," the old man advised. "That mud you got on them boots, ol' Betsy, she's seen worse. She's a workin' gal. Ain't no gentrified lady what watches her skirts none too close." He patted the weather-cracked dashboard affectionately. "Me an' this ol' girl, why, we been together a lotta years. Gotten right comfortable with one another, we have."

Still feeling a little reluctant, Delroy swung into the vehicle. The pickup leaned hard to the passenger side as his weight hit the seat.

"My, my," the old man said, his eyes widening, "you are a big 'un."

Despite the fatigue and the tension that warred with the anxiety inside him, Delroy smiled. He'd endured comments about his size all his life. He couldn't remember a time when his size hadn't drawn attention. "Aye, sir," Delroy replied.

"Your folks must have felt plumb relieved when you left the house." The old man smiled, revealing a few yellowed teeth in his wrinkled prune of a mouth.

Delroy grinned and dropped the wet backpack on the floorboard between his feet. "Aye, sir."

"Don't keep sirring me," the old man said. "Only officers get sirred like that."

"Were you in the military?"

"Army," the man declared proudly. "Infantry in World War II. I was at Normandy."

Delroy looked at the man.

"Don't you be starin' at me, boy." The man took a tin of Prince Albert and a book of rolling papers from his top bib-overalls pocket and built a cigarette with quick, simple movements that showed a lifetime of experience. He licked the paper's edge and sealed it together to hold the tobacco. "You ain't no spring chicken your own self."

"No," Delroy agreed. "Thank you for the ride."

The old man took a lighter from his overalls, cupped his hands, and lit the cigarette. The sweet smell of tobacco flooded the pickup's interior. "Been out here long?"

"Hours. Haven't seen a soul since I left 231."

Waving the cloud of smoke from in front of his face, the man said, "Name's George." He stuck out a hand.

Delroy took the old man's hand, surprised at the strength in a hand that had gone almost fleshless with age and felt more like a bird's claw than a hand. "Says Luther on the truck."

George squinted at Delroy through the cigarette smoke that coiled restlessly inside the cab. "Luther was a friend o' mine. Up an' lost him in '91. He left me this truck. Swore her off to me while I was holdin' his hand an' he died. Only fair since I worked with him an' we paid her off together. Burned her note over at Mabel's Café in '62. 'Course, we mortgaged her now an' again to keep our business open durin' hard times. We went back to Mabel's an' burnt them notes, too. Mabel always counted on us for regular business. Me an' Luther, we lost a lotta skin from elbows an' fingers between us keepin' ol' Betsy up an' runnin'."

"Must have been quite a friend."

"He was more'n that, boy," George said. "Luther, why he was the onliest thing I had for family, time I got back from the war. Lost my daddy while I was over there, an' my momma got hit by a milk truck before I got back. I was the onliest chile they ever had."

"It's hard to lose family." Delroy settled back in the seat but had a hard time getting comfortable because a spring threatened to poke through the cover. Strips of gray duct tape appeared to be the only thing keeping the seat together.

George pulled the column shift down into low gear. The transmission groaned and whined as the gear teeth fell together. The radio crackled and spat, and John Lee Hooker faded away as B. B. King flowed from the speakers. The windshield wipers strobed across George's reversed amber reflection in the glass.

"My smokin' bother you, boy?" George put his foot on the accelerator and let out the clutch. Betsy ground grudgingly into motion.

"No." Aboard *Wasp* as well as at other posts, Delroy had gotten used to men smoking.

"Want a cigarette?"

"No, thank you."

"Only carry roll-your-owns." George shifted into second gear. The truck still felt like the makings of an avalanche gathering momentum. "If you don't know how to roll a cigarette, why, there ain't no shame in it. Be glad to roll you one."

"I don't smoke."

George looked at him again, the cigarette dangling from the corner of his mouth and ash dribbling into his gray whiskers. "You got a
name, boy?"

"Delroy."

"That your onliest name? Most folks I know gots two names."

"Harte," Delroy said. "Delroy Harte."

"I knowed some Hartes in my day. Still do. Josiah Harte, now he
was a fierce-preachin' man. Could set a congregation on fire, he
could. An' wasn't a man in town what could set at a pianer the way
that man could. He could flat tickle them ivories when he wanted."

"Aye, sir," Delroy agreed. "He could."

George nodded, remembering. "Now, Josiah, come a Sunday
morning, he'd play the Lord's music. Played it right loud and proud,
he did."

Memories threaded through the pain and confusion that paraded
through Delroy's mind. He saw his father again, standing at the pulpit, hammering home a message to his parishioners; taking a lazy father and husband to task for drinking up the family's rent and food
money; working in the garden he kept behind the church.

"But come Saturday," George said with a grin, "why, Josiah would
sometimes show up at the domino hall an' play the pianer. All us rep-
robates an' no-accounts, like me an' Luther when they wasn't no yard
work to be done, we knew the price we's gonna have to pay for
listenin' to them sweet blues. After he got through layin' out the hot-
test licks he could, after he sung Muddy Waters an' Robert Johnson
an' Lightnin' Hopkins, why then he'd commence to preachin' an'
savin' souls."

"Must have been something to see," Delroy said. He knew his father had gone down to the domino hall in town where the old men
gathered, but he'd never gone along. Now he wished he had.

"Yes, siree," George said enthusiastically. "It were something to
see. You favor him some, Delroy. You kin?"

"Josiah was my father."

George smiled. "I remember you now. The roundball player."

Delroy nodded. "That's right." He'd gone to college on a basketball scholarship and had been headed straight to the NBA. Then his
father had . . . died. Even with Glenda at his side, it had taken a year
and more to figure out what he was going to do with his life.

A somber look painted George's withered features. "He was a
good man, Delroy. An' he was a hard man to lose, him bein' so young
an' the way he died an' all."

Delroy couldn't speak. He still remembered the night he'd been told of his father's death. He'd been at college, at basketball practice, with thoughts only of slipping over to see Glenda afterwards. Delroy's mother had made the call, strong and broken all at the same time.

"They never did find the man what killed him, did they, boy?" George asked.

"No, sir," Delroy replied in a quiet voice. "They said they looked, but they never found him."

"A sad thing," George said. "A sad, sad thing."

Delroy nodded.

"So you comin' back home, Delroy?" George's cigarette flared bright orange in the windshield reflection as he took a draw on it.

"Aye, sir."

"Heard you's off in the military."

"The navy."

"Made a career of it, I've heard tell. Me an' Luther, why, we's glad to be shut of it after the war. Got tired of bein' told when to get up, what to do all day long, when to go to bed."

"It's not a life for everybody."

"No, sir, it ain't," George agreed wholeheartedly. "You got a wife back here, don't you?"

Shame flushed through Delroy as he wondered just how much the old man knew about him. Marbury was a relatively small community despite the racetracks there. "I do."

"Comin' back to see her?"

"Maybe," Delroy said. He supposed there was no way around that encounter. Unless she chose not to see him. And he had to admit that was possible. But he hadn't come back to see Glenda.

George was silent for a moment. Blues music continued to spin through the radio. "I hate to ask this, boy, but you been in touch with your wife?"

More guilt assailed Delroy. He hadn't called Glenda to let her know he'd gotten emergency leave from *Wasp*. With everything that was going on in Turkey, she'd have asked why he was leaving now. He couldn't have lied to her; he never could. At least, he'd never knowingly lied to her.

You told her you had faith, Delroy. You told her you believed as she believed. If that's not a lie, then what is? Delroy stared at his own reflection. His blue-black skin almost made him a shadow inside the pickup. Only his eyes, bloodshot and haunted, stood out in the soft darkness. *But maybe you aren't so guilty there. Those are also lies you told yourself.*

"No," Delroy said. "I haven't called her."

"Them phones. A lotta them are still outta whack. People gets so they depend on them so much it's terrible. Onliest reason I brought that up, you see, is 'cause a lotta folks—" he hesitated—"well . . . sir, . . . lotta folks done up and left Marbury."

"I know."

"They's left places all around the world. Seen that on the TV."

Delroy said nothing.

"One thing I been noticin'," George continued cautiously, "an' I might be wrong 'cause I been wrong about a lot of things, but I taken a good look at all them what's missing from Marbury."

"All the children," Delroy said. That fact still hurt him. If Terry had lived, if he'd gotten married as he'd intended, there might have been grandchildren by now. And if there had been, those grandchildren would have been taken.

"All the children," George agreed. "An' them growed-up folks what's missing, far as I can see, was all good folks, God-fearin' folk."

"Good folk, indeed." Delroy thought back to Master Chief Dwight Mellencamp, his best and closest friend aboard *Wasp*. Even though he had died hours before the Rapture, the chief's body had disappeared, too. Researching news stories, Delroy had discovered that bodies had disappeared from hospitals, morgues, and funeral homes. "That they were," Delroy said.

"An' Miz Glenda, she's a good 'un, too." George carefully looked at Delroy. "What I'm sayin' is that with her bein' one of the best God-fearin' women I know, could be she ain't home when you go there knockin'."

"I know." Delroy had already accepted that. In fact, he hoped Glenda *had* disappeared. He really couldn't see anything other than that happening.

"Just want you to be prepared is all," George said softly.

"I am." Delroy stared out at the misty rain still falling from the dark sky. "I don't plan on going into town just yet. If you could drop me at Henderson Road outside of Marbury, I'd be much obliged."

"Henderson Road?"

"Aye."

"Why, boy, there ain't nothing at the end of Henderson Road 'cept Sunshine Hills Cemetery."

"I know."

George took a final drag off his cigarette, then ground it out in the ashtray. "Goin' to pay your final respects?"

"Aye," Delroy answered, but he knew what he had planned—what he *had* to do—wasn't respectful at all. "And if I can, I'd like to buy one of those shovels you have."

United States 75th Army Rangers Temporary Post
Sanliurfa, Turkey
Local Time 0422 Hours

Keeping one hand on the Kevlar-lined helmet she wore, Danielle Vinchenzo hunkered down at the base of the only remaining wall of the small building where the OneWorld NewsNet team had been grudgingly allowed to set up headquarters inside Sanliurfa. Neither they nor the other media teams on-site were welcomed by the military, since the soldiers' first objective had been to move the civilians to safety. But they were tolerated. The power of the electronic media had become a recognized force in military warfare since the second war with Iraq.

But being a journalist doesn't make you invulnerable, Danielle reminded herself. The concussive *boom*s from a string of explosions a split second ago had rolled across the battle-torn city streets around her. Then a round of ammunition impacted against the building ahead of her. A shower of brick fragments peppered her back and shoulders, drumming against her Kevlar helmet.

Cezar Prodan, the young cameraman who had been assigned to her when she had accepted the job with OneWorld NewsNet three days ago, threw himself down beside her. He cursed in English and in his native Romanian tongue. His triangular goatee, coupled with his broad forehead, made him look a bit like a wide-eyed goat.

Curled up in a fetal position against the cracked and leaning wall, Gorca Bogasieru covered his head with his arms. Pale and overweight, he looked like a turtle that had pulled in its limbs to wait out certain disaster. His eyes were squeezed shut behind his round glasses. He spoke in Romanian, but Cezar quickly shouted him down. Gorca shifted his attention to Danielle. "What happened?"

Before Danielle could reply, a corpse plopped to the ground only a few feet from her.

Startled by the sudden movement and panicked by the grotesque sight, Danielle jerked back. Her head slammed into the wall behind her with enough force to blur her vision despite the helmet. When she drew in a breath, the stink of the dead soldier fallen from the sky filled her nostrils.

Hold it together, she told herself. *You're a professional reporter. An award winner. You saw worse than this when the SCUD attack hit Glitter City. More than that, Dani, you've got the inside track on the story here. Nobody else is capable of getting the kind of footage out of Turkey that you are. You've got OneWorld NewsNet backing you. Biggest communications net presently standing after all the disappearances. Get up. Get moving and do your job.*

She forced herself to look at the dead man. At first, she was chilled by the fact that only half the torso lay there. One of the dead man's arms was missing, as was half his face.

But something was wrong. Even more wrong than such a sight should be.

Then she noticed the blood. Rather, the lack of it.

If the man had died in the blast, his massive injuries should have been scarlet with freely running blood. It wouldn't even have had time to coagulate. But all she saw across his tattered uniform—and now she saw that it was a U.S. Army Ranger day camo BDU—were the dark black stains of blood from old injuries, long since clotted and dried. Dying orange embers in the uniform, leftovers from the explosion that had blasted him into their path, glowed briefly then faded.

Despite the embers, the explosion hadn't killed him. This man had already been dead when he'd been blown up. The realization almost sickened her.

A fresh wave of artillery fire lit up the night, punching holes in the dreadful silence that had fallen across the city after the series of explosions. Warning Klaxons screamed immediately after. Around her, all across the street, and up on the rooftops soldiers launched into motion. In a heartbeat, their uneasy battleground became a full-fledged war zone again.

Danielle adjusted her borrowed helmet and stood. Her knees quaked, but she kept her legs steady under her. She pushed her fear aside, telling herself again and again that she'd chosen to be here, that standing up now and reporting was all she needed to do to rocket her career into the stratosphere. That was what she had always wanted. All she had to do now was do her job and live through the fight.

She checked her satellite phone, patting the reinforced shell that protected the device from harm. According to Gorca, who worked as her technician and outfitter, that shell was proof against everything but a direct hit. After being in the field with her since the retreat from the Turkish-Syrian border and seeing the chances she took, Gorca had also felt compelled to remind her that she was not as impervious as her gear, despite the body armor the U.N. Peacekeepers had loaned her.

Cezar glanced up at her.

"Is that camera all right?" Danielle demanded.

"Yes." The young man nodded and held the camcorder protectively. "I think so."

"Get up. We've got work to do."

Looking past her, Cezar nodded at the torn corpses and body parts that lay strewn across the street. "Maybe now, maybe time not so good. Plenty time to film after attack."

Frustrated and furious, worn down from trying to get the story of the Sanliurfa's military occupation on the air in the middle of a raging battle and from controlling her own fears, Danielle reached for the young man. She knotted her fist in the bright Hawaiian shirt he wore under the Kevlar vest. He looked at her in shocked surprise. She got her balance, set her feet, and pulled him upright.

Danielle stood five feet nine inches tall in her stocking feet. She'd spent years working out at the gym to keep fit so she'd look good on camera, not to mention so she'd have the energy and stamina to keep pace with her high-pressure job. She was stronger than most men expected her to be. A lot stronger.

Cezar almost flew to his feet. A few inches shorter than Danielle, the young man was skin and bone, more emaciated than lanky. He wore his hair in dreadlocks, fastened by multicolored rubber bands. A bout with chicken pox had left his face pitted. She loosened her grip on his shirt and surveyed him critically. He hardly looked worth her effort. Still, he had a great eye when he was looking through a camera lens.

"Get that camera up and running," Danielle ordered. "I want footage shot here and now, bits that we can cycle into the live broadcast we're going to be doing in a few minutes."

"All right, all right." Cezar stripped the lens cover off and powered up the camera. A belt of batteries hung around his narrow hips. Light spewed from the camera as he started shooting. A bright oval of it fell across the soldier's corpse. With the disappearances of so many people around the world, the gloves were off when it came to broadcasting the harsh reality of the violence in Turkey. And OneWorld NewsNet had never been a media empire that felt the need to stint on the gory drama of any situation.

Empty brass cartridges suddenly rained down over Danielle and rattled against the pavement under her feet. She flattened herself against the wall and looked up, spotting the Ranger standing at the edge of the building cradling a Squad Automatic Weapon in his arms.

That's a SAW, she reminded herself, *not a Squad Automatic Weapon. Only a newbie calls them that.* Getting the military nomenclature right was important. After years of war coverage on CNN and FOX News, the world audience had become familiar with military aircraft, tanks, armored personnel carriers, and hardware. She knew a lot, but she was also aware that she was continuing to learn. She didn't want to make a mistake now.

She tapped the speed-dial function on the sat-phone and snaked the earpiece up to her ear. The phone rang once before it was answered.

"Yes?" The voice at the other end of the connection was dry as ash. The deadpan tone was uninflected, neutral, and impossible to place. The owner of the voice was a man named Radu Stolojan. At least, that was the name Danielle had come to know him by. She wasn't convinced that it was his real name, just as she wasn't convinced that the man ever needed to sleep. Whenever she called, he was there, always aware of her situation.

"This is Danielle Vinchenzo."

"Of course it is," Stolojan replied. "This *is* your appointed line." If he heard the artillery fire blasting into the city around them, he gave no indication.

"The Syrians have just attacked the city."

"I know. I watched them approach."

"And you didn't think to call?" Danielle choked back a curse. She'd been interviewing military cooks who worked to feed the armies that had gathered inside the city. The attack had caught her by surprise.

"There was no need to call," Stolojan replied smoothly. "I knew that if the Syrians chose to attack, you would know soon enough. You are in the middle of the fight, after all."

Danielle cursed as she stared at the corpses lying across the street. A rapid burst of gunfire—from a .50-caliber machine gun she guessed from the way the targets jerked back under the drumming impacts—knocked two marines from the rooftop of the building across the street. Two stories below, both men smashed against the pavement. Neither man moved. If the armor-piercing bullets hadn't killed them outright, the fall finished them off.

A trio of U.N. soldiers, distinctive in the bright blue helmets they wore, broke cover and raced out into the street. They dragged the marines back, securing holds on their load-carrying harnesses. Before they made the distance, the makeshift barricade that choked the street two blocks away and rendered it impassable to vehicles suddenly erupted. A huge rush of flames blew cars and tractors into the air while others skidded forward.

The ground shook beneath Danielle's feet. Fear spun a ball of bile into the back of her throat as she heard the metallic screeches of the barricade sliding across the broken and pitted pavement. She dodged to the building's side, flattening herself against the wall as a Volkswagen minivan wreathed in flames shuddered past her.

"Are you getting that?" Danielle yelled, turning toward Cezar. She didn't know if she could be heard over the cacophony.

If Cezar heard Danielle, he didn't respond. He knelt, camera to shoulder, and panned with the burning hulk of the Volkswagen as it roared past. A slipstream of embers and flaming pieces skipped after the vehicle. When the chips were down and the action was at its most intense, Cezar was the camera's eye.

The rescue effort by the U.N. soldiers suddenly turned into tragedy, the mass of flying debris catching and scattering them like tenpins. Fire clung to the clothing of two of them, but neither moved, and Danielle felt quite certain that neither would move again.

"Medic!" one man shouted into the headset he wore. "*Medic!*"

"Have we got satellite access?" Danielle asked over her sat-phone.

"Of course," Stolojan answered. "We are prepared to go live as soon as you begin broadcasting. I've already cleared you. Negotiations are underway even as we speak to run your piece on CNN and FOX News with a two-minute delay."

The delay was supposed to inspire dedicated news watchers to switch over to the cable stations that carried OneWorld NewsNet as an alternative to local or national news. The violence in Turkey coupled with the disappearances that had taken place almost immediately af-

terward had guaranteed OneWorld a large share of the worldwide
viewing public.

Nicolae Carpathia was—until a few days ago—a successful Romanian businessman worth millions. He owned OneWorld NewsNet.
The day the war had broken out along the Turkish-Syrian border, the
Romanian president in power at the time had stepped down from office and named Carpathia as his successor. In addition to running
several corporations, the young Romanian power broker was now
running a country.

And he is scheduled to speak to the United Nations, Danielle reminded herself. She'd wanted to cover that meeting, knowing that—
given the current situation—the talks would garner global interest,
but the story of the men attempting to hold Sanliurfa against such un-
tenable odds was impossible for her to resist. She'd stuck it out in the
battle zone instead of breaking off to go to New York.

A Humvee marked with the Red Cross insignia roared down the
street. The front bumper grazed the still-burning hulk of the Volkswagen, spinning the vehicle around a little as it passed.

The Humvee's driver braked in front of the downed soldiers, providing a protective barrier between them and the open end of the
street. Before the rescue vehicle rocked to a complete stop, four field
medics leaped into action, breaking out gurneys and medkits. They
shouted at each other, sorting out the quick and the dead. Another artillery round, probably from a tank, slammed into the barricade and
threw more debris back over the street.

Danielle tapped Cezar's shoulder to get his attention.

The cameraman turned around.

"On me," Danielle instructed as she took the wireless microphone
from her jacket pocket and clipped it to her collar. She keyed the
power and tucked the earpiece into her other ear. When she ran her
finger across the microphone, she heard the rasp that told her the
mike was live. Despite the danger, she took off the Kevlar helmet and
ran her free hand through her short-cropped hair, trusting that every
strand would fall perfectly into place.

Cezar stood, brought up the camera, and focused on her.

Danielle moved so that she stood away from the shadow of the
building. The burning Volkswagen gave off enough light for her to be
clearly seen by viewers. The Humvee and the medical team could be
seen in the background, illuminated by the flaming debris that lay
scattered across the street.

"Cue live transmission," Danielle said.

"Live transmission cued," Stolojan replied. "Live in three . . . two . . . one . . . go."

Cezar focused on her, framing her from the waist up so she could signal him with her left hand out of the camera's view.

"Sanliurfa, Turkey," Danielle said in a clear voice. The collar microphone was cutting-edge technology, and Stolojan and his crew at OneWorld NewsNet headquarters cleaned up all the audio transmission as the piece went out live. "Also called the City of Prophets because of the biblical history that played out here and in the outlying lands. For generations, armies have marched and warred through these mountains and across the plains. Tonight, a remnant force made up of U.S. Army Rangers, the United Nations Peacekeeping force, and the Turkish army stand together against a common foe."

Stepping back, Danielle offered a better view of the rescue attempt by the medical team. She signaled Cezar with her left hand, letting the cameraman know to shift the focus to the struggling soldiers.

"Under siege from the Syrian army," Danielle continued, "these troops have faced hardship after hardship. Only last night an air strike rocked the city, destroying buildings and supply warehouses and killing hundreds of citizens. These brave warriors have stood ready to defend the town against a ground attack. Now that attack is here."

Artillery rockets lanced across the sky in the distance. Long tails of bright fire trailed them. Less than a moment later, the shells fell amid the city again.

Danielle waited until the rolling thunder passed. She had learned through hard experience that the attacks often came in waves. Signaling Cezar, she drew his attention to her again.

"Only moments ago, the Syrians apparently launched another major offensive." Danielle pointed. "This is what remains of one of the barricades this city's defenders have erected in the hopes of holding this place."

Cezar panned from her to focus on the burning barricade. Gray smoke snaked up into the black sky. A dim yellow haze burned above the piles of rubble. An artillery shell plowed into one of the buildings, toppling the upper story down on the lower in a cascade of tumbling stone and mortar that washed out into the street.

"Prior to this attack," Danielle said, "dead American soldiers were hurled into the city by the Syrian army."

Growing braver as he lost himself in the camera work, Cezar

stepped out from cover and focused on the corpse that had nearly come down on top of them.

"These men are not new casualties of tonight's attack," Danielle announced. "The dried blood on this man's clothes is days old." She signaled for the camera to return to her. "The only place the Syrian army could have gotten dead American soldiers is from the border action that took place three days ago. The U.S. Army Rangers pride themselves on never leaving a man behind, but during the evacuation of the Turkish-Syrian border, the 75th, commanded by Captain Cal Remington, was forced by the horrific circumstances to leave their dead behind. The Syrians are using our own dead as weapons against us."

Another artillery shell crashed into the street behind her and created a huge crater. Chunks of pavement ricocheted from the nearby buildings.

"In past battles in this country," Danielle went on after the din had abated a little, "armies would lay siege to fortresses and cities. They sometimes brought the bodies of their dead foes to toss over ramparts in an effort to spread disease within the ranks of their enemies." She paused. "Tonight, there is no doubt that the Syrian army hopes to spread terror amidst the brave defenders of Sanliurfa using those same tactics."

A quick signal to Cezar alerted him again.

Danielle pointed toward the burning barricade. "Somewhere out there in that rugged, mountainous terrain, the Syrian army is marching. In interviews, Captain Remington of the 75th Rangers out of Fort Benning, Georgia, has assured viewers that his team will stand firm and that the Syrians will not be able to take Sanliurfa. Tonight, his claim is being challenged."

A fresh salvo of artillery shells slammed into the nearby buildings. Two buildings fell, tumbling in a widening rush of broken brick and shattered glass. The structures ceased to exist, becoming instead pools of debris.

Calling Cezar back to her, Danielle said, "This is Danielle Vinchenzo, reporting live from the front line in Sanliurfa, Turkey, for OneWorld NewsNet." She signaled again.

Cezar pushed the camera focus past her to the rescue operation once more; then the camera light dimmed.

"You're off the air," Stolojan announced. "Good piece. I'm sure the producers will need more footage soon."

Gunfire opened up all around Danielle. She stared at the barricade area. "I'll get it," she said. OneWorld Communications had no problem getting pushy about their news, and that was fine with her. The harder they pushed, the more she was able to get out of her team. "I take it the Syrians are on their way here?"

"Definitely," Stolojan answered.

"You've been monitoring the city?" Danielle asked.

"Yes," Stolojan assured her.

"Have you managed to keep a visual lock on Sergeant Gander?" OneWorld NewsNet's satellite resources rivaled those of most modern nations. Besides being able to broadcast live news all around the world, they also had some of the best tracking satellites in the business. The corporation's infrastructure had also seemed to be one of the most intact after the wave of mysterious disappearances had taken away a third of the world's population. She hadn't heard of any disappearances taking place within OneWorld's offices.

"Yes. We lost the sergeant for a time, but quickly turned him up again. The sergeant has primarily been with his men."

Goose Gander had become a focal point for OneWorld's stories. Since she'd first accepted the job, Danielle had been told to stay close to Goose. Valerica Hergheligiu, the woman who had informed Danielle that OneWorld Communications had bought out her contract with FOX News, had pointed out that Sergeant Gander was exactly the kind of American hero that OneWorld NewsNet wanted to stick close to. As a result, the sergeant was gaining recognition, though he didn't appear to be aware of it.

"Captain Remington, however, has been something more of a challenge," Stolojan said.

Danielle knew from her own experiences that Remington was all but impossible to keep up with. During the last two days she'd tried desperately to deal with the man. The captain willingly granted interviews, even seemed to court them, but none of the media people presently working in Sanliurfa were able to keep him in their sights when he chose to vanish.

One of the CNN reporters based in Sanliurfa had voiced the rumor that Remington was searching for a rogue CIA team within the city. Or, he said, perhaps it was a double agent that had been within the PKK, the terrorist group known as the Kurdistan Workers' Party. The story was too good to ignore, and it had been told and retold among the media, with the circumstances flipping back and forth, depending on who was telling the tale.

The selling point for the media was that the CIA might somehow have been involved with the Syrian decision to attack Turkey. If that was the case, the current war story was going to get even bigger. Chaim Rosenzweig's invention of the synthetic fertilizer had turned Israel into a veritable Eden overnight and made it into an even more dynamic economic force that had unsettled the balance of power in the Middle East. There was some suspicion on part of the Arab nations that the United States, under President Fitzhugh, had had a hand in the development of that fertilizer.

Yesterday, that CNN reporter had been found dead, his throat slit. He'd been young, convinced he was on the trail of something that would earn him a Pulitzer, and he'd taken chances by going into the rougher areas of the city where the traders and black-market dealers met. Danielle had earmarked the story to follow up on, but OneWorld had kept her busy pumping human-interest stories, such as the cooks she had been with before the attack.

"We do have Captain Remington now," Stolojan said.

"But where is Sergeant Gander?" Danielle asked.

"Two blocks east of your position. One block south. At the main barricade blocking egress from the highway."

"I'm on my way. I'll cue you when we go live. Until then, we're going to shoot some bits that I'll want to work into the story. We'll upload as we go. Get them cleaned up and I'll do voice-overs later." Danielle's mind worked furiously. She didn't know how many people comprised whatever workforce Stolojan was part of, but he seemed to have an army at his beck and call for research as well as for processing.

Staying close to the building, Danielle took the lead. Cezar and Gorca followed reluctantly.

"I heard what you said about the bodies," Cezar said. "Do you think this is why the Syrians did this? To frighten the soldiers?"

"Are you scared?" Danielle countered.

"Yes."

"Then I'd say it's working."

"I suppose."

Danielle halted at the corner leading into a narrow alley filled with debris. A rumbling noise reached her ears, one of those impossible things that happened in the lull of gunfire and mortar fire. She knew what the sound was. Even though she didn't want to, she turned toward the crashed barricade.

Dust and haze and flames filled the gap where the barricade had been at the end of the street. The Red Cross Humvee loaded the wounded and performed a U-turn just as an armored behemoth lumbered into view.

The tank was Russian-made. Danielle knew from her research that the Syrian army used primarily Soviet munitions. She didn't know if it was a T-62 or a T-72, but it was huge. The tracks gouged the street, tearing away chunks of pavement. Then the turret swiveled as the tracks locked down. The main gun took deliberate aim.

Danielle dodged around the alley corner. Realizing that Cezar was frozen, his camera resting on his shoulder as he shot footage of the tank, Danielle reached back and grabbed his shirt. "Move!" she yelled, yanking him into stumbling motion.

Gorca followed, covering his head with his hands.

The vehicle's main gun belched flame that tore away the shadows between the buildings. The blast deafened Danielle. Riding out an adrenaline spike, she tried to run down the alley and drag Cezar behind her. Her feet became entangled with his, and she stumbled over a chunk of building. She fell.

Behind her, the tank sped forward again.

Renewed fear slammed through Danielle. The occupying military force hadn't claimed their cobbled-together defenses were impenetrable. In fact, Remington had told the citizens that exactly the opposite was true.

Another round blasted from the tank. A building staggered, then fell, joining the debris on the other side of the main street.

Lying on the rubble amidst shadows too thin to offer much in the way of protection, Danielle felt certain that she was about to die. Then, ahead of her, she saw a man running toward her through the swirling fog of dust and haze.

Disheveled and wearing a torn uniform, Sergeant Goose Gander ran across the ragged piles of debris that choked the alley. He held his assault rifle in both hands across his chest. When he reached her, Goose grabbed her by her Kevlar vest and yanked her to her feet. He pushed her toward the end of the alley.

"Get out of here!" he ordered. Then he was gone, rushing headlong on an interception course with the invading Syrian tank.

Cezar started for the other end of the alley. Danielle put a hand against his chest and stopped him.

"What are you doing?" he demanded.

"Follow me," Danielle told him, starting after Goose.

"You heard the sergeant!" Cezar protested. "He told us to get out of here!"

Danielle kept moving. "The story's here, Cezar. If you don't want this job, I'm sure OneWorld can find someone else to take your place."

Cezar hesitated only a moment then followed.

Stopping at the corner, already several yards behind Goose, Danielle watched the Ranger out on the street. A gunner popped up from the turret and turned the 7.62mm light machine gun mounted there toward the first sergeant.

A row of bullets chopped into the pavement toward Goose. He never broke stride.

United States 75th Army Rangers Temporary Post
Sanliurfa, Turkey
Local Time 0427 Hours

When the Syrian soldier popped up from the T-62 tank loader's turret hatch and manned the light machine gun, Goose knew he had no choice but to continue the attack. Ducking back into the alley where he'd passed Danielle Vinchenzo and her OneWorld NewsNet team would have been impossible. He'd have slipped and fallen on the debris underfoot and been easy prey for the Syrian gunner. That fact ricocheted through his mind in a heartbeat. Grimly determined, he lengthened his stride.

"Goose, look out!" a Ranger shouted.

Already in motion and with the headset securely in place under his helmet, Goose experienced a curious Doppler effect. He heard the warning through the headset, then again from his right because the soldier was so close. The Ranger sounded familiar. Under any other circumstances, Goose felt certain he would have recognized the man's voice.

The tank continued rolling forward, leaving a widely spread set of track marks in the cracked and cratered street. Thankfully, the turret gunner had trouble bringing the machine gun to bear on Goose.

Lifting his M-4A1 assault rifle, Goose fired two three-round bursts and hoped for the best. One burst struck a flurry of sparks from the tank's armored back less than a foot from the Syrian gunner. The second tri-burst hammered into the enemy gunner's chest and popped him back over the turret.

Less than twenty yards from the tank and closing quickly, Goose said, "Tango One, this is Phoenix Leader." His breath came raggedly, tearing his words apart.

"Go, Phoenix Leader, you have Tango One."

Tango One was Lieutenant Harold Wake, the commanding officer of Charlie Company of the 75th Rangers. Charlie Company held the ground currently challenged by the Syrian push. Goose, through the extension of Captain Remington's authority, actually had command of the ranking officer. Working in the heat of battle with too few troops from too many forces made for strange chains of command.

"If I don't stop this tank, sir," Goose told the officer, feeling the shuddering weakness clawing at his knee, "you stop it."

"Affirmative, Phoenix Leader. I've got a soldier with an MPIM en route. He'll be here any second."

"Great. I gotta slow the tank at least, Tango One. Till your soldier gets here." Goose didn't want to take the chance the Syrian rolling stock would penetrate to within line of sight of the makeshift hospital.

Wake's response came back at once. "My guy will be here, Leader. You've got to get clear when he does."

"Even if I'm not . . . hospital's not far." Talking while winded came hard. "I've got a shot . . . and a plan. I'm taking it."

"Goose!" another soldier interrupted. "Gunners at the rear ob slit!"

With the shadows that filled the street under the cover of night, Goose didn't see the observation slit cut in the T-62's lower quarters at first. Then the war machine sped by the flaming wreckage of a Volkswagen minivan that had been part of the barricade. The fire lit up the oiled snouts of the submachine pistols that one or more of the tank's crew had shoved through the ob slit.

Goose stayed the course, trusting that God was watching over him now. His good friend, Corporal Bill Townsend, had been a devout Christian and had steered Goose in that direction after years of Goose's being lost in his faith and convictions. Bill had always believed that God watched over everyone, that no sparrow fell that God did not know about.

Goose still hadn't found the strength to believe as strongly as the younger man had, but he was getting there. Bill had vanished from Goose's side at the same time the air-rescue effort from USS *Wasp* had turned into a nightmare of smashed metal and broken men scattered across a barren landscape.

And his son Chris had been taken in the same wave of disappear-

ing people. That was what a quiet voice had whispered into the back
of his mind even as the battle screamed around him. With no warning, God had ripped away Goose's son with no apparent care or consideration for Megan's or Goose's pain.

Goose didn't know how he was supposed to believe in light of all
that. The sergeant settled for hoping and training to believe. Chris
was in a better place; Goose had to believe that. It was the only way he
could concentrate on saving the lives he was responsible for right
now. He pushed away the whispering voice planting doubts in his
mind. As a soldier, as a father, he had to believe.

He reached for the tank just as rapid-fire detonation from the gunners inside the vehicle popped like a string of firecrackers in his ears.
At least one of the rounds struck Goose like a sledgehammer. Thankfully, the round spent itself against his Kevlar flak jacket. The blunt
force trauma from the round was a different matter; the Kevlar spread
the impact across a greater area, but the savage power of the blow still
bruised the flesh beneath.

Staggered by pain and the force of the shot, Goose stumbled. He
pushed himself forward desperately, realizing too late that he was re-
lying heavily on his weakened knee. He held the M-4A1 in his right
hand, grabbed the tank's rear deck with his left, and managed to jam
his right boot onto the right track as it came up from the pavement.

Straining, using everything inside himself as well as the leverage
gained by leaning onto his right leg as the track swung his boot up
and provided purchase, he held on to the tank's skirting. He drove the
boot down against the whirring treads. In a heartbeat, the lunge that
had looked dismally short of his chosen objective became forward
flight with the aid of the whirring track tread. Clinging to the assault
rifle, unable to draw a breath because of the pain in his side and the
explosive movement, he fell away from the tread at the apex of the
climb and smashed against the tank's turret.

Dazed, Goose realized he lay on the tank's rear deck. He sprawled
on the surface for a moment as he regrouped. Reactive armor had
been retrofitted to the T-62. If hit by another tank round, the added
armor was designed to explode and counter the effects of the other ex-
plosives and deny penetration. Several sections hadn't been exploded, and he knew if the armor detonated beneath him it would
more than likely kill him.

"Cease fire on the tank!" Lieutenant Wake's words echoed over
Goose's headset. "Cease fire! Phoenix Leader is up there!"

Taking a deep breath, trying to get oxygen back into his lungs,

Goose stood uncertainly on the lumbering engine of destruction. He peered at the bombed-out street ahead of him, seeing several beautiful buildings that had fallen into ruin under the barrage of attacks during the last few days.

The buildings that had been set aside as hospital quarters lay only a few blocks ahead of the tank. They'd be easy prey for the T-62's upgraded 120mm main gun, and the raw weight of the war machine's forty-plus metric tons was a fearsome weapon as well. Goose had seen M-1 Abrams crews raze buildings simply by driving the tanks through them again and again, smashing walls and breaking supports till the structures fell.

Knowing he wasn't going to get hit by friendly fire helped, but Goose knew if he didn't stop the vehicle quickly, the main gun would be within range of the makeshift hospital in seconds. Once in range, the tank crew would fire on the dozens of wounded inside. None of those wounded would have a chance.

The exploding truck loaded with dead men had been a feint. During the immediate paralysis after that attack, gun crews had raked the barricaded areas and rooftops with surgical efficiency. The devastation had been as complete as if the Syrians had had a map.

Goose didn't doubt that the enemy force had just such a map. The occupying army had no control over the citizens who remained within Sanliurfa. There was every chance that the Syrians had informers planted within the city, a tactic as old as the art of war itself.

"Phoenix Leader," Remington called calmly over the headset. "This is Control."

"Go, Control," Goose responded, moving forward across the bucking tank deck.

"Leader," Remington said, "you've got a string of bogeys on the tail of the beast you went to intercept. Copy?"

Turning around, Goose stared back along the street. Four blocks away, he spotted the dim outlines of another tank rumbling through the area where the barricade had been.

"Affirmative, Control," Goose said. "I see them."

"They're making an all-out run at us," Remington said. "Going for the hospital. Probably the ammo dumps and the supplies after that."

Moving supplies around during the day had become an automatic effort. With spies and potential saboteurs in the city, the three armies comprising the defense force had had no choice about trying to protect their food stores, fuel, and munitions. That protection was noticeable to even an untrained eye. Rotating the hospital around hadn't been possible.

"I've got rolling stock headed your way," Remington said. "I've also got two Whiskey Cobras in the air. But we need to slow those machines until help can get there."

"Understood, Control."

"Stop those tanks, Leader," Remington said grimly. "Buy us some time."

Goose took a final glance back along the street. The assault on the area had been nearly complete. Buildings stood in ruins all around him. The tanks arriving in the area would have a hard time passing through the terrain before rocket launchers carried by infantrymen or on the Cobras brought them down. If he could buy some time, they might just win this thing.

But stopping the tank he was currently standing on was critical. Disabling or destroying the juggernaut of hurtling armor and artillery might bottleneck the street and provide a momentary stopgap. He started forward, climbing over the turret.

The dead Syrian's body suddenly fell out of the loader's hatch and slammed into Goose, nearly knocking him off. Before Goose could recover and bring his rifle to bear on the hatch, a man's arm reached out and pulled the hatch closed, sealing off the opening.

Goose started forward again, clambering quickly across the turret. The main gun fired again, and the sound was deafening. Goose kept his mouth open to equalize the pressure in his ears. Even then, he was mostly deaf from the detonation. The tank shivered beneath him.

On the front deck now, Goose pulled a satchel explosive from his combat gear. He'd grabbed the explosive from the munitions stores as soon as he heard the tank had penetrated the defensive line. Tracks were always the weakest areas on tread-driven armored vehicles.

Lying flat on the tank's deck, Goose primed the satchel charge for a three-second delay, held it for a quick one-thousand count, then placed the bag on the whirring right tread, praying that the explosive wouldn't immediately fall away. The links coming up from the street caught the satchel's heavy cloth and carried it back along the tread.

"Fire in the hole!" Goose yelled over the headset. He rolled to his feet and stayed low as he dove from the tank's left side. The satchel charge exploded while he was in midair.

✵ ✵ ✵

By the time Megan Gander arrived after getting the emergency phone
call about the potential suicide, the MPs had erected a loose barricade
around the Hollister home. Amber lights flickered at the tops of red-
and-white sawhorses, driving shadows back from the open areas. Soldiers stood guard outside the ropes, establishing the perimeter with
their presence and the assault rifles they carried, holding back the
neighbors but also possibly trapping the young girl inside the home.

One of the soldiers stepped forward and shone a flashlight into
Megan's face through the windshield as the wipers swept across, sluic-
ing away more of the unexpected rain. Less than an hour ago, the dark
sky had released a torrent.

"Mrs. Gander?" the soldier asked. His stance bristled with challenge and authority. Three other soldiers stood nearby to back him
up immediately if necessary. Fort Benning was on full alert.

Megan pulled up the military-issued ID she wore on a chain
around her neck and rolled down the rain-spattered window of her
husband's Chevrolet short-bed pickup. The truck smelled of Goose's
cologne. Even on the brief drive over from the base's counseling center she'd missed her husband fiercely. She still did. She wanted desperately to talk to Goose face-to-face, to feel his arms around her and
hear him telling her everything was going to be all right. And when
she wasn't thinking that, she wanted to be the one holding him because she'd heard his heart break when she'd told him that Chris was
one of the missing children.

"I'm Megan Gander," she said. Rain ricocheted from the door and
misted her face. Spring was often a rainy season in Georgia. It was
only three days since the disappearances had rocked the world and
pushed nations to the brink of nuclear disaster. Megan felt like she'd
lived through years in those few days. She was sure she wasn't alone
in that feeling.

Relief showed on the young soldier's face as he played his flashlight over the ID and matched it against the color printout in the plas-
tic-covered pouch sewn to his left forearm. Taken recently, the picture
was a good match. She wore her dark hair short so she could easily fix
it while on the go, and regular tennis and hiking with Goose while he

was on base kept her fit. Except for the clothes and the circumstances, not much had changed. Right now she wore a shapeless rain slicker over jeans and a knit shirt. The clothing was hardly professional, but it was durable enough to stand up to the demands of the eighteen- and twenty-hour days she was working in this crisis.

"Good to have you here, ma'am." The corporal put the light away. "I'm Corporal Kerby."

"You're point on this, Corporal?" Megan asked. She switched off the Chevy's engine and stepped from the vehicle. They stood in front of the residential family housing on the Ranger base.

Lightning blazed through the dark sky. Normally the stars weren't visible even on a clear night because of the light pollution from nearby Columbus, Georgia. But tonight wasn't normal. Nothing had been normal for three days.

The disappearances of some of its inhabitants had thrown the base and the city into turmoil. Not all of the power or the phones were back up. The situation was much worse in the city than it was on base. Fort Benning had fared better than Columbus because the military had backup generators.

The base currently stood on alert. Armed soldiers turned away scared citizens seeking shelter on a daily basis. Reports from base personnel still returning from the outside world, as well as television and radio news, confirmed the continued riots and looting that were sweeping the city. Some people only took advantage of the confusion to follow their baser instincts, but others reacted out of fear, trying to protect themselves and others from perceived threats and enemies. Columbus, Georgia, wasn't a safe place to be. It was also typical of the troubles in most American towns.

And Joey's out there in that, Megan couldn't help thinking. Her teenage son had gotten angry, which was nothing new in his life lately, and had left home when some of the teens Megan counseled on a regular basis showed up there. All those kids had parents or other family members who had disappeared. When word spread that Megan was still around, even more of the kids had come over to her house. She and nineteen-year-old Jenny McGrath had been busy taking care of those children for the last few days while the world tried to recover. But her only living son had run off. She needed to find him— and would as soon as the state of emergency allowed her to look. But right now she needed to deal with this emergency.

Kerby looked her in the eye. "Yes, ma'am. I'm taking point on this for the moment." Unconsciously, he glanced over his shoulder at the small house that occupied the MPs' attention. "But I'm not trained to take care of something like this." The young man was rawboned and looked tired.

"I'm sure you did fine, Corporal." Megan felt the instinctive need to reassure him. She was thirty-six, almost old enough to be his mom. She'd spent a lot more years as an adult than he had.

"Yes, ma'am. I'd like to think so." Corporal Kerby pointed his chin at the house and looked bleak. "But that's one scared little girl in there."

Megan guessed that Kerby was twenty-one or twenty-two. Leslie Hollister, the girl inside the house, was seventeen. He talked like there was a generation between them instead of a handful of years.

"You've confirmed she has a weapon?" Megan asked.

"Yes, ma'am. First thing. A member of one of our families, we're going to handle this one by the book. Private Collins, he was first man on the scene after we got the report."

Megan sorted out the details of the frantic phone call she'd received only moments ago. "Leslie had a friend with her."

"Yes, ma'am." The corporal referred to his notes, but Megan got the impression the quick look Kerby took was purely for her benefit. Securing information ranked high in standard operating procedures. "Victoria McKean. She's a member of another of the base families."

Megan remembered Tori from counseling sessions. She, like Leslie, had a history of not fitting in well with on-base military life and showing her rebellion on a regular basis. Tori had continued her sessions, though, even when Leslie had largely stepped away from them. Sergeant Benjamin Hollister was a career non-com like Goose and was currently serving over in Turkey.

If Sergeant Hollister is still there, Megan reminded herself. A consolidated list of the Rangers still in Turkey, living or dead, hadn't been compiled yet. Even when it was put together, Megan felt certain that the lists would be held as confidential and only base scuttlebutt would get the news out about who had lived, who had died, and who was among the missing. She'd felt blessed to learn that Goose was still alive, but most of that relief had fled quickly when she learned that he didn't know so many children had gone missing during the unexplained phenomenon.

"Tori's clear?" Megan asked.

"Yes, ma'am. Private Collins sequestered her in one of the MP vehicles."

"Which one?"

Corporal Kerby tapped the radio mike clipped to his left shoulder, talked briefly, then pointed at a Jeep that flashed its lights on and off twice. The lights dimmed. "There."

"I'll need to talk to her."

"Yes, ma'am." Kerby took the lead.

"Tori's parents have been notified?" Megan matched his stride.

"Yes, ma'am. Her dad is over in Turkey with the 75th. Tori's mother is at the base hospital. She's on her way over; should be here anytime. Once she found out you were involved, she said to let you talk to her daughter if you wanted to."

"I do," Megan said. "Do you know if Leslie Hollister is still alive?"

"Yes, ma'am. We've got her locked on thermographic display. She's in her bedroom."

Megan knew that thermographic capabilities enabled a soldier to track body heat through solid walls and darkness but didn't allow a clear view of the environment someone was in. "How do you know it's Leslie's room?"

"The other girl confirmed the location."

Megan folded her arms over her chest against the chilly rain sweeping in out of the night. Beyond the perimeter of the lights and the MPs, neighbors stood under eaves, porches, and umbrellas. Few of them talked to each other. Even the curiosity that normally would have filled them was lacking. It was as if the world was still holding its breath after the disappearances, waiting for the next even more horrible thing to happen.

But it's already happened, Megan thought. *They don't know it, or don't want to acknowledge it yet, but God has called His people home, and evil has been given reign over the earth.* She shivered again, but not because of the cold rain falling around her.

"Where did Leslie get the weapon?" Megan forced her mind to the present task. A girl's life hung in the balance, and she didn't know if she was physically or emotionally up to the task of trying to talk her down. Her hectic schedule during the days since the disappearances—*since Chris's abduction, and God help me for feeling that way*—weighed on her heavily, exhausted her. Almost overcome from worrying about the teen charges still left to her, she felt like a zombie, except for the sharp pain of her youngest son's absence and the uncertainty about Joey's whereabouts.

"She has a government-issued Colt .45 that belongs to her father," Kerby answered. "Sergeant Hollister registered the weapon with the Provost Marshal's office."

"You haven't seen the weapon?"

"Private Collins did, but he didn't get a good look. The Hollister girl screamed at him to leave or she would shoot him; he left. He thought it was probably the .45."

"Did Tori see the weapon?"

Kerby shook his head. Rain dripped from his helmet brim. "She saw it, but she doesn't know what it is. No familiarity with firearms. She's never taken any of the weapons classes offered on base. Not like the Hollister girl."

"Leslie Hollister has taken firearms training?"

"Yes, ma'am. Top of the class."

So Leslie knows how to use her father's pistol. That thought was as ugly and brutish as a hunk of pig iron. She knew just how ugly that was. Megan's father had blacksmithed as a hobby.

"Does Private Collins think she'd have shot him if he hadn't left the house?"

Kerby hesitated.

"There's no foul here, Corporal," Megan said. "I could ask Private Collins, but that would take time we might not have. I just want to get a feel for things before I proceed. Leslie's a juvenile. Let's worry about taking care of her first, then what impact your reports might have on her and her family."

The military was all about paperwork, Megan knew. In her job as a family counselor, she stayed enmeshed in files, forms, and follow-ups. All of those reports remained with career military men and women throughout their service. *And with their kids.*

Kerby glanced at Megan. "Private Collins was convinced she would have shot him, ma'am."

"What about Tori McKean?"

"She was glad to get out of the house."

An MP opened the door of the Jeep that had switched its lights on and off. He touched the brim of his helmet with the barrel of his assault rifle in an abbreviated salute and shone his light into the vehicle. "Mrs. Gander."

"Private," Megan replied. She glanced inside the jeep.

Tori McKean huddled in the passenger seat under a man's leather jacket. Her blonde hair, normally fussed over for hours, hung in disarray. Black mascara tracked her cheeks in thin trails from bloodshot blue eyes.

She was about the most frightened seventeen-year-old Megan had ever seen. *In the last five minutes,* she amended. Terrified kids had filled her office for the last two days.

"Tori," Megan said in a normal tone.

The girl squinted against the bright light, raising a hand to shield her streaked face. "Mrs. Gander?"

Megan closed her hand over the private's flashlight and gently pushed the light away. Getting the message, the private shut the beam off.

"That's right, Tori," Megan said. "I'm here to help." *If I can. Lord, help me help. Help me stay calm and help me think.*

"I'm afraid Leslie's going to hurt herself, Mrs. Gander."

"No." Megan kept her voice calm and firm. "We're not going to let her do that."

"I don't think you can stop her. She's not herself."

"I'm going to try." Megan reached out and took Tori's hands into her own. They were cold as ice.

"She's not herself." Tori sniffled. "It's all this . . . this . . . " She shook her head helplessly. "Nobody knows what's going on. Leslie's mom disappeared, and she doesn't know if her dad is alive or dead."

"I know. I've been talking to her privately and in group." During the last two days, there had been little opportunity for private counseling sessions. The disappearances, the outbreak of war in Turkey, and the chaos that seemed to consume the world had affected all of them. Megan had started to schedule private sessions again, but there simply weren't enough hours in the day. On top of that, half the base's counselors had gone missing.

"She's going to kill herself, Mrs. Gander." Tori clutched Megan's arms. The girl's hands knotted into white-knuckled fists. The whirling amber lights atop the sawhorses striped her face, flickering into and out of existence.

"Why?" Megan asked.

"She's confused. She's all mixed up." Tori cried and hiccupped at the same time.

With the heaviness of the rain, Megan hadn't caught the smoke stink that clung to Tori's blonde tresses. "Why is Leslie confused?"

"She just *is!*" Tori drew her hands back and wrapped her arms around herself. "Aren't you confused? I mean, you lost your little boy and everything! You can't just ignore that!"

Bright hot pain lanced through Megan. She almost turned away from the accusation in the girl's eyes. Instead, Megan mustered the strength to push the pain aside. *For right now, Chris is out of reach. Concentrate on those you can save. Right now, these girls need you.*

Megan hunkered down beside the Jeep, letting Tori have the high ground. Teens were used to adults leaning over them, browbeating them.

"You've been smoking tonight," Megan said. She kept her tone flat and deliberately neutral.

"It's incense." Tori's eyes wouldn't meet Megan's. "That's all. Just incense. Leslie was burning incense."

"That's not incense." Rain drummed against Megan's shoulders, but the slicker she wore kept her from getting drenched. Her hair, though, was a different story. She felt it plastered against her head. "You were smoking."

Tori looked like she was going to argue more, but she gave up the fight and cried like a child. "I'm sorry! I'm sorry!"

MPs had caught Tori with drug paraphernalia before. Megan knew from counseling sessions that the girl occasionally experimented with drugs.

"Was Leslie smoking, too?" Megan asked.

Tori cried and buried her face in her hands. She opened her mouth to speak but no words came out.

"Tori, you've got to talk with me. I need to know what you and Leslie were doing."

"I don't want to be in trouble," Tori cried hoarsely.

Megan cupped the girl's face in her hand. "And I don't want Leslie to hurt herself. Do you?"

Pain racked Tori's face.

"Tori, help me! Leslie's in that house with her father's pistol. She's threatened to shoot herself."

"I know." Tori took in a deep, shuddering breath. "I know. She told me she was going to shoot herself. She said she was going to shoot me, too. That's when the MP came in and got me."

Megan bridled the fear that thrummed inside her. Leslie Hollister was borderline depressive. She had great parents, but her problem was chemical, not environmental. Using drugs—something that Leslie had never done before, to Megan's knowledge—could only complicate the existing problems.

"I can smell pot in your hair," Megan said

Tori shook her head. "I don't want to be in trouble, Mrs. Gander. I swear I don't want to be in trouble. I wasn't going to do it, wasn't going to smoke anymore, but things have been so screwed up I just couldn't keep calm. I've been going to pieces on the inside. When I saw that Leslie was spazzing about everything, I thought maybe it would calm us down."

"Is pot all you were doing?"

Tori didn't answer.

Megan kept her voice gentle. "I have to know, Tori. If something goes wrong here tonight, the hospital is going to have to know. If Leslie's had something besides weed, I need to know so I can tell them."

Tears fell from the girl's eyes. She shook and quivered. "My dad is going to kill me. He is *so* going to kill me."

"Your dad isn't going to kill you," Megan said. "That's just fear talking." She knew Tori didn't believe her at the moment, but the girl had been through similar situations with her parents in the past. "You're out of there. You're safe." Megan paused. "But Leslie isn't. Help me get her out of that house and somewhere that I can take care of her."

Tori glanced at the house with teary eyes and real fear.

Megan tenderly brushed the girl's hair from her face. *God, they're all so young. How can You expect any of them to be ready to go through this?* "Tori."

Dazed, the girl looked at her.

"Help me," Megan repeated.

"We smoked some pot," Tori reluctantly admitted. "I brought some whiskey. And there was other stuff."

"What stuff?"

"Downers mostly. I thought they would mellow her out. Help her get a grip."

Except when you're a naturally depressive person, Megan thought, *they send you right through the floor.* She kept her eyes on Tori, stroking the girl's hair. "How bad is it? I have to know before I go in there."

"I thought she was going to do it, Mrs. Gander," Tori choked out. "I thought I was dead. I've never seen her like that."

"Why does she want to shoot herself?" Megan asked.

"She thinks she's dreaming." Tori's voice came out hushed and dead. "She thinks her dad's at war and her mom has disappeared because she's trapped in a nightmare. She thinks if she kills herself in the dream, she'll wake up and everything will be all right."

A gunshot blasted through the night.

Turning her head, instinctively tracking the sound, Megan knew the report had come from within the Hollister home.

United States 75th Army Rangers Temporary Post
Sanliurfa, Turkey
Local Time 0432 Hours

A gust of hot, acrid wind hammered Goose as the satchel charge exploded on the enemy tank behind him. Flames jetted harsh and bright, and for a moment he worried that he was close enough to the blast that he might catch fire. The battle roars and thunder around him evaporated, as if someone had turned the sound off. Then he realized that the detonation of the explosive had deafened him again.

Off balance, lost in the sudden war of light and dark, he hit the stone street and landed awkwardly on his left side. The impact drove the air from his lungs. Instinctively, he rolled facedown and wrapped his hands over his head, making certain his helmet remained in place as debris rained around him.

Glancing over his shoulder when the worst of the onslaught was over, Goose watched in stunned fascination as the multiton Syrian tank came up from the right side, slowly flipping like a turtle caught out on a highway. The explosion left a gaping crater in the street, and Goose knew the charge must have rotated under the tank tread at the time of detonation. Sheared and no longer a continuous belt, the loose roll of heavy links spewed forward, spilling across the battle-scarred street.

With grudging reluctance, aided by the fact that the tank's left-side track hadn't quit driving, the tank turned over onto its side. The left tread continued to spin, chewing through the street, spraying broken rock over Goose. The tank revolved, turning crossways.

Goose's hearing returned in a liquid rush that popped both ears. Someone yelled for his attention over the headset.

"Phoenix Leader! Phoenix Leader!"

Goose tried to speak then found he wasn't breathing. The impact had emptied his lungs. He forced himself up, slid his rifle around to his hands, and inhaled. Heated, sulfurous dust coated the inside of his dry mouth. His ribs protested the action even as his lungs tried to find some small measure of relief.

"Leader," Goose gasped. "Leader . . . is standing." He took another breath, this one coming easier. Pain blazed along his ribs but he didn't think any were broken. "I need your soldier with the MPIM."

The tank rocked as the left tread continued to spin. Goose knew the armored vehicle had a chance of landing right side up as much as upside down. Right side up, the tank would remain in the fight.

"Leader, this is Tango Nine," a soldier called over the headset. "I've got an MPIM, and I've got target acquisition."

The Multi-Purpose Infantry Munition system was issued to the army and the marines in 2002, replacing the AT-4 and M-72 Light Anti-tank Weapon. The AT-4s and the LAWs served as disposable, one-use-only weapons against armored vehicles and heavily fortified emplacements.

"Tango Nine," Goose said as he sprinted toward a nearby building, "you have your target. Neutralize the armor." He reached the corner of the building, put his back to the wall, and hunkered down with the M-4A1 cradled across his knees and one hand on his helmet.

"Bird's away!" Tango Nine warned.

From the corner of his eye, Goose marked the MPIM gunner's position from the weapon's ignition flare that briefly lit the Ranger dressed in full battle gear. From his position, Tango Nine had direct line of sight to the Syrian tank's guts.

Farther down the street toward the barricades, three other armored vehicles roared through the clouds of dust and layers of smoke. Muzzle flashes from the surrounding buildings marked the defenders' positions and drew enemy fire. Fifty-cal machine guns strafed the buildings and chewed holes in the walls.

The MPIM rocket slammed against the Syrian tank's undercarriage. The explosion unleashed a host of flames that enveloped the vehicle. Chunks of metal broke loose, flying into the air and streaking into the buildings and the street. The other tread didn't survive the new assault, coming apart at once and flapping with horrendous bonging noises. Propelled by the blast, the tank overturned, rocking to a halt upside down.

"Tango One," Goose called, shoving himself back into a standing position.

"Go, Leader. You've got Tango One," Lieutenant Wake replied.

"Secure that vehicle," Goose ordered.

Wake snapped orders to his unit, deploying men instantly. A half dozen Rangers abandoned their positions and rushed forward to surround the tank. They carried their rifles loose and ready, tight against their chests and muzzles down so they could swing the weapons in any direction.

"If they don't have any more fight in them," Goose instructed, "I want prisoners, Tango One." His weak knees trembled slightly under his weight and he didn't trust his legs. He wasn't sure if he could move, much less run. He locked into the side of the building to provide cover fire for the approaching troops.

"Affirmative, Leader."

Wake led the team himself. He was compact and broad-shouldered.

Goose shoved away from the building. "Control, this is Phoenix Leader."

"Go, Leader. Control reads you five by five." Remington's voice was calm and cool.

"Lead armor is down, Control. Can you confirm the number of incoming bogeys?" Goose stared through the M-4A1's open sights as he covered the Tango squad.

"Negative, Leader. I've got spotters up and active, but the smoke and dust are messing with the thermographic and IR."

The thermographic scanners read heat signatures. The infrared binoculars multiplied the available light and reduced vision to a sharply defined world of greens and blacks. Both of those enhanced-vision systems suffered when particles hung in the air. The smoke and dust generated by the explosions and the arriving vehicles guaranteed problems.

Two Syrian APCs and another tank sped along the street. The vehicles jerked and bounced as they crunched through broken debris. Two jeeps maneuvered among them, taking shelter between the larger armored vehicles.

The overturned tank's rear hatch opened and a Syrian soldier dropped through. The man landed on his head and one shoulder, rolled, and came up with an AK-47 assault rifle in his hands. Before he got a round off, two Rangers stitched him with controlled tribursts that knocked him backward.

Tank crews came with a complement of four. Two were down.

One of the Rangers barked commands for the survivors to come out with their hands up. One of the men appeared in the open loader hatch, then shoved a rifle out.

Goose knew Syrian Command would have told their men that they could expect no mercy from the Americans and United Nations soldiers after their brutal attack against Turkey. From the centuries-long struggle between the two neighboring countries, the Syrians already knew they could expect no mercy from the Turks.

Lieutenant Wake gave the order to fire. Bullets riddled the Syrian. The dead man dropped in a loose-limbed sprawl. An instant later, a sphere bounced from inside the tank.

Recognizing the threat, Goose yelled, "Grenade!"

The Ranger squad turned and broke away from the tank. The men took two strides and threw themselves to the ground, staying within the three-count. A fragmentation grenade carried a probable kill zone of fifteen meters, but most of that cleared the immediate area primarily of standing targets.

The grenade exploded. Steel shot smacked against the wall where Goose stood, cracking stone and ripping up a layer of dust and broken mortar.

"I'm hit! I'm hit!" a young Ranger yelled. Two other voices joined the first.

Goose started around the corner of the building; then he saw that the lead Syrian tank had locked down and brought its main gun to bear.

"Incoming!" someone yelled.

Taking cover again, Goose watched helplessly as the enemy fired. The last surviving member of the Syrian tank crew tried to scramble out of the vehicle during the confusion, never knowing the other one had fired. The 120mm round slammed against the overturned tank, rolling it onto the Syrian soldier who had just clambered out. The blast hammered rolling thunder between the bombed-out buildings.

The forty-ton vehicle skidded a dozen feet before it came to a stop. Long tears showed in the street where stones had ripped free.

Goose rushed forward. The Syrian tank at the other end of the street lurched into motion again. Reactive armor exploded in bright yellow and white bursts all along its back and sides, proof that the war machine drew heavy fire from defenders' guns. But even the .50-cal rounds failed to penetrate the thick hide of the snarling metal beast. The APCs and the jeeps remained in the tank's wake, letting the bigger, more protected vehicle run blocker for the attack.

A Ranger in the grenade's blast area struggled to get to his feet. Blood stained his legs. The shrapnel had struck him.

Holding his M-4A1 in his right hand, Goose ran over and caught the Ranger's BDUs in one hand and helped yank him to his feet. As the man stood briefly, Goose saw that the soldier would never make the distance under his own power. Goose squatted and threw a shoulder into the young soldier's waist, buckling the Ranger in half. With the soldier over his shoulder, Goose forced himself to stand. His injured knee trembled at the exertion, and for a moment he thought the joint might not be strong enough for the load.

God help me. I won't leave this boy out here to die. A quick glance at the Ranger's bloodied and dusty face showed that he wasn't much older than Joey, Goose's seventeen-year-old stepson.

Despite the sharp twinges of pain that felt like rat's teeth gnawing at his knee, Goose stood with his burden. He turned, ran back for the protection of the alley, and eased the wounded soldier onto the ground. Lieutenant Wake, blood glistening at his waist, grabbed another wounded Ranger by his LCE and dragged the man to cover. Shrapnel had hit the young soldier in the face and head, leaving bloody wounds. He was dazed, almost out on his feet.

"Oracle," Goose called over the headset. "This is Leader."

"Go, Leader. You have Oracle."

"I need a medevac on my twenty. I've got wounded."

"Affirmative, Leader. I've got your twenty. Medevac as soon as we're able."

"How long?" Goose sucked in deep breaths as the tank rumbled in their direction.

There was no immediate response. "As soon as they're able, Leader." The radio com operator paused, and for a moment the trained distance in the man's voice evaporated. "We're taking heavy casualties. We've got soldiers down everywhere."

Goose glanced around the corner and watched as the Syrian armored cav rolled into Sanliurfa. The Rangers were supposed to hold the city until they were relieved of duty. Now it didn't look like they would hold their positions through the night.

Brake drums from a vehicle shrilled behind Goose. Paranoid, knowing that Remington's spotters couldn't tell how far the enemy had penetrated into the city, Goose wheeled around and brought his assault rifle up.

The pickup was nearly twenty years old, an American model

Goose remembered seeing back in Waycross, Georgia. A man slid out of the door from behind the steering wheel.

A crimson flare torched the sky and brought out the urban battlefield in sharp relief. It also lit up the young driver's bruised and battered features. He was in his early twenties and looked Middle Eastern.

In spite of the man's days'-old injuries that had left faded bruises and scabs around his mouth and eyes and on his cheeks, Goose recognized him at once. *Icarus.* After only a moment's hesitation, Goose muted the mouthpiece pickup on the helmet headset. Remington had declared an interest in Icarus, and Goose knew the captain would have sent Dean Hardin or others after the agent even in the heat of battle.

The man raised his eyebrows a little, obviously surprised by Goose's choice to cut off contact with his commanding officer.

If he'd known everything about Icarus, Goose might not have cut out communications. But so far Icarus seemed content to contact him. Until Goose knew for certain what the man was up to, he was willing to delay telling Remington's knowledge of the agent's activities to preserve that tenuous relationship.

"Icarus," Goose acknowledged in a voice too low to be heard by Wake or other members of Tango squad.

Icarus grinned ruefully. "Sergeant," he said. He held his empty hands carefully away from his body.

Goose's finger rested on the outside rim of the M-4A1's trigger guard.

Icarus shrugged and glanced down at the stained and ripped United Nations uniform he wore. "With everything going on, I have to admit, I'm surprised you knew me. Still, I had to take the chance. Couldn't leave you out here. I knew you wouldn't leave your men behind."

Goose said nothing, his mind reeling from the implications of the man's appearance. Icarus remained an unknown in the mysterious events leading up to Syria's unexpected attack on Turkey. Captain Remington had taken an assignment from CIA Section Chief Alexander Cody to rescue an operative who had fallen into the ungenerous hands of the PKK, a local terrorist organization.

Abdullah Ocalan first organized the Kurdistan Workers' Party in 1974 for the purpose of creating an independent Kurdish state from land within Turkey, Iran, and Iraq. Of late, the group primarily targeted Turkey, seeking to destabilize the government through bloody attacks.

According to information Cody gave Remington, the terrorist cell Icarus had infiltrated was responsible for a failed assassination at-

tempt on Israeli statesman Chaim Rosenzweig's life. After discovering
the traitor in their midst, the terrorist organization had transported
Icarus toward Syria. Goose's mission to rescue the young agent had
triggered the frantic satellite phone call that had precipitated Syria's
no-holds-barred attack on Turkey.

Since the Rangers had pulled back into Sanliurfa, CIA agents had
searched for Icarus. Remington said the young agent had possibly gone
rogue. Corporal Dean Hardin, one of Remington's go-to men for dirty
operations, had taken point on the search for Icarus inside the city.

Only two days ago, while Goose was still reeling from Megan's
news that Chris was among the children who had disappeared, Icarus
had met Goose in a bar. While there, Icarus had revealed that two of
the CIA agents had caught up to him and he had killed them both
while escaping. Icarus also told Goose that everything that had happened—his capture and the rescue attempt—was part of a carefully designed plan. The agent had spoken of the seven years of lies and
subterfuge and unspeakable horror that remained ahead for the world.

Goose hadn't known what Icarus was talking about then, but after
attending Corporal Joseph Baker's services in the tent church these
past two days, he was finally beginning to catch on. It appeared to
Goose that they might all be caught up in something that had impacted the whole world, something that had been predicted in the Bible. Baker called those seven years the Tribulation. Icarus hadn't
called them by any name at all.

"What are you doing here?" Goose demanded.

Icarus glanced at the wounded Ranger at Goose's feet. "At the moment, I'm attempting a rescue. A medevac chopper won't get here in
time to save these men. You can't drag your wounded after you and
expect to hold a defensive line." His eyes held the sergeant's. "Then I
want to talk to you. It's time." Icarus shook his head and looked
doubtful. "It may already be too late."

"You've got one thing right. I've got to hold this line." Goose listened to the sounds of battle drawing closer.

"Then we talk. After this."

Goose wanted to shake his head. Icarus was demonstrating an un-
founded optimism regarding the current situation. As far as Goose
could see, there were no guarantees that "after" was going to happen
for him. Icarus was living on borrowed time, too.

"The CIA is still looking for you," Goose pointed out. "I've seen
Cody."

"I know. And your captain's men are looking for me." Icarus

dropped his hands to his sides. "Do what you will then. It's up to you. Help me save your men, Sergeant, or shoot me." He started forward.

Goose aimed at the center of the young agent's chest for a long, measured beat. Trapped in the war-torn city with enemies just outside the gates, Goose didn't know whom to trust. But under the open uniform jacket Icarus wore, it didn't look like he had on a Kevlar vest. Unless the agent was superhuman, a bullet through his heart would kill him.

Fear showed in the young man's eyes, but so did his determination.

Goose lowered the assault rifle and called over his shoulder. "Tango One."

"I got your back," Wake said calmly.

"Stand down," Goose said. "He's here to help with the wounded." He bent and took hold of the Ranger he'd dragged to safety. With Icarus's help, they muscled the wounded young soldier into the back of the pickup.

Wake's Tango squad gave up four more men. One was already dead, and another didn't look like he would survive the trip to the hospital. But Goose refused to abandon any of the men. That retreat from the border when they'd left so many dead behind still hurt his warrior's spirit.

Icarus clambered back into the pickup. "Want a ride, Sergeant?"

A 120mm round impacted against a building on the other side of the street. The structure swayed for a moment, then crashed down in a loose tumble of rock. A few of the stones slammed against the pickup and narrowly missed Goose and the surviving Rangers.

"No," Goose said. "I've got to finish this up."

Icarus nodded. "I'll get these men to the hospital." He put the pickup in gear. "Come check on them. I'll wait for you there. But only for a short time."

"Understood." Goose slapped the pickup's top. "Get moving."

Hesitation flickered across Icarus's features. "Sergeant . . . "

"I'll be there," Goose said.

"Do that," Icarus said. "We have to talk. There's a lot you need to know. The enemy isn't just the Syrians."

"I'm beginning to suspect that. But right now—" .50-cal machine-gun fire ripped across the front of the alley—"they're my biggest problem." Goose and the Rangers dove for cover. Turning his head toward the pickup, Goose shouted, "Move!"

Tires shrieked as Icarus threw the vehicle into reverse, laying rubber on the road as he raced back along the alley. Garbage cans scattered in his wake. He swung wide at the other end and spun out. Then he jammed the transmission into a forward gear and sped from sight.

Lying on his stomach, Goose switched his headset back on and peered out into the street. The lead Syrian tank rumbled by, bumping into the other tank Goose had disabled, then rolling past without concern.

"Control," Goose called over the thunder of the passing heavy cav.

"Go, Leader. You have Control." Remington sounded more on edge. "I lost you there for a moment."

"Momentary glitch," Goose replied and hoped that was all the decision turned out to be. Icarus might have fled if Goose had reported his presence there, and the wounded Rangers wouldn't now be en route to the hospital.

"Have that headset checked out when this settles," Remington ordered.

"Affirmative." Goose knew his friend and commanding officer despised ops that went beyond his control. "You've got Cobras still in the air."

"That's affirmative, Leader. For all the good they're doing us. With this amount of smoke and debris in the air, they can't pick our guys out from the Syrians."

"Yes, sir." Goose gazed at a flare hanging in the air overhead. "But I think I have a way of beating that." He prayed that his desperate plan would work and that he would have the opportunity to meet with Icarus at the base hospital later. Too many mysteries remained in Sanliurfa for him to feel safe, and Goose didn't know if the greater danger lay outside the city or within its walls.

❊   ❊   ❊

United States of America
Fort Benning, Georgia
Local Time 2129 Hours

Before the sound of the shot faded, Megan shoved herself forward, leaving the relative safety of the military police jeep as she headed for the Hollister house. Images of Leslie Hollister, dead at her own hand, filled Megan's mind and urged her to greater speed.

"Mrs. Gander." Corporal Kerby caught Megan's arm and brought her to a sharp stop.

Megan turned on the young man.

"You need to stop," Kerby said, maintaining his hold and stepping around to shield her from any possible gunfire that might come from the home. Light blazed through all the windows, but there was no movement inside.

"I've got to go in there," Megan said in as reasonable a voice as she could manage under the circumstances. *God, help me keep it together.* "Leslie needs help."

"I'm sorry, Mrs. Gander," Kerby stated evenly. "I can't let you do that."

Megan tested the young corporal's grip on her arm. She couldn't match his strength. Wordlessly, two other MPs created a human shield between her and the house. She knew they wore Kevlar body armor under their slickers, but all of them were risking getting shot. They served as protection, but she knew they stood as a barrier as well.

Eyeing the corporal fiercely, Megan put steel in her words. "Let me pass, Corporal."

"No, ma'am. I—"

"I came out here to help that girl," Megan interrupted. "And I'm going to help her."

"I'm not going to throw away two lives," Kerby stated. "Not when I can save one."

"She could be hurt." The words came thickly to Megan. She'd seen pictures of people who had died from self-inflicted gunshot wounds.

"Yes, ma'am. I know that. But right now you're safe." Kerby lowered his voice. "I know Goose, Mrs. Gander. And I know he wouldn't like it if I allowed any harm to come to you."

"Mister—" Megan kept her tone calm despite the fear that thrummed through her—"you can get out of my way and let me do my job, or I'm going to walk right over the top of you. If you can stop me, you're going to have to hog-tie me to keep me down."

Shock registered on Kerby's face. "Ma'am?"

Megan stood her ground. "You heard me, Corporal. This is *my* situation. *My* mission. You called me into this. I'm here to help that child, and I'm not going to let you stop me. I won't hesitate about filing a grievance with your superior officer if you continue to get in my way."

Kerby blinked at her but didn't move.

"Take your hand off my wrist, Corporal," Megan ordered. "Do it *now*."

With obvious reluctance and a little anger, Kerby released his hold. "Yes, ma'am."

"You've got Leslie Hollister under surveillance with thermographic sights?" Megan asked.

"Affirmative." The corporal's reply was grim and officious.

Megan felt her heart hammering within her chest. "Confirm her status." *Find out if she shot herself.* But Megan couldn't bring herself to say those words. Even the thought of the deed was too horrendous.

Kerby clicked the walkie-talkie handset on his shoulder but never moved or looked away from Megan. "Eyes, what's the sit-rep?"

The walkie-talkie blared a reply that Megan heard. "The subject fired a round into the wall."

"What's the subject's status?"

"She appears to be unharmed."

Kerby dropped his hand from the walkie-talkie.

"Why did she shoot the wall?" Megan asked. Kerby relayed the question.

There was no answer.

"Eyes," Kerby prompted.

"I don't know the answer to that."

Megan let out a pensive breath. She locked eyes with the corporal. "The only way I'm going to do that girl any good is to get inside and talk with her."

"Yes, ma'am." Kerby opened the flap of his pistol holster. "Maybe you shouldn't go in there empty-handed." He started to remove the pistol from the holster.

In sick disbelief, Megan caught the man's hand and stilled it upon the pistol butt. "So what? If she doesn't harm herself, *I'm* supposed to do it?"

"Ma'am, that's not what I—"

Megan got control of herself. "I know that's not what you meant. But harming her isn't an option."

"With all due respect, Mrs. Gander, I don't think you know what that girl is currently capable of doing." Kerby's eyes turned wintry hard and bright. "During the last two days, I've worked three murders and six suicides here on base. I've never done that before. Most of them were people I knew in mess hall or from around the family areas of the base."

Megan had heard about the murders and suicides. Her current caseload dealt with three teens whom the horrible events affected. Like the corporal, she had known most of the people involved.

"She won't hurt me," Megan said.

"You don't know that."

"I've known Leslie for months."

"And she's been a troubled kid. I know. I was warned on my way here." Kerby held the pistol out.

"Corporal," Megan said in as level a voice as she could muster, "I have no intention of entering that house armed."

"I could go with you."

"You could not." Megan stepped forward, taking one step to the side around the corporal. One of the other men reached for her.

"No," Kerby said. "Let her go."

"Doug," one of the other MPs said, "we let her go in there and she gets hurt, it's gonna roll over on us."

Kerby looked at Megan. "My decision, then. Anything rolls downhill on this one, it rolls on me."

"Thank you, Corporal," Megan said.

Kerby shook his head. "No, ma'am. I won't take any thanks from you. Not until you and that girl walk back out of the house in one piece." He touched two fingers to his helmet in a salute. "Just make sure you do that, ma'am."

"I will." Megan turned and walked up the short sidewalk to the porch. On either side of the walkway, yellow and red tulips stood tall and proud. The life expectancy of a fully blossomed tulip was only a week, two weeks at best. But they were a great way to start an early spring after a long winter. Now, however, the cheerful and hopeful flowers seemed out of place.

Anxiety knotted a greasy ball in Megan's stomach when she caught scent of the sickly sweet smell of marijuana on the other side of the door. What Corporal Kerby had said made sense. Megan didn't know what she was walking into. And with drugs in Leslie Hollister's system, Megan didn't know what frame of mind the girl was in.

Yes, you do, Megan chided herself. *She's scared and hurt and confused. You've seen a lot of teenagers like this over the last two days.*

But none of those had held a gun in his or her hand.

The thought was at once chilling and sobering. Megan's hand felt as heavy as an anvil as she lifted it to knock on the door. Knocking somehow seemed more homey, more relaxed, than ringing the doorbell. Her knuckles rapped against the door.

She waited, aware of the silence after the sound of the last knock faded. Security lights pinned four of her shadows to the front of the house. She remained aware of the stares of the silent neighbors just outside the perimeter the MPs had established.

She made herself be patient. She tried to listen for movement inside the house, but she couldn't hear over the noise pollution of the MPs' radios.

Dry-mouthed, her knees shaking slightly, Megan lifted her hand again to knock. During the first day after the disappearances, Megan and the other counselors had gone in after kids who had barricaded themselves in their homes. None of them wanted to believe some unknown force had taken away their families and friends.

Then a young girl's voice called out, "Who is it?"

Thank You, God. Thank You for Your mercy. Megan breathed out a sigh of relief and felt her eyes brim with hot tears. She tried to speak, found herself choked, and tried again. "It's Megan," she replied. "Megan Gander. You know me, Leslie."

Only silence answered her, interrupted by the undercurrent of walkie-talkie white noise and idling jeep engines.

"Leslie," Megan tried again, "can you hear me?"

Another long silence ensued. Just as Megan was about to try again, Leslie called back, "I hear you."

"Are you all right?"

A painful mewl came from the other side of the door. "No," Leslie choked out. "No, I'm not all right."

"I came to help you."

"I just want to wake up, Mrs. Gander. I swear, I've tried and I've tried, but I can't wake up."

"Leslie," Megan said in a soft but firm voice, "I want to talk to you."

"Can you wake me up? I'm trapped in this nightmare, Mrs. Gander. I've had nightmares before, but nothing like this. I need someone to help me. I'm just so *afraid*." Her voice ended in a mournful howl.

Megan pressed her palm against the door and willed herself to be strong. She felt overwhelmed. Ever since Gerry Fletcher had slipped from her grip atop a base apartment building and seemingly fell to his death four stories below—except for the fact that only his clothes hit the pavement—her whole life seemed out of control.

"It's okay," Megan said. "We're all a little afraid right now."

"We don't need to be *afraid!*" Leslie shouted. "We all just need to *wake up!*"

"Leslie, I'm coming in there. I want to talk to you." Megan reached for the doorknob and found it unlocked. She twisted it and walked inside.

Even though lights glowed throughout the structure, the Hollister home filled Megan with fear so cold the effect made her shiver. Away from the protection of the MPs, anything could happen now.

Movement on her left startled her. Her heart exploded into action in her chest as she turned around to face the perceived threat. Panicked, Megan raised her arms to shield herself from attack.

Instead of Leslie Hollister, though, Megan found herself facing her own reflection in a mirror on the wall. Evidently Linda Hollister had placed it behind the couch to make the room seem larger. Still, the unexpected movement had proven horrifying and Megan had overreacted. Adrenaline charged her system, almost making her nauseous and causing her hands to shake.

That was when Megan realized she was in over her head. A teen with a gun and a death wish probably ranked high as one of the situations a family counselor least wanted to face.

Or is least equipped to handle, Megan thought. She turned from the mirror, striving to calm herself with a slow and careful breath. She wanted to leave, and she wanted to leave *now.* Kerby's assessment of the situation was correct. She *didn't* belong here. Feeling guilty, she turned to the door, hoping she could make her way outside and have the time necessary to think of another plan.

"Mrs. Gander." Leslie's voice coming from the back of the house was shaky and sharp.

Megan halted, then tried twice before her own voice worked. "Yes."

Leslie spoke in a hoarse whisper. "I was just . . . you know . . . checking."

"Checking?" Megan echoed.

Leslie sniffled. "Checking to see if you were still coming. To see if it was just you."

The pain and loneliness and confusion in Leslie's voice nearly broke Megan's heart. She felt defeated. There was no way she could walk away from this girl. She turned toward the back of the house, knowing she was probably driving the MP squad crazy. "It's just me, and I am coming."

"I don't want nobody else in here." The trembling sound in Leslie's voice intensified. "If you've got somebody with you . . . if you do . . . "

"I don't have anyone with me," Megan said into the ominous silence that followed. "I'm alone."

"If someone comes with you, it's gonna be bad." Leslie's words broke and grated.

God, Megan prayed as she continued on trembling legs and knees that felt like watery ligaments, *watch over us. Give Leslie the strength and guide me as I try to find a way to free her from the fear she feels. I don't want to be shot, and I don't want her hurt.*

Megan knew if Leslie fired on her, the MPs would rush the house in an effort to save her. Nothing would hold them back at that point. For the first time, she realized how much she had upped the stakes by choosing to pursue the face-to-face confrontation with Leslie. Megan looked around the house. *She'll be all right. We'll be all right. She was raised by good parents. She just needs someone to talk to her and explain what's going on.*

Although small and modest like most of the other base houses, the Hollisters had made their home comfortable and cozy. The living room held solid, carefully chosen pieces of furniture—a wide couch and matching his and her chairs facing an entertainment center filled with electronics.

A collection of family pictures adorned the wall, showing the three Hollisters on vacations or at events. The images made Megan feel sad. Despite the challenges Leslie faced and those she had presented to her parents, Leslie had enjoyed a good life.

But that was over.

No, Megan told herself. *Not over. Just changed.* She remembered the church sermons she'd attended that talked about the glories that awaited believers in heaven. *And the best is yet to come.* She just had to find a way to convince Leslie of that.

The living room adjoined the dining room, carefully presented and clean. Pictures of fruit and farmhouses hung on the walls. Linda Hollister had enjoyed success as a homemaker. The woman's mark showed in every room in the house.

Megan halted at the hallway off the living room. Bedrooms lay at either end behind closed doors. Television voices emanated from both rooms. More family pictures covered the hallway walls, showing generations of family in black and white as well as color. The family, both sides evidently, sported a long line of military men in uniform, on battlefields, and in front of tanks, ships, and planes.

"Leslie," Megan called.

"My room's to the right, Mrs. Gander." Leslie's voice sounded smaller and more scared.

"All right." Megan followed the hallway to the door. She placed her hand on the knob, watching with bright interest as her hand shook. "Leslie."

"Yes."

"I'm outside the door."

"It isn't locked."

"I'm coming in."

"Okay."

Please don't shoot. Megan took a final deep breath and told herself that talking with Leslie Hollister in her room wasn't that much different than talking to someone in her base office. Only it was.

She turned the knob and pushed the door open. Instinctively, she held her hands up and out at her sides and stood her ground, praying that her trembling knees wouldn't give out.

Posters of half-naked rock-star singers and actors covered all four walls. Guys in Speedos with wildly dyed hair and body piercings and tattoos warred with guys in unbuttoned flannel shirts, tattered jeans, and cowboy hats. Leslie's interests apparently leaned toward a little bit country and a little bit rock and roll.

Megan recognized fewer than half the faces on those posters, but the room possessed a familiar feel. During her teen years, she had covered her walls with posters of rock bands and Chippendale models. Her father had railed against them when he had found them, but her mother had campaigned for her right to self-expression. Teens struggled for individuality, and in doing so, tended to be like every other teen, never knowing they were so like their parents at the same age. Only the accessories were different.

A notebook computer lay open on a small student desk next to a compact vanity cluttered with cosmetics, brushes, and curling irons. Small stuffed animals adorned the desk and the vanity. Pictures—primarily Polaroids but sharing space with 35mm shots and what looked like computer printouts—ringed the mirror of the vanity like a border, tucked in under the corners of the frame holding the reflective surface secure.

A small entertainment unit held a TV, DVD player, and an orange-and-white boom box that looked like the head of a robotic insect. Silent images flickered across the television screen. Megan's quick glance showed her that the news story covered the military action taking place in Turkey. The station ID, FOX News, occupied one corner, but the main slug showed that the footage currently showing came from OneWorld NewsNet.

The footage revealed that—except for explosions and tracer fire—it was dark in Turkey, but it was a day ahead in Fort Benning. Tomorrow had arrived there, and for a moment the idea that Megan was watching tomorrow's events today again struck her as ludicrous.

The television held a hypnotic intensity for her. Joey had told her how he'd seen Goose on a live broadcast right after the action erupted along the Turkish-Syrian border. In the days that had passed, few in-depth news shorts regarding the conflict hadn't contained the striking image of Goose hauling the wounded marine from the downed helicopter right after the rescue attempt fell from the sky. It was an image that had caught the scattered attention of the world. At least, the part of the world that had fathers and sons in the military.

"Mrs. Gander."

Guilt washed over Megan as she turned to face Leslie Hollister. Megan hadn't forgotten the girl, but in that frozen moment with the television images, nothing else had mattered.

Leslie sat on the floor with her back against the wall near the foot of her unmade bed. Plates and bowls of barely touched food—potato chips, Twinkies, miniature chocolate bars, and microwave meals—shared the bed and floor space with clothing. Plastic bottles of juices, soft drinks, and sports supplements added to the mess. The lingering acrid bite of marijuana smoke hung in the air, mixing with the turgid stink of incense.

Judging from the rest of the house and the pictures of Leslie and her friends taken in the bedroom, the room usually didn't look as disheveled. Leslie Hollister's bedroom was as much a battlefield as Sanliurfa, Turkey.

Realizing that, and hoping that she could do something to alleviate the girl's painful confusion, Megan stood facing the young teen. "Leslie." Despite the automatic impulse, she didn't ask how the girl was doing; they both already knew the answer to that.

Pale and bordering on anorexic, Leslie sat with her knees folded up nearly to her chin. Her long blonde hair, frizzy and uncombed, draped her blade-thin shoulders. She wore silver-gray capri pants and a teal sleeveless sweater. A tiny gold cross rested at her throat, shining against the sweater fabric. A silver toe ring glittered on her left foot.

Her face appeared as pasty as bread dough. The bloodshot blue eyes were washed out and almost colorless except for the red. Her mouth was so grim and thin it looked like a bloodless straight-razor slash.

The .45 semiautomatic pistol Leslie held cupped in both hands atop her knees made her look even smaller.

❁   ❁   ❁

United States 75th Army Rangers Temporary Post
Sanliurfa, Turkey
Local Time 0438 Hours

Captain Cal Remington stood on top of the three-story building and surveyed the battlefield that had taken over the city he was supposed to defend. He choked back the rage and frustration that filled him. He swore inside his head, thinking dark and vile things, but never gave vent to any of the words over the radio link.

Command had given him a losing proposition. And now fate— and the blasted Syrians—seemed determined to add insult to injury. He didn't let himself think of the men dying under his command out in the streets of Sanliurfa. He couldn't. Thinking like that made every decision he made too personal, too heavy.

On making the decision to become an officer, he'd stepped away from personal involvement with the men under him. They were tools, just like the vehicles and weapons he put into the field. He trained himself to think like a strategist and realize that acceptable losses had to be made to attain an objective.

Or to hold on to one, he told himself bitterly. What he was going through now, though, wasn't anywhere in the neighborhood of acceptable.

The holding assignment Command he currently headed up wasn't one he'd have wished on anyone. He was in charge of cannon fodder, strictly a time-delay tactic, and he knew it. The losses galled him. He didn't mind losing men to hang on to something or to reach a goal, but losing them just to run in place was too much.

Only the fact that Icarus and Section Chief Alexander Cody of the Central Intelligence Agency remained within the city as well offered him any solace. With them present, there was a chance Remington could salvage something from the godforsaken mission. The CIA agents searching for their wayward undercover man, missing since the action that possibly precipitated the Syrian attack against Turkey, worked to keep a low profile with all the international media people in place in the city. But they couldn't stay off the Ranger captain's radar once he'd identified them.

Remington had assigned teams to keep Cody and his men under surveillance. He'd also set up checkpoints around the city, identifying everyone who came and went to the best of his ability. The United Nations teams and Turkish army entrenched with them helped.

With all the traffic into and out of the city, Remington knew he couldn't be certain he hadn't missed the man, but Cody's agents remained in place. Remington used their presence as a litmus test. If Cody and his team disappeared, then undoubtedly Icarus had disappeared as well.

But Cody was here now. So were his agents. It stood to reason that Icarus was also.

The Ranger captain wanted Icarus, wanted to know why Icarus had run from the agency after he'd sent a Ranger team in to rescue him, wanted the covert agent's secrets and the power those secrets would bring. If Remington was doomed to ride out the onslaught massed outside Sanliurfa's borders, he was determined to have something to show for his time. Icarus was a big prize. Remington was certain of that.

The deaths of two CIA agents in Sanliurfa the same night of the attack lent even more credence to that belief. Lieutenant Nick Perrin, the man Remington used for covert activities of his own—including the search for Icarus and the surveillance of Cody's CIA team—believed that the agents had found Icarus and he'd killed them to effect his escape. If the Rangers still had access to the satellite network owned by OneWorld NewsNet, searching the city would have progressed more easily. They didn't have that access, though.

Remington directed a few more curses at Nicolae Carpathia, the CEO of NewsNet and the man responsible for the decision to withdraw that satellite access. A leading businessman in his country, Carpathia had received the presidency of Romania on a silver platter when the president had stepped down and named Carpathia as his successor the day before the attack. The satellites on loan from OneWorld had given Remington an edge over the Syrians, who had lost their own access to the limited sources they had when the disappearances had occurred. The satellites would have continued giving the U.S. military the edge inside the city.

CIA Agent Cody had put Remington in contact with Carpathia. At first Carpathia had oozed generosity, saying he was interested in having a Western influence in the Middle East. Then Carpathia had developed an international social conscience less than seventy-two hours later. Remington still wasn't certain of the reason for that. However the change of heart had come about, the timing roughly coincided with Carpathia's receipt of an invitation to speak before the United Nations in New York City. President Fitzhugh had helped roll out the red carpet.

In the meantime, the 75th Ranger Regiment bled and died as sacrificial lambs.

Perspiration slid down Remington's body under the heavy Kevlar and BDUs he wore. Dust and smoke caked his face and exposed skin. His mouth was parched and dry, and he thought he would never again taste anything but dirt.

But his mind worked. No matter what else went on around him, he considered the actions he had open to him. The Syrian army's use of the American dead left behind from the border conflict had caught him by surprise and he felt embarrassed by that. Armies in the Middle East had used the bodies of fallen comrades against city defenders even back into biblical days.

Remington stared after the Syrian tanks and jeeps that rumbled deeper into Sanliurfa. He regretted the men that died under the onslaught of Syrian armor, his Rangers as well as the United Nations soldiers and the Turkish military. Dying here tonight meant that those men couldn't die again later when he might need them even more. He was quickly running out of resources, and that fact was an increasing irritation to him.

An AH-1W Whiskey Cobra gunship cut the air over his head.

Hovering low, the helicopter presented a fat target to the Syrians invading Sanliurfa as well as the troops stationed outside the city. Three other Cobras flew low over the city, cutting the area into quadrants. Bullets struck sparks as they ricocheted from the helicopter's sides or punctured the metal and passed through. Enemy small-arms fire provided some danger, but the Syrians boasted .50-cal sniper rifles that were capable of punching through the light armor the helos carried.

"Phoenix Leader," Remington said. "This is Control."

"Go, Leader." Goose sounded confident but a little agitated. There was no indication that the earlier break in communication would repeat.

Remington looked to the east where the Syrian armor had rolled through the barricade. All he saw was a roiling cloud of dust lit by tracer rounds and flames from the surrounding gutted buildings. "I've got the birds in the air awaiting your go."

"Affirmative. Preparing to light up the lead target."

Remington jogged to the building's edge and peered down. Goose's plan was desperate, but it had merit. The ability to think on his feet, to assess an unfavorable situation and find leverage within it was only one of the many reasons Remington had kept his friend close after completing Officer Candidate School and working his way up to captain's bars.

"Nighthawk Leader, this is Control. Are you patched into the loop?" Remington glanced up at the nearest helicopter. He didn't know if that was the gunship that held the Whiskey team leader. All the Cobra pilots were marines from USS *Wasp*.

Captain Falkirk, the ship's captain, and Colonel Henry Donaldson, the commander of the marine contingent on board the seven-vessel 26th MEU(SOC) deployed in the Mediterranean Sea, had given generously of their men and equipment, but they had their own problems. With the rash of disappearances around the globe, the U.S. military had taken severe hits, leaving holes in the supply infrastructure as well as in front lines in all hot zones. Supplies came late or not at all, and Remington knew that the U.S. ships had become targets for terrorist organizations as well as for the Syrian navy.

"Nighthawk Leader reads you, Control." The radio communications carried the tinny sound of static.

"Phoenix Leader is ready." Remington checked the Syrian line to the south and saw that the armored division held steady.

"Roger that, Control. Light 'em up, Phoenix, and we'll take 'em down."

Remington silently hoped the marine pilot proved as able as he sounded confident. Glancing back toward the point the advancing rolling stock inside the city had reached, only blocks from the hospital, Remington said, "You're greenlighted, Phoenix Leader."

"Affirmative," Goose replied. "Nighthawk, the bogeys are running double-stacked, standard two-by-two deployment. Don't know if you'll see that from up there."

"Not a problem, Phoenix. We just appreciate getting to do some good in here."

The Syrian armor also ran without using the main guns or the machine guns at the moment. Remington knew the teams were conserving ammo rounds, using the forty-ton behemoths to take out buildings, vehicles, and fighting positions. The enemy armor ran silent and deep through the sea of smoke and dust, invisible to the forward-looking infrared and thermal-imaging capabilities of the helos.

"Fire in the hole," Goose announced.

Remington didn't see the MPIM squad that Goose had assigned to the task of firing on the lead Syrian tanks, but he saw the halo of fire that ignited between buildings a few blocks over. The dusty haze made clear sight of the area impossible, but there was no mistaking the red ball of fire that leaped up from the MPIM's target.

Goose had suggested using 40mm red phosphorus rounds to mark the locations of the armor for the aerial units. Red phosphorus was an incendiary, normally used for clearing trenches, bunkers, and buildings with the blazing explosion the grenade meted out. With the action shaping up to take place in the streets of Sanliurfa, the Rangers carrying M-79s, M-203s, and MPIM grenade launchers had taken to the field with the 40mm munitions.

The bright light of the phosphorus contained in the grenades would normally disable infrared devices and throw off thermographic imaging. With the dust and smoke hanging thick in the air, those systems were out of play. Now, however, the phosphorous grenades showed up brightly against the dingy shadows that filled the city.

A bright red bubble of light nestled in the street only two blocks from the hospital buildings.

Remington waited because there was nothing else he could do.

"Phoenix Leader," the marine helo pilot called with a trace of enthusiasm, "stand clear of that hot zone. We see your target designation and we have the ball."

"Affirmative, Nighthawk. We're clear."

As Remington watched, the Whiskey Cobra twisted in the air and dove, making a run above the street where the invasion had come from. Equipped with a three-barrel, rotary 20mm cannon mounted on the turret that the gunner operated with a chin mount, a pair of LAU-68 rocket-launcher pods on the inside of the stubby wings, and eight TOW missiles on the outside of the wings, the Whiskey Cobras were deadly aerial predators.

But only if they acquired their targets.

Goose's plan was simple. The 40mm phosphorus rounds did some damage to the Syrian tanks as the burning chemical clung to the tanks, but primarily Goose intended to use the phosphorus to mark the tanks.

As Remington watched, three flaming hulks closed in on the hospital.

"Nighthawk Leader to Nighthawk Two, I have the point tank. Close down the retreat."

"Will do," the second helo pilot replied over the headset.

The helicopter decreased speed and tilted down to bring its weapons to bear. In the next instant, the marine pilot unloaded his turret gun and fired rockets into the fiery tank. Explosions ripped across the street. Not all of them hit the tank, but enough did.

Slammed again and again by the 20mm cannon and the 2.75-inch antitank rockets, the Syrian tank crumpled and died. Before the other vehicles had a chance to scatter, the second Whiskey Cobra ripped into their flank and put down the rear vehicle.

"*Hoo-ah!*" a Ranger yelled over the headset.

Despite the desperate straits his team was still in, Remington couldn't help smiling. Goose had come through again. The first sergeant wasn't a master tactician—more of a paint-by-numbers soldier in planning—but he was at his best when his back was up against the wall. He was the most dependable man Remington had.

"All right, Rangers," Remington said. "Isolate your targets and co-ordinate the strikes with the marine wing. We'll see if we can hold the line against the rest of the rabble waiting outside the gate."

"Affirmative, Control," the marine helo pilot replied. "We'll get other birds in the air now that we know we can be effective. Let's turn this thing around."

Remington gave orders to the various units scattered around the city, then turned his attention to the specialty squad he'd assigned to mark the forward line of the Syrian cav waiting out in the darkness. Captain Mkchian of the Turkish military had managed to bring some heavy artillery pieces into the city that Remington hoped might yet provide a nasty surprise for the Syrians.

Remington's headset chirped for attention while the second set of helos swooped down to attack another group of Syrian rolling stock. He switched over to the other channel, prepared to sound irritated if it wasn't important.

"Control, this is BirdDog." Birddog was Lieutenant Nick Perrin, the man Remington had put in charge of keeping tabs on the CIA agents.

"I'm listening, BirdDog." Remington waited impatiently, knowing there were a hundred things he needed to do.

"Spotted our guy, Cap'n."

"Who?"

"The primary. Couldn't get to him in time to stop him. Had to waylay a member of the competition."

Stifling curses, Remington asked, "Do you still have the primary in sight?" The primary was Icarus, not one of the CIA agents.

"Negative. The primary had a vehicle. My squad and I are on foot. But I'm pretty sure I know where he's headed."

"Where?"

"The hospital. He was carrying wounded. Men from Phoenix Leader's squads."

Goose? Remington couldn't believe it. Goose knew Remington wanted Icarus for questioning. Goose was under orders after their face-to-face in the bar two days ago to bring the man in no matter what.

"Phoenix Leader saw the primary?" Remington asked, still believing that there was some other explanation.

"Affirmative, Control. They talked while they loaded wounded. There's no way Phoenix Leader didn't know who he was talking to."

Anger swelled up over Remington like a tidal wave, rising high above him then crashing down. He didn't know why Goose had betrayed him, but he was going to find out.

United States of America
Fort Benning, Georgia
Local Time 2143 Hours

"I came alone," Megan pointed out to Leslie Hollister as she stood across the bedroom from the girl. The audience of male rock stars and actors kept silent watch. "Just like you asked."

Leslie nodded. The pistol shifted in her hands with the slight motion.

Megan's breath caught in her throat, and she resisted the instinctive impulse to retreat into the hallway. *Just go easy*, she admonished herself. *Talking to kids is always the same. Doesn't matter if they don't like something about themselves or if they are holding weapons.* Even though Megan knew what she was telling herself was true, she also knew that a teen who had a weight problem or an esteem issue generally wasn't equipped to take the counselor's head off with one shot.

The realization was sobering.

Leslie blinked back tears. Her hands twitched uncontrollably. "Mrs. Gander . . . " She tried to talk further, but her voice deserted her.

Megan waited quietly and tried to show confidence. There was nothing she couldn't handle. Leslie Hollister had to feel that. Every time Megan worked at counseling a child, she had to make that child feel that way. Usually that appearance started because she honestly believed she could handle the situation. She'd never had to work so fiercely to generate that feeling within herself.

"Mrs. Gander," Leslie tried again. "I just don't . . . don't understand."

"I know," Megan said softly.

Leslie yanked a hand back and covered her mouth in an effort to control herself. "My mom . . . three days ago, my mom . . . "

Megan forced herself to wait. "I'm right here, Leslie. Take your time."

Leslie's hand holding the pistol shook violently. The .45 slid from her knee and fell. She yanked the big weapon back up, narrowly avoiding contact with the floor.

Releasing a pent-up breath, Megan asked, "Leslie, would you mind putting the pistol down while we talk?"

Suspicious paranoia darkened the girl's face. She pulled the pistol closer to her chest. "Why?"

"Because having it here makes me nervous." Megan carefully chose not to call the weapon what it was anymore. Referring to it with a bland pronoun robbed the pistol of some of its importance. It became an object, not an invincible force. *Not something that can't be overcome if we work on it together.*

"It makes me feel safe," Leslie declared. She tightened her grip on the pistol butt. Rebellious defiance shone in her bloodshot eyes.

"Why?" Megan asked.

"Because as long as I have it, I have a choice."

"A choice about what?"

Leslie scrunched her eyes closed. Tears leaked down her sallow cheeks. "About whether I keep dreaming or I wake up."

Megan pointed to the floor. She ignored the bed; too much clutter rested there that might fall and prove a disastrous distraction. "Can I sit?"

Leslie hesitated then nodded. "Yeah. Sure. Okay. I mean, this is my dream." A weak smile played across her lips but never touched the hurt in her eyes. "But I gotta tell you, Mrs. Gander, never in a million years would I have figured you'd ever be sitting in my bedroom."

Slowly, keeping both hands visible, Megan lowered herself to the floor in a lotus position. She'd studied yoga for the relaxation techniques. For the past few years, since Chris's birth, spending time at that pursuit proved impossible. But the skills remained.

"You believe you're dreaming," Megan said.

A troubled look formed on Leslie's face. "Of course I am." She worked her jaw. "I mean, there's no way all this is real. My mom couldn't just . . . just . . . *disappear* in the middle of the night like I dreamed she did."

"Do you remember being in group the day after your mom disappeared?" Megan had gathered all of the base's surviving kids together

with help from Jenny and the other counselors who hadn't disappeared and had been on base.

Leslie shook her head. "I dreamed that."

"What did you dream about that meeting?" Megan knew she
couldn't force the girl to remember everything to realize that what
was going on now was real. Leslie bordered on being hysterical at the
best of times, and the drug abuse and the recent events hadn't helped
her faulty grip on reality. She had to be led back to the now.

"You got us all together." Leslie's brow furrowed. "Told us that the
disappearances didn't just happen on base. That they'd happened all
around the world."

Megan nodded encouragement. "That's right. I did, and they did."

The statement caused Leslie to shake her head vehemently. "No.
This is just a dream."

"You were watching television that night," Megan stated calmly.
"Up past your bedtime."

"I do that a lot."

"You and your mother argued about that earlier."

Leslie stared through Megan, nodding and starting to rock herself.
"Yeah. We argued about that a lot. She hated—*hates*—trying to get me
up in the morning." She hugged herself with her free arm and gazed
around the room. "Now I can hardly wait till she comes and gets me
out of bed. Out of this. I can't believe it's taking so long."

Megan ignored that and kept pushing Leslie forward. "You heard
a noise that night."

"My mom," Leslie agreed. "I swear I heard her call out to me."

"You thought you were in trouble."

"Oh, yeah. I hit the remote and blanked the TV quick as I could."

"But your mom never came to check on you."

Slowly, Leslie shook her head. "No. And she always checks on me
when she thinks I'm up. When she *knew* I was up late—when she
knows I'm up late."

"But not that night."

"No."

Megan made herself breathe despite the desperate tension and
fear that filled her and thrummed like a live thing. She kept her voice
low and hypnotic, neutral and no threat. Leslie had experienced trouble sleeping lately. She looked worn-out now. Because of the drugs in
Leslie's system, Megan hoped the girl would go to sleep listening to
her voice.

"You went to check on your mom," Megan reminded.

"Yeah." Leslie remained a knotted ball rocking against the wall.

"What did you find?"

"I thought she'd be sleeping. I mean, if she wasn't awake checking on me, she had to be sleeping. But I thought maybe she was having a nightmare. I wanted to check on her, make sure she was okay. She's had it rough since the Rangers deployed. My dad being over there in Turkey—it worries her, you know." Leslie grimaced. "I mean, of course you know. Your husband is over there."

"Yes, he is. I worry all the time, and I've gotten to talk to him."

Leslie focused on her. "Has he said anything about my dad? About whether he's okay or not?"

"He hasn't," Megan said. "Goose is in Sanliurfa. Your dad is with a team in Diyarbakir."

"I don't even know where that is."

"It's is the eastern part of Turkey. Diyarbakir is a large area. An important place. Goose's team is being kept separate and out of close contact with the Rangers stationed in Diyarbakir and Ankara." Megan knew that from the news coverage.

According to the media, primarily OneWorld NewsNet, Sanliurfa was a lost cause, a sinking ship that the Americans, Turks, and United Nations were struggling to get to in order to rescue the border militias that had gotten stranded there. She also knew from her infrequent conversations with Goose that the story wasn't entirely true.

"I wish I could talk to my dad," Leslie said.

"Maybe we can make that happen," Megan suggested. "Communications around the world are steadily improving."

Leslie shrugged. "That's just in this dream. Maybe when I wake up I'll find out I was dreaming that, too." She scratched her leg absently with the pistol.

Megan waited a moment then said, "Could we put that away now?"

"No." Leslie hauled the pistol back into her stomach. "I like holding on to it."

"It's a dream, remember? You have all kinds of powers in dreams. You could fly out of this room. You don't need that."

"No." Her features turned hard.

Megan gave up that front for a moment. "You went to check on your mom that night."

"Yeah."

"Do you remember what you found?"

Leslie tried to speak, couldn't, then swallowed hard and tried again. "My mom was gone."

"Yes."

"I thought maybe she'd gone to the kitchen for a drink of water," Leslie whispered. She looked through Megan again, trapped by the memory. "But that didn't make any sense because if she'd gone to the kitchen I'd have heard her door open."

"You were watching TV."

"She would have heard the TV. She'd have come into my room to check on me and probably ground me for a week." Leslie shifted her attention to Megan. "I looked in her bed and found her pajamas. That was weird. If she'd left her pajamas in bed, that meant she was walking around the house naked. And that would be like . . . like . . . just *gross.*"

Megan took in a breath and let it out.

"But she wasn't walking around the house naked," Leslie said. "She was just . . . just . . . "

"Missing." Megan tried to keep her voice low to lessen the impact, but she knew at once that the effort was futile. She'd tried to find a new way to talk about the disappearances for two days.

Looking totally miserable, Leslie nodded. She squeezed her eyes tight again and shook as she cried silently.

Resisting her maternal instincts, so sharp now because Chris was missing and Joey had left and Goose was in danger, Megan made herself remain seated instead of crossing the room to put her arms around the girl.

"I found Mom's wedding ring in the bed, Mrs. Gander." Leslie snuffled and wiped her tears from her trembling chin with a hand. "Mom never took her ring off. *Never.* She said Dad had put it on her hand and she would never take it off."

"I can only imagine how hard that was for you, Leslie." Megan struggled with her own memories of finding Chris's clothes after Joey had told her of the disappearances in the base child-care facility.

"It was terrible. Worse than when our cat had kittens and I found one of them dead." Leslie shrugged, looked up at the ceiling, and wiped mascara from her eyes, smearing black across her cheeks. "I've dreamed some pretty horrible stuff before. I've dreamed my mom has died in a car wreck, drowned in the ocean, and was in the World Trade Center on 9-11. I've even dreamed she was killed by monsters that came out of my closet." She paused and glanced at Megan for reassurance. "I guess every kid has those dreams."

"Every child fears the loss of a parent." *Just as every parent fears the loss of a child,* Megan thought. After each of her boys had been born, months had passed before she'd gotten a full night's sleep. She'd constantly gotten up to check on them, afraid that they'd called out to her and she hadn't heard them, afraid that they'd stopped breathing. Goose had helped her with Chris, something her ex-husband had never done with Joey.

"But maybe not to monsters out of the closet," Leslie suggested with a slight grin.

"Maybe not to that," Megan admitted.

Leslie looked around the room. "It's kind of weird, you know. How long this dream has lasted. Usually they seem to last only a few minutes. No more than a few hours. But this has lasted for days. Somebody once told me that you always know when you're dreaming because you can never see a clock in a dream." She gazed at the digital clock on the small nightstand by her bed. "I've been watching clocks and watches for days."

"I don't think that's especially true. I've had dreams where I could tell time."

"When the clock thing didn't work, I tried other stuff. Stuff I knew would usually draw my mom down on me in a heartbeat. Stuff she usually has like mutant's powers for, you know?"

"A mother's radar."

"Yeah." Leslie shrugged helplessly. "But it didn't work. Nothing I tried did. I mean, I thought that me filling the bedroom with food and dirty dishes would get my mom in here for sure." Leslie paused. "She hated that."

Megan surveyed the carnage. "Looks like you went all out."

"I did." Leslie gave an embarrassed grin at praise for something so blatantly wrong. "I figured even in a dream, Mom would be here in a second."

"But she wasn't."

"No." Leslie shook her head. "So I called Tori over."

"Why?" Megan was curious about that, trying to put all the pieces together.

"Because Mom doesn't really like Tori. Mom knows Tori smokes, which she doesn't approve of."

"But she didn't know that Tori smoked pot."

"No way." A little calmer now, Leslie wiped her face. "If Mom knew Tori smoked pot, Mom would have never let Tori into this house."

Megan was silent for a time. Rain continued to sluice down Leslie's bedroom window. The amber lights mounted on the saw-horses outside streaked the running water as regularly as a metronome.

Lolling her head against the wall, Leslie yawned. She covered her mouth and said, "Excuse me. That one snuck up on me." The effort seemed entirely normal except for the bullet hole in the wall that her movement had revealed.

The sight of the bullet hole jarred Megan. She tried not to focus on it. "You're tired."

"Yeah. Can't hardly keep my eyes open." Leslie shifted again.

"Have you ever gone to sleep in a dream?"

"That doesn't make sense. You're sleeping when you're dreaming. So you have to go to sleep to dream."

"No," Megan said patiently. "Have you ever dreamed of going to bed and going to sleep? I have."

"That would be too weird." Leslie stifled another yawn.

Megan made herself smile, but she knew if she could get the girl to lie down for only a few minutes the present situation would defuse itself. After that, she'd have some time to think and plan on how to help her. "Maybe not. Maybe it's like resting twice as much."

Leslie struggled against the wall as if trying to find a more comfortable position. "That sounds stupid. I'm sorry if that sounds rude, but this is my dream. Maybe I won't even remember it when I wake up, and I hope to God that I don't, but I know for sure that you won't remember it."

The childish logic brought a smile to Megan's lips, but at the same time the statement made abundantly clear the fact that the children on base were inadequately prepared for what had happened.

"Maybe you should try going to sleep," Megan suggested.

Leslie stared at her from under drooping eyelids. "What?"

Megan gestured to the bed. "Try sleeping. Maybe you'll wake up as soon as your head hits the pillow."

After a brief hesitation, Leslie said, "That just sounds wrong."

"It's worth trying." Megan gestured. "Turning your room into a disaster area and having Tori over didn't seem to do the trick."

Leslie frowned. "No." She paused. "There was an MP in my room. I think I remember dreaming that."

"Yes."

"He took Tori." She held up the pistol. "I made him stay away from me. He didn't like it, but I made him."

Megan nodded.

A frown knitted Leslie's brow. "Is Tori in trouble?"

"Are you going to dream her into trouble?" Megan didn't want to deal with the reality of the situation. She had no idea how the base officials would handle what happened here in the Hollister home tonight.

"No. Tori was just trying to get me to calm down. Before she came over, I was seriously freaking."

Megan silently gazed at the bullet hole in the wall behind Leslie and doubted that things had drastically improved with Tori's arrival. Megan stood and offered her hand, but didn't try to encroach on Leslie's space.

"Let's get you to bed," Megan suggested.

Looking at the bed doubtfully, Leslie asked, "What if it doesn't work?"

"It will."

"How do you know?"

Megan felt suddenly inspired. "Because you can dream me the power to put you to sleep." She'd had those empowering conversations with Chris when he'd had night terrors, coaching him on how to train his subconscious mind to deal with his fears and worries. Working with Chris was easy, though. Her son had loved superheroes. She'd encouraged him to dream himself up superpowers. *And to know that God loves him,* she reminded herself.

"Powers," Leslie repeated.

"Yes. I'm sure that you can."

Leslie frowned. "You think?"

Megan shrugged. "Why else pull me into your dream?"

"If I was looking for someone to fix everything, why didn't I dream my mom into this? She's the one that should be here. Not you."

"Because this is a nightmare, not a dream." Megan knew that she spoke the truth. If God had indeed raptured His church as she believed, the world remained a nightmare for those left behind. "C'mon. Get up."

Leslie dragged herself from the floor. Her attention suddenly shifted to the flickering amber lights chasing themselves across the rain-spattered window. She leaned into the glass. The pistol rested on the sill between stuffed animals placed in a row.

God, Megan thought as her heart lurched inside her chest, *please don't let any of those young men out there panic.* As tense as the situation was, she was afraid that one of the MPs might misread the situation and shoot Leslie Hollister through the window.

❊ ❊ ❊

United States 75th Army Rangers Temporary Post
Sanliurfa, Turkey
Local Time 0448 Hours

"Ready, Sergeant!"

Goose provided cover fire against the advancing line of Syrian infantry that flanked the T-72 tank rumbling down the street only a block from the hospital. Keeping the M-4A1's muzzle belt high on his targets, he swept the Syrians with sustained three-round bursts.

The nine other Rangers he'd gathered in his squad did the same, fanning out across the alley they'd taken refuge in. They had to stay bunched in order to keep from getting scattered when the marine helos vectored in on the enemy vehicles, and to provide a safer fire zone.

The Syrians went to ground, spreading across the street and taking advantage of cover offered by rubble and burning vehicles. Other Syrian soldiers followed close behind the T-72 to prevent close engagement with the city's defenders.

"Private," Goose snapped, feeling the assault rifle cycle dry. He stepped back to cover and shucked the empty magazine, changing it over for the full one taped to the first.

Private Al Goodwin stared at Goose through a mask of haze and blood. He looked impossibly young, but the MPIM he carried canted up across his chest lent him authority.

"Yes, Sergeant," Goodwin responded.

"Hit it." Goose flattened against the wall as Goodwin stepped forward and leveled the MPIM.

"Fire in the hole!" Goodwin yelled. Almost immediately, the MPIM chugged in his hands and a flash roiled through its snout.

The 40mm grenade sailed across the fifty-foot distance. Fighting in the streets kept the combatants close. By rights, the Rangers' skirmish line was ten feet inside the blast radius of the grenade, but the wall protected them.

Goose slitted his eyes and locked them forward. A heartbeat later, before Goodwin had much of a chance to even step back, the phosphorus round exploded, throwing out harsh red light over the immediate vicinity. The heat of the blast swirled over Goose as debris slammed against the wall.

"Private," Goose prompted.

"Yeah, Sergeant," Goodwin confirmed, nodding enthusiastically. "I got him. Dead center. There's a lake of red phosphorus burning on that tank's hide. He's marked. He can run, but he can't hide." He was wired on adrenaline, his words coming in a torrent, but he maintained control.

"Good job, soldier." Goose watched as the incandescent red glare of the burning phosphorus staggered across the alley's mouth. The light revealed the whirling clouds of dust and smoke that filled the air. He didn't look around the corner because he didn't want to lose his night vision.

Sporadic small-arms fire from the Syrian infantry chopped into the alley walls, chipping stone and mortar loose and striking sparks. Tracers burned lines of sight back to the shooters. The tank's engine growled as the driver changed gears. Goose didn't know how much contact the Syrian armored units had with each other, but they had to know that the rolling stock that had invaded the city were getting systematically hunted down and killed. Only a handful of them remained, and soldiers were stalking them now.

"Nighthawk," Goose called over the headset.

"Nighthawk here." The marine's reply came strong and confident.

"We've lit up the cake."

"Affirmative, Phoenix. Nighthawk's coming in to blow out the candle. Get clear."

Overhead, a pair of Whiskey Cobras leaned into the thin dry wind and came around on an approach path only a short distance above the rooftops.

"We're already gone." Goose threw his free hand into the air and waved the nine men he'd organized into a squad back into the alley.

The Rangers moved in concert, falling into the point-and-wings formation automatically. They ran by the light of the city that burned around them.

Long and narrow, the alley offered little protection or options for cover. When the tank crashed through the wall of the building behind them, locked down, and swiveled the turret around, Goose knew they were in trouble. Pools of red-flamed phosphorus fire burned and wavered on top of the T-72.

"Down, Phoenix," the marine pilot commanded curtly. "We're cutting this one close."

Goose shouted, ordering his group to ground just as the lead Whiskey Cobra tilted in midair and came about. He dove for the cobbled alley floor just as the 120mm main gun roared behind them. The shell wobbled through the air only a few feet above their heads, then slapped into a curving wall less than thirty feet in front of them. Broken rock and mortar spanked the ground all around the Rangers.

A fist-sized chunk of stone landed on Goose's back. He saw the stone roll away but realized he hadn't heard the impact over the buzzsaw roar of the 2.75-inch rockets from the Whiskey Cobra's wing pods. He pushed his head up and looked back.

The Syrian tank sat shivering, riddled with damage and flames and no longer in motion. Drops of burning red phosphorus still clung to the tank, but a lot of them stood out against the dark alley walls and on the cratered ground ahead of it. The tank sat inert, no longer a threat, thrust through the building wall the driver had taken out in pursuit of the enemy vehicle. Canted sideways amid the rubble, it resembled a ship that had run aground on a reef.

"Up," Goose commanded. "Now." He pushed himself up, setting the example. "Move out."

Gathering their feet beneath them, the Rangers moved out down the alley.

"Oracle," Goose said, jogging with his troops and trying fiercely to ignore the rat's teeth gnawing at his knee at every impact against the uneven ground.

"Go, Phoenix Leader. Oracle reads you five by five."

The thunder of the Whiskey Cobras swept by overhead, already en route to their next target.

"I'm hunting," Goose said.

"Negative. All enemy tanks have target groups assigned. The marine wing is working the takedowns."

Goose felt a moment of relief. He switched channels on the headset. "Control, this is Phoenix Leader."

"I hear you, Leader."

Goose immediately recognized the unaccustomed cold neutrality in Remington's voice. In nearly twenty years of friendship and service, Goose had heard that tone directed at him less than a handful of times. His relationship with the captain, even when they'd been enlisted men and sergeants together, had contained confrontational situations but always with mutual respect. Questions filled Goose's mind, but he shelved them. Whatever the problem was, he and Remington were too professional to let it interfere with the present op.

"We've taken down our last target," Goose said. "Awaiting orders."

"Fill in the gaps, Leader. I want this city secure while we shove their front line back and earn a little grudging respect from the Syrians."

Getting dismissed so casually with no real agenda set was unusual as well. Remington always kept Goose at the forefront of any action. Goose knew Remington was aggravated, but he didn't know why. However, the fact that the captain was able to feel aggravation during the current situation was a positive note in one respect: it meant the captain was fairly certain they were going to survive.

In the next instant, the heavy artillery Captain Mkchian had managed to bring into the city opened up with drumming full-throated roars. Still in the alley, Goose couldn't see the immediate effects of the heavy long guns, but he got the impression the damage was substantial when other Rangers started cheering over the headset.

Goose flipped over to the fire-control channel on the headset and listened to the confirmed hits among the second wave of Syrian armor. Mortars and howitzers screamed into the night, launching from behind the front line and carrying to the enemy troops a mile away. Marine sniper squads deployed after the first few minutes of the attack had set up nests in the broken terrain outside the city and used the big Barrett .50-cal sniper rifles to pick off Syrian artillery teams.

Judging from the amount of damage the embattled Rangers, marines, U.N. Peacekeepers, and Turkish army were reporting, Goose felt certain the tide of the battle had turned. Knocking out the Syrian armor gave all the fire teams the room they needed to breathe. When it came to sheer tactics and number crunching, no one beat Remington. Goose took a small amount of pride in that because the captain wasn't just his commanding officer but his friend.

"Man down! Man down!" someone ahead yelled.

The Rangers went to ground immediately, dropping into squatting defensive positions with their assault rifles at the ready.

Sweat ran down Goose's face. Squatting on his injured knee was pure agony. The cortisone shot he'd received only a few days ago wasn't standing up to the demands he was putting on the joint. He peered through the M-4A1's open sights and waited.

The point man, Charlie Jointer, crept like a crab to the body lying at the corner of the alley opening onto the street. He prodded the inert man with a boot, keeping his rifle directed at the man's center mass.

Flickering flames provided enough light for Goose to see that the man was dressed in civilian clothes—khaki pants and a lightweight shirt. He also wore a light jacket even in the heat.

"He's alive," Jointer called back. "But he ain't one of ours. Maybe American or European."

"Okay," Goose said. "Everybody up and moving."

The Rangers rose as one and advanced. Explosions rang out around them, but there was no sign of the enemy.

Reaching the man, Goose studied his features. He didn't know him, but he knew the look of him. Scruffy and unkempt to a degree, the man looked like any number of people—residents as well as travelers trapped by the sudden attack and stranded in the city—who holed up with the military awaiting rescue.

"Kinda weird," Jointer said to Goose. "Guy like this being out here all alone." He looked down the street as if looking for more bodies.

"His friends could have left him," Hershel Barnett offered. Big and solid and usually solitary, he wasn't noted for optimism.

Breathing shallowly against the aching pain in his knee, Goose knelt. He kept his assault rifle canted up in the ready position and searched the body with his free hand.

The man wore a shoulder holster under his left arm and a paddle holster at the small of his back. Both holsters were empty. Dark bruises covered his face and a split along his right cheek needed stitches.

"Looks like somebody pistol-whipped him," Barnett said. He'd grown up in the wildcatter oil fields near Houston, Texas, and knew a lot more about violence than the army had ever taught him. Goose had known the man at a glance. They shared small-town roots and similar backgrounds.

"In the middle of an attack?" Jointer shook his head. "Doesn't make any sense."

Goose ran his finger inside the man's mouth, popping the jaws open to make certain there was no obstruction. He held his rifle between his knees and used his pen flashlight briefly. There was no obstruction and the dental work was definitely American. Europeans still used a lot of gold instead of the porcelain American dentists used. He took his finger from the man's mouth.

"Trust me," Barnett said, "somebody took the time to pistol-whip him like that, they had a reason." He shrugged. "Would have been simpler to kill him 'cause this guy ain't gonna let something like this go. He knows who's responsible, he's gonna go after them."

Goose pushed himself to his feet. A bad feeling came over him because he was fairly certain the man was one of the CIA agents looking for Icarus in Sanliurfa. Goose knew Icarus was desperate enough to kill to save himself. Whatever secrets he held were big and dangerous to more than just himself, or else the CIA wouldn't have searched for him so thoroughly and Icarus wouldn't have taken such pains to hide.

But the beating looked fresh. Whoever had administered it had gotten bloody.

Goose tried to remember if Icarus had looked bloody but couldn't. Still, Icarus had driven; he wouldn't have stopped to beat a man on foot he could easily escape from.

Then someone else had administered the beating. With growing discomfort, Goose figured he knew who was behind that cold-blooded act. Remington was searching for Icarus, and he had assigned some of the company hardcases to look for the man. This attack breached the grudgingly granted no-man's-land between the CIA and Remington regarding the Icarus matter.

"Get him up," Goose growled. "Let's get him to the hospital. The defensive perimeter there could use some shoring up." Reports flashed constantly over the headset, relaying information about incoming wounded and continued flurries of attacks by Syrian infantry trapped inside the city.

If Icarus was true to his word, the man was waiting there. But it didn't mean he was going to tell Goose everything—or anything. Icarus would tell only whatever suited him.

This time, Goose was determined not to let Icarus get away. Whether he answered questions or not, Icarus was no longer going to be a player.

❊   ❊   ❊

United States of America
Fort Benning, Georgia
Local Time 2148 Hours

"Leslie, why don't you come away from that window?" Megan suggested. She stood still, knowing if she closed on the girl that she could upset the delicate balance they'd maintained over the past several minutes. But she was also afraid one of the overzealous or overwrought MPs outside might chose that moment to neutralize the potentially explosive situation inside the Hollister home.

"The MPs are still here?" Leslie lifted her left hand, the gun-free one, and shaded her eyes against the pulsing amber lights that came from outside.

"Yes." Megan resisted the immediate impulse to go to the girl and pull her from the window.

"This is really weird." Leslie turned from the window, lurching a little unsteadily. The pistol hung heavily at her side. "I've never dreamed in this much detail before." She looked at Megan with rising panic in her eyes. "What if I'm not dreaming? What if I was in a traffic accident? What if I'm in a coma, on life support in the hospital or something like that? Maybe that's why I can't wake up! Maybe that's why I'm dreaming so vividly!"

"Leslie." Megan struggled to make her voice reasonable. "You're not in a coma. There's been no accident."

"You'd say that, though," Leslie accused, growing increasingly hysterical.

"Why would I say that?"

"Because." Leslie sounded petulant and frantic. "Because maybe you're the thing that's trying to keep me in here."

"What thing?"

"The sedation." Leslie waved, obviously pulling at straws. She shifted her weight from foot to foot restlessly.

Panic swelled within Megan, but she knew she was siphoning off most of the emotion from the girl.

"Don't you see?" Leslie wailed. "The doctors could be working on me now! I could be in the ER on base while they're trying to save me!"

"Leslie, listen to me. That's not what is happening."

Leslie pushed her sweaty hair back from her forehead. "You can't say that! You don't know that!"

Megan knew the girl's voice carried through the window and could probably be heard at least by the MPs if not the surrounding neighbors.

"You're *me!*" Leslie went on. "You can't know anything more than I know! That's impossible!"

"Leslie, you've got to stay calm."

The girl started to pace like a caged animal, but she kept her distance from Megan.

Megan respected the distance. In other counseling sessions under tense circumstances, she'd seen teens exhibit the same restlessness. The need to move seemed ingrained in so many of the young who had emotional problems and needs. That instinct made dealing with them even more problematic.

"I've got to get out of here," Leslie said, shaking her head. "I can't stay like this. I'll go crazy."

"It's going to be all right," Megan said.

Leslie wheeled on her, stepping into the intervening space between herself and Megan. "How can you say that? You don't know!"

Megan held her ground, feeling a queasy sensation coil in her stomach. With Leslie approaching her with a weapon in her fist, Megan felt certain the MPs could scarcely contain themselves.

"Leslie, you've got to stay calm," Megan said. She didn't move, fearing that any sudden attempt on her part to get away from the young girl—any visible sign that she wasn't somewhat in control of the situation—would trigger the MPs into action. Maybe Kerby even had a sniper standing by, ready to kill or incapacitate Leslie Hollister if she looked like she was going to be a threat to the neighbors or his squad.

"I can't be calm!" Leslie roared. Tears poured down her face. "I can't wake up, Mrs. Gander! Don't you get it? I'm trapped here!" Her voice broke. "I just want out of here! I want my mom!"

Leslie raised the pistol toward Megan's face.

Despite the fear that filled her, Megan stood on trembling legs. Her lungs felt like a vise had closed around them, making breathing almost impossible. *Don't shoot! God, please don't let her shoot, and don't let those young men outside make a mistake!* Tears blurred Megan's vision, and it was all she could do not to give in to her own panic.

Shaking with anger and fear, clearly out of control, Leslie shoved the pistol barrel against Megan's cheek.

"Don't do this," Megan said softly. "Please don't do this. You're making a mistake. Everything is going to be all right."

Leslie quivered. Her eyes narrowed. More tears coursed down her face. "Will I wake up if I shoot you?"

Mastering her own rampant emotions, Megan prayed that she wouldn't faint. "No." She put as much conviction into her answer as she could.

"I don't believe you."

"I know."

Leslie wiped at her mascara-smeared face. "I tried to shoot myself earlier."

Megan remembered the deafening report and the hole in the wall.

"I couldn't do it," Leslie said. "I was just too afraid. I kept hoping everything would get better."

"It will. But you've got to trust me."

Leslie shook her head. "But that's the problem! Don't you see, Mrs. Gander? You're not you!" She snuffled and hiccupped and cried out in frustration. "You're me! And *I* can't wake up!"

Before Megan realized what was going on, the gun barrel was pulled away from her cheek. Too late, she saw that Leslie had turned the weapon on herself, burying the muzzle against her stomach.

The sharp explosion echoed within the room.

Horrified, Megan reached for the teenager as she twisted away and fell. But as Megan closed her hand on Leslie's arm, the girl jerked away from her, propelled by an outside force. Even before the sound of the rifle shot penetrated the bedroom and the broken glass from the shattered window tumbled to the floor, Megan knew that one of Kerby's team had fired, thinking that he was saving Megan's life.

Leslie's body sprawled across the floor. Her blonde hair fanned out around her, making her look impossibly young, as blood gushed onto the carpet.

Sunshine Hills Cemetery
Outside Marbury, Alabama
Local Time 2148 Hours

"I'd feel better if I could pay you for the shovel." Delroy Harte stood in the drizzle beside the old truck at the front of Sunshine Hills Cemetery. Wild and frenzied, the wind yanked at his slicker and buffeted his back. A jagged blade of lightning ripped through the black sky, followed immediately by a thunderclap. The rain had abated somewhat, but the storm remained, regaining strength.

George spoke through the open window. "An' I don't feel right about chargin' you for the use of one knowin' you ain't set on keepin' it." The old man took a last drag on his hand-rolled cigarette and filled the truck's interior with the warm orange glow. As he exhaled, he pinched the cigarette out between a callused thumb and forefinger, then fieldstripped the charred and spit-wet remnant so the tobacco and paper blew away.

Over the years, Delroy had seen several soldiers practice the same procedure out in the field. "That a habit?"

"Smokin?" George lifted his eyebrows in surprise. "Been doin' it for years."

"Stripping the butt away like that." Delroy nodded toward the overburdened ashtray sticking out of the pickup's battered and sun-ripened console. "Looks like you normally use the ashtray." Observing men's mannerisms had become second nature to him as chaplain. Most sailors aboard a ship weren't predisposed to saying when they had a problem or what that problem was.

George looked at the full ashtray, then back at Delroy. "Hadn't paid

attention. Guess I been doin' that for some time these past few days."
He glanced around the cemetery. "Just don't feel safe here, I reckon.
Guys in-country, where they ain't supposed to be, fieldstripping ciga-
rettes comes as easy as manners at your momma's table."

An old habit of soldiers in dangerous places, Delroy thought. *Trained
to move on and leave no trace of themselves behind. Over fifty years later
and the life-or-death training returned as if learned yesterday. Comes from
serving in the war, and from getting left behind. He knows this isn't a safe
place.*

"These here times, Delroy," the old man said in a soft voice barely
audible over the crack of the branches slapping each other overhead,
"why I'm afeared they ain't safe for man nor beast."

"God sees us through the darkest times," Delroy said automatically.

George squinted and studied Delroy with bright interest. "You
really believe that?"

"I'm working on it."

"An' you a-standin' there with that shovel in your hand." George
shook his head sadly.

Guilt flushed through Delroy; he knew then that the old man had
guessed what he planned on doing, but he made no apologies for his
decision. He had to know. He had to know for a lot of reasons.

Glancing ahead where the ancient pickup's dulled yellow head-
lights played over the wrought-iron gates of Sunshine Hills Cemetery,
George said, "This here ain't no place to be in the dead o' night, boy."

"It's the place I have to be for right now."

"Be better to come back in the light o' day."

"Can't." Delroy couldn't imagine accomplishing the task he'd set
before himself in broad daylight. He was also afraid that if he got a
good night's sleep, fatigue wouldn't again numb him enough to allow him to set foot into the graveyard. He tightened his grip on the
weathered shovel handle.

George sighed and crossed his arms over the steering wheel again.
"I wouldn't like it none, but if you needed me to, I reckon I could wait
out here for you for a spell."

Delroy shook his head. "Couldn't ask you to do that."

The pickup's windshield wipers slowly swept the drizzle from the
smoke-stained glass in brief waves. "You wasn't askin'. It was me was
offerin'."

The prospect of remaining alone in the graveyard left Delroy edgy.
Still, he couldn't ask the old man for that. And no matter how things

✵ ✵ ✵

United States of America
Fort Benning, Georgia
Local Time 2149 Hours

"Oh, God," Megan cried as she stared in horror at the girl lying in the pool of blood spreading across the light-colored berber carpet.

As that frozen moment released, the sound of the second shot invaded Leslie Hollister's bedroom. The crack of the rifle came flat and horrible.

Megan turned toward the window and faced the sudden onslaught of bright light that blasted through the sea green, sheer curtains. "Don't shoot!" She held her arms up. "Don't shoot! She didn't hurt me! You shouldn't have shot her! You shouldn't have shot her! There was no reason!"

Shapes raced in front of the harsh spotlight. A girl's scream ripped through the night.

Ignoring everything taking place outside the window, horrified at what had happened to Leslie, Megan turned to the girl. As a counselor, she'd taken several first-aid classes, including what to do for gunshot victims. But she'd never seen a gunshot wound up close and personal until tonight.

Stop the blood. That's the first thing. Megan dropped to her knees beside Leslie.

The girl still breathed.

Thank You, God, Megan prayed. *Please stay with us. Please help us.* The suddenness with which Leslie had decided to shoot herself still staggered Megan. She'd watched the girl turn the pistol on herself and hadn't believed she would pull the trigger.

Frantic, trying desperately to stay calm, Megan knelt and pulled the girl's shirt up to expose her midsection. Blood ran everywhere. The hole looked big enough for Megan to put her fist into. For a moment she thought she was going to get sick. She grabbed a pillow from the bed nearby and shoved it across Leslie's middle to slow the bleeding. The pillow started to soak through immediately. She looked at the girl.

Leslie's eyes flickered and went out of focus, quivering in their orbits. Her breathing rasped and caught in her throat.

"Leslie." Megan pressed on the pillow in an effort to staunch the flow of blood. *God, it's everywhere. You've got to help me. Please help me. This girl isn't supposed to die. How can You let her die like this? She's just a child.* For a moment she experienced déjà vu, remembering how she had felt on the rooftop three days ago when Gerry Fletcher started slipping from her grasp, started sliding into that four-story fall to his death or serious injury.

She'd lost Gerry, but the boy had never hit the ground. The Rapture had swept across the world in a twinkling and stolen Gerry from that fall.

There's not another rapture, God, Megan reminded. She kept the pressure steady, hoping it was enough. "Leslie."

The girl shuddered and stopped breathing for just an instant.

"Leslie," Megan called louder. "Stay with me. You stay with me now."

Leslie's head rolled toward her. Her eyes tried to focus. She gagged; then a worm of blood crept from her mouth and leaked down the side of her face.

Panic set in. Megan figured that the bullet had pierced one of the girl's lungs. If that was true, Leslie's lungs would fill up with blood in a matter of minutes and she would asphyxiate. Megan tried to remember what to do, tried to remember if she was supposed to turn Leslie over or try artificial respiration or—

Without warning, the MPs, with their rifles up and ready, suddenly filled the hallway.

In some distant corner of her mind, Megan heard them talking quickly over the walkie-talkies, reporting the situation to the provost marshal's office, requesting backup and an ambulance.

Megan looked up and saw Corporal Kerby leading the MPs. The young soldier's eyes reflected shock, but he conducted himself with confidence and purpose. Two other MPs stood on either side of Kerby, pointing their weapons at Megan.

"Back away from the girl, Mrs. Gander." Kerby's tone was polite but firm.

Megan couldn't believe what was happening. "She's bleeding."

"I know that, ma'am." Kerby came into the room, but he remained left foot forward so he presented a smaller profile. "Back away from the girl now."

"She shot herself."

"We need to take care of this situation, ma'am." Kerby kicked the pistol away from Leslie's outstretched hand. It slid across the carpet to another MP, who entered the room. "Secure that weapon, Private."

Dumbfounded, Megan watched. She hadn't even thought to knock the pistol away.

The new arrival put a foot on the pistol. "Weapon's secured, Corporal."

"Don't touch it. Forensics will want to examine it. They don't need to sort through your fingerprints, too." Kerby looked at Megan. "Mrs. Gander, I need you to move. If you don't, we will move you."

The concept was so alien to Megan that she had trouble comprehending. She couldn't leave Leslie; she had taken responsibility for the girl.

"If I have to move you, ma'am," Kerby went on, "I'm going to have you handcuffed."

"Do you think I did this?" Megan asked. "Do you think I shot her?"

"Ma'am, I need to contain this situation." Kerby's voice remained low and controlled, but Megan heard the fear in his words striving to get out.

"One of your men shot her." Megan couldn't stop talking.

"Ma'am," Kerby said, "you're hysterical."

"She could be dying," Megan said more forcefully. *God, make them listen to me. They're not hearing me.*

"Corporal," the MP on Kerby's left said.

Kerby gave a reluctant nod.

The MP slung his weapon and took a pair of disposable handcuffs from his belt. Megan recognized what they were because she'd seen them placed on kids she had counseled over the years.

"You can't do this," Megan said. "I'm just trying to help."

The private lunged forward, caught Megan by one hand, and levered her over facedown on the carpet. Instinctively, Megan fought. The private put a knee in her back to hold her in place, pinned her hands behind her back, then fastened the cuffs around her wrists.

"You're making a mistake," Megan said, but she knew her voice was too high, too forceful to sound anywhere close to acquiescent.

"Yes, ma'am," Kerby agreed hoarsely. "I reckon I made that mistake the minute I let you force me into allowing you into this house."

Megan struggled against the cuffs, but they only bit deeply into her flesh and refused to give.

Outside, a siren screamed into the night.

Lost and panicked and hurt, Megan turned her head and stared at Leslie Hollister. Bloody froth bubbled at the girl's lips as Kerby worked on her.

God? God, where are You?

❀   ❀   ❀

Sunshine Hills Cemetery
Outside Marbury, Alabama
Local Time 2153 Hours

Delroy moved through the dark cemetery by memory and with the aid of the flashlight he'd packed for the occasion. The white halogen beam cut through the darkness, chasing the night back into two-dimensional cutouts between headstones and statuary, between plants and hedges. He struggled to keep his imagination from filling those impenetrable expanses with terrifying creatures. He felt like a child again, afraid of the dark and the sleeping dead.

Crickets chirped around him and bobcats screamed like dying women in the distance. The constant rain dripping from the tall oak, pecan, and cedar trees that cloistered the area created a rhythmic snare-drum effect as the drops splashed against stone and the muddy ground. The air came thick and damp, and he had to drag it into his lungs.

Gray patches of thin fog wound like a river through the headstones and family crypts that jutted up from the hilly land. Twice, feral red eyes gleamed back at Delroy when the flashlight beam caught them. He never saw what the eyes belonged to; whatever the creatures were, they scampered off quickly into the underbrush that ringed the graveyard.

Sunshine Hills Cemetery was blatantly misnamed. Trees shrouded the area, towering over the hilly and rocky land so that shadows lingered even on the brightest day. Night never truly went away from the cemetery.

Generations of dead lay in the ground and in vaults all around Delroy. Josiah Harte had delivered several graveside services here during his tenure as preacher. Delroy had accompanied his father to those services only if the deceased was someone he knew from the congregation. Josiah Harte had buried several indigent and unclaimed bodies that occasionally had shown up in the medical examiner's office. A lingering sadness had always accompanied Josiah from those funerals, and Delroy remembered his father had come home a little bit less of himself for a time.

When Delroy had asked his mother why the funerals had affected his father so when he hadn't even know the men and women that were laid to rest, she had quietly taken young Delroy aside and told him,

"He's your daddy, Delroy, and sometimes maybe you just think of him only that way. But your daddy is a *special* man. A *good* man." Etta Harte's eyes had glistened as if she was going to cry when she'd spoken, and Delroy could still remember the lump that had risen in his throat.

"But though your daddy is a man and likes his music and his baseball on the radio and his son and his wife, first and foremost, your daddy belongs to Jesus. The Savior took your daddy into His family a long time ago. Gave him a calling that's as strong as any hurricane you ever heard tell of. We're just blessed that Jesus saw to it your daddy has a heart big enough to love all of us as much as he loves working for the Lord." She'd paused and wiped away the tears that had trickled down Delroy's cheeks.

Delroy still didn't know why he had cried, but the emotion had come over him quick and strong.

"When your daddy has to bury one of those unmourned people," Etta Harte had continued, "he feels like he's missed his calling, like he hasn't worked hard enough at what Jesus called upon him to do. He feels sorry for those people, because maybe they didn't know the love of the Lord and that their souls would have been saved if they only had given themselves to Jesus."

And here you come, Delroy chastised himself as he walked across the cemetery grounds, *bringing your doubts and your fears to this place. To your father.* He felt nauseous, but he blamed it on fatigue rather than guilt.

Josiah Harte's grave lay in the back of the cemetery. Other Hartes lay to rest there, as well as Delroy's mother's side of the family. The land also had a history. Even before the Civil War, ancestors of both families had worked in the cotton fields, living and dying on farms, then getting put into ground where no one wanted to plant a cash crop because of the trees and the rocks.

Sunshine Hills had started out as an unnamed black cemetery in its early years, but after the Civil War's reconstruction brought the carpetbaggers from the North, poor whites were buried there, along with once-affluent whites who had lost all their wealth. Interment there was delivered as punishment and insult to the privileged white who had lived in Marbury and the surrounding areas.

Gradually over the years, the stigma had finally washed away, and the cemetery was no longer thought of as black. But only family members of longtime residents were ever buried there. Sunshine Hills remained small and special within the community, a tie to a way of life that was long past but never forgotten.

Josiah Harte's murder nearly thirty years ago had stirred up all that turmoil again. The late sixties and early seventies had tried men's souls as civil unrest had threatened to split a nation again.

Rain leaked down the back of Delroy's neck under his slicker collar. It felt like an icy tentacle spreading against his skin. He rubbed his hand over the area and felt the moisture soak into his shirt. There was nothing comfortable about tonight.

Thunder suddenly broke loose in the dark skies. Lightning flashed and turned the landscape into a sharp relief of white and black. For a moment, no gray existed.

Delroy came to a brief stop, feeling his resolve start to shake a little. Then he took a firmer grip on the shovel and started forward again. What he had to do lay before him, and he knew he couldn't avoid it.

Gravel covered the narrow path between the markers, but the constant rain had still managed to turn the earth to mud. Muck clung to his boots and made them feel clunky and heavy.

Another flash of lightning revealed Josiah Harte's final resting place. Near the grave, a statue of Jesus held a shepherd's crook and a small lamb. Weeks after Josiah's brutal murder, the church had raised the money to place the statue. Etta Harte had planned on making payments on a small marker for her husband's grave. She hadn't asked for anything, even though everyone in the community knew how much the reverend had given to those who had needed.

The sight of the grave weakened Delroy's resolve. How could he visit his father's grave with the intentions he had in his heart? If Josiah yet lived, Delroy doubted he'd have had the nerve to ask his father's blessing in what he was about to do.

But maybe he'd have had the answers to quiet the aching doubt in your heart, Delroy thought.

He stopped for a moment in the shelter of a pecan tree twenty feet away. Standing still was a mistake, though. The wind cut more deeply and even the rain seemed to gain intensity. He let out a long gray breath that disappeared in patches, then walked to the foot of his father's grave.

As Delroy stood there, hot tears filled his eyes. He worked to get his voice out. "Hello, Daddy." He didn't know if that salutation was right under the circumstances. This wasn't a visit like the ones in the past. He wasn't here to simply pay respects; he was here to do something unthinkable and possibly blasphemous. "Pastor Harte."

Shame filled him because he didn't know the proper way to address his father. Truth to tell, even at twenty-one Delroy hadn't grown into a man's responsibility and had remained a boy in so many ways. His life had consisted of Glenda and basketball, chasing a girl and playing ball.

Lightning flashed again and laid his tall, broad shadow across his father's grave.

"Daddy." Delroy's voice was so thick he could hardly speak. "I miss you. Never have stopped missing you. I could have used your counsel a thousand times for every year that's passed since you were taken from us." He paused, feeling his hands shaking with fear and uncertainty. "I wish you were here now to talk with. But you're not."

Thunder pealed.

Deciding to be as honest as he could because he had always had that with his father, Delroy said, "Daddy, I've come to you now because I'm lost." He let the tears come because he could no longer stop them, surprised that there were so many. Five years had passed since he'd honestly let himself go. All the grief had stayed bottled up inside. He'd kept it in so long that he'd gone numb. He'd seen other men do that and had counseled them not to, but he'd never thought that would happen to him. For him, keeping himself together was all about control.

But control was just an illusion, wasn't it, Delroy? He swept the flashlight beam over his father's headstone, remembering how he'd had to touch the carved letters even many months after his father's burial just to know that they were real.

JOSIAH C. HARTE
PASTOR, FATHER, AND HUSBAND
ABOVE ALL THINGS, BELIEVER

The sight of his father's grave had made death seem so permanent. Delroy had struggled to find himself in the choking mire of pain and loss that had closed in on him for years afterward. It wasn't until he'd decided to become a preacher that some of that misery passed.

"I'm sorry so much time has passed since I've visited you," Delroy said. "I've not been a good son." A sob broke at the back of his throat, and he waited for control to return before going on. "After Terrence— after I lost my boy—" His grief overcame him. He closed his eyes and wished that he could feel his father's arms around him. No place in the world had ever felt safer.

Stained, pale white flower petals gleamed in the light near the headstone. Someone had visited recently.

"Daddy, you were a fine preacher," Delroy said. "The best I've ever heard. I never told you—and God knows I should have—how proud I was to see you take that pulpit on Sunday mornings and sing and preach the Word of God. I swear I'd never seen anything like it, nor have I seen anything like it since. The Lord spoke to you and through you. I truly believe He did."

Some of the petals broke away from the flowers the rain had beaten down into the mud. They floated away like small boats.

"But I don't think even you could have explained what happened to Terrence," Delroy went on. "A father should never outlive his son, Daddy. I tried to tell myself that Terrence had gone to be with you and the Lord. But, Daddy—" pain choked him up—"Daddy, he didn't know you. You never took Terrence fishing the way you took me fishing. Never heard your stories or sat with you on a riverbank while you cooked our catch. Never heard you sing gospel songs in the quiet of the night when we camped out. Terrence didn't know you, and I miss him so much. I *still* miss him. Taking him like that wasn't right, Daddy. There's a hole inside me that nothing can fill."

Feeling weary and hopeless, Delroy knelt, no longer trusting himself to stand. He placed the flashlight on the ground so the beam washed over the headstone. He laid the shovel beside him. The muddy ground soaked the knees of his pants with wet and cold.

"Daddy, if you were here, maybe things wouldn't seem the way they do," Delroy said. "You knew all about the end times. You always told me they were just around the corner, that we would live to see them. You were right, even if I never believed it. You almost lived to see them, too."

The heartbreaking images of his father's body laid out on the stainless-steel table returned to Delroy with savage force. Since a murderer had taken Josiah Harte's life, the state medical examiner's office had taken the body for an autopsy. The funeral home, the people who had known and loved Josiah, hadn't gotten his body until after the forensics investigators had finished.

"I know you're in heaven, Daddy," Delroy croaked. "And I know you've looked down on me from time to time. I swear I could feel you then. I can look back and probably name the days when I felt close to you. I only hope you're not watching over me tonight."

Delroy leaned forward and placed his hands on his father's grave. He wasn't surprised to find that he was shaking.

"I failed you, Daddy," he whispered, too ashamed to admit that out loud. But he knew he had to say it. His father had always seemed to know even the things he had tried to hide. "I never once told you that I wanted to become a preacher. I didn't know it myself. All I ever wanted for myself when you were alive was a career as a professional basketball player."

Josiah Harte had sat in the bleachers at a number of county league, junior high, high school, and college games.

"I was selfish as a young man, Daddy, and I know you saw that in me. But I wouldn't listen. The sad thing was that I didn't learn enough then or even when you were taken from us."

Delroy closed his fists in the mud at his father's grave. "I was self-ish in my grief, too, Daddy. When I lost Terrence, I just couldn't see anyone else. Couldn't see Glenda, couldn't see Momma. Couldn't see anybody but that hole that his passing left. His absence was too big, too painful. I couldn't get around it."

Delroy remembered how Glenda had tried to talk to him during those dark days. But he'd turned away from her, taking the first step of all those that had separated them over the last five years. Even on a ship halfway around the world from Glenda, he'd never put as much distance between himself and his wife as he had standing side by side on the day they had buried their son. He couldn't give himself over to her because he'd feared that he couldn't pull himself back together.

"And now I come to you tonight," Delroy said in a hoarse whis-per, "shamed and hurting because I don't have the faith that you did. I've never had it. I never knew God. I can see that now. Not like you did. I don't even have the faith that God cares about us."

Grief and fear doubled Delroy over. He cried, dipping his head in close to his chest. Rain pelted the back of his slicker and ran down the back of his ears. He gave himself over to the emotion, letting it wrench him and tear him apart. The hours of flying, the miles of walking, and the days of worry and agony came together and taxed him to the point of exhaustion. He rested his head on his forearms, almost passing out.

"I've seen news reports since I've been back stateside, Daddy," Delroy whispered. "People everywhere have disappeared. Unborn children were taken from their mothers' wombs. Funeral homes and morgues have had the dead disappear on them, too."

During the last few days, Delroy had concentrated his attention on stories concerning the missing dead. That was when the idea for his present course of action had called out to him.

"There's no explanation for those missing bodies, Daddy. I have guessed that they were all God's people called up to heaven, too."

The wind whistled through the trees and the rain shifted, coming in from the north now, blowing harder and turning colder.

"I'm serving aboard *Wasp* right now," Delroy continued. Lightning flashed and thunder pealed. The rain ran across the muddy ground only inches from his face. "I had a good friend pass away the day before the—the—" he couldn't even bring himself to say "the Rapture." "—before the disappearances. You'd have liked Dwight Mellencamp. The chief was a good man."

Taking a ragged, deep breath and feeling the cold, wet night air crawl into his lungs, Delroy pushed himself up to a kneeling position. He stared at his father's headstone.

"Dwight's body disappeared, Daddy. I was there when it happened. I saw it and I still don't know what it was that I saw." Delroy's voice caught. "He was a Christian man. He and I had long talks about the Bible. He knew about the end times, too."

Rain slid down Delroy's face. The flashlight brought out the headstone in sharp relief. More of the flower petals ripped free and floated away on the runoff.

"With Dwight's body disappearing along with the bodies of all those other people, I knew I had to come here. I didn't have a choice. Revelation doesn't say that people would disappear when the Rapture came. The book doesn't mention that they'll leave their clothes behind. It just says that God will call His church."

Delroy's voice quit for a moment before going on. "There's so much that we didn't know. I wish I had known it would happen like this. But they *are* called the mysterious ways of the Lord, aren't they? Maybe He judged that the whole truth would wreak havoc in His church. I just don't know what to think. Not about my part in all of this. With my head I believe in God, Daddy, and I believe that this *is* the Rapture, but I can't seem to find that faith in my heart. Maybe I'm wrong, but it seems to me that at some point we should just *know*."

Slowly, Delroy pushed himself to his feet. He took up the shovel and the flashlight. "I've got to see, Daddy. That's all. I've just got to see." Delroy paused. "I raised Terrence the best I could. Watched my boy become a man, and then watched that man walk off to become a warrior. He died in battle. He was a hero, a man to be remembered. Like you. You would have liked him, Daddy. You would have loved him. I hope—I hope that the two of you have met by now."

Almost overcome by the emotions that raged within him, Delroy tilted his face up at the dark heavens, letting the rain pock his face. He felt the cold drops burst and spread against his skin.

"There's a war coming on, Daddy," Delroy said softly. "The hosts of heaven and the demons of hell. They're going to fight right here and right now. For seven years, the people left behind are going to see some of the greatest evil atrocities ever committed. Souls hang in the balance. Not all of them will know the love of Jesus and His salvation, and they will be lost. It's already too late for so many."

Thunder hammered the skies. Lightning flashed again and another roll of thunder followed in its wake.

"I brought Terrence up in the church, Daddy. The same way you raised me up. But—" Delroy stopped and brushed the hot tears from his eyes—"but I know how weak a man sometimes is. I'm weak. Not nearly as strong as you thought I was." His voice didn't work for a moment. "I raised Terrence in the church, but I don't truly know if he knew the Lord. Just as I don't know if I ever truly knew the Lord. I baptized that boy and I heard his prayers, but maybe I failed him. Just like I failed myself."

Thunder cracked and pealed.

"Daddy, here I am in this graveyard, wet and without you or the Lord. I am miserable, and I know now that I am lost. I don't know what I'm supposed to do." Delroy fought back the pain that threatened to choke him. "I know you believed I was saved, too, but I wasn't. I know it has to be a terrible thing to see me here like this, to know that I doubted God so much that He left me behind. I've shamed you, and for that I hope you'll forgive me." He wiped the tears and the rain from his face with a big hand.

"I hope you'll understand why I've got to do what I'm going to do." Rain pelted Delroy, smashing hard against his face and getting into his eyes. "I hope that you'll find it in your heart to forgive me." Taking a fresh grip on the shovel, Delroy turned and walked to the grave two plots down. The one in between was reserved for his mother. Etta still lived in Marbury in a self-assisted home.

At the foot of the chosen grave, Delroy shone his flashlight over the headstone:

LANCE CORPORAL TERRENCE DAVID HARTE
SON, SOLDIER, HERO
BELOVED ALWAYS AND MISSED DEARLY

Delroy stood at the foot of his son's grave for a moment. He heard the sound of the rain all around him. Tears coursed down his cheeks.

"God, forgive me," he whispered. "I know what I'm about to do is

an affront to You. I know I can't ask Your blessing in this, but I do beg
Your understanding."

Firming up his resolve and his conviction, Delroy set the flashlight on the ground so the beam spread over the grave. He pulled on
the gloves that George had lent him; then he took up the shovel. He
placed the keen blade on the ground, then leaned on it and plunged it
deep into the dark, wet earth.

United States 75th Army Rangers Temporary Post
Sanliurfa, Turkey
Local Time 0510 Hours

Goose swept his gaze around the makeshift operating theater set up inside the basement of one of the city's more prestigious hotels. Beds filled every available space, but severely wounded and dead still lay in the floor in places. Cries of injured men and women filled the large room, while doctors and nurses shouted information to each other across patients. More litters arrived, transferred from the triage stations on the first-floor level.

The wounded weren't just military; a few were citizens and tourists who hadn't yet found a way or a time to depart. Some were journalists that Goose had seen working over the past two days. Recognizing them, Goose wondered what had happened to Danielle Vinchenzo. The young journalist tended to insert herself and her team into the thickest action. He had no doubt that reporting from the front lines where the Syrian tanks had crashed through was her idea. But he hadn't seen the woman or her team since then.

While making the rounds, Goose also checked in with standing security teams, making certain they held the line. The combined military forces in the city had immediately elected to set up their own surgery areas instead of using the Turkish hospitals. Sanliurfa's hospitals became targets for the Syrian air force the next night after their retreat and had taken major damage during each successive raid.

Triage teams manned the doorways into the building. Incoming wounded were marked before they came inside. Shorthand written across their foreheads with washable markers indicated to surgeons

and nurses what had to be done, whether to attempt to save a life or
administer painkillers till they passed. Life and death was reduced to
a symbol or two. In the middle of bloody and pain-filled chaos, the
surgical teams somehow managed to eke out a sense of professional
care and compassion that amazed Goose even after his other battlefield experiences.

"Control," a man called over the headset Goose wore, "I'm starting to see movement along the Syrian front line."

"I do too," Remington replied.

"They appear to be pulling back."

"Affirmative, Tango Leader," Remington replied. "Stay on them. I
want laser-assisted targeting for the howitzers for as long as you can.
We've earned their respect for the moment, but they'll be back. We're
standing between the Syrian war machine and everything their gener-
als need to control. I want to take down every unit of their armored
cav that we can while we have the chance under the cover of darkness."

"Roger, Control. Tango Team will continue to flag 'em and tag
'em."

Tango Team, Goose knew from the defense briefing Remington
had put into effect nineteen hours ago when news of the Syrian armored advancement was received, was a scout team lead by Lieutenant
Carlos Mendoza of the 75th. The team all rode Enduro motorcycles
tricked out with infrared lights for night riding. They also carried Litton
PAQ-10 Ground Laser Target Designators. The GLTDs used by Lieutenant Mendoza's team marked targets and relayed coordinates to Captain Mkchian's artillery teams, allowing them almost pinpoint
accuracy. Judging from the communications traffic Goose had been
privy to, Mendoza's team was turning the Syrian armored cav into sitting ducks for the Turkish howitzers and mortars.

The constant thunder of the artillery cascaded over the city, echo-
ing hollowly down in the basement.

Pain ratcheted through Goose's knee as he walked, causing a
slight limp. He tried to remain distant as he recognized the Rangers
who were wounded or dead, but he had difficulty doing that. He
knew most of them personally, from ops out in the field to basketball
and volleyball games back at Fort Benning. So many of them were
young men, and too many of those were dead and dying, or horribly
wounded.

"Bleeder," a surgeon called out as a line of blood shot up from a
patient's open chest cavity. He ignored the stream of blood splashing

his chest and neck, reached into the man's body, and closed the artery with his fingers. "Forceps. Close that off. I'll suture once we get him stabilized."

A young male assistant leaned in with something that looked like scissors. The stainless steel gleamed until the moment the blood pumped onto it when the surgeon released his hold.

Goose kept moving, listening to the chatter across the headset. Teams were shutting Sanliurfa down section by section, taking out Syrian soldiers trapped behind the lines. Many of the enemy soldiers fought to the death when cornered, but there were already a few prisoners in custody. There was a chance the intelligence teams could gather information about the Syrian army's strength and movement.

An orderly hustled by Goose with an IV rig in his hands. Glucose and blood were in short supply. The surgical teams would struggle to get through the night.

And tomorrow's still coming, Goose reminded himself.

Feeling useless and guilty for coming down into the main operating theater, Goose walked out of the room. He'd arrived only a few minutes ago and his thoughts had immediately turned to Icarus. The man had stated that he would make contact at the hospital.

Could have been a mix-up, Goose told himself. *There are other triage areas in the city now. Maybe Icarus went there.* He couldn't get the man's cryptic warning out of his head. Finding the CIA agent in the alley so near to where Icarus had confronted him had left Goose unsettled. The possibility existed that the CIA team had intercepted Icarus, and the man his squad had found in the alley was a casualty of that encounter.

But why leave a man behind? That didn't make sense. Unless the other CIA agents had believed the man dead—or they'd been pressed for time by one of the teams Remington had in the field searching for Icarus. Few soldiers were aware of the tension between Remington's covert teams and the CIA agents. Goose knew about them, but he also knew Remington deliberately kept him out of that action. The only time the captain had ever assigned Goose to a private mission like the search for Icarus was when Remington was certain Goose believed in what that mission's goal was.

Icarus's choice to make contact with Goose hadn't set well with Remington from the outset. If the man was looking for a safe house from the CIA, he could have asked Remington. Goose had pointed out that Icarus had talked to him under duress, claiming that he was armed with an explosive device.

That hadn't mattered to Remington. Goose knew the captain considered him tainted as a result. Goose also had a tendency to think for himself at times too, and Remington never assigned him to a mission that Remington totally wanted to control. Remington sometimes used information he got from unconventional sources to his own benefit. Goose had never been comfortable with that, though several times that information had provided key turning points in an engagement or op.

Goose was distracted from pursuing the line of logic concerning the man his squad had found by a squawk from the headset.

"Phoenix Leader," Hershel Barnett called.

"Go."

"The prince came by and kissed Sleeping Beauty. He's about nine kinds of mad about being held for questioning. Throwing around his threats about us infringing on his constitutional rights and so forth."

"Has he identified himself as an American citizen?"

"Says he is. Accent's about right. But you know that the spies they turn out of spy school these days sound like Kansas City radio DJs. Maybe he's American and maybe he ain't."

Goose knew Barnett was deliberately baiting the man they'd brought to the hospital. Judging from the sheer torrent of verbal invective unleashed in the background, Barnett had succeeded.

"I'm on my way."

Another series of artillery blasts reverberated through the building. The thunderous roars were partially muted so it was impossible to tell if they were made by howitzers firing or warheads landing within the city.

Goose navigated the long stairwell up to the main floor. He favored his injured knee by using the handrail and leaning part of his weight on it. What he most needed was rack time and a chance to get his knee elevated. Though they weren't part of the original construction, the building had elevators. Getting stuck between floors in case of a power outage wasn't an ideal situation, so he'd opted for the stairs.

Goose stepped into the service area and took a left. He passed by the arched doorway to the huge hotel lobby.

Trimmed in classic art deco, the hotel lobby stood out immediately as a fantasy landscape for tourists, a trip back in time to a foreign land where *Lawrence of Arabia* and *The Ten Commandments* had been set. Posters of both movies, as well as *Cleopatra* and *Ben-Hur*, held positions of prominence in the lobby. Palm trees in ornate pots reached for the main chandelier high above the floor.

It was a place, Goose knew, that he would like to have brought Megan to, the kind of place where normal life and all its problems evaporated at the door. They'd never had a real vacation since their honeymoon. Because money had always been tight, they had never felt comfortable with spending so extravagantly. Now, however, Goose wished he had taken Megan someplace like this. The chance might not ever occur again.

And Chris wouldn't be there with them.

Goose's heart ached at the thought. Desperately, he pushed the troubling thoughts away. He couldn't afford to think about Chris's absence now. He had to survive; then he'd see what he could do about seeing Chris again.

The allure of the hotel was conspicuously absent at the moment. Patients without life-or-death wounds lay on the marble floor on makeshift litters and mattresses culled from beds throughout the hotel. The living shared space with the dead, which were covered with sheets. Some of those sheets bore bloodstains that testified to terrible wounds and painful deaths.

A mix of Rangers, marines, Turkish military, and U.N. forces guarded the hotel's doors. Rangers held command there at Captain Remington's insistence. Heavy plywood covered all of the elaborate windows on the main floor. Guards posted on the top three floors made constant security sweeps. So far, none of the Syrian forces had managed to reach the building. Patrols had stopped the closest tank less than a block away. The south end of the hotel had taken a couple of severe hits. Military firefighters had put out the blaze that threatened to consume the building.

The hotel security office was located behind the main desk. Two Rangers stood guard at the entrance. A simple desk took up the back third of the small office space. The desk held security camera monitors that rotated through all four upper floors of the hotel and the basement. Two Rangers sat at the desk watching the camera sweeps, keeping constant radio contact with security teams throughout the building.

The unknown man Goose's squad had picked up in the alley sat in the center of the room in a straight-backed chair that didn't look comfortable to any degree. His bruised face had swelled considerably. Black-and-purple splotches covered most of his features. Dried blood mottled the long tears and split skin. He held a chemical ice pack along his jaw.

Barnett lounged against the wall and smoked a cigarette.

The man glared up at Goose. "You in charge of this operation?"

Goose returned the man's gaze full measure. "Yes."

The man nodded, but the movement looked painful. "They're not letting me leave."

"They were told not to."

"Why?"

"Because we found you, unconscious, in the middle of a battle-field."

"So what?" the man asked belligerently. "You put me under guard to make sure I stick around long enough to say thanks? Well then, thanks." He started to get to his feet.

Barnett leaned forward casually and shoved the man back into the chair. He landed heavily, and the chair legs screeched across the stone floor.

"What is wrong with you people?" the man demanded. "First you save me; now I'm getting the tough-guy treatment."

"What's your name?" Goose asked.

The man didn't hesitate. "Winters. Mike Winters. I'm an American citizen. From Newark, New Jersey. You don't have any right to hold me here like this."

"Well, Mr. Winters," Goose said, "at the time we found you, you didn't have any ID."

Winters made a show of reaching into his pants pocket. He looked surprised when he came up empty. "My wallet must have fallen out." Then he glared suspiciously at the Rangers in the room. "Or maybe someone stole it."

"At the time we found you," Goose repeated in a slower, more forceful voice, "you didn't have any ID."

"Then I guess I lost it while I was running for my life," the man said. "Just my bad luck. That doesn't explain why you're holding me."

"I notice you normally carry a couple of sidearms."

"Not normally."

Goose shrugged and acceded the answer. "You did tonight. And if you don't normally go armed, tonight was a special occasion."

Winters shifted a little, rocking from side to side and grimacing. The holsters he wore offered mute testimony that he had carried weapons.

"I like to be safe," the man said.

"Safe would have kept you inside tonight," Goose said.

"The building I was staying in was bombed. Killed a whole room full of people. I was lucky I wasn't killed."

The man was lying. Goose's sergeant's nose for trouble and false-hoods told him that. "Safe would have had you out of the city days ago."

"I got trapped here during the attack."

"A lot of people left immediately afterward. Before the Syrians started running jets through Turkish airspace and taking out convoys headed north."

"I wasn't in the city then."

"Where were you?"

Winters waved a hand. "South."

"What were you doing?"

"Business."

Goose waited a beat, took a look at the empty shoulder holster the man wore, and asked, "What kind of business are you in, Mr. Winters?"

"Photography. I'm a photojournalist."

"Whom do you work for?"

"I'm independent. I work for myself."

"You didn't have a camera with you tonight."

Winters hesitated. "I did. It must have gotten stolen."

"I thought so," Goose said. "An attack like this, there'd probably be a lot of news agencies willing to pay for pictures."

Shifting the ice pack along his jaw thoughtfully, as if suddenly realizing he'd stepped out onto dangerous ground despite the innocuous line of questioning Goose had introduced, Winters nodded. "Yeah. A lot of 'em."

"How much film were you carrying?" Goose asked.

Winters shrugged. "Don't know. A bunch."

"Where is it?"

"I suppose it was stolen with the camera."

"And your pistols."

"Yeah. And my pistols. Maybe you should be out there looking for whoever jacked me instead of giving me the third degree."

"I don't do police work," Goose replied. "I'm here to help my captain maintain a strong position inside this city and resist occupation by enemy forces."

Winters relaxed a little in his chair. "Looks like I'm keeping you from your job, Sergeant Gander. I'm not the enemy."

"Part of my job responsibilities here includes running security and identifying potential threats," Goose said.

"What does that have to do with me?"

Goose ticked points off on his fingers. "You don't have any ID. You were heavily armed for a civilian, even under these circumstances. You were in motion in this city, carrying out your own agenda when common sense would have dictated that you hole up until the worst of this situation was over. You don't come across like any photojournalist I've ever met, and I've come across a lot of them since the op here began. You're demanding to leave immediately instead of taking comfort in the fact that—at present—you're safe from attack."

"That's all circumstantial. Doesn't mean anything."

"You were in the same area as me," Goose said softly. "And you know my name."

Hesitation froze Winters for an instant. He tried to cover. "You gave me your name."

"Private," Goose said, raising his voice slightly.

"Yes, Sergeant." Barnett looked directly at the back of Winters's head.

Goose knew the man felt the private's stare because he squirmed uncomfortably and couldn't resist a glance over his shoulder. "Did I give this man my name?" Goose asked.

"No, Sergeant."

"Did anyone else in this room give this man my name?"

"No, Sergeant. I've been doing the only talking in the room."

Goose shook his head and maintained eye contact with Winters. "No one gave you my name."

"Maybe we met somewhere before," Winters suggested. "You said yourself that you've seen a lot of media people. We probably met in Glitter City or possibly when I was doing some shooting on the front line."

"I didn't see you."

"Sure you did. You just don't remember me." Winters gestured to his face. "I bet I look like raw hamburger right now. If you'd seen me before this happened you might have remembered me."

"Before what happened?"

Winters didn't miss a beat, flowing smoothly into the question Goose thrust in the middle of the conversation. "Before I was beaten up and robbed."

"Did you see the person or persons who did this?"

"No. It was dark. Maybe he followed me."

"He?"

Shrugging, Winters said, "He, she, it. Pick your pronoun, Sergeant."

"Followed you from where?"

"The bar."

"You were in a bar?"

"I told you I was in a bar."

"No," Goose said, "you didn't." He paused. "What bar would that be?"

"I don't remember. Some hole-in-the-wall that survived the bombing."

"Until tonight."

"That's right," Winters agreed testily. "Until tonight."

"I don't forget faces," Goose said. "I've never seen you until tonight. But I find it interesting that you know who I am."

Winters didn't say anything.

That, Goose knew, showed training. A normal individual caught in a lie tended to try to overexplain or modify his or her answer to take care of any discrepancies. Winters was trained to refuse the knee-jerk reflex.

"Did you see who attacked you?" Goose asked.

"No," Winters replied.. "I told you that."

The answer came too quick and too certain. Goose's instincts told him the man had lied again. "Do you think whoever did it meant to kill you?"

"No. Probably just wanted to get the camera and pistols."

"And the film," Goose said. The answer wasn't a complete lie. Winters—and Goose doubted that was the man's real name—knew who had attacked him but not if that person intended to kill him.

"Yeah."

Goose surveyed Winters's face. "That's a lot of damage for a guy who was just intending to rob you. Someone who spends that much time at that kind of beating usually intends it as personal."

"It could have been a rival photojournalist," Winters said. "Things have gotten crazy in this city."

"A rival journalist who decided to take on a guy carrying two pistols."

Winters nodded and decided to stay with his lie. "A really desperate photojournalist who'd broken his own camera or didn't get the pictures of the attack that I did."

Raised voices sounded out by the main desk. Goose glanced in that direction and saw the two Rangers posted at guard confronting a tall athletic man with dark hair going gray at the temples. He wore a tailored canvas jacket covered in dust and splintered wood. He stood toe-to-toe with the Rangers, obviously not intimidated.

Winters started to get up again. Goose noticed the look of recognition in Winters's eyes.

Barnett dropped a big hand on Winters's shoulder. "Siddown, Mikey. You haven't been dismissed yet." He shoved the smaller man back into the chair with a thump.

Goose walked to the doorway. "Something wrong here, Private?" He locked eyes with the civilian.

The Rangers stood with their M-4A1s at the ready, far enough back from the man that he couldn't impede their ability to use the assault rifles. Three men in lightweight jackets flanked the tall man. All of them had flat-eyed stares that reflected only cold dispassion. Goose had seen the same lack of personal attention in the eyes of trained guard dogs.

"This man says he wants to speak with you," one of the privates answered.

Goose stared the man in the eye. "Did he ask for me, Private? Or did he ask for whoever was in charge?"

"He asked for you, sir. By name."

Goose pinned the tall man with his gaze. "Did he identify himself?"

"No, Sergeant."

The man regarded Goose with cold disdain. "You think maybe we can cut the chitchat, Sergeant Gander?"

"Sure," Goose said. "Tell me who you are, prove it, and we'll negotiate how chitchat-free we can become."

"Maybe we can talk in private," the man suggested.

Goose walked by the desk, not bothering to try to clear the security office as he guessed the man was hoping he would do. The Rangers held their post. The three bodyguards followed their leader.

"You said in private," Goose reminded. "If you start playing the intimidation game with me, I'll fill this area with Rangers and conduct this conversation with a bullhorn while we try to figure out who you are."

Irritably, the man waved off his three associates. They retreated reluctantly but interposed themselves between the man and Goose and the Rangers posted at guard. The psychological impact was clear: Goose was cut off from his men; any help he expected on that front would have to go through them first.

Goose held his M-4A1 comfortably by its pistol grip. One step would put the man between him and his three bodyguards, partially blocking their fields of fire. In addition—judging from the bulky heft of the man's upper body, Goose was willing to wager that the man wore some kind of body armor.

The three men looked at each other wordlessly, then relaxed their stances. They no longer looked as threatening.

Goose figured that his psychological impact was clear, too. Pistols just didn't measure up against an assault rifle in an armed confrontation. *Okay, boys, all the marbles are on the table. Let's see how the ante goes.*

❋   ❋   ❋

Sunshine Hills Cemetery
Outside Marbury, Alabama
Local Time 2221 Hours

The earth from the grave site turned easily. Delroy removed shovelful after shovelful of dark loam, adding to the tall heap to one side. Most of the dirt stayed in place, but occasional trickles ran back into the deep hole he'd made.

Rain had saturated the area for days. When the gravediggers had cut the hole in the ground and filled it back in, the replaced soil was free of rocks and roots. The rain had helped when Delroy first started digging, but now the constant flow of water into the open hole hindered his progress. Black rain that barely reflected his flashlight beam pooled at the bottom of the hole, rendering the earth the consistency of soup if he didn't dig deep and hard beyond the surface.

Delroy's back and arms and legs ached from the unfamiliar exertion. Back on *Wasp*, he kept in shape, playing pickup basketball and handball with the other officers and enlisted. Three times a week he went through the weight machines. Five times a week he jogged *Wasp*'s landing deck. Sometimes he jogged in the morning, starting before daybreak and ending when the sun crested the eastern skies, seeming to come up out of the sea or from whatever landmass that lay to the east of the ship.

But he'd never before dug a grave.

Or dug one up, he amended silently. He took a fresh grip on the shovel and thrust it deep into the earth again. Sweat covered his flesh under the slicker and his wet clothes. Thankfully, the chore also warmed him against the cold chill of the night.

He swept the shovel aside and dumped the latest load atop the hill of dirt that was slowly but surely turning to mud. The drowned earth under his feet sucked at his boots as he shifted.

The hole was three feet by three feet so far, and nearly as deep. The work had gone quickly, but his reserves were going just as quickly. Emotion further exhausted him, growing stronger and stronger the deeper he went, wearing him out even more quickly.

Relentless, he thrust the shovel back into the grave. The blade struck an unyielding surface with a clank.

Delroy's heart leaped into his throat as he realized that he might have already reached his son's casket. Many graves weren't truly six feet deep. He froze. His stomach churned, filled with acid, and a rancid taste coated his mouth.

"God help you, Delroy," he whispered to himself. "Are you ready for this?"

Terrence had died in the Middle East five years ago, his squad ambushed by terrorists the U.S. Marines had gone to disenfranchise from the local populace that had kept them hidden. The wounds Terrence had died from had necessitated a closed-coffin ceremony.

Delroy had never gotten the chance to say good-bye to his son properly, never had the chance to kiss him good-bye one last time. But he'd also been spared the harsh sight of seeing Terrence dead. All Delroy had seen was a flag-draped coffin that scarcely seemed big enough to hold his boy who had been so big in life.

Raw pain surged through the chaplain anew. Just when he had decided that he had never before hurt so much in his life and surely couldn't ever hurt that much again, the thought of seeing his son's badly maimed corpse hit him with the unstoppable force of a battleship under speed.

He reeled and swayed, holding onto the shovel with both hands. "God, help me."

Only the drumming rain and the low whisper of the wind washing through the trees answered him.

Delroy felt more alone and cut off from the world than he ever had. It was even worse than when he had returned to his quarters after he'd received notification of Terrence's death. He'd been at a new posting, with no one really close to him, bereft of family and friends until the helicopter had started him on his trip back home.

Lightning blazed against the sky. When the thunder came immediately afterward, the basso boom sounded right above him. The vibration reached through his whole body, jarring him solidly.

Looking into the dark sky above the small bubble of pale yellow illumination afforded by the flashlight lying on the other side of the grave, Delroy took a long, ragged breath. "You took him from me, Lord. I wasn't ready to let him go, but You took him anyway. He was just a boy." His words caught as fresh tears filled his eyes. "*My* boy. You had no cause to do that. I'd worked long and hard for You, and You took him from me anyway."

Thunder rumbled in the distance, but there were no answers in the dark sky.

Delroy wiped the fresh tears from his face. "I want answers, God. I want to know what is going on. I want to know if the Rapture really did occur or if I've been fooling myself about everything my daddy taught me."

That's not true, Delroy told himself. *You know that's not true. Here you stand, lying to the Lord and you're standing in your own son's open grave to do it.*

Realization of what he was doing filled Delroy with weakness. He tried to hang on to his resolve. "God, forgive me. I beg You. But I'm weak. I know that You've raptured Your church and that I've been found wanting, but I need to know—" His voice broke and he couldn't go on. He felt the hard surface grate against the shovel's blade as he shifted. "I just—I just need to know if my boy made it to You. That's all, God. I just need to know that You've taken him into Your embrace and are watching over him because now I can't."

He turned his attention back to the ground. Placing his foot on the shovel, he thrust again, changing the angle. This time the shovel slid freely, rasping along an object hidden in the muddy earth. As he turned the shovel over, he saw that what he'd found was a rock.

The rock was flat and smooth, obviously one that had spent years at the bottom of a creek bed or a river. Now here it was, where no rocks were supposed to be, miles from any creek or river. The rock was large, as big as a hubcap, and at least thirty or forty pounds in weight.

Words from the past, from a talk Delroy had shared with his father, came back to him. At eight or nine years old, Delroy's curious mind had constantly created questions for his father to answer.

"But how do I know to believe in Jesus and the Lord, Daddy?" young Delroy had asked. They'd sat on a creek bank only a few miles from the church and the little house out back where Josiah Harte preached the Word of the Lord and raised his family. They both held cane fishing poles Pastor Crook had made as presents the previous

Father's Day. Pastor Crook had trained Josiah in the ways of the church.

Josiah had worn the old felt hat festooned with handmade flies and lures that his wife said she hated because it made him look unkempt. Etta Harte had prided herself on her sewing and ironing, and she'd always made sure her man looked his best when he went out her door. Josiah had worked his line, setting the hook into the deep water beneath a log where Delroy had spotted bass only the day before.

"You don't know how to believe, Son," Josiah had replied.

"I know, Daddy," Delroy agreed. "That's what I'm telling you. I don't know how to believe. So how am I supposed to learn to believe?"

"You can't learn to believe."

Delroy had fumbled with that thought for a moment or two, testing it for inconsistencies. "Well, you did."

"Nope."

"Then how come you believe in the Lord so all-fired much if you didn't learn how?"

Josiah had turned to his son with a big grin. He rubbed a hard hand across Delroy's head. Working with fences and lumber and occasional construction to help out with congregation members' projects over the years had left thick yellow calluses on his hands.

"You sure do a powerful lot of thinking, Son," Josiah had said.

"Yes, sir. That's what I intend to do."

"Thinkin' ain't always good for a man. That's one thing you can purely do too much of if you ain't careful."

"You always tell me to think about what I'm doing."

Josiah had shrugged in resignation. "Well, Son, now I guess that would be about right. Your momma's always after me about that, wanting me to think more. So I guess maybe you an' me come by it righteous enough. But we didn't come out here to think. We came to fish."

"I know, Daddy. I just can't help myself."

Josiah had sighed, and even then Delroy had known his father was resigning himself to another interrogation. "No, I suppose you can't. So what did you want to know?"

"How'd you get to learn how to believe so much?"

Josiah had hesitated a moment. "You might not be ready for this, Delroy."

"You saying I ain't old enough, Daddy?" Age hadn't been something that Delroy let stand in his way in those days. His mother had taught him the word *precocious* because she was always calling him that and he'd asked Lutie the butcher what it meant one day while buying a chicken for the family stewpot.

"I didn't say you weren't old enough."

"Then what are you saying?"

"God talks to you at different times in your life," Josiah had said. "All you got to do is listen to Him."

"I been listening. But He ain't said a word."

"Maybe now just ain't the time. You're still a little young."

"So God don't like talking to kids?"

Josiah had frowned long and hard. "God loves His children. Don't you ever go lettin' nobody tell you any different."

His father's swift and fierce reaction had scared Delroy a little. "No, sir. I won't."

Josiah had tried to return to his fishing, but Delroy knew that he'd come too far for his father to simply leave the matter lie. Delroy bided his time, knowing his father would get back to the conversation even though he was a little uncomfortable with it.

"I didn't learn," Josiah finally said after long minutes of silence.

"Didn't learn what, Daddy?" Delroy had tried to appear innocent.

"I didn't *learn* to believe. I *chose* to."

"Chose to what?"

"Chose to believe in the Lord God Almighty. Ain't that what we're talking about here?"

"Yes, Daddy. But you ain't giving me no answers."

"I'm givin' you all the answer there is. All the answer a man should ever need."

"Well, then, I must be stupid because I don't know what you're talking about."

Josiah had never liked it when Delroy called himself stupid. At eight or nine, the threat of thinking of himself as stupid was always offered as bait to get his father to open up more when he became reluctant about a discussion topic.

"You see?" Josiah said. "That's why I said you should wait on this here conversation."

"Till when, Daddy?"

Josiah had scratched his head. "Well, you right about that. No man ought to wait on something like this. Not if he's smart enough to be askin' questions about it." He'd looked around, then pulled up a flat stone from the creek bank. With a practiced effort, he'd sent the stone skipping across the creek. Every time the stone had touched the placid water surface, it bounced upward again, getting a little closer to the other side with each hop.

"Way to go, Daddy," Delroy had crowed with childish glee. "That was a good one. You almost throwed that rock to the other side."

Josiah nodded. "Now, when I tell you, I want you to close your eyes. Then open them again when I say so."

"All right." The exercise had seemed like a game. Delroy had always loved games. He'd closed his eyes and waited, hearing the *whip-snap* of his father's shirt in the breeze.

"Now, Son, open them eyes and tell me what you see."

Delroy had, and he'd seen the stone skipping across the creek even farther than the first one. "I see a stone hopping on the water."

"Yes, sir, you do. Now tell me who threw that rock."

Delroy had looked at his father warily. He hated it when people pulled tricks on him. The answer was so simple, so straightforward that there had to be a trick. But there also was no other answer. "Well, you did, Daddy."

"Did I now? Did you *see* me throw that rock?"

"No, sir. You told me to keep my eyes closed."

"Then you *believe* I throwed that rock."

Delroy had nodded. No other possibility existed. "Yes, Daddy. I believe it was you throwed that rock."

"An' you'd be right." Josiah had smiled. "An' you there talkin' like you're gettin' stupid. I can't fool you."

"No, sir." Delroy had felt mixed up. He wasn't quite happy with his success because he didn't know what it meant. "I still don't know how you learned to believe in the Lord."

"I know that, Son. That's what I'm tellin' you. When the time comes, the Lord'll make a miracle for you. Something that only you an' Him will know ever happened. Maybe you'll be stubborn about it, because when you get down to it, most folks are. An' maybe you'll be blessed enough that the Lord won't have to take time outta His day to come pound it into your head. Now, mind you, He will do that 'cause He loves you an' He knows some folks just need a powerful lot of convincin' 'cause they's stubborn."

"What kind of miracle will He make for me?"

"Don't know. Miracles come in all sizes. Some big, some small. Sometimes you won't even see 'em till you're well past 'em an' happen to look back one day 'cause you know you up an' missed somethin' in your hurry."

"And then you'll know, Daddy?"

Laughing, Josiah had grabbed his son in a bear hug. "'Course you won't know. Ain't you been listenin'? You see your miracle, you still won't know. If you see somethin' that there ain't no explanation for, why you'll know an' it won't be faith no more at all now, will it? It would just be something you know. No faith there in that, Son."

"No, sir. I guess that's not likely."

"Knowin' ain't the same as believin'. Never was supposed to be. It'll be up to you to believe because you choose to. You got to learn to trust in the Lord, that's all."

Delroy had thought about that for a while, long enough to watch his daddy miss getting a fish. "Believing seems like a lot of hard work."

"Well, Son, it is. But it's kind of like goin' up a long, tall hill. Once you get to the top an' actually do believe, why the way just gets easier. 'Course, that don't mean there ain't gonna be some rough spots along the way. Always gonna be rough spots. I never knew a time without them myself. That's what keeps you strong in your belief."

"Seems like the easiest way for me to believe is for you to make me. Just tell me to."

"I have told you that, haven't I?"

Delroy had raised his narrow shoulders and dropped them. "Yeah, Daddy. I guess you have."

"Well, then, an' it ain't workin' for you, is it? Otherwise we wouldn't be havin' this here conversation instead of fishin', would we?"

"No, sir."

"Belief's a personal thing, Son. Anybody you ask about it, why they got a different story for how it come upon them. That's the way it's supposed to be. Men get together an' talk about belief an' witness about the power of it, women too, but belief's about the most personal thing there is in all the world. Even after you get it, you'll find it's a hard thing to hold on to sometimes 'cause you're so busy tryin' to find other things to shore it up so you don't have to worry about makin' a fool out of yourself for simply trustin' in the Lord. That's why so many people hang on to superstitions an' such. 'I ain't blessed by the hand of God,' they say; 'I just got lucky today.'"

"Like Mr. Childers and the pocketknife his grandpa gave him?" Roy Childers had raised cotton, and everytime the weather got too dry or too wet, folks saw him around town constantly rubbing the old pocketknife his grandfather had given him, summoning up the good fortune his grandfather had told him was in the knife.

"Yeah," Josiah had answered. "Exactly like Mr. Childers. I seen a lot of things durin' my time in this world, an' mostly I seen a lot of scared people makin' excuses to themselves why they should believe in the Lord. Now that there, that's too much work. Especially when all they gotta do is just let go an' believe. That's all you'll ever have to do, Son: just believe in the Lord God Almighty an' He will keep you in His grace when things turn bad, an' He will give you direction when you feel lost."

Thunder startled Delroy from his reverie. He watched rain spatter the large stone that shouldn't have been in his son's grave. Mud dissolved and ran off the stone, leaving the smooth white surface behind. For the moment, his doubts and fears and feeling of betrayal dissolved as well. Peace settled over him, something he thought he'd never again feel.

Shaken, Delroy knelt while using the shovel for support and touched the stone to make sure it was real. There's no way this should be here. No way at all. *And no way you should be here doing this blasphemous thing you've set before yourself, Delroy Harte. You got to get up out of this hole. Stop now before you dig yourself any deeper.*

The problem was that he couldn't make himself step away when he was so close. At least, not immediately. He'd traveled so far, and the answer to so many of the questions he'd had for such a long time lay within his grasp. He stood, frozen, feeling the rain bead up on his skin and run under his clothing, chilling him to the bone. Believing, trusting, after everything he'd been through, was so hard.

But the rock remained where it shouldn't have been, as if guarding his son's final resting place.

Daddy, did you find believing easy day after day? I wish I could talk to you now. We never talked about this. You just always seemed so strong, and you always brought out the best in everybody around you.

Delroy took a long, shuddering breath and released his grip on the shovel. For now, he was through. He couldn't go any further without giving up everything his father had tried to teach him. He wasn't ready to do that yet, to dishonor his father's memory like that or to completely remove his trust in God.

But at the same time Delroy knew that Terrence's grave would remain here, and he would suffer from the temptation to come back and try again. If he could just make it back to the *Wasp*, the temptation would be removed at least for a time.

God, please help me remain strong. Keep my feet on Your chosen path. Continue to show me the way as You have shown me this tonight.

"A rock?" a dry, grating voice mocked from behind Delroy. "You're going to get superstitious over a rock? You're a fool, Preacher. Probably the biggest fool I've ever seen."

Recognizing the voice, Delroy whirled around and raised the shovel defensively, holding the handle across his chest so he could use it to block an attack. The thing was *here*. It *had* followed him from Washington, D.C.

"My name is Alexander Cody," the man told Goose as they stood in the hallway outside the hotel security room where Mike Winters was being held under arrest. "I'm with the CIA."

"You've got ID?" Goose asked. He framed the question politely, the way he'd been trained to do, but his curiosity had sparked considerably. He'd never met the CIA section chief who had asked Remington to send a squad to rescue Icarus, but he'd heard about him. Only Remington's cyber teams and security detail had seen the man.

Moving carefully, evidently aware of the way Goose had positioned himself so that he blocked the view of the three men with him, Cody reached under his jacket and took out a slim Italian leather wallet. He flipped it open and revealed a photo ID that declared he was Alexander M. Cody, a special agent with the Central Intelligence Agency.

Goose sincerely hoped Icarus wasn't anywhere near the makeshift hospital in the hotel. If the rogue agent got picked up, Goose figured he'd never know what the intrigue was all about. The CIA or Remington would make the man disappear.

"What can I do for you?" Goose asked.

Cody put his wallet away. "You're holding one of my men."

"Where?" Goose chose to play the blockheaded military personality, the no-nonsense, no-imagination riff that gave the military a bad name at times. In his occasional experience with government spooks—National Security Agency, Drug Enforcement Agency, as well as the

CIA—the agency people acted elitist, presenting themselves as far supe-rior to men in uniform. They liked to cut through rank and file to get special services from men in uniform.

"In there." Cody pointed to the security office. "That's my man."

"Mike Winters is one of your agents?"

"That's not Mike Winters."

Goose shrugged. "Then we have a problem, Agent Cody. That man says his name is Mike Winters."

"Winters is his cover identity." Cody spoke slower now, as if he guessed the concept was more than Goose was capable of easily han-dling.

"He doesn't have CIA ID like you do. In fact, he doesn't have any ID."

Cody sighed. "Of course he doesn't have ID that states he's a CIA agent. You send an agent out in the field with ID where he's going to run the chance of being apprehended, you might as well put his ID on a toe tag. It'll save you a step when you have to recover his body from the morgue."

"I'll need to see proper ID on him before I cut him loose."

Cody massaged his head like he was getting a migraine. "Look, Sergeant, I really don't need this. What I need is my man. And I need him right now."

"No can do," Goose replied. "Not until I can positively ID him for my report."

"What report?"

"In case you hadn't noticed, Agent Cody," Goose stated, "we were attacked tonight. Hostiles battled their way into this city and made straight for our hospital and fuel stores like they had a road map. Someone told the Syrians those locations."

Cody looked perplexed for a moment; then understanding dawned in his cold gray eyes. "You think my agent had something to do with that?"

"I think the man in that room might have."

Cody pointed into the room. "That's my agent, and my agent didn't have anything to do with leaking strategic information to the Syrian army."

"I don't know that. I don't even know for certain that he is your agent. As a matter of fact, you don't know that he is either. You haven't been in to talk to him, and I'm betting he looks different than he did the last time you saw him."

Angrily, Cody pointed to the man sitting in the chair inside the room. "I'm telling you that is my man."

"Yes, sir," Goose replied. "I'm hearing you loud and clear. But maybe you're not hearing me: I want that man identified before I release him to you or anyone else."

Another artillery wave blasted through the city, sounding closer than the last. The waves had slowed, but they hadn't become less deadly.

Cody flinched, drawing back to the safety of a nearby wall.

Goose thought that was interesting. Evidently the man hadn't often been on the battlefield, yet here he was in the thick of one of the worst Middle East engagements the U.S. had taken part in. Goose also didn't miss the fact that the three men who accompanied Cody had reached under their jackets out of reflex. They were wired and ready to go.

Cody cursed as he recovered, raking the walls with his gaze as if they might give way at any moment. He returned his attention—and his ire—to Goose.

"I don't *want* that agent IDed in your report," Cody said.

"That's your prerogative, Agent Cody," Goose replied. "But if you don't identify him, he's staying here till I can prove to my commanding officer that this man had nothing to do with the information the Syrians got tonight."

"Just because you don't know him?" Cody glared at Goose. The CIA section chief's left eye twitched.

"I'll start with that," Goose said. "I'll add to it that the circumstances surrounding his discovery by my squad and me were suspicious."

"What would *not* be suspicious tonight, Sergeant?"

Goose nodded as if in agreement. "Exactly my point, sir. I'm glad you understand my situation."

"No!" Cody exploded. "I'm not here about your situation."

"Why are you here?" Goose asked. "And if that man is your agent, what was he doing out on that street by himself?"

Cody drew himself up. "I don't answer to you, Sergeant."

"No, sir." Goose emphasized the imaginary rank, knowing his refusal to comply with the man's authority would rankle him further. "I was just thinking that if I knew why one of your agents was out there by himself, obviously the victim of some kind of violence—"

"There's violence taking place all over this city," Cody objected.

"—the victim of *personal* violence," Goose stated. "Maybe that would be enough for my report."

"You're interfering with a CIA operation, mister."

"I don't see it that way. Holding this city, that's a military operation—" Goose paused—"sir." He counted on the polite and calm yet firm manner he maintained to get under the man's skin.

"I'm here to take care of my operation."

"And I'm here to take care of mine."

"My operation—"

"Doesn't take precedence over the 75th Rangers' peacekeeping efforts at this moment," Goose interrupted.

"Captain Remington wouldn't have you stand in my way like this, Sergeant."

Goose frowned. "I don't know that, sir."

"I did you guys a favor by hooking your captain up with Nicolae Carpathia to get you satellite access when you needed it."

That was something Goose hadn't known. Remington had never revealed his sources or how he had managed to pull the feat off. Until Carpathia had provided the satellite access, Goose hadn't been aware that Remington had known the new Romanian president drawing all the media attention with his trip to the United Nations in New York. Remington liked rubbing elbows with the upwardly mobile, people who could do things for his career. But Goose didn't know when Remington would have gotten the chance to meet Carpathia.

"We appreciate the favor," Goose said. "Those satellites made a difference. Saved a lot of lives. Probably would help now if we had access to them again."

"You guys owe me," Cody said. "*Big-time.* If I hadn't intervened, you might have all gotten killed." He blew out his breath in obvious disgust. "You guys sure don't have much of a spirit of cooperation, do you?"

Goose refused to be baited. "When the situation eases up, we'll contact the captain and get his opinion. Until then, we do things my way. The way I think Captain Remington would want them done."

"Then let's contact Remington."

"The captain's busy, and this situation—for the moment—is contained. I'll wait for him to contact me."

"This is insane. You're standing in a city filled with strangers, and you pick one man out of that city—*my agent*—to take into custody?"

"Fewer and fewer strangers all the time," Goose pointed out. "We'll get them down to a manageable level."

The privates guarding the door looked at each other and silently cracked up just behind the three CIA agents keeping Cody under surveillance. The Rangers stopped laughing and straightened their faces when they saw Goose had noticed them.

Cody stepped away, put his hands on his hips, and paced three long steps away like a baseball coach who couldn't believe the call an umpire had made. Then he paced back. He put his face closer to Goose's, drawing himself up to take advantage of the handful of inches of difference between them.

"What would you do if I just took that man, Sergeant?"

"Won't happen." Goose kept his voice crisp and clean. He gave no indication of the tension or curiosity he felt, and he didn't back away from the physical intimidation game the CIA agent was trying by invading his personal space.

Goose considered his options. Icarus was supposed to meet him here at the hospital. The possibility existed that Cody and his team had already apprehended the rogue agent. If they hadn't, though, Goose intended to make enough of a scene that Icarus would stay away. Goose had no reason to trust Icarus, but his instincts about the younger man had been good, and his gut told him now that Cody didn't have the young agent's best interests at heart. As a career sergeant, Goose had learned to pay attention to his instincts.

Cody eyed Goose speculatively. "What are you saying, Sergeant? Would you shoot me if I stepped into that room and tried to take that man?"

"No, sir," Goose said. "Not without first warning you that was going to happen if you chose that course of action." He paused, leaned forward to invade Cody's personal space, and stared deeply into Cody's eyes. His voice was calm and polite when he spoke. "Just so you know, sir? *This* is that warning."

✧ ✧ ✧

Sunshine Hills Cemetery
Outside Marbury, Alabama
Local Time 2229 Hours

The creature that stood a few feet away at the edge of Terrence Harte's partially open grave looked like a man, but Delroy knew that image was a lie. He'd seen something of what the thing really looked like at the Pentagon. He tightened his grip on the shovel and held it before him.

Lightning flashed and stripped away some of the human characteristics the foul thing chose to wear. The pale skin turned translucent and revealed the spiderwebbing of reptilian scales beneath. The corners of the eyes and the mouth drew back, elongating until they showed snakelike characteristics. The image blurred constantly, going from human to monster between heartbeats.

For the first time, Delroy realized that he stood almost three feet deep in the hole. He was in a barely defensible position; the creature that faced him had the advantage of the high ground.

"You're going to believe in a rock that some lazy gravedigger could have thrown into that hole just because he dug it up and didn't want to trouble himself to carry it away?" the thing demanded.

Delroy couldn't speak, but he felt the rock he'd uncovered sitting solid and heavy behind him. He thought he'd finished with the creature back in Washington. *But you felt it coming after you, didn't you, Delroy? You knew it had your scent. That's why you've been looking over your shoulder for days.*

A grin spread across the creature's face. A forked black tongue played over its thin lips. "Isn't that idolatry, Chaplain Harte? Worshiping an image of anything that isn't the God you profess to believe in?"

"Get away from me," Delroy ordered. Fear of the thing and what it might do filled him. The fear wasn't for himself; it was for the final resting places of his loved ones and his family. There was no telling what the creature might choose to do to the graves. He stepped back farther in the hole, straddling the rock.

The thing leaned forward and smiled again. Another flash of lightning turned the head more wedge-shaped, stripping away the false humanity and exposing long teeth. "I have to admit, you surprised me by coming here. Didn't think you had something like this in you. Thought you'd head on back to that ship once you finished your business in D.C."

Delroy's heart hammered frantically in his chest. When he'd last faced the thing in the Pentagon, the creature had tried to kill him. And it had been seen by a Joint Chief, the one man Delroy needed to convince of the Rapture.

"Going back to the ship could have been interesting," the thing said. "Personally, I was looking forward to it. Your ship buddies are having a lot of problems there. The war effort—" it shrugged—"other . . . *things.* I would have enjoyed adding to those problems."

"What do you want with me?" Delroy demanded. The creature's words tore into him, making him feel even guiltier that he'd asked for and received permission from Captain Falkirk to check on his family before returning to *Wasp*. Under the circumstances, with all the disappearances around the globe and information slowly grinding through the communications channels about who remained, Falkirk had hesitated only a little before agreeing.

The thing grinned. Blue eyes glinted in the reflected flashlight beam, then lightning flashed and turned the eyes into fiery amber slits that ran up alongside its head. "What do I want? I want you to suffer, Chaplain. Then I want you to die."

"Why?"

Coiling with a grace that was more than human, the evil being squatted down at the edge of the grave, resting on the knuckles of its left hand. Or perhaps it rested on a paw.

"Because that's what I was sent to do," the thing answered. "Because I exist to accomplish that."

"Who sent you?"

The thing shook its head. "That would be telling."

"You're insane."

The thin, brittle laughter that issued from the thing's mouth ricocheted from the nearby trees. "Sanity and insanity and every degree between are human conditions, Chaplain. I've never been human. I've never been that vulnerable or weak. Only worn the flesh and got the T-shirt." It paused to lick its lips with the forked black tongue. "I'm evil, and I glory in being that. I love wielding fear and violence, threat and half-truths. Those are the tools of my trade." A mocking smile framed its lips. "Tactics not totally unlike those practiced by some of the leaders of your calling." It took a deep breath through its slitted nostrils. "And I love the chance to walk the earth again. People here are . . . foolish . . . and frail. Easy to destroy or to kill."

Delroy noticed that the thing wore a black T-shirt and khakis. People passing this creature on the street wouldn't give it a second look. Though it got rained on, the creature showed no signs of being wet. Water rolled off its skin and clothing without leaving anything behind, like water from a duck's back.

"Go ahead and open the grave," the thing suggested with a coaxing, crooked little smile. It flicked a forefinger toward the hole Delroy stood in. "That's what you came here for, right?"

Delroy stood and held the shovel like a weapon. Back in the Pentagon, the creature had told him that all the people who had been left behind after the Rapture were only prey, meant to be hunted by it and others like it.

"Open the grave, Chaplain," the thing taunted. "See if that God of yours saw fit to pull your son's remains from that box and take him to heaven."

Delroy waited. He knew he could not run. Even if the creature had been human, he could never elude it in the brush. It moved too quickly. He was too tired and there was no safe place to run.

"Or maybe when you open that box, you're going to find your boy still there." The thing smiled. "Wouldn't that be something if he didn't make it to heaven either? if he was still stranded here? Like father like son, I guess."

"Terrence was a good man," Delroy said, unable to restrain himself, even though he knew the creature only baited him. "He gave his life to save the lives of other members of his squad."

"Stupid bravery is going to buy his way into heaven?"

Delroy started to speak but couldn't.

"Even I know that a hero's death isn't going to guarantee you a place in heaven, Preacher. I'm familiar with the childish ideology you follow. You believe you can get to heaven by simply believing Jesus died for your sins. I'm telling you now that He was nothing more than a scared man the day the Romans hung Him on that cross. You want to know who deified Him? Hawkers. Men who chopped up that cross and sold kindling as religious objects. Just men out to make a profit."

"You're lying," Delroy said. "Everything that comes out of your mouth is a lie."

The thing raised an arched eyebrow. "Is it?"

"Yes."

"Your son was a good man, and he was a good soldier." The creature raised its hands. "See? Is that a lie?"

Delroy forced himself to remain calm and watchful.

"If your son was such a good man," the thing challenged, "why are you here? Why did he have to die if he was being noble and protective of his friends? Why didn't God simply spare him?"

Delroy couldn't answer. He didn't know, and that truth was too hard to speak out loud.

The thing lifted a handful of mud and let it splatter from its palm to the grave's edge. "Dead is dead, Chaplain. Is it really better to have a dead hero for a son instead of just having a dead son? I mean, what's the upgrade in that?"

Delroy gripped the shovel more tightly and held his tongue. He moved carefully within the hole because the mud and the rain made his footing treacherous. He wondered whether he could trust the sides of the hole to hold his weight if he attempted to scramble out.

"Go ahead," the thing challenged with a mocking grin and a tone that invited mean-spirited playfulness. "Open the box and let's see what's inside. I'm interested. Really."

"No," Delroy answered.

The thing opened its hand and let the remainder of the mud fall from its grip. Nothing remained behind to stain its flesh. "You're pathetic." It scowled. "You come here, desert your post in the greatest time of need the crew has ever seen, and you wimp out on testing your faith."

Delroy waited.

Sighing, the creature said, "Maybe I should have waited. Maybe you would have convinced yourself to keep digging without any help from me."

"No. I was done with that."

The thing walked around the edges of the grave, its hands clasped together behind it like a schoolteacher on hall patrol. "You dug that hole in the ground and are standing in your son's grave. When exactly did you start believing again?"

"Now."

"Convenient, don't you think? Seems like believing for you people always comes when it's most convenient. Ever notice that?"

The accusation stung, but Delroy's fear and wariness were greater. Still, he stayed with the truth. "I realized how wrong I was."

"I don't believe you. There you stand with that shovel in your hands." It gestured to the hole. "Your son's casket can't be much farther down."

Delroy turned, taking small steps in the loose mud and pooling water so that he constantly faced the creature. "You came here to see me fail. That didn't happen. That's not going to happen."

The creature smirked. "You haven't failed? C'mon, Delroy, you're still here after all those people disappeared. You failed a long time before you got here." It lifted its arms and gestured to take in the graveyard.

Lightning split the sky for a second before a thunderous cannonade shook the earth. Electricity danced along Delroy's skin while sparks spat from the thing's hair and mouth.

"A navy chaplain who can't find a billet in heaven after decades of service?" It shook its head. "Now that's truly a sad thing. You'd think God was more generous than that."

"My being here is my fault." Delroy kept shifting. The loose mud beneath his feet became even more treacherous.

"Your fault?" It lifted its shoulders in an exaggerated sigh. "You're stupid to blame yourself. You can't help it because you don't believe. Look at everything you've been through. You're lucky you've been able to hide your true feelings this long."

"I do believe." Delroy's protest sounded hollow in his ears.

The creature covered its ears. "Lies. You and I both know you're telling lies. If you believed, you wouldn't be here. You'd be up in heaven right now. Reunited with—" the thing made a show of reading the gravestone at its feet—"Terrence. Terry. Your son." The amber tinted eyes fixed on Delroy again. "Instead, you're here. With me." A malicious smile framed the creature's face. "Or maybe you'd be up there and notice ol' Terry was among the missing."

"No."

"You came out here tonight to see if his precious soul was saved. All you've got to show for your trouble is a big rock." The creature kicked mud into the grave. As soon as the brackish earth touched the rock, though, rain washed the mud away. The creature cursed. "You don't think he's up there. You think he's down here, locked in the earth."

"My boy is up there." Delroy clung to that thought because it was the only thing keeping him sane at the moment.

"Really? And what do you think he's doing right now?" The creature cocked its head to one side. " 'Hey, Gramps, good to meet you. Don't know what's keeping Dad. He should be here any minute.' " It paused. "Only you're not coming, are you? Not now. Not *ever*."

Guilt flooded Delroy as heartache and uncertainty nearly crushed him. His faith was lost to him. He wasn't sure he knew how to believe anymore. Even with all the proof around him—with the mass disappearances and even this malevolent creature stalking him, he still found it hard to believe that Jesus had died on the cross for him. God existed, but maybe He didn't care as much as everyone wanted to believe.

"Do you think maybe that's what's going on up there, Chaplain?" the creature continued in a belligerent tone. "Big family reunion? Only you weren't invited?"

Pain locked Delroy's throat up tight.

"Your father must be feeling pretty disappointed right now," the creature said. "There he is, surrounded by all these people he's saved for the Lord, and his own son didn't catch the ship when it sailed."

Delroy firmed his trembling jaw. *God, help me. This is so hard. I know my father loved me. I want to believe You love me, Lord, but it's so hard. Help me to hang on to that. Let me start with that and continue to build till I'm strong again.*

"Nope." The thing shook its head. "You're right to blame God for all your troubles, Delroy. After all, He gave you those troubles, all that sorrow and grief. More than any one man should carry."

"No." Delroy's angry response was a choked whisper.

The creature stood still and gazed down at Delroy. "Sure He did. God let that man murder your father all those years ago. God let those terrorists kill your son. And God left you behind three days ago when the least He could have done was take you up with all the others." The forked black tongue slithered over its thin lips. "If you're looking for someone to blame for your troubles, Chaplain, blame God. He's supposed to be taking care of you. I submit to you that's not what's happened. How many people have you seen that God has saddled with that much bad luck?"

Swayed by his anger, Delroy felt pulled toward the creature's way of thinking. God *was* powerful. There was a *lot* He could have done. If He'd wanted to, if He'd cared enough about Delroy.

"God has His plans for people," the thing said. "That's what I keep hearing all you people say. All you *would-be* believers. That's just you trying to make something important out of the brief flicker of existence you've been given." It scowled. "I'm telling you now that He doesn't even care you exist. *If* He even knows."

It would be so easy to blame God, Delroy knew. He'd seen people do it all the time. Sailors he'd counseled had blamed God for losses and fears and changes in their lives when Delroy had talked with them. People who had attended his father's church in Marbury had blamed God for the bad things that had happened in their lives, too. For a time, Delroy had blamed God for his father's murder but had somehow found his way around that.

Until tonight.

Or maybe I never did, Delroy told himself. *Maybe I was only fooling myself.*

Terrence's death, so unexpected and so unfair, had caused those strong feelings to rear up again, and that unresolved anger had carried Delroy far from the Lord, although he still ministered in His ways. He'd been on autopilot, giving lip service to something he no longer truly believed in.

A memory returned to Delroy as he shifted. Josiah's own father,

Jonah, had lived as a hard man. He'd drunk and gambled and lived a life of violence, raising his family amid poverty and abuse, neither of which he tried to alleviate. During that time, Jonah had barely acknowledged his son.

When cancer had finally taken Jonah, Josiah had spent those last days with his father, caring for him and ministering to him in spite of the fact that his father had cursed him and God. At the end, though, Jonah had come to know Jesus and was saved through his son's work. The old man had died peacefully in Josiah's arms.

Later, in the quiet of the funeral home after the families had all gone and Josiah had sat with Jonah composing the eulogy he would deliver, six-year-old Delroy had returned to find his father still there. Without a word, Delroy had tiptoed over to Josiah and stood beside him. Tenderly, Josiah had picked Delroy up from the floor and set him in his lap. He'd wrapped his arms around his son and held him tight. Delroy had felt warm and safe in his father's embrace, and he knew even then that his father had taken comfort from his presence.

"Are you okay, Daddy?" Delroy had asked. "You've been crying a lot."

"Not all of these tears are sad tears, Son. Some of 'em, why they're tears of gladness because I know my daddy isn't hurting anymore. It's just hard to let him go."

"I didn't want to let Grampa go either, Daddy."

"I know. But we had to."

"See? You're crying again, Daddy. Me and Momma, we're worried about you. She says she's never seen you so brokenhearted."

"I'll be okay, Son. God will heal my heart the same way He healed Grampa Jonah's there at the end. The Lord will take away all the pain an' fear an' anger. I just gotta be a little bit patient till He gets around to it. I know Gram'pa Jonah's in a better place, but it still hurts turnin' loose."

"He was your daddy."

"Yes, he was."

Delroy had sat quietly with his arms around his father. Even now he could remember the smell of his father's aftershave, the same brand of bay rum the barber used when they got store-bought haircuts on days that Etta was too sick or too busy to do the job herself.

"Don't you wish God had made Grampa Jonah love you sooner?" Delroy had asked. "Instead of waiting all this time? Wouldn't that have been better?"

Tears had glimmered in Josiah's eyes, but he'd looked at his son and nodded. "Yes, I do, but I'm thankful for bein' with Grampa Jonah as much as I could. I was there for him at the end, an' that was important for both of us to end this thing right. Mighty important."

Delroy felt cheated. His father and his son had died away from him, both of them meeting violent ends with no family around to see them through their final moments. Neither event had been fair.

"See?" the creature asked in a soft voice, tearing into Delroy's memory. "You know God doesn't care about you. You know what I'm saying is true. If He's given you any notice at all, it's only been for the sake of torturing you on a more personal level."

Pain and confusion reeled over Delroy. He'd never truly gotten over either of those deaths and he'd known that long before tonight. But he was certain he had never felt those losses more strongly than he did right then.

"How dare God take your father and then your son," the creature said softly, barely audible above the steady rainfall. "How dare He do that when you have given Him so much of yourself."

For a moment, Delroy was mesmerized by the solemn conviction in the thing's voice. Everything it said sounded so right and true. His mind felt thick; thinking past his pain and anger got hard.

"God," the thing continued in that soft, understanding cadence, "had no right to take them. He chose to break up your family. He even turned your wife against you so you ended up alone."

The last part jarred Delroy's thoughts. Glenda hadn't left him; he'd walked away from her, burying himself in his pain and his work, and insulating himself from all the confusing feelings he'd had over Terrence's death.

"She stayed there, content in her service to God and she left you all alone," the thing whispered. "She didn't feel any pain because her blindness made sense of their deaths. But you know better, don't you? You know that God doesn't care about you—or anyone. Worse yet, she wouldn't allow you your grief either, constantly at you to 'trust the Lord.' I know she tried to talk you out of—"

"No," Delroy said, pulling back from the creature, suddenly aware that he had started leaning toward it.

The creature smiled sadly, and without the lightning to slash away the human image, the expression looked warm and inviting. "It's God's fault, Preacher. You know it is. All of this is."

"People faultin' God, Son," Josiah had said on a number of occasions. "You ever notice how much trouble people get theirselves into when they start that? An' as soon as they get theirselves well an' truly into trouble up to their eyeballs, why they start gnashin' their teeth an' pulling their hair out an' callin' on God for help they accused Him of not givin' in the first place."

Delroy staggered back from the creature, his father's words ringing in his head. That day at the funeral home, he'd asked Josiah why God hadn't found him a better daddy, the way God had found him a good daddy. Delroy had said that God should have known Josiah was going to be a preacher and would need a good daddy to raise him up right and treat him nice.

"Maybe it wasn't about a son havin' a good daddy when I was born," Josiah had answered with a slight smile. "Lookin' back on things here at the end, I'm thinkin' maybe the Lord knew what He was doin' all along. Wasn't a boy needin' a good daddy when this was all said an' done. Was a troubled an' lost daddy what was needin' a good son. You see, God made me strong enough an' believe enough that I helped my daddy finish his life off right with death lookin' him in the eye ever' day. I helped my daddy find Jesus when he needed Him most. An' I'm mighty pleased about that. Mighty pleased. Pastor Crook always told me the Lord would never give me more'n I could take care of when he helped me move into our church. Just never planned on what the Lord had to give me bein' this much. No, sir, never planned on that at all. But that's the way it is, Son: them surprises an' curveballs an' change-ups the Lord keeps throwin' at you just to keep you good at your game."

"Dig, Preacher," the creature coaxed. "Dig up this box and expose the lies your God has put before you. Set yourself free."

Glenda. Delroy kept his thoughts centered on his wife, remembering how strong her faith had been. It was the faith that she exhibited, the unshakeable certainty that everything was unfolding exactly as God had planned, that had ultimately torn them apart. She had accepted their son's death; Delroy had not. He felt betrayed by her acceptance, then shamed because he could not find it within himself to forgive God while she trusted God's hand in the matter.

Delroy didn't even know if she was still . . . here. She had a phone. He had the number. But he had never called before leaving Washington. He couldn't remember the last time he'd talked to her. All he could recall was the continued pain and confusion and frustration that even long-distance contact had caused.

Delroy backed up in his son's grave. His thighs hit the back of the hole and he almost tripped. He turned, planting the shovel handle down to use as a support to step out of the hole.

Before he could get clear, the creature moved with incredible speed to face him. "Where are you going?" it demanded. Angry sparks showed in the amber eyes as lightning blazed. Thunder underscored the question.

"Out of here," Delroy answered. He had to tilt his head up to look at the creature. Rain spattered across his face and into his eyes.

"Dig."

"No, sir." Delroy looked at the hole around him and shook his head. "I'm done here. This was a mistake. I was weak. I should never have come." He shifted and tried to step past the creature. This close to the thing, Delroy smelled the sour stench that emanated from his opponent. He didn't remember that from their first encounter.

Moving explosively, the thing planted both hands in the center of Delroy's chest and shoved. Delroy felt tiny claws bite into his chest, but he scarcely had time to notice them because he came up off his feet. He sailed backward, then landed off balance on his back in the watery mud at the bottom of the hole.

The creature leaned in closely, bending at the waist and shoving an accusatory forefinger forward. "You're going to dig, Preacher."

Delroy didn't respond, but he heaved himself to his feet. The layer of mud that clung to him made him feel incredibly heavy. He gripped the shovel and swung it with all his strength, catching the thing in the ribs. The creature fell backward.

Surprised by his success, Delroy hesitated a moment. Then he turned and stepped across the rock toward the other end of the grave. He lifted his foot, planted it into the soft earth, and shoved up, powering himself out of the hole. He swung his head around, trying desperately to get his bearings and find the cemetery entrance as he fled.

"*Preacher!*" the thing roared. Then it filled the air with foul curses. Footsteps slapped against the wet graveyard grounds as it pursued him.

Captain Cal Remington surveyed the computer screens in the situation room hidden in a basement café deep in the heart of Sanliurfa. His team operated smoothly, efficiently using the limited capabilities they had access to.

Infrared images of the city relayed from FLIR mounted on the marine helos scrolled across the screens. Other images came from Rangers in the field carrying digital cameras mounted under their assault rifles that connected to the modular computer/sat-com feed on their LCEs.

All of the communications relays pumped through rooftop-mounted dishes scattered throughout the city. The network wasn't much compared to the speed and scope offered by satellite relays, but the system kept the command center from being deaf, dumb, and blind.

White noise from the radios and clipped pieces of chatter filled the room.

Buried deep in the ground, shored up by thick stone slabs, and having a manhole that led into the city's sewer system for a quick escape or in the event the building was targeted by Syrian artillery and brought down, the room was a perfect place to run ops control from.

The only thing the room didn't have was air-conditioning. Fans pushed the air around but did little to cut the heat. Body odor mixed with the stink of overheated components. Cables, bundled together with OD green tape and held in place with tent stakes, crisscrossed the room. The generators used to run the operation occupied a room upstairs, but the steady vibration remained detectable even over the hum of the computers and the sharp barks of the radio communications.

"Foxtrot Four has wounded," a Ranger called over the channel.

"Affirmative, Foxtrot Four," one of the dispatch officers responded immediately. He tapped keys on the computer in front of him.

The screen blinked, closing out four windows that showed two aerial and two ground shots of the main areas that had gotten hit by Syrian troops. The next image was relayed in IR black and green, showing bodies strewn under a badly damaged building.

"Who are the wounded?" the dispatch officer asked. His voice sounded strained, and the effort to keep himself calm showed frayed ends.

"Nobody on Foxtrot. We're looking at civ casualties." The Ranger's voice hesitated a little and lowered. "Got two kids in here, Dispatch. I think one of 'em's already dead."

A woman's harsh screams and pleas for help in English, French, and Italian came over the channel.

The dispatch officer punched another series of keys. A small window opened and revealed Foxtrot Four's GPS location. Thankfully, he could access the global positioning satellites easily.

Remington missed the quick and quantitative information offered by the usual network of spy satellites that special forces units used while on a mission. Still, as far as he could tell, the operation was limping along just as it was supposed to be.

For cannon fodder and a distraction, the 75th Rangers maintained a lively game. Remington took pride in that, but the fact didn't remove the sting of facing a losing situation.

"Foxtrot Four, I've got your twenty locked," the dispatch officer said. "Be advised that a medevac is en route."

"Roger that, Dispatch. We're going to stand hard here. I've got a medic in my squad. Maybe we can help out till the evac arrives."

Remington almost stepped over and ordered the squad into motion. Staying with civilian casualties was a waste of time. He needed the city secure. Compassion at this point would only make things worse. Then he remembered that several reporters and news teams remained within the city. Getting reported on national television ordering troops away from civilians, especially if one of them was a journalist, would leave him seriously compromised. He held himself back, took a deep breath in through his nose, and let it out through his mouth.

Holding Sanliurfa for the next few days wasn't just a military operation. When he was done, if everything went his way, he figured he
could become something of a media darling. Promotions and cushy
careers followed media darlings.

"We're live," another dispatch officer said.

"Radio?" someone asked. "I've heard some radio reports broad-
casted from inside the city."

"No. Television. OneWorld NewsNet."

Remington turned to face the computers that were dedicated to
monitoring the media sources transmitting out of the city. FOX News
and CNN managed to get sporadic stories out live, but most of what
they could send were finished stories through burst transmissions.

OneWorld NewsNet remained the consistent source the world
turned to for news in the Middle Eastern theater. Of course, even then
Remington didn't know how large a share of the overall world audience OneWorld pulled. News from the rest of the world painted a picture of riots and fear. Cities had declared martial law and curfew, then
discovered they didn't have the emergency people to properly administer those conditions even after calling in the National Guard.

The anchor on the OneWorld NewsNet station looked professional, edgy, and sharp. He was dark-haired, dark-eyed, serious, and
intent—the kind of guy people sitting in their living rooms could
trust. He sat in front of a Mercator map that displayed the globe in
cutouts like orange sections. At first glance, though, the news logo
had often struck Remington as a row of closed fangs.

Remington worked the time difference in his head and realized
the time was after 10 P.M. back in the States. Back there, it was still yesterday. At that time of night, though, the news teams brought out
their big guns.

"As you know," the anchor said, "OneWorld continues our coverage of the outbreak of war in the Middle East with our reporter in the
field, Danielle Vinchenzo." He placed his hands together, a practiced
effort at being solemn. "Danielle, are you with us?"

"Yes, Addison, I am." The audio transmission popped and stut-
tered a little, but definitely less than the efforts put out by the major
American networks.

"We've shown viewers at home that traumatic footage your team
shot of the attack there at Sanliurfa," Addison said. "As you might
imagine, the station has been besieged with calls wanting to know
more about the American soldiers over there."

As the anchor spoke, a window opened on-screen. Remington

watched as footage rolled of a Syrian tank crashing through a building then firing its main gun. The explosion of the shot was muted, but the flash of the shell overpowered the low-level-light video pickup and turned the screen white for a second.

The caption War in Turkey lit up the bottom of the screen, followed by the silhouette of a man in full battle gear carrying another man in his arms.

"What is that?" Remington asked.

"An icon," one of the dispatch officers answered. "That's Goose. They cut it out of the footage of the attack at the border. When the aircraft from *Wasp* dropped out of the sky. They're starting to use it all the time now. Kind of identifies what we got going on over here."

Anger and frustration filled Remington. With that one rescue, with those few seconds of imagery, Goose seemed to have captured the world's attention regarding the Syrian-Turkey conflict.

And Danielle Vinchenzo seemed to have an obsession with the first sergeant. Even after Remington had given blanket orders to his troops that their contact with the media from this point on was to be limited, Vinchenzo had managed to keep Goose in the limelight.

As Remington watched, Goose momentarily filled the screen, in hot pursuit of a Syrian tank. Then the screen cleared and the broadcast switched to a street scene with a Sanliurfa slug line. The silhouette of Goose blinked into place at the end of the slug.

"As you could tell from the earlier footage," Danielle Vinchenzo said, "American forces, their Turkish counterparts, and the U.N. contingent assigned on a peacekeeping mission in the area took a pounding. Squads continue to comb the wreckage for survivors as well as for enemy troops caught behind the lines when Sanliurfa's defenders managed to break the Syrian attack and push their line back."

Sporadic gunfire chattered in the background. A few howitzer shells still took to the air from Mkchian's artillery banks.

"Has there been any indication of what losses the troops have suffered?" Addison asked.

Remington mentally cursed the news anchor. The last thing he wanted the media to do was release stats on the op. Syrian army intelligence was probably up early this morning catching all the news broadcasts they could to gather information.

Back in the Gulf wars, more so with the second than with the first, the media had worked with the military forces on the ground. The fall of Baghdad had been a carefully orchestrated event in some ways, both for the military and the media.

"I don't have any numbers for you yet," Danielle answered, "but I hope to have them soon. From my impression, walking around just this small section of the city, the losses have been considerable."

The camera panned to take in the fallen buildings across the street. Flames clung stubbornly to two burned-out husks of cars.

"I intend to talk with First Sergeant Samuel Gander at his earliest convenience," Danielle said, "to see if I can get more concrete news."

Remington blew out an angry breath. He didn't know why the woman wasn't coming to him. He was captain in charge of the American forces occupying the city.

The headset chirped in his ear. He seethed as he watched the news broadcast roll on. "Control," he snapped.

"This is BirdDog," Perrin said.

"You'd better have good news, mister," Remington growled. "Tell me you found your target."

"No, sir," Perrin said. "I can't tell you that. But I did find out something else you might be interested in."

Remington waited.

"Seems Phoenix Leader has arranged a tête-à-tête with the alphabet group."

The implications of Perrin's statement spilled through Remington's mind like a passenger-train pileup. "Why?"

"Don't know," Perrin said. "What I've heard is that Phoenix Leader found one of the alphabet guys in the street near where he talked to the target. He took the guy into custody and is refusing to give him back to the alphabet section chief."

The ramifications shifted constantly as Remington pushed them around. The captain wanted to know what Goose had learned and what he had to say to Agent Cody.

"Is there any sign of your target?" Remington asked.

"No, sir." Perrin paused. "The guy Phoenix Leader has in custody? He's the same one I encountered earlier."

"When you saw Phoenix Leader talking to the target?"

"Affirmative."

What are you doing, Goose? Remington wondered. *Covering your tracks? Or making a deal with the devil?*

"Anything you want me to do, Control?" Perrin asked.

"Negative. Keep them in sight."

"Phoenix Leader doesn't look like he's going anywhere. He's camped out in the security office of the hospital."

"Don't lose them if they try to leave," Remington commanded, turning and heading for the door. "I'll be there in five."

At the door, Remington took a final glance at the OneWorld NewsNet channel. Danielle Vinchenzo was still talking. The icon at the end of the slug line remained in place.

And Cal Remington was figuring it was about time to do something with his first sergeant. If he couldn't get Goose to play ball and keep him informed, then he was going to break him.

❋   ❋   ❋

Sunshine Hills Cemetery
Outside Marbury, Alabama
Local Time 2232 Hours

Delroy ran, not daring to look back over his shoulder at the thing that chased him through the cemetery. *God, help me. Keep that thing from me.*

The spongy ground absorbed the rapid impact of his frantic steps. Twice, the ground slid out from under him, causing him to stumble. He kept his attention focused on the trail leading out of the cemetery.

Marbury was miles away. He knew he'd never make it, but he had no choice except to try. There was nowhere else to run.

Before he had covered fifty yards, a hand closed over Delroy's shoulder and yanked him around. He tried to bring the shovel up but couldn't move fast enough. The thing's hand exploded into his face, slapping him so hard that he thought his neck was broken. Overcome by exhaustion after pushing himself so hard and so long, Delroy didn't have much to give. He lost the shovel and dropped to one knee.

"You're not getting away that easily," the creature said, coming for him. "Me and you, we've got some excavating to do."

Delroy pushed himself up from the ground. He'd fought the thing before in Washington. He knew from experience that it was more powerful and quicker than he was. But he couldn't find it in himself to just lie down and die.

He threw himself forward, staying low. He roped his arms out, catching the creature's legs and powering through. Unable to stand against Delroy's assault, it went down. Moving quickly, his breath coming harsh as a blacksmith's bellows, Delroy scrambled up and straddled it. He beat the thing with his fists, driving punches home to its head, working into the same kind of rhythm he'd used in boxing. A human opponent would never have survived the brutal attack.

The creature appeared dazed, but its head was impossibly hard. Delroy felt certain he was going to break both his hands and not have anything to show for his efforts. Despite his best punches, the creature didn't show any bruising or split flesh.

Then it twisted beneath him, throwing Delroy up and forward, shrugging out from under his greater weight. Gasping for air, Delroy struggled to get to his feet and made it on his second attempt. The evil thing was already up. It kicked him full in the face.

Caught off guard, Delroy felt an explosion of pain fill his head. He whipped backward. Salty blood from his split lips coated his teeth. He went down. Immediately, he rolled to his side and tried to push himself up. Before he got to his feet, the creature kicked him in the back and sent him forward.

The yawning grave lay before him.

"You're not finished yet, Preacher," the thing roared. "You've got a job you've left undone here tonight."

Delroy pushed against the earth as he tried to rise. The muddy earth caused his hands to slip. Before he could fall against the ground, the thing caught him by the neck of his slicker and yanked him upward. For a moment, Delroy believed the thing had crushed his windpipe and he was going to suffocate. Then he drew in a long breath.

The thing turned him in its impossibly strong grip. Face-to-face, Delroy felt its hot, fetid breath against his battered face. A sour stench filled the chaplain's nostrils. In that moment, he recognized the stench. When he'd visited a congregation member who had worked in a meatpacking factory, the same smell had filled the killing-room floor. Lightning flared and stripped away some of the creature's human appearance.

"I came a long way to find you," the creature said. "There are other things I could have been doing."

Delroy found the strength to throw a punch that caught the creature in the jaw. Even hanging loose by his opponent's grip and not properly braced, the punch had enough force to turn its head.

The creature cursed, then turned back to look at Delroy with blazing amber eyes. "You're a stupid man."

"I beat you," Delroy wheezed. "Back in Washington, I beat you."

The thing grinned. "You think so?"

Delroy's sense of victory melted.

"Do you think we really wanted the people left behind to launch a

full-scale nuclear attack?" The thing shook its head slowly. "The people left behind are ours to torture and play with. We're going to break
them, and we're going to turn them away from that precious God of
yours. We're going to teach them that God never cared for any of
them. Just as I'm teaching you tonight."

Delroy swept his left arm up, then turned abruptly to the right and
brought it down. The martial arts move broke the creature's grip on
him. He staggered back and lifted his hands as he slipped into a
boxer's stance.

The thing slapped Delroy's defenses away as though he were a
child. It grabbed the front of his slicker and flung him toward the
yawning mouth of the grave thirty yards away.

Propelled by inhuman force, Delroy flew twenty yards through
the air, then bounced across the muddy ground like a stone skipping
water. His breath left his lungs in a rush. Still, he tried to get up. The
creature met him with a kick that drove him back to the grave's edge.
Hammered backwards, Delroy fell. He tried in vain to get up. There
was no strength left in him.

"C'mon, Preacher," the thing snarled. "Time to open the box."

"No." Delroy said defiantly.

The evil creature leaned down at him, tilting its head from side to
side. "I'll kill you." It unfurled its hands. The lightning stripped away
the look of human fingers, revealing the lizard's claws that lurked beneath.

"Then kill me," Delroy whispered.

It pressed its face next to his. The nose slits flared. "You're afraid. I
smell it on you."

Delroy didn't bother to deny the accusation.

"I won't kill you," the thing said. "I want you to know the truth.
Once you know the truth, you can set the record straight about your
God." It reached for him.

Delroy tried to fight, but he was too weak, too hurt, and too
afraid. It seized the front of his slicker and lifted him bodily from the
ground. Almost casually, it threw him into the grave.

He fell into the pool of water, now three inches deep. The brackish
taste of mud mixed with the salty flavor of blood in his mouth. His
nose swelled and one eye nearly closed. He flung himself to one side,
watching in terror as the thing followed him into the grave.

"Dig," the creature commanded. "Use your hands."

"No." Delroy glared at it but didn't try to say anything more because he knew his voice would break.

"I'll bury you in here," the thing warned. "Do you want to die?"

Delroy truly didn't know the answer to that question. Everything had come home to him these past three days. In the Bible, Jesus had been reborn in three days, walking from the tomb after His death on the cross to the astonishment of even His disciples.

No one had believed in Him.

Delroy tried to put himself back into his father's Sunday school class. He tried to remember how safe he had felt on those mornings while listening to his father tell stories about creation, about Noah and the ark, and the parting of the Red Sea. God had been so real in those stories, so near. And now, well, now God seemed a million miles away.

The creature screamed in inarticulate rage. As easily as Delroy would turn a child over, the creature flipped him facedown into the muddy water and put a knee into his back. Delroy was so tall his legs stuck out of the grave, but his face was under water. He tried to lift his head clear. The creature grabbed the back of his head, wrapping impossibly long fingers around his skull. Claws pricked Delroy's flesh. The thing forced his face more deeply into the water.

"I'm going to drown you, Preacher, if you don't dig up this grave."

Delroy struggled, but the muddy sides of the grave gave way every time he tried to use them to lever himself up from the water. His head pounded and his lungs burned from the lack of oxygen. The foul water burned his eyes. He gasped reflexively and bubbles escaped his mouth.

Just as he was about to give in and take a breath, the creature pulled his face clear of the water. His chin remained immersed.

"Dig," the creature ordered.

Delroy thought hard, wondering why the creature was going to such lengths to make him cooperate. It could easily kill him. Why was exhuming Terrence's coffin so important to it? And why didn't the creature dig it up itself?

The thing shoved his face back into the water. Again, just when he was about to start drowning, his opponent lifted his face clear.

"Give it up, Preacher. Your faith is misplaced. I'm teaching you the only things you need to believe in right now. Dig up the coffin and know the nature of all the lies that have been told to you."

Delroy didn't speak. He concentrated his efforts on drawing air into his lungs. The thing shoved his face back into the water a third time. This time when it pulled him up, Delroy was choking and spluttering on water he'd sucked in.

"You're a fool, Preacher. Too stupid to even be afraid."

Lacking the strength to argue or even aid in his own salvation from the water, Delroy hung in the thing's grip. He wanted to pray, but he didn't believe anything he had to say would ever reach God's ears. He'd been abandoned in the cemetery.

Suddenly the weight of the creature was gone from his back. For a moment Delroy believed he'd just started slipping into unconsciousness and was less aware of his surroundings as a result. Weakly, arms trembling from the effort, he pushed himself up from the water. He sucked in a breath, looking over his shoulder as lightning ripped through the dark heavens.

The creature was gone.

Suspicious that the thing's disappearance was a trick, Delroy waited, taking a moment to recharge his lungs with air. He lacked the reserves of strength to move quickly. In fact, he didn't know if he would be able to move at all for a while.

He didn't know what had happened to the thing. It had disappeared back in Washington, too. But someone had seen the creature then. He wondered if it lacked the power to appear to anyone else. But no one else was around.

God—?

The possibility surfaced in Delroy's frenzied thoughts an instant before he felt something move in the earth between his two braced hands. Instinctively, he glanced down.

A black-taloned hand shot out of the mud in front of Delroy's face. Adrenaline slammed through his system anew, filling him with the strength to pull back. However, before he could get away, the hand reached past him and cupped the back of his neck.

The creature's face surfaced in the water pooled in the grave. Predatory cat's eyes gleamed amber in the flashlight beam. Fangs filled the thin-lipped mouth. Unable to move with the hand holding the back of his head, Delroy watched in horror as the creature glared up at him.

"Now," the thing growled, "now you're going to see what's below."

The creature yanked Delroy's head down again. This time it didn't stop with just putting his face into the water. The creature dragged Delroy's head and shoulders deep into the rain-drenched mire.

Delroy felt the cold mud all around him. Then he touched the smooth metal surface of Terrence's coffin. He couldn't see anything, including the monster that dragged him through the dirt, but he smelled the damp earth. Thunder cannonaded, sounding more distant because he was inside the earth instead of above it. Then a glow filled the coffin and he saw Terrence through the metal wall.

Delroy's mind told him there was no way he saw what he saw, but his eyes took in the stark image of his son lying in the coffin. *God, why have You forsaken me?*

"He didn't make it to the party," the creature whispered into Delroy's ear. "Everything you were afraid of—that your son didn't find his belief, that you weren't as good a preacher as you believed yourself to be all those years ago—it's all true."

Terrence's body showed the ravages of the horrible wounds that had taken his life. No amount of mortician's wax could cover the grievous burns that covered his body, or the bullet holes that had left his face shattered and inhuman. His left arm was missing.

Delroy tried to scream but couldn't. No one had told them that Terrence hadn't come back whole, only that his wounds had rendered viewing impossible.

"The military didn't tell you," the thing hissed in Delroy's ear. "Didn't get all the parts back. Couldn't find them."

Delroy wanted to escape but couldn't.

"What is that, Preacher? When someone willingly doesn't tell you something they know you would want to know? Lying by omission, right?"

Horror gripped Delroy as fiercely as the creature that held him.

"But it gets even worse," the thing said gleefully. "Your son came back missing a few parts and he didn't make it to heaven, but the worst thing of all is that he *knows* he's lying in his grave."

Even as the creature's words registered in Delroy's mind, mixing with his silent screams, Terrence opened his left eye. The other eye was a burned-out pit.

"Dad?" Terrence croaked. He tried to rise but could only move a few inches. "Dad!" His ruined face filled with panic. "Dad, get me out of here!" He pounded his fist against the top of the coffin. The rapid-fire thumps filled Delroy's ears. "Dad! Dad, help me!"

"Are you going to leave him there?" the creature asked over Terrence's screams. "Are you going to leave him trapped, Preacher? Or are you going to free him?"

In the next instant the light inside the coffin dimmed. Delroy felt water and mud all around his face. He arched his back and rose, lifting his face clear of the water pooled at the bottom of the grave.

His breath came back to him in a rush. Terrified, he pushed himself out of the grave, swinging his body around and grabbing for the flashlight that remained at the grave's edge. Mud caked his face and burned one eye.

He aimed the flashlight at the bottom of the hole where the creature had pulled him under. The beam reflected in the dark water that shimmied as it settled. There was no hole like he thought there would be.

"That's impossible," Delroy said, hoping that it truly was. Still, he couldn't shut out the vision of Terrence trapped in the coffin under the muddy earth.

"*Are you going to leave him trapped, Preacher?*" The creature's words taunted Delroy, even from his memory.

The creature was gone. Or at least it was in hiding for now.

Delroy listened. He heard pounding, but he told himself that it was his heart, not his dead son's fist slamming against the coffin top.

Breathing hoarsely, unable to calm down, Delroy played his beam over the cemetery grounds and spotted the shovel where he had dropped it during the fight with the creature. On his third attempt, Delroy got his feet under him and lurched out of the hole. He grabbed the shovel and headed back to the grave. He started to clamber back down, unnerved by everything he had experienced.

"*Son.*"

Delroy heard his father's voice. He froze and looked at his father's grave. *He's not there. If anybody made it to heaven, my daddy did. That was just the wind. That's all. Just the wind.* He returned his attention to Terrence's grave. The image of his dead son—*wounded, God, he's only wounded*—trapped in his grave filled Delroy's mind. He felt compelled to start digging. He lifted the shovel.

"*One thing you always gotta remember, Son. Satan, why, he was made for lyin'. He's got his powers, terrible powers to do many things, but none of 'em are as strong as his lies. Because when Satan lies to you, it's gonna be when you most want to believe him. Nothin' he's gonna tell you ever gonna be the truth. See, he weaves lies outta your own hopes, fears, an' dreams, outta what you think you saw an' what you think you want to see. That's how he works. That's how he always works.*"

The words weren't new. Delroy remembered them from a conversation he'd had with his father when he was nine.

Delroy made himself look at the grave and reason things through. *There's no way Terrence is down there. I know my son. He was a good boy. He went to church and he honored the Ten Commandments.* But at the

APOCALYPSE CRUCIBLE   161

same time he realized that Terrence might not have been a true believer. No man could ever really know another's heart.

Captain Mark Falkirk's warning about "pretty good Christians,"
people who led good lives but still didn't challenge themselves to
fully trust and believe, echoed inside Delroy's head. Was that what
Terrence had been? A pretty good Christian? Was that what Delroy
had been, too? What happened to those who died without ever truly
believing, when God raptured the world? Were they left behind like
Delroy, but remained dead and buried deep in the cold, hard ground?

Delroy's heart ached. He didn't know, and that was the worst of it.
No, he amended quickly as the rain continued to fall from the black
sky, *the worst of it would be if Terrence really was trapped down there.* He
closed his eyes, feeling the pain that throbbed through his body from
the beating he'd taken. He fully expected the creature to return and
finish what it had started.

But it didn't.

Weary and scared, feeling bereft and abandoned, Delroy dropped
to his knees at the foot of his son's grave with the shovel in his fists.
He bent his head to shield his face from the cold rain and told himself
he was going to pray. Only he couldn't find the words.

He knelt in the night only a few feet from where his child lay buried and reminded himself over and over again that the thumps hammering his eardrums were his heartbeats and not the sound of his
son's fist striking the coffin lid.

United States of America
Fort Benning, Georgia
Local Time 2234 Hours

Megan sat in the hospital waiting room between two MPs that Corporal Kerby had assigned to accompany her after they had left the
Hollister home. Kerby hadn't said that she was under arrest, but the
way the MPs offered to get her coffee from the break area and followed her to the bathroom, dealing with the uncomfortable situation
of her doing something they couldn't do for her in a place they
couldn't go by standing guard over the ladies' loo, made it clear that
though she wasn't technically under arrest she was at least being
closely supervised.

She didn't let the presence of the two young MPs bother her.
Other MPs stood guard in the base hospital so she felt she almost
blended in. The disappearances brought out full-blown cases of panic
and paranoia as the people left behind tried to figure out what they
were supposed to do. A quartet of young men sat quietly talking, each
of them with a Bible in hand. One of the major concerns everyone
had was that the disappearances would start again, maybe taking just
as many people.

Hoarse screams shattered the steady undercurrent of whispering
voices as a straitjacketed man was wheeled through the room on a
gurney. Three orderlies and a nurse accompanied the screaming man.
All of them looked worn-out.

General Amos Braddock, the base commander, had encouraged
the staff to sleep in the hospital and have their families come visit
them. The hospital staff shored up their diminished personnel with

men and women on base, including the teens who were holding their own emotionally.

People sat in the waiting room to find out about friends and loved ones who had gotten injured when cars and trucks had gone out of control and airplanes had dropped from the sky. A number of casualties and losses had occurred at the post's airfield. Thankfully the disappearances had happened late at night or more aircraft would have fallen.

The gurney slammed through the double doors on the other side of the room. The man's screams faded as the doors closed and the orderlies wheeled him farther away.

"Man," one of the MPs whispered to the other one, "wouldn't want to be that guy."

"Wouldn't want to be one of the guys Kerby had with him tonight, either," the other whispered back. "With that girl getting shot, they're going to catch some serious—" He stopped speaking.

Megan felt their gazes on her as they realized they'd spoken without thinking. She didn't look at them, didn't give any indication she had heard the comments. There was no sense in all of them being uncomfortable.

Televisions hung from swivel mounts in two corners of the room. The blue-white ghostly reflections of FOX News on one set and CNN on the other hung in the windows in front of Megan. She didn't want to watch because the stories that broke in the media seemed never to end.

Mostly the coverage consisted of canned footage of horrible crashes in huge metropolitan areas, passenger jets lying in flames in fields or across highways or buried in cities. The wreckage continued along major harbor areas in San Francisco, New York, New Orleans, Seattle, and other ports as suddenly unmanned ships crashed into bridges, docks, and other ships. The chaos and destruction never relented. Riots added fuel to the fire in several areas. Even Columbus, the city nearest the post, knew unrest and violence. Local television stations covered that, though few news teams ventured out into the hardest-hit areas.

The reporters sought out interviews with witnesses now. A steady parade of frightened people flashed across the screens, each with his or her own story of personal tragedy and loss. Even veteran politicians had trouble keeping their emotions together when they backed the president's stance that everything was under control.

That was a lie, Megan knew, but it was a lie that a lot of people would want to believe. "No, it's not going to hurt," was the biggest lie of all, followed by "Everything's going to be all right." She wanted to scream. *Lie to me. Make me feel better.* Nothing was ever going to be the same again. She felt that. Everyone could. Not many were ready to deal with it, though. She'd thought she was prepared, even after losing Chris, until Leslie had shot herself.

On one of the television screens, CNN covered the press releases given by President Fitzhugh regarding the no-holds-barred investigation into the worldwide disappearances as well as Nicolae Carpathia's junket to New York City to address the United Nations in a few days. No one, it seemed, yet knew why the Romanian president would make the trip now.

Despite the cold terror that she held locked up inside herself with iron control, Megan couldn't help but pay attention to Carpathia. Over the past few days, the man had gained increased presence in the media, becoming linked more and more to the effort to recover from the disappearances. Nothing was said about what shape that recovery was going to take.

Carpathia was a youthful-looking man, appearing slightly younger than his early thirties. Cameras were generous to him. His blond hair looked like spun gold when it caught the light. No one knew exactly why Carpathia was coming to the U.S. to speak to the U.N., or why President Fitzhugh worked so hard to make the man feel invited.

Still, the few times that Megan had caught prerecorded interviews with the Romanian president, she had noticed the calm presence Carpathia seemed to exude. He seemed like a man who could get things done, a man who'd never known defeat, but she had no idea what his plans were. But whatever they were, they would have no impact on her life at the moment.

Somewhere in the hospital, Leslie Hollister fought for her life. The image of the young girl lying so slack and bloody on her bedroom floor never left Megan's mind. After making certain that Megan wasn't hurt, one of the hospital orderlies had given her a set of green scrubs and asked her to change clothes, telling her she couldn't sit in the waiting room as bloody as she was. No one wanted the other occupants more upset than they already were.

Leslie's blood had soaked into Megan's underwear, her skin, and her hair. Clotted and dry now, the blood felt raspy against her skin. Even repeated washings in the bathroom hadn't removed the stains. More blood etched her nails, dug in deep now where she wouldn't be able to reach it without a cuticle brush. The smell of blood lingered on every breath she drew.

Megan blinked tears from her eyes and let out a long, low breath that attracted the attention of the MPs assigned to her. She ignored them and concentrated on the televisions.

On the other set, FOX News recapped the Syrian attack on Sanliurfa, using footage from OneWorld NewsNet. The icon of the soldier's silhouette carrying another soldier caught her eye and made her think of Goose.

On the screen a photojournalist's camera captured the image of a Syrian tank rolling through the wreckage of a street. The cameraman was evidently on a rooftop because the camera looked down onto the street. A group of soldiers stepped around the side of a building and fired a shoulder-mounted weapon at the tank. When the projectile hit the tank, red flames leapt up. A moment later, a heavily armed attack helicopter swung into view and opened up with its rocket pods, reducing the tank to a rolling pile of flaming wreckage. No one inside the vehicle could have survived those blasts.

Those watching the television set in the waiting room viewed in mute horror.

Casualties among the military groups, Megan understood from the earlier story on the radio on the way here from the Hollister home, ran high in Sanliurfa. Communications within the beleaguered city had suffered again as a result.

Megan prayed for Goose's safety. But even as she did so, she felt even more uncertain whether the effort was worth the time it took. God, she felt, hadn't shown up in Leslie Hollister's room tonight. Guilt ripped through her for thinking like that, but she thought it anyway. If God had taken an interest there, she hadn't seen it.

Still, the image of Gerry Fletcher plummeting from the rooftop only to disappear a heartbeat before he hit the ground bounced crazily through her mind. She had seen the boy disappear. Spotter lights manned by MPs had held the boy in their glare as he fell. Gerry was there one instant, and gone the next. Jenny had pointed out that God had taken Gerry then to prevent him from experiencing real death.

But Gerry experienced the horror of the fall, didn't he, God? You let him feel that, didn't You? Megan didn't mean to be so angry, but the longer she sat in the waiting room—not knowing if Leslie was alive or dead—the more frustrated and hurt she became.

What surprised her was the aching feel of loneliness that pummeled her. She'd never felt particularly close to God, not the way Bill Townsend talked about, but she hadn't known she was so far away either. She missed Bill. If he hadn't disappeared in Turkey, he'd still be with Goose. Having Bill watching Goose's back would have provided Megan with an ease of mind. Now everything she cared about was scattered. Goose, Joey, Chris—all of them gone from her so she couldn't immediately make sure they were all right. She felt broken and shattered and barely held back the tears.

What did I do, God? What did I do that was so bad?

"Mrs. Gander."

Startled, Megan looked up at the young MP on her left, realizing that it wasn't the first time he'd called for her attention.

"Yes, Private," she responded in a voice tight with emotion.

"I was asking if you'd like some more coffee, ma'am." He pointed to the empty paper cup she held in her hands, then held up his own. "I was about to go get some myself. Thought if you could use some more, I could get it for you."

Megan handed the private the cup. Getting her coffee would give him something to do. There was no reason for both of them to sit here while the anxiety built up.

"Yes. Please."

The MP took the cup from her. "I'll be right back."

Megan nodded.

The private glanced at the other MP, who nodded only slightly to indicate that he was awake and knew he was flying solo for a time.

Coffee wasn't going to make Megan feel any better and she knew it, but holding the cup at least gave her something to do with her hands, and the warmth would steep some of the chill out of her fingers. She wished she could hold Chris. Even though he was five and big enough to run through the house with a cape from an old Halloween costume as fast as any other superhero in the neighborhood, he still consented to being held by Mom sometimes. Occasionally, though only when he least expected it because he still fought against it, he fell asleep in her arms while they watched cartoons.

The thought of never having an evening like that again cut through Megan. She couldn't remember how much time had passed since Chris had last fallen asleep in her arms. Her caseload as a counselor on base had taken up so much of her family time that sometimes days had seemed to blend into each other, becoming seamless. Family evenings often got hectic all by themselves, but the addition of the work she brought home cut into those precious hours. Before being deployed to Turkey, Goose had made the most of those times, playing with Chris in the backyard when it wasn't raining or too cold.

Joey had, as usual, stayed in a funk, going to his room and separating himself with a wall and loud music. Even if Megan hadn't spent years as an experienced counselor, she would have seen the jealousy that Joey had for his younger brother. A little jealousy was normal, but Joey had let his eat at him. He hadn't shown those feelings to Chris, though, except for times when he built a little more distance between himself and his little brother. Becoming a teenager was hard enough, and the added strain of a little brother coming along so late in life had taken a toll as well.

If his father had stayed in his life after the divorce, Megan thought, *maybe Joey could have better handled Chris' birth.* Then she stopped, bringing herself up short. Her next leap of guilt would be to question her judgment about the divorce, whether everything was her fault. Her first husband hadn't involved himself in Joey's life or hers for years, and he had always claimed he'd divorced her because she had never made space or time for him. *What if that was true? What if the divorce was all my fault?*

Marrying Goose had trapped him in trying to raise another man's son. At first, Goose had acted uncertain about that responsibility, and Megan's own inability to simply let go and trust Goose with Joey hadn't helped. When things were good, Goose was Joey's best bud. But when things had turned for the worse and Joey was a problem in school or around home, Megan had insisted on handling the discipline herself. Discipline was her responsibility as Joey's mother. She hadn't wanted to push that chore off on her husband as she'd seen so many other wives do with their children. And Goose didn't handle things the way she did. Goose was sometimes too direct, too honest. He let people know how he felt about something instead of hinting at it.

After living with Goose these past eight years, she knew her husband to be fair and just, but she'd made excuses, telling herself that Joey wasn't used to having a man around the house. For a while, she hadn't let Goose have a free hand with Joey, and that choice had limited the relationship they could have had now.

I made a mistake there, too, she told herself.

By the time she realized what she was doing and that Goose had followed her lead, all of their relationships were pretty much in place. But it was—for the most part—quiet, and they'd made the best of it. Actually, judging from so many cases she saw in her office, they'd gotten through the blended-family issues better than most.

The family dynamic had worked well enough until Chris was born. Then Goose stepped into the role of father with a natural ease that had proven surprising. Megan had noticed the change, the closeness between Chris and Goose, at once. There was no distance between Chris and his father. Megan hadn't stood between them in any way. Goose wouldn't have let her, and she'd never felt the need to protect Chris the way she had Joey. She knew that Joey had seen the difference, too.

Blended families, Megan knew from studies as well as from experience, were the hardest things to make work. Roles and rules seemed to operate on a sliding scale, shifting constantly on a day-to-day basis as everyone concerned tried to find commonalities, a set of rules they could all live by, and goals to make it worthwhile. The stress increased when the natural triangles that occurred worked two-on-one against each other.

Joey had lost a step in the family. Nothing Megan or Goose could do could have prevented that from happening, and she knew that now as she took herself apart with every piece of psychological ammunition she could lay hands to. Watching Leslie injure herself brought Megan's insecurities to the forefront until it was almost too much to deal with. All her own shortcomings, all her failures, seemed strung together in Megan's eyes. She'd pieced them together with quiet and thorough skill as she awaited word on Leslie Hollister and remembered the events in the room again and again.

When it came down to it, Joey wasn't an only child anymore. After eleven years with his mother and three years with Goose, Joey had been forced to make room for his brother since Chris's birth.

Goose had tried to stay close to his stepson, but being raised in the country outside Waycross, Georgia, then spending his next years as a career soldier, he lacked experiences he could share with Joey. Joey had grown up in the city, in malls and arcades, in a high school that had more students than the whole populace of the small town Goose had grown up in. If they weren't involved in sports events, they hadn't had much in common.

It's all your fault, Megan told herself. *You let Joey slip through your fingers. Now he's out there somewhere, all alone and hurting.*

Arms aching for Chris, wishing she could listen to his soft breathing and know that he was all right, Megan looked out the hospital window and wondered where Joey was. Her family was missing in action, and she'd never before needed the comfort and support they could offer so very much.

The private returned with two cups of coffee. Megan took one and thanked him politely. She held the cup in both hands, feeling the warmth and knowing the liquid was too hot to drink for the moment. Wearily, she closed her eyes, breathing out to clear her lungs and working on a relaxation technique she taught in classes. The effort didn't work. Leslie Hollister, bleeding and still, lay waiting in her mind's eye.

❀ ❀ ❀

United States 75th Army Rangers Temporary Post
Sanliurfa, Turkey
Local Time 0537 Hours

Goose stood in the center of the security office and watched the security cameras the Ranger team used to manage surveillance all over the hotel. Litters of wounded continued to flow into the building, get marked for surgical attention by the triage teams, and get carried away to the appropriate waiting areas.

As he watched, Goose silently prayed that numbness would kick in and take away the horror and frustration that filled him. A soldier best served on a battlefield when somewhat detached from his immediate emotions. He'd experienced the battlefield calm several times before, but those times were generally during the heat of an engagement, not in the aftermath. Once a battle was over, the true cost of the action showed up on the bottom line in spent lives and wounded.

Later, he knew, other squads would bring in their dead. Detail leaders would assemble lists of Killed In Action and Missing In Action. Then the process of sorting the KIAs and MIAs out from the new wreckage of the city would begin.

Artillery continued to boom and fill the hotel with noise, but the frequency had dropped. Captain Mkchian and the Turkish artillery units obviously wanted to make a definitive statement to the retreating Syrian troops. But the ammunition they used was precious and possibly irreplaceable before the Syrians gathered for their next attack. All communications over the channels open to him indicated that the Syrians were in full retreat.

The CIA agent, Winters, sat in his chair. He continued to hold the chemical ice pack to his jaw. Beads of condensation ran down his neck.

Since Cody had appeared in the hallway, Winters hadn't said a word to Goose. Maybe he was confident that Cody could get him released. *Or he's afraid,* Goose thought. He didn't know which.

Barnett stood behind Winters and leaned against the wall. His presence next to the smaller man remained a constant threat, but Winters didn't acknowledge that either.

The CIA team was hiding something, Goose knew, and his mind kept prying at what it might be. Icarus's abduction, the satellite phone call that might have precipitated the Syrian strike into Turkey, and the game of cat and mouse playing out through Sanliurfa's war-torn streets danced through Goose's mind.

Icarus was a key player. Keeping the rogue agent out of CIA hands was important for the moment.

"First Sergeant."

Goose looked at the Ranger private manning the security station. "Yeah."

"Captain Remington is here." The private pointed at one of the screens.

Crossing the distance to the security desk, Goose looked at the screen. Electronics teams had moved some of the security cameras outside the building when they'd converted the hotel into a make-shift hospital. The fields of view overlapped so no blind spots existed.

Captain Remington stepped from the Hummer's passenger seat and walked purposefully into the building. The private made the necessary adjustments to the camera feeds to stay with Remington.

Interest and a little trepidation thrummed inside Goose. The captain hadn't mentioned that he planned on visiting the hospital. Remington hadn't communicated on the way over either. Usually the captain stayed with the nerve center even after the close action was finished. And usually nearly every move Remington made Goose knew ahead of time, either by knowing the man or by being kept informed.

Remington's presence now was a surprise.

Somebody bumped the table stakes, Goose guessed. He hadn't relayed the information that he had one of Cody's agents in custody. That fact wasn't a salient point during the battle for the city. Cody and his team were an internal problem, small when compared to the effort required to hold Sanliurfa.

Only Remington's presence testified that wasn't true. He wouldn't have come to the hospital to inspect the wounded and the dead. That wasn't his way. He would wait until the company officers made the reports their staff sergeants gave them.

Goose's mind cleared as anticipation filled him. From over his shoulder he studied Winters. The CIA agent's eyes showed bright hope. Catching Goose staring at him, the man smiled.

"Officer's coming," Barnett bawled. "Button it up and dust it off."

The Rangers inside the security office attended to their attire out of habit.

Goose walked to the doorway and peered out.

Remington moved briskly down the hallway in stained BDUs. Enlisted saluted him as he approached. His jaw was a hard, clenched line.

"Captain," Goose greeted, firing off a quick salute.

"First Sergeant," Remington returned as he came to a halt in front of the door.

Goose noticed there was no immediate command of "at ease," the way Remington normally handled their relationship. He stayed at attention as did the enlisted men around him and inside the security office.

"You've got a man in custody in this room, First Sergeant," Remington said.

"Yes, sir," Goose replied, keeping his eyes locked and level.

"Why wasn't I informed?"

"Sir, this man's arrest had nothing to do with the battle, sir." Goose replied in crisp tones, maintaining the complete professionalism Remington demanded.

"That was your assessment, First Sergeant?"

"Yes, sir."

"And you chose not to bother me with this detail?"

"Sir, not while you were otherwise engaged in maintaining the safety of this post, sir."

Remington gave a grudging nod. "Point taken, First Sergeant."

"Yes, sir."

Nodding toward Winters, Remington asked, "Have you identified this man?"

"He says his name is Winters, sir."

"And who is Winters?"

"He won't say, sir, but CIA Section Chief Alex Cody tells me the man belongs to him."

Remington's eyebrows lifted. "Cody did, did he?"

"Yes, sir. He asked that I remand Mr. Winters to his custody."

"*Asked*, First Sergeant?"

"Captain, Section Chief Cody made it plain that he was dissatisfied with my reluctance to hand Mr. Winters over to him."

"I suppose he would be."

"Yes, sir."

Remington studied Winters. From the corner of his eye, Goose noted that the CIA agent no longer looked as hopeful as he had.

"Have you seen this man before tonight, First Sergeant?"

"No, sir."

"Do you believe that he is a CIA agent?"

Goose considered that, wondering if Remington knew something that he didn't. "I decided that wasn't my decision to make, Captain. Thought I'd leave it up to you."

"You were holding Mr. Winters here for me."

"Yes, sir. I planned to notify you of Mr. Winters's arrest when you signaled an all clear."

"Have you talked with Mr. Winters?"

"Mr. Winters is reluctant to talk, Captain."

A cold, cruel smile spread across Remington's lips. "All right, First Sergeant, I'll take over."

"Yes, sir."

Remington stepped into the room. Barnett and the privates manning the security station remained at attention.

"At ease," Remington said.

The enlisted men relaxed.

Goose followed Remington into the room, staying at the captain's six almost two strides behind.

Remington turned around and locked eyes with Goose. "I'll take it from here, First Sergeant."

"Sir?" Goose stood his ground. As fatigued as he was, comprehension came slowly. He'd fully expected to be present while Remington dealt with the prisoner.

"You're dismissed, First Sergeant. Get my squads back together and get the defense of this city back in shape. I want the security perimeter reestablished, and I want to know how badly we were hurt by that attack. And I need that information five minutes ago."

Stung by the unexpected dismissal, Goose saluted. "Yes, sir." He put the toe of one boot behind the other and executed an about-face that strained his injured knee. He kept his head up as he walked out of the room. Remington was angry over the situation and was taking some of that out on him now, but it didn't make sense for the captain to send Goose away. Remington's dismissal was meant as an insult, a reminder of who was in charge.

As Goose stepped into the hallway, he spotted CIA Section Chief Cody making a beeline for the security office. His three agents followed in his slipstream.

Limping slightly, Goose continued toward the main room. It was going to be interesting to see who won the battle of wills between the captain and the CIA agent. But it was a grim reminder that more was at stake than Goose knew.

The tensions inside the city were building as quickly as those outside the city. Goose wouldn't have wanted to take bets on which one was going to blow first.

United States of America
Fort Benning, Georgia
Local Time 2241 Hours

Megan's cell phone chirped for attention and roused her from her re-
curring nightmare of Leslie Hollister's shooting. The unexpected
sound startled her.

Over the last few days, cellular service had remained impossible.
The circuits that were still up after the disappearances were often
taken over by FEMA, the Federal Emergency Management Agency. Repeated interviews with FEMA spokespeople had assured listeners that
the service would be returned as soon as possible.

Megan placed her coffee on the floor as she reached for her purse.
She took the phone out and flipped it open. "Hello."

"Megan?"

"Yes." Megan recognized Jenny McGrath's voice. Joey had
brought her to the post during the night of the disappearances. He'd
taken her out to a club that night, using a fake ID and staying out way
past his curfew.

At first, Megan had partially blamed Jenny for Joey's wayward-
ness, but meeting the girl had changed that opinion. She was beautiful and outgoing, and only nineteen.

Jenny had told Megan everything about her relationship with
Joey. There hadn't been much to tell. She had known Joey liked her,
and she'd liked him. But Jenny had no intention of getting serious
about anyone because she didn't have time or interest. Megan had in-
tuitively known there was more to Jenny's story, but she'd also known
Jenny wasn't going to talk about things until she was ready. For the

moment, Megan was just glad that circumstances had placed Jenny there to help out.

Once the post was locked down and no one without military ID was allowed in, Megan had persuaded Jenny to stay with her. Jenny lived alone with her father. With the phones out, no way existed of knowing whether her father was at home. Megan hadn't wanted Jenny to leave until they could be sure she would be all right. For the moment, the city was no place for a girl alone.

Jenny had proven to be a godsend. She had a natural affinity for other teens, and she seemed able to handle any crisis that came along. Surprisingly, she knew a lot about cooking and cleaning that aided in supporting all the teens who filled the Gander household.

Several people had opened their doors to kids who were left without parents or guardians and didn't want to stay at home alone. At present, the Gander house was full nearly to bursting, but even in the packed home Megan still felt the absence of Chris, Joey, and Goose.

"Are you all right?" Jenny asked. Voices sounded in the background.

"I'm fine," Megan answered. She tried to make sure her voice sounded confident.

Jenny hesitated. "I didn't know if the cell phone was working. When I couldn't reach you at the office, I thought I'd give it a try."

"I'm glad you did. I hadn't even thought of trying to use it. We'll need to call around to the people helping us and let them know the cells are up. At least for now." One of the first things Megan had done when she organized the support teams for the teens and adults struggling to come to grips with what had happened was put together a phone tree with home, work, and cell phone numbers.

"I will," Jenny promised. "First thing after I get off the phone with you." The voices in the background sounded louder.

"Is everything okay there?" Megan asked. She suddenly realized that she should have called to let Jenny know she wasn't going to be home anytime soon. Guilt assailed her. Somehow she couldn't seem to do anything right.

"Everything here is chaotic," Jenny assured her. "But we're good. Nothing to worry about."

The voices dimmed a little and Megan guessed from the steady hum of the washer on spin cycle that Jenny had stepped into the utility room. The washer and dryer ran constantly, struggling to keep up with the need for clean clothes for the teens.

"What you're hearing," Jenny went on, "are the sounds of a Mo-

nopoly game in the kitchen and a DVD audience in the living room."
She sighed. "There's popcorn everywhere."

"It's okay," Megan said. "It'll clean."

"I know. I'm not really worried about it. It's just constant, you
know. No matter what, nothing ever really seems to get done."

The guilt Megan felt cut more deeply. She should have seen this
coming. Jenny was hardly any older than most of the teens there.
Helping out around the house was a tremendous responsibility for
the young woman.

"When was the last time you were out of that house?" Megan
asked.

"I haven't been."

"I'm sorry. I should have thought to relieve you."

"You've been busy."

"I know, but—"

"Megan, I called to see how you were," Jenny interrupted politely.
"I just heard about the girl who was shot."

"Leslie," Megan said automatically. "Leslie Hollister." It seemed
important that people know Leslie's name. Megan didn't want her—
Leslie—to just be a statistic.

"How is she?"

Megan's throat tightened, and she had to work to force the words
out. "I don't know. She's in surgery. They're supposed to let us know.
I'm sorry. I should have called. I should have known you would hear
about—about—" She couldn't say "the shooting," and anything in
place of that term seemed too dismissive.

"Calling here would have been like the last thing on my mind if I
were in your shoes. How long until you know something?"

"I don't know. I'm not going to leave—" her voice tightened up
more—"I'm not going to leave until I find out how this . . . this is going to go." She refused to let herself be negative. Leslie Hollister was
going to make it. "Not until I hear that Leslie is stabilized."

"Don't worry about anything here. We've got things under control."

Someone whooped enthusiastically in the background.

Megan felt an immediate backlash of anger at whoever sounded
so delighted. Everything in the world had changed. Her family was
scattered, some of them maybe lost . . . forever. There wasn't a teen in
her house who hadn't lost someone. It just didn't seem fair that anyone would be happy.

She took a breath, held it a moment, then let it and her anger out.

What she was hearing, she knew after years of counseling and raising kids of her own, was the resiliency of youth. Nothing lasted forever in a young person's life. Everything changed every day. They just made the adjustment and kept moving. Youth was a river, a constant stream that flowed wherever it could.

But not all of those young people can make those adjustments, Megan reminded herself. *That's why Leslie is here.*

"How about you?" Jenny asked. "How are you doing?"

"I'm fine," she said. *Yeah, right.*

Jenny was silent.

Megan knew at once that the young woman didn't buy into her fib. There was something about Jenny McGrath, some skill or sense that could see deeper than most people twice her age.

"Okay," Megan said, "I'm not fine. But I'm holding up."

"I could probably get away from here for a little while. Stacy and Richard can keep the household running. Not much to it, really. Just make sure everybody uses the popcorn button on the microwave and keeps spills to a minimum."

Stacy and Richard Delmonico were two of the most responsible teens in the group. They were brother and sister. Their mother was a career drill sergeant currently assigned TDY to Fort Sill. Their father was in Nevada visiting his ailing mother. So far neither parent had called, but a lot of phone lines were still not functioning. In spite of their own worries about their parents, the two kids had stayed calm and helped greatly around the Gander household.

"I appreciate that, Jenny. Really I do. But I wouldn't be good company."

"That," Jenny said, "would be my part of the bargain. I could even bring you something to eat. I bet you haven't eaten yet."

"No," Megan admitted. Around the house, she sometimes forgot to eat even though she helped prepare so many meals for the teens. Every time she did forget, Jenny always seemed to be there to remind her.

"I've got homemade chicken noodle soup. I could bring you a thermos."

Megan's immediate impulse was to say no.

"Is anyone with you?" Jenny asked before Megan could answer.

Megan glanced at the two young MPs. "No." They weren't her friends. The only friends she had at the hospital had disappeared or were swamped with emergencies.

During the past few days, Megan had greatly missed Helen

Cordell, the night-shift supervisor who had worked at the counseling center and the base hospital. Helen had, like so many other people Megan had known, disappeared. Megan hadn't seen the clothes that Helen had left behind, but she had heard stories of their discovery.

"You could use a friend," Jenny said decisively. Another whoop went up from the Monopoly crowd as someone went directly to jail. "And I could use a break from Camp Gander. Just for a little while. Gotta be quieter at the hospital, right?"

"Right," Megan said.

"I'll nuke the soup. Be up there in a few minutes."

"Thanks, Jenny."

"No prob. I'll see you soon."

Megan clicked the phone off and started to return it to her purse. Then she realized that if her cell was working Joey's might function as well. She punched in her son's number and listened, hoping that he would answer so she would know he was all right. Then she could open negotiations to get him back where he belonged.

❖   ❖   ❖

United States of America
Columbus, Georgia
Local Time 2243 Hours

Joey Holder woke slowly, fighting his way through cottony layers of fatigue and a hangover. He was beginning to recognize the symptoms after the last couple days, but he still wasn't used to them. He'd never been a drinker, and had never gotten interested in overindulging—until two days ago.

Occasionally he'd sipped alcohol one of his buddies had swiped from home, but he'd never gotten inebriated. He knew his mom would probably know immediately, and he figured that Goose might just kill him on the spot.

Opening his eyes wide in the darkness, Joey stared up at the ceiling. Demons and devils stood out in glowing purple, green, and red on the walls. Horns and chains covered the fantastic and hideous creatures. Seductive women in wisps of electric blue clothing accompanied the monsters.

I'm in hell, Joey thought in wide-eyed panic. He surveyed the gruesome creatures. Then he calmed himself, remembering the posters on the walls and the ceiling in the borrowed bedroom where he slept. He just hadn't noticed they were black-light posters. In fact, he barely remembered stumbling into the room at all that afternoon.

He rolled his head, noting that he hadn't even made his way to the bed before collapsing. He lay on the floor within arm's reach of the bed. A headache pounded at his temples. When he swallowed, he felt like he was trying to choke down a dead cat covered in talc. Most people probably didn't know what it tasted like, dry and bitter and thick, but Joey could still remember when he was really small and had licked the talc container.

At least I didn't puke my guts up tonight, he told himself. That had happened yesterday morning. He'd woken up in his own vomit and freaked out. He hadn't even known he was sick; the whole night before was a blur.

He sat up slowly, knowing there was no avoiding the pain of the hangover. Once the room stopped swimming, he pushed himself to his feet and stood swaying. He kept a hand on the wall for balance and tried to remember where he was. The group he'd fallen in with moved around a lot, shifting from house to house, never staying in the same place twice. Generally, they'd worn their welcome out in each place.

The bedroom evidently belonged to a young person. Probably a teenager, Joey judged from the black-light posters and the drum set in one corner. A gun rack mounted on the wall held two bats, one wood and one metal. A skateboard and a BMX bike occupied space near the head of the bed.

Joey didn't recognize the room. He glanced at the pictures on the wall. Most of them were of a redheaded kid with a gap-toothed grin. He looked maybe fourteen or fifteen, but Joey had never seen the kid in his life.

Shaking his head and regretting the movement instantly when renewed pain slammed against the inside of his skull, Joey moved toward the doorway and down the hall toward the voices and the sounds of cars crashing and guns blasting. They were video-game noises, much different than the real thing.

During the last three days since storming out of his house in anger, Joey had learned a lot about real car crashes and real guns blasting. Columbus was filled with violence. Most of that was controlled during the daylight hours, but at night the city became a hunting ground for predators and looters and people determined to survive even if that survival meant others suffered.

At least, that was what it seemed like. Joey had stopped living in the daylight hours and roamed the city with his newfound friends at night.

Joey paused at the doorway of the living room. Six people sat in the large room in front of the home entertainment system. On the big-screen television, a character ran forward and blasted three aliens with a shotgun. The aliens exploded in violent bursts of orange blood. The animated figure ran between them and picked up a medpack that boosted his health level nearly back up to full.

"Dude!" one of the guys yelled. "That was so cool! I just knew you weren't going to make it past those guys! You were, like, in the last minute of your life!"

"You just gotta have the eye," the game player smirked. He paused the game and took a drag on the cigarette hanging from his lips. "The eye . . . and the nerve." The cigarette tip flared orange, lifting his stark features out of the room's darkness. His face was all bone and angles and tight flesh. "I got 'em both. Not gonna leave anything but a bunch of dead aliens behind me in this game."

The game player was lanky and tall. He sat in the middle of the floor wearing only a pair of black-and-white, zebra-striped pants. Tattoos covered his arms, chest, and back. The black ink stood out starkly against his pallid skin. His shaved skull gleamed blue from the television glow. Joey didn't know the guy's real name. All he knew him by was Zero.

"Hey, Joey," Derrick Hanson called from the couch.

Joey glanced at him. Derrick was the only one of the group that he really knew. The other five were either friends of Derrick's, or friends of friends of Derrick's.

They'd fallen in together three days ago at Cosmic Quest, an arcade-and-game store in downtown Columbus. The store had been closed then, and Joey guessed it was probably still closed. Some of the businesses in Columbus had reopened, primarily supermarkets and supply stores that were encouraged to do so by city, state, and federal agencies. National Guard units worked security at those businesses, protecting the stock and making sure everyone had a chance to buy what was needed.

A lot of small places didn't reopen because they didn't have protection. Despite presidential and FEMA spokesperson reassurances, panic—and looters—still filled the streets. Protesters gathered every day and every night, demanding to know what was truly going on.

Derrick was from Fort Benning, too. His father was a lieutenant currently stationed in Germany. His mom had worked at the hospital. She'd been one of those who had disappeared. If Derrick missed her—or even thought of her—he'd never mentioned it.

Squat and broad from power lifting in the gym, Derrick looked like a bulldog. He was broad shouldered and narrow hipped, but had short legs. Normally his hair was brown, but tonight it was green and bright orange, colored by special-effects, temporary dye.

"Hey," Joey replied. He didn't advance into the room. Even after three days with them, he still didn't feel like he belonged. They were crass and vulgar. He didn't have a problem with that, but he remained a little uncomfortable with their behavior.

Still, after leaving the post, he hadn't had many choices. He didn't want to go back to his mom. Not yet. Part of it was because Jenny might be there and he'd feel embarrassed about how that whole deal had turned out. Part of it was because he didn't feel like listening to his mom, or being grounded when the whole world seemed like it teetered on the edge of extinction.

And a big part of it was that Joey didn't want to see all those strangers in Chris's room, sleeping in Chris's bed. Not when Chris was supposed to be there. Not when he couldn't help thinking that if he'd been home on time that night instead of out breaking curfew, he might have gotten to see his little brother one last time.

The sadness and guilt that suddenly coiled in Joey's stomach made him sick. He put a hand to his mouth.

"Dude," one of the guys said, "don't do that in here."

"If he blows," another one said, "I'm not cleaning it up."

Joey got control of himself with difficulty. He swallowed the sour gorge of bile at the back of his throat. "No sweat," he told them in a strained voice. "I'm okay."

"You sure?" Derrick asked.

Joey knew Derrick didn't really care how he felt; he just didn't want to be embarrassed in front of the others. "I'm sure."

"Good." Derrick settled back in the deep sofa.

The others eyed Joey suspiciously. Again, that feeling of not be-longing resonated within him. But he chose to ignore it. There was nowhere else to go, and he didn't want to be alone. But it reminded him how little he knew them.

He'd spent time with them at Cosmic Quest for months, playing with them and against them at various games. During those times, Joey had felt cool, one of the gang. Zero, with his barely submerged challenge and hostility, earned a lot of respect in the arcade center. He didn't spend much time with many people. Getting in Zero's crowd was something of a coup.

And knowing that they were guys that Goose and his mom wouldn't approve of was an added luxury. Joey didn't fully understand the anger he felt toward his mom and his stepdad, but he knew it was their fault. They weren't giving him what he needed. Joey didn't exactly know what he wasn't getting, but he knew Chris was getting it all.

"Well, well. Lazarus lives." Zero flashed a thin smile. He held a game pad in one hand and a cigarette in the other. Ash from the cigarette dropped onto his crossed legs.

Joey crossed his arms over his chest. Getting Zero's full attention was always uncomfortable. The guy had dead black eyes set deeply into his hard-planed face. Normally even within the group he seemed tuned to his own inner frequency. Since the disappearances, he'd somehow seemed more alive, more a part of the everyday world.

"Yeah," Joey agreed.

"So how's the head?" Zero asked.

Joey knew Zero didn't care. He hadn't found anything yet that Zero cared about. "Hurts."

Zero grinned, exposing a broken left incisor. "I bet. You know what you need, don't you?"

"What?"

"Hair of the dog that bit you." Zero nodded to one of the other boys. ".Bones."

Bones leaned forward and took a liquor bottle from the coffee table in front of the overstuffed couch. Stacks of plates, containers, and potato chip bags covered it. The mess matched the rest of the house, standing out starkly against the neat carpet, furniture, and overall look of the room.

"Here." The boy held the bottle out in a knobby fist. He was tall and gangly, with ears that flared out like sails beneath a shaggy mullet. He wore baggy jeans and a black shirt left open over a black T-shirt featuring a dragon breathing fire on a knight. His name was Jonas but everyone called him Bones. He lived for role-playing games and was a laser-blasting menace on Marauders, a popular science-fiction-based shooter video game.

Joey held up a hand. "No thanks."

"Better hit it, man," Bones said. "Trust me. It'll cure that hangover headache right up." He uncapped the bottle and took a swig. "Me, I'm all about prevention. Don't ever sober up and you'll never face a hangover. That's one thing I've learned." He laughed.

Joey shook his head and regretted the instinctive action when flashing sparks danced in front of his eyes. He held back a groan of pain with effort.

"Want something to eat?" Derrick asked. "Still got plenty of TV dinners in the freezer. Fish sticks. Corn dogs. These people were really loaded up on stuff."

These people? That caught Joey's attention. He looked around the room. "So . . . where are the parents?"

"Parents?" Bones shook his head and snickered. "Ain't no parents here, man." He put on a pronounced Hispanic accent. "We don' need no *stinkeng* parents."

The effort drew a chorus of laughter from the other boys. Joey knew none of them were sober. Only Zero appeared unmoved by the joke. He kept his dead black eyes centered directly on Joey.

Of course there were no parents present, Joey realized. The house wouldn't have been a mess and the guys wouldn't have been smoking and drinking if there were parents around.

"Whose house are we in?" Joey asked. Last night's intoxication had left him blank about that.

"Dude," RayRay said, "ain't every house we come to we gotta have an invitation to. We ain't vampires." RayRay was athletically trim with a ghost of a mustache that barely stood out against the yellow coloration of his skin. His dark bronze Afro stood up four inches.

"Invitation," Joey repeated. Only then, like the final number of a school combination lock dropping into place, did he realize what RayRay was talking about. *They broke into this house. We broke into this house. We're trespassing in someone's home.* Panic fired up inside him. His immediate reaction was to leave—right now, before the police showed up. But with Zero's blank eyes on him, somehow Joey couldn't do it. Slowly, very slowly, he forced his tense muscles to relax.

United States 75th Army Rangers Temporary Post
Sanliurfa, Turkey
Local Time 0546 Hours

Cal Remington turned at the sound of his name.

CIA Section Chief Alexander Cody made all due haste in his approach. He held a bulky sat-phone in his right hand.

"I want this room secure," Remington said to the two privates manning the doors.

"Yes, sir." Both men snapped into position with their M-4A1s across their chests.

Cody read the movement at once and pulled up little more than arm's reach from the Rangers. He spread his hands in obvious disbelief. "Captain, is this really necessary?"

"Not as long as you respect the security I've placed on this room," Remington stated evenly.

The three men behind Cody spread out. All of them wore stone faces and kept their arms folded across their chests. Under their jackets, the weapons in their shoulder holsters were only a few inches away.

Remington shifted, turning so he was in profile. His right hand rested easily on his hip above his holstered sidearm. He kept his eyes on Cody, but his peripheral vision would alert him the instant any of the three men made a move.

"You're holding one of my agents," Cody protested.

"I was told you didn't convince my first sergeant of that," Remington said.

"My verbal ID isn't enough?"

"Not for me."

Cody cursed with enough effort that he turned red in the face. "I helped you, Captain. When no one else would lift a finger to aid you or your men along the border during the attack, I put you in contact with a man who could and did help you."

"You did." Remington nodded briefly. "However, that man isn't a United States citizen."

"So *now* you're suspicious of him?" Cody looked like he couldn't believe what he was hearing.

"I was suspicious then. At that point, the satellite systems worked to my advantage. Now, when I need them just as badly, I find that I don't have access to them."

"He explained the reasons for that. Surely you can understand the position he's in."

Remington noted that they carefully skirted around Nicolae Carpathia's name. "I understand the position he's placing himself in. I don't see that he has to be there at all." The United Nations appearance Carpathia planned didn't make sense to the Ranger captain.

Cody's eyes glittered. "There's an opportunity there. He's seizing it."

"Why?"

Cody pursed his lips, then let out a long breath. "I can't talk about that."

"But you know."

"I know some things, Captain."

"And the U.S. president supports this?"

"He does," Cody said. "Haven't you been watching the news?"

"I've been busy."

"So have I." Cody leveled a finger at the man sitting in the chair inside the security room. "So have my men."

Remington waited.

"Captain," Cody said in a softer voice, "I'm as shorthanded as you are. But taking one of my men is like you losing a company."

"I'm at less than half my strength after the disappearances and casualties," Remington said. "I'm stuck here, defending a city that is going to fall no matter what I do, with orders to make that loss last as long as possible." The captain put steel in his voice. "Don't you dare compare your situation with mine."

Cody held up his hands in supplication. "Captain, I don't mean to insult in any way."

Remington stepped forward between the two privates, emerging from the defense they offered. He stopped when he was almost nose to nose with the CIA section chief. "What is your mission here?"

"You know my mission here. I'm trying to recover a rogue agent."

"A rogue agent," Remington growled, "that you had me risk the lives of my Rangers for. You led me to believe we were rescuing someone."

"You were. Your men did. Those terrorists would have killed him. I'm sure of it."

"Your guy ran. The first chance he got, he ran."

Cody took a breath.

"The next day in Sanliurfa," Remington ground on like an M-3 Bradley armored personnel carrier, "two Americans were killed. Your rogue agent was seen entering the building where their bodies were found."

"I don't know what you're talking about."

"Lie to me," Remington threatened with slow deliberation, "and things just get harder." He held up his left hand, his forefinger and thumb an inch apart. "I'm this far—*this far*—from having you and your junior G-men slapped into custody until I finish my mission here."

"That would be a mistake." Cody's eyes turned icy with menace.

"Mister," Remington declared forcefully, "just about everything involved with this situation is a mistake. Not one of those mistakes has been mine. And I won't make one now."

"My mission here is very important, Captain."

"Prove that to me."

Cody blew his breath out. "I can't."

"Then you step back out of my face, Section Chief Cody."

Cody didn't move. "Captain, we're working on the same side."

"I don't know that."

"I assure you."

"Tell me what you're doing here."

Cody shook his head. "I can't."

"Then we don't have anything to talk about."

"Captain, you can't do this."

Remington raised his voice. "Corporal Hardin."

"Yes, sir." At the other end of the hallway, Corporal Dean Hardin stepped around the corner. Four men flanked him. They all held assault rifles at the ready, butts pulled back into their shoulders.

"Show Section Chief Cody and his men to the front door," Remington said. "I don't want to see them in this building again."

"No, sir, Captain," Hardin said, moving forward slowly with his weapon leveled on the CIA agents. "You won't, sir. I'll make certain of it myself, sir."

Hardin was lean and wolfish. The Kevlar helmet he wore further shadowed his dark features. Bruises from the violent encounter he'd had with Goose still showed on his face.

Goose had caught Hardin robbing American military corpses after the disappearances caused the air support from USS *Wasp* to crash into the hills near the Turkish-Syrian border. Remington knew all about Hardin's self-serving ways. They weren't noble, and many of them weren't legal, but they were all useful. As long as Remington maintained control over them.

"Captain," Cody implored.

Hardin reached the rearmost CIA agent, who wasn't moving. Quickly and mercilessly, Hardin swung his weapon around and buttstroked the agent in the face.

Blood erupted from the agent's face, and he dropped to his hands and knees. A silencer-equipped pistol tumbled from inside his jacket.

Hardin shot a foot forward and captured the pistol under his boot. He reversed his assault rifle and brought it to bear. "The next one of you doesn't listen when Cap'n Remington tells you to hit the road, I'm going to open up and let a little daylight through. *Capisce?*" He glanced at Cody over his gun sights. "That goes for you too, Chief."

The agent on the ground groaned in pain. Blood dripped to the floor.

"While we're at it," Hardin said, grinning, "why don't you all just clap your hands to your heads. You know the drill."

Reluctantly, the CIA agents put their hands on top of their heads.

"Billy," Hardin said, "help that boy to his feet. But stay out of my field of fire."

One of the privates came forward and helped the dazed CIA agent to his feet.

"Chief," Hardin said in an easy conversational tone, "you might want to get your boy to the infirmary. The Sanliurfa citizens are still keeping theirs open. Maybe you can get some joy there. Looks to me like he's definitely going to need some stitches. And his jaw might be busted."

Remington noted the gleam in Hardin's eyes. The corporal liked the violence. During his years as a Ranger, Hardin had made it as far as corporal five times. He'd been busted down in rank each time. After getting caught robbing the dead as he had, he deserved to be broken in rank again. If it had happened during peacetime, Remington probably would have done exactly that. But here and now, with circumstances the way they were in Sanliurfa, Remington wanted Hardin in place.

"Now," Hardin said, "y'all get moving before I have to turn plumb nasty."

Grumbling and cursing beneath their breath, the CIA agents started moving.

"A moment, Corporal," Remington said. He stepped in front of Cody. "Your people have been running rampant through this city. That stops. Today. *Now.* You keep them out of harm's way."

"Captain."

Remington put his finger to his lips like he was shushing a child. "Don't talk. You'll just offend Corporal Hardin and he'll feel compelled to make you respect his commanding officer."

Hardin grinned broadly.

"When you decide you can tell me exactly what's going on here," Remington said, "you come see me. Then we'll negotiate what rights and privileges you have open to you while we're here."

Cody swallowed hard. His eyes flickered. He clearly didn't like being dictated to.

"I want you to stop hunting for Icarus," Remington commanded. "We'll find him."

Cody opened his mouth and started to speak.

"Bad idea," Hardin said softly. "Bad, bad idea."

Cody's lips flattened and became a hard, thin line.

"Do you read me, Cody?" Remington asked.

"Yes," Cody replied, "but—"

Hardin stepped forward and rammed his rifle butt into Cody's midsection. The CIA man doubled over and retched. Before he could fall, Hardin caught him by the jacket collar and held him up.

"The answer's 'Yes, sir,' " Hardin said. "Or 'Yes, Captain.' You got that?"

Cody nodded and whispered hoarsely, "Yeah, yeah, I got that."

"Let's hear it," Hardin suggested.

"Yes, sir," Cody said.

Hardin straightened Cody up. "Good. Can you stand on your own?"

Cody nodded.

"Outstanding," Hardin said. He released Cody and stepped back. "Sir, are we done here?"

"We're done," Remington said. "See to it these men are taken out; then rejoin me in this room."

"Yes, sir." Hardin put a hand in the middle of Cody's back and shoved him forward.

Cody glanced back over his shoulder as he stumbled down the hallway. Hardin said something to the man and he turned his eyes forward.

Watching the agent, Remington knew he'd probably made an enemy for life. But that was fine. During his climb to his captaincy, he'd made more than a few enemies. One more wasn't going to matter.

Turning back toward the security office, Remington caught sight of Goose standing at the other end of the hallway. Silently, the captain cursed himself. Goose had seen everything, and he could tell from the set of Goose's body and his small frown that the first sergeant didn't approve. Over the years, they'd butted heads several times while serving together.

You're not looking for approval from him, Remington reminded himself when he felt a twinge of guilt over the free hand he'd given Hardin to act. *When you first put on lieutenant's bars, you stepped up past First Sergeant Goose Gander. You don't answer to him. You never have.*

"I thought I gave you an assignment, First Sergeant," Remington said in a loud voice.

"You did, sir," Goose responded. "On my way now. I just thought there might be a problem, sir."

"There's not a problem here that I can't handle."

"No, sir," Goose said. "I guess there's not. Sir." He turned and walked away.

But you, Remington thought at Goose's back, *you're going to turn out to be a problem, aren't you, Goose?* The captain took in a deep breath and released it.

Normally during situations of high stress, he and Goose remained on the same page, reading each other's thoughts. That was why Remington had temporarily bumped Goose up to the unofficial role of second in command of the unit during the Sanliurfa occupation.

But the Icarus issue had divided them. Remington didn't know how that had happened, but he knew it had. It remained to be seen how big a rift that issue put between them.

Gathering his thoughts, Remington turned and faced the CIA agent, Winters, in the security room. Defeat colored the man's face. Watching his superior get manhandled so easily hadn't generated any feelings of confidence about his current state.

Remington strode into the room and stopped in front of the man. "Winters, is it?"

The CIA agent nodded.

"I'm going to conduct an interview, Winters," Remington said. "I'm going to ask questions, and you're going to answer them."

Winters licked his lips. "If I can."

Remington regarded the man. "If you can't, Mr. Winters, neither of us is going to be happy about that."

❈   ❈   ❈

United States of America
Columbus, Georgia
Local Time 2249 Hours

Guilt hammered at Joey as he gazed around the room with new understanding. They weren't supposed to be there. They hadn't been invited. They were trespassing. If the police caught them, they would go to jail. That thought filled him with cold fear. He couldn't believe Derrick and the others could sit there so calmly.

"You weren't really of this world when you got here, were you?" Zero asked in a soft voice. His gaze remained riveted on Joey.

"Didn't remember breaking in," Joey admitted.

Zero shrugged but maintained eye contact under the stark ridge of brow over his blade of a nose. "Lotta people ain't home now, Joey. Got a lotta places we can go that nobody needs any more."

"The police—"

"The police," Zero said in a harsher voice, "aren't a problem. You think they're going to leave the supermarkets and gasoline-storage areas and airports to come looking for guys smart enough to find themselves a place to stay during all the chaos going on out there?"

"Especially teenagers." Bones took another drink from the bottle. "We got a right to find food and shelter for ourselves. And we ain't hurt nobody."

"The people who lived here," Zero said, "don't need this home anymore. We found their clothes in the big bedroom. Pajamas lying on the bed. They disappeared in their sleep just like a lot of other people."

Joey glanced around the room. Family pictures on the mantel over the fireplace showed at least three generations. A picture of Jesus Christ hung above them, His hands together as He looked up. As Joey gazed at the picture, he knew a moment of peace, but the confusion inside him won out as soon as he took his eyes off the painting to see the confusion around the room.

"Do you understand what I'm talking about, Joey?" Zero's voice held a hint of warning.

"Yeah," Joey said, knowing he could give no other answer.

Zero smiled. "Good. You might just survive this thing."

"Did you find out what was causing the disappearances?" Joey asked. He knew Zero kept up with the news. Somehow, if he knew who the mysterious enemy was, he felt certain he would feel better about the whole situation.

"No," Bones said. "There's all kinds of people on television making all kinds of claims about who did this. A lot of them don't believe the president when he says that Russia wasn't behind it. I mean, who else has that kind of tech?"

"China," Maxim said, "for one. North Korea for another." He was normally quiet, always watching. Zero and the others adopted him into the group because he was so knowledgeable about games and game systems. He had a habit of sitting around flicking disposable lighters, watching the flame for a moment, then blowing it out.

Zero was the oldest of the group at nineteen or twenty, but Maxim was second in line. He wore thick glasses, black button-up shirts, and long hair. He never discussed the three scars on the right side of his face, but Derrick had told Joey that Maxim's dad, an ex-convict, had given him the scars when he was ten.

Dropper shifted on the couch. He was the biggest of the group at six feet four. Solid and heavy, he was built like a Mack truck. Close-cropped blond hair framed a round face that at first glance looked innocent. But there was little that was innocent about Dropper.

Joey thought Dropper's name might have actually been Tony or Anthony or Andrew, but no one called him by that name. His father was a cop, but he lived with his mom and ended up getting kicked back and forth between his parents. Everybody called him Dropper because when he fought he usually dropped his opponents after a few punches.

"You guys are forgetting a basic thing," Dropper rumbled in his deep voice. Joey had learned the big youth had a keen and incisive mind, despite his slovenly looks.

"What's that?" Bones asked in a challenging manner.

Dropper swiveled his attention on Bones. The slender youth drew back into himself as if trying to fade into the couch.

"We have that kind of technology too," Dropper said. "The United States government. What's going on out there, it could just be the result of something the U.S. government did. Of course, we wouldn't want to claim it was us."

"I think you're all wrong," Zero stated.

All of the others, Joey included, looked at Zero. During the past few days, Zero had kept to his own counsel, volunteering no idea of what he thought caused the disappearances or how he felt about them. If Zero had lost anyone, no one knew it.

"Okay," Bones said. "I'll bite. What caused all the disappearances?"

"Aliens," Zero stated.

Of all the explanations Joey had heard, that one was the dumbest. Still, he remained quiet. No one ever argued or disagreed with Zero; there were stories about people who had that and ended up getting their heads busted.

"Aliens," Bones repeated. Maybe he'd drunk enough that he wasn't thinking straight, which Joey knew was possible, or maybe he'd grown braver about his responses since he'd accompanied Zero full time for the last three days.

"You have a hearing problem?" Zero demanded.

Bones quickly held his hands up. "Nope. Not me. Just, you know, trying to get around the whole aliens-concept thing." He paused. "Kind of out there, don't you think?"

Zero fixed the other youth with a cold stare. "You don't believe me, Bones?"

"I'm just thinking, you know, that maybe if it was aliens that did this, we'd know by now."

"Not if they didn't want us to," RayRay said nervously.

"The air force would have seen their ships," Bones replied.

Shut up, Joey thought, looking at the dark anger that filled Zero's hard-planed face. *Quit while you're ahead.*

"Cloaking devices," RayRay said. "Air force wouldn't have seen them if they'd had cloaking devices."

"They're not Romulans," Bones insisted.

"We got cloaking devices." RayRay tried valiantly to battle Bones's arguments. "Got them spy planes and boats that radar can't detect. Ain't so hard to believe that somebody would figure out how to do it in outer space. I mean, aliens are from outer space, for crying out loud. They're going to know lots of stuff."

Maxim and Dropper gazed at Bones with avid interest. Even Derrick seemed hypnotized by the possibility of impending violence.

And Joey knew that was going to happen. Zero wouldn't put up with anyone challenging him. Not even Bones.

Bones blinked, suddenly aware of Zero's intense scrutiny. His survival instinct kicked in. "Oh," he said hoarsely. "Cloaking devices. Yeah, I guess that could be it."

Tension hung in the room for a moment.

"Why aliens?" Dropper asked.

"Because I can't figure out who else would do something like this," Zero answered. "I've turned this thing over in my head every which way. You see, something this big goes down, you gotta look for the angle. What the prize is. The people who have the most to gain from something like this." He nodded to the television. "I've been watching the news."

Joey remembered the other nights they'd stayed in other homes. Zero had watched the news then, too.

"The way I figure it, nobody has anything to gain by disappearing so many people all at once." Zero lit a fresh cigarette. "The whole world is in chaos. Sure, maybe the president and his flunkies will be able to get everybody back up to speed in a few days, but look at everything that's been lost: airports, airplanes, buildings." He shrugged and blew out a cloud of smoke. "People."

"Assets," Dropper said.

Zero smiled. "Exactly. You figure the United States is getting ready to take over Russia or one of those other countries, the last thing they'd do is cripple themselves. Right?"

"Right," Bones answered.

Joey wasn't so sure. He was still leaning toward the accidental use of a superweapon himself. Some kind of new weapon of mass destruction that no one had ever heard of. He didn't know what, but that theory beat the alien thing all to pieces. Weapons were part of his everyday life at Fort Benning, but he'd never seen a single extraterrestrial.

"That leaves aliens," Zero said. He held up a hand. "Now I know you want to ask: Hey, Zero, if it's aliens that did this, why haven't those aliens come forward and made their demands?"

That, Joey thought, was only one hole in Zero's theory.

"It's because they don't know how to talk to us," Zero said. "All these video games we play? In those games the aliens already know our language." He made his voice deep. "'Die, Earthling.' 'I'm going to disintegrate your world.' Like Marvin the Martian or something. But that ain't how it would be in the real world."

A real world of aliens, Joey couldn't help thinking. But he saw the avid fire in Zero's black eyes and knew the youth was consumed by his idea. Maybe it was the liquor, or maybe it was something else.

Over the last three days, Joey had seen Zero taking pills as well as drinking. He couldn't remember seeing Zero sleep this whole time.

"I mean," Zero said, "when the Spanish went over and conquered the Mexicans, they didn't know their language either. Right?"

The Spaniards hadn't conquered Mexicans, Joey knew. They'd conquered the Aztecs and Incas.

"What they did," Zero continued, "is demolish the Mexicans, then teach them their language. So they could talk. Tell them what they wanted and stuff."

"That's right," Bones said. "They came over and wiped out the Incas and—and—the Mexicans."

"Right," Zero said, warming to the subject. "They taught them their language and made them their slaves. That's what's going on now."

Joey seriously doubted that, but he didn't dare voice an objection. This was something scarier—something *worse*—than that.

"What would have to happen for the aliens to take over," Zero said, "is that the aliens would have to make a statement. A show of force. Prove to the world leaders what they can do." He waved a hand. "All this stuff that's happened, you think there aren't believers in aliens out there now?"

Everyone waited.

"There are believers," Zero said. "And I bet the president and some of the others are just waiting for first contact. Only the aliens are going to do some recon first. Same way we do when we team-play Maelstrom Force. Get the lay of the land, so to speak, before you risk a lot." He smiled. "But you know what else they're going to do?"

"What?" Bones was totally into his supportive mode now.

"They're going to want to make contact with earthlings that they can deal with," Zero answered. "Guys who can give them information about stuff, and who can talk to the rest of the world for them."

"Negotiators." Bones's voice held a note of awe, and he smiled broadly.

"Right." Excitement rattled through Zero. He pushed himself to his feet with an effortless flexing of muscle. The rumor was that he had been some kind of big-deal martial arts student before he dropped out of the dojo. "But it's going to be more than just negotiators. Those people who talk for the aliens? They're going to be ambassadors in a whole new world."

Uneasiness wormed through Joey as he watched Zero. The kid had totally wigged out. Whatever grasp of the situation, of reality, he'd had until this point was gone.

"So you know what we're going to do starting tonight?" Zero asked.

Dropper cracked his knuckles.

No one said anything. Joey figured they were all scared to voice any opinion on the matter.

Zero hissed in exasperation. "We're going to look for the aliens. C'mon. This isn't brain surgery here."

"Okay," Bones said nervously. "Say we find these aliens. *Before* anybody else finds them. Including the military. What then?"

"Then," Zero said, pacing the floor, "we offer our services. In exchange for being made ambassadors." He grinned. "That's the angle, guys. You always gotta try to cut a piece of the action for yourself. Otherwise you're always the guy getting beat up."

Nobody looked excited about the prospect. Joey felt even sicker at his stomach.

"The whole find-the-alien thing," RayRay said. "You know, maybe that won't work out like we're thinking it will. I mean, maybe these alien dudes won't exactly be friendly. They could be figuring that they can do the whole thing themselves."

"Yeah," Bones added. "If we find 'em, they might try to make us part of the examples they leave behind."

"Right," RayRay said. "Like that alien psycho dude in Tormentor of Thraxtor did to all his victims. You know, when he chopped off the heads of those guys, put them on pikes, and used them to line the walls of his fortress to warn everybody else away."

The Tormentor of Thraxtor was a video game that had enjoyed several weeks of fame at Cosmic Quest. Bloody and vicious, it had attracted the attentions of most of the teenage boys in the metro area. It had also received a special note of condemnation from one of the local papers. Of course, the condemnation only served to increase the game-playing public's awareness of and interest in the game.

Zero's eyes turned cold. "That would be their mistake then." He turned and lifted his shirt from the floor.

Joey spotted a gleam of an oily metallic surface only an instant before Zero unlimbered a large handgun from his shirt. Zero leveled the pistol at the television set where an alien stood frozen on the screen when he'd paused the game.

The shot sounded like a cannon in the enclosed space. A bright flame shot from the barrel. The bullet hit the television screen and exploded the set, leaving a gaping hole where the video-game picture had existed only a moment ago.

Zero turned to them with a smile on his face and the pistol waving before him. "I'm gonna be an ambassador. Or a prince. Some alien tries to make me his little trophy prize, I'm gonna blow his head off."

No one spoke for a time.

Finally, RayRay said, "They still got cops, you know. In this neighborhood, I mean. A neighbor could call in on that shot. We know there's a few neighbors left. We've seen them, and there are lights on out there now."

"All the more reason for us to get up and get moving," Zero said. He glanced around the house. "We're about done with this place anyway."

Joey thought about going home. Any place was safer than being with Zero. Maybe it was the whiskey and the pills Zero was taking, or maybe the whole disappearances thing was catching up with him, but Joey felt like Zero had lost it. If he had been dangerous before, he was decidedly more so now.

But Joey shut down that line of thinking. Home wasn't an option for him. His mom had turned away from him when she'd taken in all those other kids. She hadn't even thought of him, hadn't considered how he'd feel about getting invaded and sharing everything in his home—including his mom.

He also felt certain she blamed him for not being there when Chris . . . vanished. He was supposed to have been there. If it were him, he knew he'd blame himself for not being there to take care of his brother.

He already did.

Even if he'd wanted to go back to Fort Benning, he'd lost his military ID somewhere since he left. Maybe an MP would look him up in the computer and let him enter the post, but more than likely that wouldn't happen. From the scattered news reports he'd seen on local television stations, Fort Benning remained under siege by frightened citizens begging and fighting to get in.

Still, he'd have to find a way to get across the city and back to the post before he could do anything. Predatory groups still roamed the streets, though. Murders and personal violence had escalated. Going through that dangerous landscape alone wasn't an option.

With a sinking feeling, Joey knew he was trapped with the others. At least for the moment. He stared at Zero and the broken television, feeling that things were only going to get worse.

United States 75th Army Rangers Temporary Post
Sanliurfa, Turkey
Local Time 0552 Hours

"Goose, wait up. *Goose.*"

More than anything, Goose wanted to ignore the sound of that voice because it could only mean trouble. So he pretended not to notice even though doing so made him feel bad. His father had raised him to be respectful of women.

A Ranger private parked in a Humvee across the street spotted the first sergeant. At Goose's signal, the private put the vehicle in gear and spun it around, bringing the Hummer to a stop in front of Goose. The driver was bloodied and covered in soot, evidence of his proximity to the front line.

"First Sergeant Gander," the private greeted.

An M-1 Abrams rumbled down the street. The heavy treads smashed through piles of debris that littered the pavement and filled the immediate vicinity with rumbling and cracking. One of the stores still burned. Flames twisted along the outside of the building like they were trying to escape. Fire teams worked to control the blaze.

Goose lifted his leg gingerly and slid into the passenger seat. He put his M-4A1 buttstock down between himself and the driver.

"Where to?" the driver asked.

"Away from here," Goose answered, taking his Palm Pilot from the chest pouch of his BDU. "I'll call it on the fly, Private. I just want to feel the wind in my face."

"All right, First Sergeant."

Anger seethed inside Goose. He didn't like getting cut out of the investigation into the CIA's operations inside the city. And despite his years of training and having the mind-set of an enlisted man, he didn't like the way Remington had handled his dismissal in front of an audience. For a long time, they'd shared a deep friendship. Perhaps that friendship hadn't extended beyond the postings and battles they had gone through together, but it was there at those times.

It'll be there again, Goose told himself. *Once we get around this, if we're not dead, it'll be there again.* His friendship with Remington, despite their differences on a number of things, was part of the bedrock of his military life.

Goose's friendship with Bill Townsend had been on a different level. Bill had gotten involved with all aspects of Goose's life, from the military to the family. And if Bill were still here instead of among the MIAs reported after the rash of disappearances, Goose knew his friend would tell him to relax and let Remington have his way for a while. They were all headed in the same direction.

Goose couldn't shake the idea that Icarus knew more about the vanishings than anyone else Goose had so far talked with.

"Goose."

"First Sergeant." The driver nodded toward the approaching woman. "Lady there seems to want to talk to you."

Reluctantly, Goose shifted his attention to Danielle Vinchenzo. She wore fatigues and a Kevlar battle helmet. A few strands of her short-cropped brown hair poked out from under the helmet. Dirt or blood streaked one of her cheeks. Her cameraman followed her, panning the street and the soldiers.

"Maybe I don't want to talk to the lady," Goose growled.

"Might at least take a minute, First Sergeant," the private said, gazing across Goose. "You got to at least tell her that running around in these streets ain't no place for a lady."

"I don't think she'll listen to me," Goose said. He was certain about that. Danielle Vinchenzo had a habit of reporting right from the middle of a battle. Talks with some of the other reporters from FOX News where she had worked before taking the new assignment with OneWorld NewsNet had revealed that her behavior in the Sanliurfa situation wasn't new. She'd taken that tack dozens of times before. She wasn't one to go along with the flow when she felt she had a story. A maverick, one of the journalists had called her.

But she was easy on the eyes, another had said. She pulled in ratings for news stations. A woman in the middle of a war zone was attention-getting enough, but Danielle was also bright and articulate and knowledgeable.

Goose's opinion was that she was also dangerous to herself. And, just maybe, to the people around her.

Danielle stopped at the side of the Humvee. "I didn't think you heard me."

"I'm busy, ma'am," Goose replied, not addressing the question of whether he had heard her or not.

"Are you on your way somewhere?"

The cameraman hunkered down to line up a shot on Goose.

Pointing at the camera just as the bright cone of light flared out at him, Goose said, "No."

Danielle adjusted her helmet and squared her stance. "Cezar."

"Yeah," the cameraman replied.

"Off."

The cameraman looked petulant. "But you said you wanted footage of the sergeant. Said he was your golden boy."

"He's a first sergeant, not a sergeant," Danielle said. "There's a distinction. I said, off. I meant it."

"You meant it when you said you wanted the footage, too." Shrugging, Cezar turned the camera off and walked away. "When you decide you want to get back to the job, I'll be over here." He walked a few paces away and lit a cigarette.

A cargo truck pulled to a stop in front of the Humvee. Soldiers representing the American, Turkish, and United Nations forces bailed from the truck and began unloading gurneys of wounded soldiers and citizens.

"We're in the way," Goose said. "Got people here with jobs to do."

"No problem." Danielle vaulted with lithe ease into the rear of the Hummer. She settled in. "Let's go."

Irritated, Goose swung around in the seat to face her. "Miss Vinchenzo, what do you think you're doing?"

"Following up on my story."

"Get out of the vehicle."

"No." Determination showed in her dark eyes.

Goose was surprised to see suspicion in the woman's gaze as well. "Ma'am, you'll either leave this vehicle under your own steam or I'll have you escorted off and placed under guard till I figure out what to do with you."

"What is the CIA doing here?" Danielle demanded.

Shock locked Goose's mind down for a moment. He took a breath to figure out his course of action.

"Don't bother to deny it, First Sergeant," Danielle said. "I saw the man myself."

Goose rubbed his face with a hand. The rough contact awakened pain in a dozen cuts and scratches. Stubble rasped against his callused palm.

"Is the U.S. military working with the CIA?" Danielle asked.

"In the defense of this city," Goose replied, "no, ma'am."

"Then what is that CIA agent doing here?"

"You'd have to ask him, ma'am."

"Can't tell, First Sergeant? Or won't?"

"The U.S. military has conducted strategic missions with CIA assistance even before the second Gulf war, ma'am. If they're here, I'm sure their presence is a planned insertion. I'm likewise certain that if they wanted their ops plastered across the media they'd have called and scheduled an appointment with you."

Danielle didn't react to the sarcasm. "Do you know that man?"

"No. He introduced himself. That's all."

A frown knitted Danielle's brows together. "What were he and Captain Remington arguing about?"

Goose hesitated.

"I saw them myself," Danielle said. "You can deny it if you want to, but I'll know you're lying. You were standing right there. I saw you take a step forward when the CIA guy closed on Remington."

Stepping up to the defense of his friend and superior officer was a reflex. "Ma'am, you'd have to discuss that matter with Captain Remington. Or with the other gentleman."

"*Gentleman.*" Danielle snorted, folded her arms across her chest, and leaned back. "One thing I can tell you, First Sergeant, is that man is no gentleman."

Goose's anger subsided immediately as interest flared to take its place. He looked at the driver. "Private, give me some space."

"Yes, First Sergeant." The private switched off the Hummer's engine and left the vehicle.

Goose swung his attention back to the reporter. "Do you know that man?"

Danielle gazed at Goose in open-eyed speculation. "What name did he give you?"

Shaking his head, Goose said, "No, ma'am."

"Need-to-know basis, huh?"

"Yes." Goose shifted in the seat, trying in vain to find a more comfortable spot to ease the throbbing pain in his knee. "Now if you don't mind, I've got ops to attend to."

"We need to talk."

"We talk too much," Goose said. "I don't have time to give right now."

"Then we'll talk later."

Goose chose a more diplomatic course. "Later." That was his answer, but his intention was to stay too busy until she gave up on talking to him again.

"That's lip service, First Sergeant." Danielle glared at him, but her instant anger was distracted, too.

"Ma'am," Goose said, "I've got wounded men out there and a defensive line that's been hurt badly. I need to get to them."

"Goose." Danielle's voice was softer, punctuated by a sudden distant roar of an assault rifle on full auto. "That man, whatever name he gave you, he's dangerous. I've seen him before. In Romania while I was covering a terrorist group the government ordered killed." She paused. "I was working with an informant. The informant told me about the man I saw talking with Remington in the hallway. The next day, my informant was dead. Someone had hung him inside the shower at his hotel long enough to nearly asphyxiate him, then slit his jugular and let him bleed out. He didn't die easily."

The declaration, devoid of emotion, shocked Goose. The woman had seen more than he would have thought. "What does that have to do with the man you saw talking to Remington?" Goose carefully left out the fact that he'd had a conversation with Cody.

Danielle's eyes turned cold and hard. "I believe he killed my informant. I think it was, in some way, my fault. My director wanted some edgy copy. I gave them the story about the potential CIA link to the terrorist group, to the fact that our government possibly had a hand in the political unrest in Bucharest." She paused to swallow. Her left eye twitched. "I didn't warn my source. When I couldn't get hold of him, I went to the hotel where I'd put him up. I was the one who found his body."

"I'm sorry," Goose said.

"I checked him into that hotel, you see," Danielle said. "So it was my fault. My company credit card was easily traced. I was reporting on rogue American CIA efforts, right? I should have known they could easily trace the cards I was using."

"You think the CIA killed him."

"Yeah." Danielle nodded. "The terrorists would have made a bigger deal of it. They'd have killed my source and thrown his body into a public area with a note pinned to his chest with a knife."

"But the CIA—"

"They wanted things kept quiet. The execution was clean. The Romanian police—" Danielle shrugged—"the government does a lot of business with the United States. Movies. Tourism. And they didn't want terrorists there anyway. The murder was kept quiet. Even the network I worked for treated the story strictly hands-off. My source was a footnote. Nothing." Her voice tightened. "And I got him killed."

Goose looked away from the woman and focused on the hotel. "You think that man in there—"

"He was there." Danielle's voice was firm. "He was *there*, Goose. I know that. I saw him. Once. But I saw him."

Switching his gaze back to her, Goose said, "If you only saw him once—"

Her eyes held his. "I'm sure, Goose. It was him. Before the events were over in Romania, he and his team left a trail of bodies behind them. I never found the witnesses or the kind of proof that I needed to go on the air with the story, but I know it was them." She drew in a ragged breath. "If this guy is here now, he's not here to help the military. No matter what he says. He's following someone else's orders."

"Whose?" Goose asked.

"Fitzhugh's, maybe. There are a lot of rumors around that the American president's hands are dirty in international politics. Or someone else." Danielle bit her lower lip. "Maybe not. Maybe it was just independent action. Some of these CIA guys? They're powers unto themselves. The American government doesn't want to know every dirty little trick those agents play to get the job done."

Goose remembered some of the horror stories he'd heard from the old guard about Vietnam. The CIA had been responsible for a considerable amount of carnage in that war.

"And if a president does want to know," Danielle continued, "you can bet that he doesn't want anyone else to. Not everyone in the agency is like this guy. Only a few of the black ops field guys. But I'm telling you now that this is one of those guys you don't want to trust. No matter what he offers you."

Goose kicked that around in his head. Cody had obviously gone to Remington to retrieve his captured agent. Remington had refused. Both of them, he was sure, were after Icarus. But his mind seized on another important fact that he didn't think Danielle Vinchenzo had yet acknowledged.

"This guy knows you," Goose said.

Danielle started to disagree.

Goose cut her off. "If he killed your source in Romania, he knows you. If he thinks you're a risk to him, things could go badly for you. And if he was following your credit card, like you say he was, it might even be you he wanted back in Romania. I'd watch your back."

She wrapped her arms around herself. "Okay."

"Don't let him see you as a threat," Goose advised. "You're a reporter. Here. Doing a story on the Syrian push into Turkey."

Danielle didn't say anything.

"Stay away from him, Miss Vinchenzo," Goose said. "Stay away from him until we figure out what to do."

Raising an eyebrow, Danielle asked, "*We?*"

Goose sighed. He was getting drawn into a lot more than he wanted. There were too many sides being drawn inside the city, and the Syrian army stood just outside the walls waiting for an opportunity to kill them all. Keeping straight the alliances he had made was going to be hard.

"*We*, ma'am," Goose told her. "On this issue, I'm with you to a limited extent. And the first time you cross me up, I'm gone and you're on your own."

She returned his gaze full measure, then gave a nod. "Fair enough, First Sergeant. But that threat's a two-way street. I trusted you enough to warn you. I don't like being wrong." Without another word, she placed a hand on the Hummer's side and heaved herself from the vehicle.

Surprised, and maybe feeling a little threatened, Goose watched her go. She never turned back, never looked over her shoulder. He sat back in his seat and called for his driver.

❋   ❋   ❋

United States of America
Fort Benning, Georgia
Local Time 2255 Hours

"Jenny! Hey, Jenny!"

Holding the saucepan with both hands as she poured chicken noodle soup into the olive-drab thermos standing on the kitchen counter, Jenny looked over her shoulder but managed to keep an eye on the pouring at the same time. The soup smelled great, and she hoped Megan was in good enough spirits to appreciate it.

"What?" she asked.

Casey Schmidt held the cordless phone up. "Phone. For you."

Teenagers clustered around the kitchen table still playing Monopoly. The game had progressed quickly. Motels sprang up everywhere around the board.

"Gimme a sec." Jenny finished pouring and put the saucepan in the sink on top of the mountain of dirty dishes that never seemed to go away despite her best efforts. She and the dishwasher were barely able to keep up with the demand for clean plates, bowls, and silverware. She tried to clean pots and pans as she went.

Megan and the other counselors were talking about getting school going again to provide a larger area for the teens and also to provide a stable environment. At least the cafeterias at the facility there were equipped to handle the feeding workload.

The microwave timer dinged for attention. One of the guys got up from the table and pushed by Jenny. When he opened the door, the smell of buttered popcorn filled the room in a fresh warm wave.

Jenny sealed the thermos and wiped her hands on a towel. She made her way toward Casey and the phone.

"Who is it?" Jenny asked. Her first thought was that it was Megan calling to let her know not to come to the hospital because Leslie Hollister had died. Jenny didn't know what she was going to say if that was the case.

"A guy," Casey answered. She was thirteen and gangly with a serious overbite. Having her blonde hair pulled up in pigtails made her look even younger.

"Did you get a name?"

Casey shook her head. "He didn't give it. Just said he wanted to talk to you." She eyed Jenny speculatively. "Do you have a boyfriend?"

"No," Jenny said crisply.

During the last few days she'd been inundated with personal questions. That came from her acceptance as an authority figure, Megan had said. Kids wanted to know adults so they could better understand them and the perimeters they were allowed, and then how far they could push those perimeters.

Jenny figured it was a lot like a prisoner finding out how far he could push the jailer. "I don't have a boyfriend." She took the phone before Casey could ask why not, which she was certain would be the next question out of the younger girl's mouth. Holding the handset to her ear, Jenny said, "Hello."

"Jenny? Is that you, girlie?"

As always when she talked with this man on the other end of the phone connection, Jenny's stomach twisted with relief and dread. She felt relieved because she knew he was still there. Not vanished. Not dead. But she felt dread because of all the bad memories of him. As soon as she felt that, guilt came charging up from the rear to the head of the line.

She worked to keep her voice calm and level. "It's me."

He waited a second, and she could imagine him taking a puff from his cigarette. "Do you know who this is?" He'd been drinking. She knew at once because when he drank, he liked to play games that he thought were cute.

"Of course I know who this is, Dad." Jenny hated his games. Sometimes he did it to prove how much smarter he was than she, and sometimes he did it to be cruel.

"Thought maybe you might have forgot. It's been days since I seen you."

"I called every day, Dad. Three and four times a day after the phones here started working again."

"Yeah. Yeah, I noticed that. Weird how CallNotes work. I mean, you can leave a message even when a guy's phone isn't working. 'Course, he don't get it till the phone's up and working again."

Jenny turned and made her way to the utility room. The noise from the Monopoly game and the crowd of movie watchers made having a conversation almost impossible. Not wanting anyone to see her talk to her father because he always had such an emotional effect on her, and especially when she was tired, she opened the utility-room door and stepped out onto the small stone patio Megan had told her Goose and his friend Bill had laid one summer.

Plants lined the patio area. A plastic tarp covered the gas grill. Dishes that people had abandoned littered the patio table and chairs. Farther back, a tire swing hung from a thick branch, a sandbox held a collection of Tonka toys, and a small fort flew a black pirate flag that had faded in the sun. Jenny had seen a picture of Chris and Goose inside the fort. Both of them were dressed as pirates, carrying plastic swords and wearing eye patches.

"Are you all right?" Jenny asked.

"Do you care?"

Guilt slammed into Jenny like a fist. Even though she knew leaving Fort Benning was next to impossible and would have caused stress between her and Megan—in addition to leaving Megan overwhelmed by the number of teens she presently had staying at her house—Jenny had felt glad to have a reason not to leave.

"Of course I care."

"Seems to me if you cared, you'd have come home sometime over these last few days." Her father's accusation was flat and hard.

"I couldn't come home. Have you watched the news?"

"You know I try to stay away from that. Buncha depressing people with sad lives is what it is."

Like yours is any better, Jenny couldn't help thinking before she could stop herself. Then she immediately felt bad. He was her father and she was supposed to love him. *I do love him,* she told herself fiercely. And that was the truth. However, the truth was that she also didn't like her father much most days. Loving someone and liking him were totally different.

She said, "I know you don't make a habit of watching the news, but with everything that has gone on, I thought maybe you might have watched."

"I didn't." He paused, and this time she could hear him take a drag on the cigarette.

"A lot of things have gone on. Things that you should have known about."

"Oh, I know about them," her father said. "Had a guy come to my door a day, maybe two days, after you left. A church guy. Started telling me that the world had up and ended and we were all going to hell. Now ain't that somethin'? Man shows up at your door and tells you you're going to hell."

Goose bumps prickled across the back of Jenny's neck. "Did you do anything to that man?" Her father had attacked door-to-door salesmen and bill collectors who had shown up at their home before, and had spent time in jail and in anger-management classes as a result.

"Nope," her father declared. "You'd have been proud of me, girlie. I didn't lay a finger on him. 'Course, it helped that he was a lot younger and faster than me." He cackled with maniacal glee. "But Dog, now, he gave that feller a run for his money before he reached his car. Yes, sir, ol' Dog surely did."

Jenny walked to the edge of the patio and sat cross-legged on the stones. The greasy smell of the gas grill tickled her nose. Even miles away from her father, she felt helpless and trapped.

"Where are you at, girlie?" he asked in a soft and hoarse voice. "You had me scared plumb out of my wits. Truly you did. Thought you was up and gone like all them other folks. Somebody told me only the good folks disappeared. Figured surely you'd be one of 'em."

Jenny closed her eyes and wished that she'd been taken with all the others. From everything she was seeing, the good people, the ones who had truly believed in God, were the ones who had vanished.

Was it that I didn't believe in You enough, God? Or was it that I'm just not good enough? According to a lot of people, Jackson McGrath wasn't worth the gunpowder it would take to blow him up. Many of those people had assigned the same kind of worth to his daughter. She'd heard stuff like that from the time she was just a girl.

"So, girlie," her father said, "when are you coming home?"

Home. The thought summoned up images of the battered and paint-faded apartment she and her father were currently renting. They didn't have enough money or credit between them to actually own a house, and that was a sad piece of business. But her father had ruined his credit even before Jenny was born, and he'd ruined hers last year within months of her turning eighteen. Collection departments still sometimes called her at home and at work if they could find out where she was working. Kettle O' Fish, the restaurant where she'd worked with Joey was new, so the collectors hadn't caught up with her yet.

"As soon as I can," Jenny said.

"Yeah?" His tone became doubtful and aggressive. "And when would that be?"

"I don't know. I'm at Fort Benning. The military police have the post locked down."

Her father was quiet for a moment. She heard his lighter flick and knew that he'd lit another cigarette. "Do you need me to come get you out of there, girlie?"

"No. I'll—"

"They can't just keep you locked up there. Ain't const-constitutional." He slurred his words slightly.

Her father always managed to speak properly until he became falling-down drunk. She figured he'd been drinking while she was gone, but hoped that he hadn't. Pressing her ear closer to the phone, she heard country-and-western music in the background. She knew the sound; she'd heard the music plenty of times before because her father liked to frequent those places where it played at all hours on a worn-out jukebox. "Where are you?"

"Home. I'm to home is all."

"No you're not." Some of the frustration and anger that swept over Jenny washed away the guilt that had weighed on her since she'd recognized her father's voice.

"Girlie, are you calling me a liar?"

"If the shoe fits." She expected him to blow up at her and hang up. But since she'd grown up and started paying part of the bills at fifteen, she'd stood up to him. Her behavior had made him angry, but her independence had also made him fearful. That was why he'd started his latest pattern of manipulations.

Instead of getting angry or threatening her, he waited a bit, just long enough, then he laughed like they'd just shared a good joke. "Never could fool you, could I?"

Not often, Jenny silently agreed. *Only those few times I made the mistake of thinking I could trust you. Memories of those times still hurt.*

"I'm at this little place around the corner from the house," her father said. "Can you believe it? All these people up and disappeared and ain't nobody quite knows why. Big businesses all over the city are closed down right now, but this little place just kicks the doors open and welcomes in the weary and the worried. It's funny when the most dependable place in the world is a joint."

The places her father frequented were always around the corner from the house. Even when they were halfway across Columbus.

"Which little place?" Jenny asked. She knew dozens of them: bars, saloons, taverns, and pubs. Over the years, she'd pulled her father out of too many of them. Even if he couldn't drive, even if he couldn't walk, he always remembered how to get hold of her at home or work or school.

"Butch's or something like that. A hole-in-the-wall is what it is. Got no class at all. Change the roll of toilet paper in the john and you've upped the décor. Wouldn't bring a dog here. But they got a pool table, a jukebox, and a lady bartender that's full of sass. My kind of gal, only she don't know it yet."

And if the lady bartender was looking her father's way, Jenny knew he'd give her a big wink. Just to keep her on her toes, according to him.

"You shouldn't be there," Jenny said, but she knew her protest was already a lost cause. Her father always found a reason for patronizing those kinds of places.

"The end of the world is upon us, girlie. Where else am I gonna be?"

"You might try church." Jenny didn't know where that suggestion had come from. She'd tried to get her father to church before but he wouldn't go. He'd never accepted Christ's mercy or been baptized.

"If I was to walk into a church," her father said, "the building would more'n likely fall down around my ears." That set off another gleeful cackle.

He's had a skinful, Jenny thought morosely. "Dad, listen to me. You should go home. Just put the beer away and go home."

He took a deep breath. "Well, now, I would. I'd do exactly that. Except there ain't nothin' and nobody there. Get mighty tired of looking at four walls. I got to tell you that."

"It's not safe to be out at night." Jenny had paid attention to the news all evening. Violence still filled the streets. The police and the National Guard advised everyone to stay home and had imposed a curfew. But the news stations reported that large groups hunted through the streets.

"Just as safe being here as it is at home. And the company's looking mighty fine. Ain't you, darlin'?"

A woman's voice sounded indistinct in the distance against the background of country-and-western music.

"Dad, please. For me."

Her father was quiet for a moment. "Can't."

"Why?"

"I'm scared to."

Jenny remained silent, praying that he wouldn't start in the way she knew he was going to.

"You know why I'm scared, girlie?" her father asked in a tight, hoarse voice.

"No." She had no choice about answering. This was her part of the cycle her father had thrust them into. Her hands shook, and she felt the hot warmth of tears on her cheeks. Just like always, she felt so helpless. She hated that feeling more than anything.

"I'm scared," her father said slowly, "because I almost did it this time. When I thought you was gone."

Jenny shook as she cried. She wiped tears from her face with the back of her free hand.

"I couldn't bear it, girlie, if I knew you were gone. It would cut the heart right out of me."

Jenny knew her father meant what he said. Some days she felt that the only reason he was still alive in spite of his pain and his weakness and his alcoholism, with the misery of guilt that echoed those character flaws, was because she was there. Most of the bills got paid, mostly on time, and meals were put on the table because of what she could provide. She knew he couldn't take care of himself.

"I almost did it," her father repeated. "Had that pistol settled in nice and tight up under my jaw. I was just four pounds of pressure away from saying sayonara."

"Dad." Jenny's voice came out as an agonized croak.

"You don't have to worry about me," her father said. "I'd never have felt a thing. Here in this world one minute and on to the next faster than a New York minute."

Jenny pulled her knees up to her chest and wrapped her free arm around her legs. She pulled tight, hugging herself.

"You know the only thing that kept me from doing it?" her father asked.

Pain seized Jenny's lungs so tightly that she couldn't answer.

"I couldn't do it, girlie, because somehow I knew you was still here." He cackled again. "Ain't that something? Somehow, I knew you was still here and it was just a matter of time till I found you. I went home today and the phone was working. Found your messages on the answering service, and here I am talking to you. That's almost enough to make a man get religion."

Shaking and scared, Jenny wiped her face. "Dad, I love you. I don't want anything to happen to you. Please, please *don't*—"

"Why, girlie, they ain't nothing going to happen to me. You just get on back home and everything's going to be right as rain."

"I can't leave here yet," Jenny said. "The army isn't letting anyone in or out of the post tonight." She snuffled.

Her father was silent for a moment. "That's fine then, girlie. I'll just hook up with you tomorrow. I'll give you a call and drive on out that way to pick you up. Then you can tell me how you ended up on an army base in the middle of all this confusion."

"All right."

"And this here bartender, why she's taken a shine to your old man. I can tell. I know when women are interested. Maybe we'll both have stories to tell tomorrow."

"Just take care of yourself," Jenny said.

"You got a deal. I'll call you tomorrow." He paused. "I mean, unless you don't want to see your old dad."

"I do," Jenny said, and the answer was half right. She wanted to see him, but she didn't want to see him, too. Her heart ached, but she didn't trust him. She felt bad about that. He was her father, and he had taken care of her the best he could after her mom had run out on them. But his best wasn't very good. Still, despite everything, she loved him. As usual when she talked to her dad, she felt as if she were all ripped up inside. "I do want to see you," she managed to say. A big part of her even meant it.

"Then you be ready tomorrow, girlie, because I'll be out there tomorrow bright and early to pick you up."

"All right, Dad," Jenny whispered. "I'll be here."

Her father said good-bye and hung up.

For a while, Jenny sat on the stones of the Ganders' patio. She hugged her knees to herself and stared up at the star-filled sky. Not all of the power was back in the city yet, and the base ran black at night. Most of the light pollution was gone and the stars shone brightly.

She cried for a time, till that pain was once more used up and she felt empty. She could cry it away for a time, but it always returned because the hurt never healed. She didn't want to lose her father, and she didn't want to hate him. But she was scared that she was going to do both.

"I don't have anything to say to you, Captain Remington."

Standing in front of the CIA agent seated in the chair, Remington looked down at the man, reminding the guy who had the upper hand. A large part of command, of the whole issue of control, was about body language. He was standing, free to walk around, and the agent didn't dare move from the chair. Even his superior officer had gotten the boot.

"You do," Remington accused.

"My superior—"

"Is off nursing a sore stomach," Remington interrupted. "If he'd had any real weight to throw in this operation, I'd have already felt it."

Winters leaned back a little in the hard wooden seat, as if realizing only then that he was within striking range of the Ranger captain. "You're making a mistake."

"Am I?"

"Yes."

"Then you're in for a world of hurt," Remington stated flatly. "Because I don't see it that way."

Winters tried another tack. "We're on the same side."

"And whose side would that be?"

"The side of the United States government. The *good* guys."

Remington paused as if he were thinking the answer over. "Uh-uh. I'm stuck here in this city, dying by inches with an enemy army camped outside my doorstep, and you're withholding information that I need."

"I don't know anything that will help you with your operation here."

"Tell me about Icarus."

Winters hesitated. "I can't."

Corporal Dean Hardin stood at Winters's side. Staring at Remington, Hardin lifted an eyebrow. Remington blinked slowly. With an economy of motion, Hardin shifted his weight and threw a hard left fist straight into Winters's jaw.

The blow caught the CIA agent unexpectedly and spilled him from the wooden chair. He groaned and coughed, choking on blood from his busted lips and nose. Hardin stepped forward and kicked him in the stomach with his combat boot. When Winters tried to cover up in a fetal position, Hardin simply stepped behind him and kicked him in the kidney.

A cry of pain ripped from the CIA agent's bleeding lips.

Remington grew conscious of the attention Hardin's brutality was receiving from the two privates seated at the security camera network. Despite the horror that the city had been through after the latest attack, they still appeared somewhat uncomfortable with violence on a more personal level.

The captain looked at the privates and demanded, "Are you going to be spectators or security personnel? Or maybe you want to spend the next few days waiting on the Syrians to attack again while pulling KP?"

Threatened with the kitchen shifts, the privates turned their attention back to the security network.

The corporal against the back wall shifted slightly.

Remington pinned the man with his gaze. "You got a problem, mister?"

"Sir, no, sir." The corporal tapped the front pocket of his BDU. "I was just thinking about lighting up." He glanced down at the groaning CIA agent on the floor. "Looks like maybe I have time, sir."

Remington studied the man, recognizing him after a moment. "Corporal Barnett, isn't it?"

Barnett nodded but didn't make eye contact, staring past Remington's shoulder as every enlisted man was trained to do when dealing with officers in a potentially confrontational encounter. Eye contact was there only if a soldier was in a personal situation; otherwise an officer could read challenge into a too-level stare. "Yes, sir."

"Smoke 'em if you got 'em, Corporal," Remington said.

"Yes, sir. Thank you, sir."

Remington watched as Barnett reached into his BDU pocket, extracted a crumpled cigarette pack, and shook out a cigarette. He lit up in cupped hands while Winters continued to breathe in short, painful gasps. Barnett didn't seem to care about the discomfort the CIA agent was in.

The captain tried to remember if Goose had any solid connections with Barnett. Remington was certain Goose knew the man, but Goose had a way of knowing every man in the 75th.

Once he had the cigarette going, Barnett put the lighter away and resumed his position against the wall behind the prisoner. He glanced at the CIA man on the floor, but no emotion touched his eyes or his face.

"Corporal Hardin," Remington said, "get that man back in that chair."

"Yes, sir." Roughly, Hardin squatted down, took a two-handed grip on the agent's jacket, and yanked the man to his feet. Winters tried to take his weight on his own legs, but Hardin shoved him backward into the chair. Blood ran down his face and dripped onto his shirt. His eyes looked glazed, but there was a healthy dose of panic in them now.

"We'll try this again." Remington stepped back in front of the man, taking up his personal space again.

Winters looked up at him like a whipped puppy and tried to slide back in the chair.

"Tell me about Icarus," Remington ordered.

"What do you want to know?" Winters asked.

Quick as a striking snake, Hardin backhanded the CIA man in the face. The blow was calculated and measured, hard enough to turn Winters's face and cause enough pain to bring tears, but not hard enough to knock him from the chair.

Over the years, Remington had come to appreciate the different degrees of cruelty Dean Hardin could exhibit on command. Hardin's whole world centered on himself, but he knew he couldn't make it through life alone, so he allied himself with the strongest men around that he could tolerate or who'd give him freedom enough to take care of himself. Remington wouldn't have been Dean Hardin for anything, and wouldn't have risked being personal friends with the man, but the Ranger captain was plenty willing to utilize the other man's capacity for violence.

"*Sir*," Hardin said, speaking to Winters. "'What do you want to know—*sir?*' The man's an officer. Respect that."

Straightening cautiously, raising his shoulder to block another such blow, Winters asked, "What do you want to know? Sir."

"Outstanding." Hardin grinned coldly and patted Winters on the cheek like a cherished pet that had learned a new trick.

Remington recognized the fear in the CIA man's eyes and knew the emotion came out of self-preservation, one of the most powerful tools in an interrogator's arsenal. Fear bent and broke men more than physical hardship ever did. Remington believed people were born into the world with fear, and everything they learned from the time they drew their first breath only strengthened that fear.

The world doesn't care if you live or die, Remington thought. *That's lesson one, and welcome to our little refresher course.*

"Have I got your attention now, Agent Winters?" Remington asked in a brusque voice.

"Yes." Realizing his mistake almost at once, Winters threw a quick, fearful glance at Hardin. "Yes, sir."

Standing at parade rest, rocking back and forth on his heels so he would be read as a constant threat on Winters's personal radar—able to strike without warning at any given instant—Hardin smiled slightly and gave a brief nod.

"Good," Remington responded. A kind word reinforced the reward system that usually balanced a punishment situation. The Ranger captain stood squared up, officious, exuding command. He was also a walking poster child for freedom and power to the CIA agent at the moment, a reminder of all that had been stripped from him. "Special Agent Cody is in pursuit of a covert agent here in this city?"

Winters hesitated. The brief indiscretion earned him a quick slap from Hardin. Winters cursed, and Hardin started to strike him again, causing the man to flinch.

"Wait," Remington said.

Hardin halted.

Remington fixed Winters with his gaze. "The next time I won't stop him, and he won't stop with just slapping you. Understood?"

"Yes . . . yes, sir."

Satisfied that the reward/punishment coda was properly installed, Remington repeated his question.

"Yes, sir," Winters said. "Agent Cody is here to intercept a rogue agent."

"A rogue CIA agent?"

"Yes, sir."

"By whose authority?"

"Sir, I don't know."

"Or is he working to clean up his own mess?"

"I couldn't tell you that, sir. We, my team and I, we take our orders from Agent Cody. We take those orders directly, sir. It minimizes the probability of our exposure, and we're usually never in a situation that our government can own our actions or us. Sir."

Remington paced in a measured cadence, his brain working quickly to assess the information he was getting. "You stated that Cody was here to intercept the rogue agent. Where is that agent bound?"

"I don't know, sir." Winters glanced fearfully at Hardin.

Remington hesitated just long enough that Hardin executed a vicious slap, knocking Winters from the chair again. Winters fell with a thud and groaned. Blood dripped from a new cut beside his eye.

"Wait," Remington said. "I believe him."

"Sorry, Captain," Hardin said. "I thought he was shining you on."

The corporal's response was a carefully orchestrated one they'd used before. If Remington let a lull happen in the conversation after a negative answer, Hardin dealt out punishment.

"We'll go with my feelings, Corporal." The statement made it clear that Remington could serve as the CIA agent's savior as well as punisher.

"Of course, sir." Hardin reached for Winters and hauled him to his feet and the chair again. "I'll await your orders, Captain."

"You said *intercept*," Remington reminded.

"*Intercept* is the term Special Agent Cody is using." Winters turned his head and wiped his bloody mouth on his shoulder.

"But you don't know whom, or what, Icarus is on his way to."

"No, sir."

"Do you know what Icarus's last mission was?"

Winters flexed his puffy lips as if trying to get used to their new size. "He infiltrated a group of terrorists. Sir. The PKK. They're Kurdish terrorists."

"I know that, Agent Winters." Remington restored the man's rank to inspire confidence. The address was subtle but rarely went unnoticed in tense situations where an interrogation subject examined the smallest word, the tiniest movement for hope that he or she would survive. "Icarus succeeded in penetrating one of the cells that were assigned to assassinate Chaim Rosenzweig."

"That's right, sir."

"Icarus helped foil that effort and was in turn discovered as an enemy agent."

An uneasy look flickered across Winters's face. "Agent Cody thinks that didn't happen exactly that way. Sir."

Remington stopped pacing and stared at Winters.

Shrugging, looking totally pathetic and helpless, Winters licked his bloody lips and said, "Agent Cody thinks Icarus was compromised."

"By the terrorists?"

"By the Syrians, sir."

Interest flared white-hot inside Remington. If such a thing had happened, it offered a possibility he might exploit. "Explain."

"Icarus called in the hit on Rosenzweig late, sir," Winters replied. "Almost too late. The assassins had the Israeli in their sights when covert ops took them down." He hesitated, causing Hardin to shift toward him again, then ducked his head, burying his face in his shoulder in an effort to protect it. "Don't hit me again! Please, don't hit me again!"

Remington held up a hand to stop Hardin and kept it up long enough that Winters saw it when he peeked up to see why the corporal hadn't hit him.

"If you don't know," Remington suggested, "tell me what you think."

"I think that Icarus is a double agent," Winters said in a rush. Blood flew from his lips as he spoke. "A week or two before the assassination attempt, while Icarus was still in deep and we had no plans of retrieving him, some of our operatives caught wind of an alliance between the terrorist groups in the Middle East. The PKK, Hezbollah, Hamas, Al-Qaeda. Some of Hussein's bullyboys and warlords that got missed during the second Iraq war."

"They've been networking for years," Remington said. "That's nothing new."

"Networking," Winters repeated. "Yes, sir, they have. But the word we were getting was that they'd lined up with Syria in a big way. Supposed to be an operation like no one had ever seen before. And something else was in the wind."

"What?"

Cautiously, Winters shook his head. Hardin started forward, giving Remington plenty of time to raise his hand to stay the blow.

"What?" Remington asked. "What was in the wind?"

"Don't know, sir," Winters said, then rushed on. "My guess is that it was the Syrian attack. Maybe it was supposed to set off a wave of attacks throughout the Middle East. Maybe it still is."

"Why would they risk that?"

"I can't confirm this, sir."

Remington nodded.

"The terrorist groups had heard that President Fitzhugh had made a deal with the Israeli government."

"What kind of deal?"

"For the fertilizer, sir. The fertilizer that Rosenzweig created. Heard he was going to use it to turn the western states into a Garden of Eden. Increase the U.S.'s capability to produce food. That stuff would make a lot more farmland. The price was that once Fitzhugh got the formula for the fertilizer, he was supposed to use American troops to launch a full-scale attack against terrorist training grounds all over the Middle East. Against known leaders. That's why Fitzhugh was posting U.S. Army units alongside so many United Nations Peacekeeping teams. He wanted his army in place for the time when he gave the word. And when he did, there was going to be a bloodbath."

❋   ❋   ❋

OneWorld NewsNet Mobile Platform
Sanliurfa, Turkey
Local Time 0608 Hours

"Danielle, are you listening to me?"

Ignoring Cezar's pleading voice and the desperate look in the young cameraman's face, Danielle took out her sat-phone and started punching buttons.

"Danielle," Cezar protested, "you can't be serious. I mean, c'mon. You're throwing out some of my best stuff here." He peered anxiously at the video monitor in front of him.

Since leaving Goose, Danielle had returned to the Winnebago Adventurer OneWorld NewsNet had provided the team two days ago to use as a rolling news department. At thirty-seven and a half feet long, the recreational vehicle painted a huge target for the Syrian aircraft that routinely flew strike missions into the city.

In addition to providing dish access to the OneWorld NewsNet geosynchronous satellite 23,500 miles out in space, the Adventurer also served as a photo- and video-processing lab, a cutting room, and—with the addition of a small blue screen and news desk on the other side of the computer equipment along the slide-out portion of the wall that replaced the lounger/bed—a compact studio for interviews as well as tactical breakdowns of what was happening in the city.

When she'd first seen the vehicle, Danielle's breath had caught in her throat. She'd heard of the comfort levels OneWorld provided their employees and news teams in the field, but she'd had no clue to the lengths the corporation was prepared to go.

Though space was cramped, the Adventurer had a bedroom, a bath, and a galley as added comforts. The powerful 8.1-liter Vortec V-8 engine had powered the vehicle all through the city over the last two days as the news team pursued breaking stories. The recreational vehicle was also covered in bulletproof armor plating and fitted with bulletproof glass just like an executive limousine.

That bit of foresight had saved their lives more than once. Still, Danielle wasn't sure how long their luck would hold. The armor showed scars from numerous bullets and shrapnel, but Danielle had yet to see if the Adventurer could survive a direct hit from a rocket launcher. Radu Stolojan assured her it would. Personally, she was quite content to leave the OneWorld NewsNet liaison's claim untested.

Air-conditioning chugged through the big vehicle, distancing the crew from the dry heat that lay over the city, heat that would only grow worse with dawn already rising in the east. The smell of spiced meat from the galley reminded Danielle she hadn't eaten since the day before.

"Danielle," Cezar pleaded.

"Later," Danielle replied, turning away from him and clapping her free hand over her ear as she leaned her head against the satphone and waited for the connection to go through.

Cezar cursed as petulantly as a foulmouthed child.

The strident double ring of the European phone line echoed in Danielle's ear. She hoped Stolojan didn't answer the phone. As her liaison with the network, he remained steadfast and conservative in his approach to the news. Stolojan didn't like going off on tangents, which, as every good investigative reporter knew, was the only way to go if he or she wanted a shot at an exclusive story. Hidden secrets didn't just jump out at a reporter and yell for attention.

Danielle had learned in short order to follow her instincts, and with the presence of the CIA man she'd encountered in Romania, her instincts for a hot news story had practically gone off the measuring scale.

"Hello," a woman answered.

Thank You, God, Danielle thought as she recognized Lizuca Carutasu's soft voice. Lizuca held down the OneWorld liaison desk from 11 P.M. to 7 A.M., but Stolojan seemed like he never slept. Occasionally, when working on human-interest pieces that she knew Stolojan might object to, Danielle had intentionally called during those hours because Lizuca helped her get the information she needed.

Getting information about a CIA agent who liked to play mystery guy was a lot different than lining up interviews with clergymen and former high school teachers of the young United States military men serving in Sanliurfa.

But I don't plan on telling her this guy's CIA, do I? Danielle felt a little guilty about that. However, like any successful reporter, she'd learned to turn her guilty conscience off and on a long time ago.

"Lizuca," Danielle said.

"Ah, Danielle," the young woman replied. "You are safe, yes?" Her English was somewhat accented, but her youth and enthusiasm came through perfectly.

"Yes," Danielle said. "For the moment."

"Things over there, they look very bad. I am very much worried for you, yes? I am praying every hour for your safety."

"Thank you," Danielle said. "Your prayers must be working. I'm still in one piece."

"Good. Because I think you being in many pieces would not be a good thing." Lizuca paused. "Is joke, yes?"

"Yes," Danielle said, unable to tell the young woman she didn't much feel like joking.

"I have not gotten through to Mrs. Samuel Adams Gander," Lizuca said. "I have been trying very hard. I seem unable to find her close to a phone when I call."

"That's okay. Stay with it and let me know if she'll consent to do an interview." Danielle wanted the interview as a human-interest piece to flesh out the viewers' awareness of First Sergeant Goose Gander. The man was a hero even before the media had made him out as one, and Danielle wanted to know what he was like at home.

"*Danielle*," Cezar called again. "You need to watch what these . . . these . . . *butchers* are doing to my beautiful work."

Danielle held a hand up to the cameraman. Finding a quiet place to work inside the RV was almost impossible. Noise from the passing military vehicles outside the Adventurer still invaded.

"Lizuca, I want to send you a digital photograph." Danielle

reached into the pack she carried. In addition to the spare headset microphones, handheld microphones, and makeup, she also carried a micro-digital camera that had seriously set her finances back but had also proven worth its weight in gold since she'd had it.

"Of course, Danielle. Is this part of a news story?"

"Not yet." Danielle made her way around Cezar, who mewled at her with a pleading face and looked as though he were about to cry, to one of the notebook computers the news staff kept charged and online at all times. "I want you to do some research on this guy."

"Of course. Do you have his name? It would be easiest, I think, to begin there."

"I don't have a name." Danielle hooked a USB cable to the digital camera, opened the appropriate program on the computer, downloaded the picture from the camera, then shot the digital image into cyberspace as an encrypted burst. "That's one of the things I want."

"I see." Lizuca sounded doubtful. "This task you put before me, it is quite difficult, yes?"

"Yes," Danielle answered. "Difficult, but not impossible. One-World has huge video archives, and they've got search programs espionage agencies around the world would give their eyeteeth for."

"Yes, but those things are necessary to doing good business. We are not spies."

Cezar made wild gestures toward the monitor where the video editors worked on the footage of the night's attack. The cameraman bit his knuckles in frustration, then clapped his open hands together in obvious supplication.

"I know we're not spies," Danielle said to ease the woman's mind. Half-dozen countries around the world had claimed at one time or another that OneWorld NewsNet was an espionage unit working for Western powers. The news corporation's reporters had broken several big stories about biological weapons and terrorist movements that had sent United Nations and United States troops into the Middle East, Eastern Europe, and Africa during the past few years.

UPLOAD COMPLETE printed across the notebook computer's LCD screen.

"Do you have the picture?" Danielle asked.

"It is coming through now."

Danielle covered the sat-phone's mouthpiece and glared at Cezar. "Calm down. The piece they're editing is for the midnight updates for CNN and FOX News. We're saving your brilliance for OneWorld."

Cezar looked relieved as he glanced back at the computer monitors. "Those are for CNN and FOX?"

"Yes. You don't think we're going to give them all your hard work,
do you?"

"Oh." Cezar crossed his hands over his chest. "That is all right
then."

"I thought it would be."

"Danielle," Lizuca said, "I have the picture now. He is a very evil-
looking man, yes?"

Danielle didn't exactly get *evil* when she looked at the CIA agent.
Conniving, maybe, and certainly self-serving. She studied the image
on the digital camera's view screen.

"Run that image through the search programs," Danielle said.
"Let me know the minute you find anything out."

"My shift here, unfortunately, is almost over. It is possible that I
won't be able to finish this before it is time for me to go home."

"Want overtime?" One of the first things Danielle had negotiated
for herself was the ability to pass out overtime to research assistants.

"Of course. Money is money, Danielle, and though Mr. Carpathia's corporate policies are very generous, I find I can always use a
little more. I am supporting my mother and three sisters, yes? And
there is a dress I saw just last week in a shopwindow that is—how do
you say?—to die for, yes?"

An artillery round exploded in the distance, causing everyone in
the RV to look up apprehensively.

Not exactly the way I would have put it, Danielle thought as fear drew
a chill across the back of her neck. She tried to blame the air-conditioning, but she knew what had caused the feeling.

"I will find out who this man is," Lizuca promised. "If he is in
OneWorld's digital archives, yes?"

"Yes," Danielle replied. "The minute you find out—"

"I will call you. I give you my promise, yes?"

"Thanks."

"It is—how you say?—no problem. Stay safe. I will be praying for
you, yes?"

"Yes," Danielle said. She broke the connection, took a final look
at the mystery man's picture, and thought, *Whoever you are, I'll have
you. It won't be long. Not with OneWorld's resources.* She felt good about
that, confident. She clicked off the camera, keeping the picture stored.

She thought about the man Captain Remington was questioning,
and she wished she were a fly on the wall for that. Secrets were no

doubt popping loose in that room. From what she'd seen of the Ranger captain, he was an unstoppable force once he got started.

The problem with secrets, Danielle knew from her career as a journalist, was that once they started coming out, usually they couldn't be stopped. And secrets had a tendency to change everything.

❋   ❋   ❋

United States 75th Army Rangers Temporary Post
Sanliurfa, Turkey
Local Time 0612 Hours

"Only a fool would believe he could pull something like that off." The response was the only one Remington could think of as he considered the possibility that President Fitzhugh had entered into an agreement with Israel to lash out in a concerted effort against major terrorist organizations in exchange for Chaim Rosenzweig's chemical wonder.

Believing that Israel would want to do that was no problem. Ever since 1948, when the nation had been forged from the ashes of the Second World War and been placed like a dagger in the heart of the Middle East, Israel had cried out for security and prayed for death to her enemies. Her enemies' prayers ran along the same lines, of course.

"The State Department convinced Fitzhugh he could get it done, sir," Winters insisted. "At least, that was what I heard. Plans have been in the making to continue American police action throughout the Middle East."

"To protect the oil concerns."

Winters nodded. "China has been growing, Captain Remington. So has their need for petroleum products. Studies indicate that in a few years, they'll need and use as much crude as the United States currently does. Our usage is probably going to grow. We're not slowing down our energy use or finding alternate energy sources the way analysts have suggested since the early 1970s."

Remington was aware of the growing energy-crunch situation. Besides being informed through military connections, similar concerns were voiced in the international media, though not much attention was paid in the United States to the fact that the Chinese were about to become a major competitor for that oil. No one much wanted to rattle Joe U.S. Citizen about the coming petroleum wars with China. In time, Remington figured, the United States government would lobby for an increased military presence in the Middle East on behalf of big business, and the votes would get counted at the gas pump as U.S. consumers felt the bite.

"China jumped into the Afghanistan situation as opposed to the American military strikes," Winters said. "They took a stand, but didn't pony up the army. But they made every effort they could to glad-hand the Afghanistan government."

"To build up a rapport they could utilize later." Remington had talked about those prospects with other career officers who had years to go before they pulled the pin.

"Yes, sir."

The Chinese government's efforts to win over the Middle East had consumed much of China's diplomatic time and financial resources. Those behind-closed-doors discussions had included trade concessions that favored the Middle East as well as overland and sea access between China and Singapore. Not to mention the fact that it was cheaper to ship to China than to the United States. The Middle East had quietly entered into a seller's market as the demands started pushing past their ability to produce.

"The strikes against Al-Qaeda and Osama bin Laden," Winters continued, "just added fuel to the fire, sir."

Remington knew the agent didn't even recognize the irony of the metaphor he'd used. "What does this have to do with Icarus?"

"Remember what I said about Icarus being a double agent, sir?" Winters wiped his mouth on his shoulder again. Blood streaked his shirt. "Agency resources—HUMINT, SIGNIT—all involve traces of a terrorist organization that's grown since the U.S. Army took down Iraq."

Human intelligence and signals intelligence were part of Remington's operations as well. HUMINT involved spying, individuals inserted into an area or bought off by an espionage agency. SIGNIT referred to high-tech machines like spy satellites and low-tech devices like simple phone taps. The military used them these days, too, but most of that information was gathered by outside agencies—at least until the military occupied an area. Then they supplemented what they received with efforts by their own people trained for those jobs.

"American strikes against the terrorists were the catalysts for the growth," Winters whispered. "Like hitting the common flu with antibiotics every time someone gets a sniffle. We didn't kill them all and they had no choice but to go more underground, get craftier, and grow stronger."

During the last few years, Remington had heard a lot of the same scenarios spelled out by paranoid officers and intelligence operatives. But as far as he could see, there hadn't been any real evidence of such growth.

"The terrorist groups have banded more tightly together during the last year," Winters said, "and Syria stepped into a leadership role."

"No," Remington objected. "If that had happened, I would have known. A lot of people would have known."

"You didn't," Winters responded with a little heat; then he bowed his head when Hardin moved toward him. "*Sir.* You didn't know. The people who thought they knew? They weren't talking. They had orders not to talk. You can bet on that." He paused. "But others knew. That was Icarus's true assignment, Captain Remington: he was supposed to find out how big that terrorist organization had gotten."

"But he didn't do that."

"No, sir. He didn't. Turns out, Icarus *was* a double agent."

"That was confirmed?"

"Yes, sir." Now that he'd decided to talk, Winters seemed to have no problem spilling his guts. "Only hours before the attempt on Rosenzweig, an agency informant gave us information that Icarus was a double." He coughed and spat out a blob of blood. "Know why we continue to call him Icarus, Captain?"

Remington made no response.

"Because we don't know his real name. After the agency got the tip, they pulled Icarus's jacket and went through his file again. All the information on him was false. Looked good on paper because there had been a guy by the name he was using at one time. Somewhere along the way, Icarus—or someone working with Icarus—killed him. Then Icarus replaced him."

"How?" Remington marveled at the concept.

"We're the agency, sir." Winters grinned a little, getting some of his confidence back now. "Guys like us, guys who do deep recon, surgical strikes, who know *governmental disavowal of actions* is our middle name—sir, we don't have friends. If we did, we give them up and don't make anymore. If we have family, we walk away. As soon as you step into the truly covert action in the CIA, man, you just don't exist as a person anymore."

"A strength," Remington said, recognizing the behavior for what it was, "and a vulnerability."

"Right." Winters warmed to the story now that Remington seemed won over.

"How did the agency know Icarus's identity was false? It could have been bad information. Or even a ruse on the part of someone else."

"Someone else who, sir? Not the terrorists. They don't have ways into our encrypted computer files." Winters shook his head, then seemed to immediately regret the effort. Hardin's blows had that effect on people. "No. The agency turned up evidence that Icarus wasn't who he said he was. Went back to a girlfriend he dated in high school. The agency's got a long reach once they start. Found cards he'd sent her while in high school and college. Letters."

"Fingerprints," Remington said, his clever mind catching the direction the conversation was going.

"Exactly." Winters smiled, but the effort was lopsided because of his swollen and cracked lips. "They took his fingerprints from the cards and letters. They didn't match the ones the agency had on file. Wasn't the same guy. You ask me, they were lucky this woman hung on to those things. But sometimes they do."

Remington didn't have firsthand knowledge of that. He'd never been around women who cared that much, or even claimed to have cared that much. Keeping letters and cards was something the woman Goose had married would do. The gesture was romantic, but that also meant she was clingy—a real problem, to Remington's way of thinking.

A career military man didn't have any business being with a clingy woman. Even Goose's standards and goals had changed since his marriage. He'd lost some of his game and some of his edge, had a tendency to think about things more completely now, seeing the whole picture instead of just focusing on the mission like an enlisted man worth his salt should.

"So where did Icarus come from?" Remington asked.

"We don't know that yet, sir. Agent Cody believes that most of the guys we use in the Middle East are Syrians. Or other Middle Eastern guys the Syrians have bought out. Or are just believers. Jihad, you know. Guys who figure fighting the holy war against Christianity and the Western powers is in their blood."

Remington paced for a moment again, turning everything over in his mind, searching for the angles that would pop the story into pieces and expose any lies Winters had told. But there were no weak places. Despite the lack of physical evidence, the story was convincing.

"I saw real-time video of the takedown when my Rangers rescued Icarus." Remington remembered the scene vividly. A copy of the op still existed on VCD in his personal files. "Icarus was badly beaten. Looked like he was lucky to live through it."

"For a man next to death's door, he's getting around pretty good, don't you think? We haven't caught him yet."

"Why would the PKK want to kill him?"

"Because we leaked information he was a CIA plant," Winters explained.

✻   ✻   ✻

OneWorld NewsNet Corporate Offices
Bucharest, Romania
Local Time 0617 Hours

Lizuca Carutasu hummed as she worked. She liked American pop tunes, and the one she hummed now had hit the Top Forty on morning-drive stations in America. She knew that because she listened to the radio through the Internet.

Lizuca was twenty-three years old, a slim-hipped brunette with hopes of seeing America at some point. She'd studied the movies, which was how she had improved her English, and bought Western clothes, which were still frowned upon by her mother, who was very much a traditionalist. Oldest of her four sisters, she was also considered the rabble-rouser by her mother because Lizuca had no interest in simply marrying a man in order to get a house and raise children the way it was done before the people rose from the streets and took back their country from the despot Nicolae Ceausescu in 1989.

Not having been alive during those times, Lizuca knew little of how desperate simply surviving had been, but she imagined that life had been hard. What she could not know of the executions and mass murders and food lines, she heard about from her mother and her aunts.

Sitting at the desk near the eastern wall of the tall and imposing building that housed OneWorld NewsNet on the top three floors, Lizuca had a good view of the city and Cotroceni Palace, which was now the presidential residency and a museum. She loved the glass porch with its stained-glass windows. One of her favorite places to visit while shopping in City Centre was the botanical gardens.

Shopping. The thought pleased her. The overtime Danielle offered for her research assignment—even though the man was evil-faced and would no doubt cause nightmares for her if he'd done something truly atrocious, which he had to have done because those were the people news stories were done about, yes?—would surely buy the new dress she'd been looking at for the last few weeks in the shop-keeper's window.

Even this early in the morning, the office buzzed with activity and the strong smell of coffee.

Lizuca had a small desk, but she shared it with no one else. When she left her shift, no one sat in her chair or moved her things around. Files and supplies stayed exactly where she left them. Provided she locked the drawers, of course. Other people in the office shared their work space with second shifts.

As she sat in her chair and watched the computer search the video archives for the picture of the man Danielle had sent her, she pinched off another piece of the cheese pastry her mother had baked last night and sent with her for breakfast.

Lizuca would have preferred going out for breakfast before return-ing home, but her mother watched her spending habits with a miser's eye. Her mother didn't consider the money Lizuca made to be her own but rather the family's. Lizuca was the only one with a good-paying job.

With all the disappearances around the world, so many of them in Romania as well, Lizuca didn't feel like arguing with her mother. She was glad that her family remained intact. Her father had died nine years ago, and things had been especially hard for them even though freedom fighters had removed the Communist government.

The blue bar graph indicating the amount of video library covered moved slowly, ticking off completed percentile points.

Lizuca considered trying the home number she had for Mrs. Sam-uel Adams Gander again, thinking perhaps with everything that was going on in America—all the unrest and accidents—that it might not be too late to call.

"Miss Carutasu."

Startled by the low, menacing voice, Lizuca turned in her seat and saw Radu Stolojan standing behind her.

He was tall and powerful-looking in his habitual black suit. He wore his curly hair in a short crop, like the Greeks. Despite the fact that he worked primarily daylight hours, his pale skin showed no tan, as if he took pains to avoid the sun.

"Yes, Mr. Stolojan." Lizuca tried desperately not to choke on the bit of pastry she'd been chewing.

"What are you doing?" Stolojan crossed to her desk, staring at the picture inset in the upper left of her computer monitor.

The picture of the evil-faced man looked back at her accusingly. "Research for Miss Vinchenzo," Lizuca answered.

"She asked you to research him?"

"Yes, sir."

"Do you know who this man is?" Stolojan demanded.

"No." She was going to say more but Stolojan cut her off.

"Does Danielle Vinchenzo know who this man is?"

"No, sir. I mean, I don't think so. She said she didn't have his name. She wanted to know if OneWorld had anything on him in the video archives."

"This," Stolojan said, reaching out and tapping keys on her keyboard, "is a waste of time." The search ended with a sputter and the picture blanked. He continued tapping the keys, opening the files and locating the folder where she had stored the digital image. A few keystrokes later, the image was gone completely from the computer's drives.

"Yes, sir. I'm sorry, sir. I didn't know, sir." Lizuca felt terribly embarrassed. There was no way anyone else in the room could not have heard Stolojan chastising her. That hurt. She prided herself on being professional, a good employee, and a strong asset to the corporation.

"In the future, Miss Carutasu," Stolojan said as he turned and headed back to his office, "I expect you to clear any projects Miss Vinchenzo might assign you with me before you begin them."

"Yes, Mr. Stolojan."

Stolojan spared her one more look at the door to his office, then turned and closed the door.

Even with the door closed, Lizuca knew Stolojan watched the news office. Spy cameras were spread throughout the building: in the main rooms, the bathrooms, the break areas. No one went anywhere inside OneWorld NewsNet that Stolojan didn't have the ability to see them.

She kept herself from crying in her embarrassment through sheer willpower. Part of her couldn't help wondering why Stolojan had shown such a strong reaction—at least, the reaction was strong for him—to the picture. It was as if he knew who the man was.

And that he didn't want anyone else to know.

Lizuca brought up other screens on her monitor and busied herself with the mundane work that constantly lay at her fingertips. Inside her heart, she was torn. Even after just three days, she enjoyed working with Danielle Vinchenzo very much, and Danielle had told her that, if she could, she would take her back to the United States with her when she went.

The thought burned within Lizuca, as did the realization that Danielle evidently thought the man she'd been researching was good story material. Danielle Vinchenzo had a nose for news. Lizuca looked at Stolojan's closed door. Maybe Stolojan didn't think the story had merit, but Lizuca believed in Danielle.

She turned her attention back to her computer and to the time/date stamp in the lower-right corner. What Stolojan didn't know about her was the habit she had of e-mailing important things to herself that she didn't want to lose. She still had a copy of the picture of the evil-faced man. And she had access to OneWorld's vast video archives while off-site. All she had to do was retrieve the picture and continue her search on her own time. Perhaps she wouldn't get overtime or the new dress immediately, but she trusted Danielle's instincts.

If the story panned out and she was able to identify the man, Lizuca felt certain that something interesting would come her way. The time/date stamp rolled over one more minute, putting her that much closer to the end of her shift. She awaited the time anxiously.

❄ ❄ ❄

**United States 75th Army Rangers Temporary Post
Sanliurfa, Turkey
Local Time 0620 Hours**

Icarus was sold out by the CIA. Somehow, the thought didn't surprise Remington as much as it should have. Maybe subconsciously he'd already figured that out. If Icarus was in place and secure, who else could have done the deed? He listened intently as Winters continued his story.

"We knew before the Rosenzweig assassination was supposed to go down that Icarus was a double. But the decision was made to leave him in place until Rosenzweig was safe."

"Icarus could have burned the agency then," Remington said.

"Yes, sir. But he didn't. His information about the hit and the PKK terrorist cells involved was on the money."

"Don't you think that was strange? Doesn't Cody?"

"No, sir. See, hitting Rosenzweig wouldn't do much."

"Because the fertilizer had already been invented and changed Israel's political and economic situation in the Middle East."

"Exactly. Assassinating Rosenzweig? Well, that would be more of a—" Winters searched for words.

"A consolation prize," Remington supplied.

Winters nodded. "You could call it a political statement. And maybe a warning, a way of putting other people, other countries, on notice."

"Why didn't you wait for Icarus to cut loose from the PKK instead of burning his cover?"

"Icarus had already missed exfiltration ops. No one felt they had a handle on him."

"Why did he miss exfiltration?"

"He said the PKK was suspicious of everybody after the assassination cells were taken off the map. Left messages in drops telling Cody that he couldn't get away, that he was scared if he tried the PKK would kill him."

"And Cody believed him?"

"No, sir. Icarus's choice to stay deep only reinforced the idea that we were on the right track. Finally. Until the information popped about Icarus, rumors about the growing terrorist conglomerate and the Syrian link were just rumors. A ghost that couldn't be laid to rest."

"Only it wasn't a ghost."

"No, sir."

"After you burned Icarus's cover, why go after him?" Remington knew there was more to the story.

"Icarus knew too much."

Remington's look asked the next question.

Winters hesitated. "Part of Icarus's assignment was to compromise the terrorist communications," Winters said. "As he worked his way through the PKK organization, he planted back doors and viruses in their computer networks. They used their own hardware and they used cybercafés. If the agency couldn't access the information the terrorists were using, the agency wanted the ability to shut their systems down."

"Terrorist cells aren't known for communicating a lot," Remington said. "That's one of the basic precepts for breaking them into autonomous groups. If one cell operates independently, doesn't know anything about any other cells, they can't give them up if they're compromised. That's what makes them so dangerous."

"But there's been a changing terrorist front, remember? Sir." Winters cleared his throat. "They were communicating. Still are. More now than ever. The agency wanted the back doors and viruses left intact. The thinking was that if Icarus got loose and contacted his true masters, they might make those back doors and viruses go away."

"They still could."

"Maybe. But it would be hard. It *is* hard."

"The Syrians could tell the terrorist groups what's going on."

Winters gave him a cold, jackal's grin. "Think about it. The Syrian military attaché or the State Department or the War Department—whatever they have over there—they're telling their new terrorist buddies, 'Oh, we know we let a spy into your group, but it was to help us spy on the Americans. Surely you can see you would have benefited from that, too. And, yes, we know we let a lot of your people get killed or captured by the Americans and Israelis when they tried to assassinate Chaim Rosenzweig. But don't worry; we'll fix everything.' " The CIA agent shook his head. "Let them try selling that one. Me, I wouldn't want to do it. End up getting a front-row seat as a target at a firing-squad detail."

"If Icarus got back to the Syrians, he could shut those subroutines down?"

Winters nodded. "That's what we've been told."

"So why isn't Icarus streaking for the border?" Remington asked. "Why is he staying in Sanliurfa?"

"Maybe he hasn't been able to connect with his exfiltration contact." Winters remained quiet for a moment.

Remington waited, letting the silence stretch out between them till it seemed to fill the room.

"And maybe there was something else," Winters said. "Maybe Icarus has already been in touch with his exfiltration guy."

A cold feeling threaded through Remington's stomach. "What are you talking about?"

"I'm talking about First Sergeant Gander's connection with a rogue agent, sir," Winters replied in a neutral tone that offered no hint of accusation or reproach. "This is the second time Icarus went looking for Gander."

Remington hadn't been aware that the CIA knew about Goose's confrontation with Icarus in the bar the night they'd arrived in Sanliurfa.

"What are you thinking, Agent Winters?" the Ranger captain asked.

The sharp tone in Remington's voice was all the warning Winters needed. He lowered his voice more. "Sir, it wasn't me thinking. It was Agent Cody."

"Cody thinks Goose is a spy?"

Winters considered his answer, then gave it with obvious reluctance. "That is one possibility that explains the repeated contact with Icarus, sir."

Remington cursed. "Look," he said when he slowed down, "First Sergeant Gander is a lot of things—pigheaded and too content to remain enlisted to suit my tastes—but he is every inch an American fighting man." The image of Goose carrying the wounded marine OneWorld NewsNet currently used to cover the Turkish-Syrian confrontation slipped into the Ranger captain's mind. "He is not now *and* will *never* be in any way disloyal to his country. I'll stake my life on that any day of the week."

"I believe you, sir," Winters said, but even though Remington knew the CIA agent was doing his best to sound sincere, it was plain he held some serious reservations.

"Goose—First Sergeant Gander—isn't seeking Icarus out," Remington said. "In both instances, Icarus has approached him."

"Yes, sir."

But both times Icarus had been able to find Goose while Perrin and his team and the CIA hadn't been able to locate Icarus.

That fact rankled.

Remington paced, breaking away from Winters because the sight of the man angered him so much he was afraid he was going to lose control. Losing control in front of people wasn't something he did.

He scanned the security-camera monitors, watching the vehicles arrive with more wounded and dead, then leave quickly. Concentrating on his breathing, he calmed himself and looked at the screens but not really seeing the figures.

Despite all the pluses Goose brought to the combat field, Remington knew he had to figure in all the minuses Goose brought as well. Goose wasn't at his best. He'd lost his son to whatever force had caused the mysterious disappearances. He had, for whatever reason, become a fixation point for a rogue CIA agent who was a walking target and yet another reason for the Syrians to invade this city that the 75th and other military units had fought and died and killed to keep. He was an enlisted man currently filling an officer's post, which didn't sit well with the other officers no matter how much combat experience and know-how Goose brought to the table.

And Goose was Cal Remington's friend. In some ways, when it

came to their military life, they couldn't have been any closer, even if they'd been brothers.

But Goose's weakness made Remington weak. Goose's borderline insubordination about the CIA agent made Remington's command weak.

And weakness gets you killed, Remington reminded himself. *No matter how good you are. Friendship or no friendship, Cal, you didn't come all this way to die. And you're going to wear general's stars before you cash in your chips. Your command is going to stay strong. You are going to stay strong. No matter how many bodies you have to climb over, no matter if these rivers run red with blood. You're a survivor. So . . . survive.*

Something had to be done about Goose, and it had to be done soon. Before things had a chance to get worse. Because that was one thing Remington was sure of: things were definitely going to get worse.

United States of America
Fort Benning, Georgia
Local Time 2338 Hours

Megan spotted Jenny's reflection in the dark glass as she entered the hospital waiting room. For a moment, Megan watched the young woman, not knowing what made her hesitate. There was something just . . . *different* about Jenny McGrath. Something different in the way she held herself and the way she acted. Something different, even, from the way she had sounded on the phone.

You're imagining things, Megan told herself reproachfully. *That's just paranoia kicking in.* But she didn't fault herself. With the way things had turned out tonight and the long hours she'd been putting in every day since the disappearances, her own emotions over losing Chris, and dealing with Joey and Goose away from the home in dangerous circumstances, it was no wonder that she was paranoid. The miracle was that she didn't need full sedation. And soft restraints. And a straitjacket.

Jenny peered around the nearly filled-to-capacity waiting room, holding the thermos and a brown paper bag.

Several of the young soldiers looked at Jenny, and Megan didn't blame them. She knew why her son had been infatuated with the young woman; she was nothing short of beautiful.

Standing, Megan turned to face Jenny and called her name.

A relieved look flashed across Jenny's face, but she didn't let it find a home there. She was too composed to let something as vulnerable as relief show. Since Megan had known the young woman, she'd recognized that about her. Jenny always put on a strong front, showed a little attitude. Whatever her weaknesses were—and Megan was certain they were there—Jenny kept them quietly under wraps.

Jenny joined Megan, and they sat in the chairs between the two MPs assigned to keep Megan in the waiting room.

"Crowded," Jenny observed in a whisper.

"Tonight . . . hasn't been a good night. For a lot of people."

The young woman glanced at the two MPs. "Fan club?"

"Not exactly."

Understanding dawned in Jenny's eyes. "Somebody figures it's your fault Leslie Hollister is in here?"

Megan started to hedge, but she realized immediately that Jenny would see right through her best efforts, and she was hardly at her best. "If it's not my fault, then maybe it's partly my responsibility. I was in the room when Leslie shot herself."

"You went in there because she was in trouble. Blaming yourself is wrong. *And* it's stupid." Jenny glared at the two MPs, who decided to find different parts of the room to look at.

It's the military, Megan wanted to tell her. *It has to be someone's fault.* But all she said was, "We'll just take this one step at a time for now."

Jenny nodded, then concentrated on opening the thermos.

Seeing the container immediately reminded Megan of Goose. When he was stationed at the post, he never went anywhere without it. He carried coffee in it fifty weeks out of the year, but during the last two weeks before Christmas, Megan always filled the thermos with homemade cocoa. It had been one of her private ways of making sure Goose remembered that Christmas was a special and blessed event.

Jenny looked awkward. "It was okay to use this, wasn't it? I mean, I didn't think to ask."

"It's fine," Megan said. "Just caught me a little off guard."

"It's Goose's, isn't it?"

"Yes."

"I wasn't thinking. Brain-dead or something. Sorry."

Megan touched Jenny's shoulder. "Don't be. If it hadn't been the thermos that reminded me Goose isn't here, the TV would. The news channel televises a recap on the attack in Sanliurfa every fifteen minutes."

Carefully, Jenny poured the hot chicken noodle soup into two plastic cups she took from the paper bag. "Thought I would join you. If you don't mind."

"I appreciate the company. Miss dinner?"

Jenny smiled, but the effort was off, weaker than Megan had ever seen. "I'm thinking I missed lunch, too," Jenny said, "but that might have been yesterday."

"Lunch *was* yesterday. We're already into a new day."

Jenny shook her head. "Not until I've gone to sleep. Clock-watching just gets me confused. It'll be tomorrow when I wake up. And not one moment before."

Megan accepted the cup of hot soup and inhaled. Her stomach growled eagerly. "This smells wonderful."

"Thank you. I found the recipe in a cookbook in the library when I was a kid. I always liked it."

"It smells homey and substantive, like something your mother would have taught you to make."

Jenny broke the eye contact and rummaged in the paper sack again. Megan watched the young woman's feelings slide back behind protective shields that came up like a conditioned reflex. "My mother—"

Not *Mother* with a capital *M*, or even *Mom*, Megan noted. And there's anger there too.

"—didn't really stick around to teach me cooking or laundry." Jenny took two sandwiches wrapped in wax paper from the paper sack. "Or how to fix my hair."

"Ah. That would explain the purple tint," Megan said automatically, then wondered immediately if she had gone too far.

Instead of taking offense, Jenny grinned.

"I was teasing," Megan said.

"I know." Jenny held out one of the sandwiches. "BLT?"

"Yes. Thank you. I was afraid for a moment it might be peanut butter and jelly."

"That was a temptation. PB and J would have been quick and easy. Frying bacon with a houseful of teenagers banging around is about as much fun as juggling cats."

"I didn't mean to put so much on you."

Jenny sighed and stared at the cup of soup in her hands. Her hands shook slightly. "That came out wrong. I didn't mean that. I just . . . I just . . . have a lot on my mind right now."

Megan waited. The rumble of voices sounded all around them as people whispered and talked.

"Can I help?" Megan asked.

Jenny slowly tore her BLT in half. "I wish you could, but you can't."

"Try me."

With quiet focus, Jenny pulled a lettuce leaf from her sandwich and ate it.

"Something happened since you called me," Megan said.

"Maybe."

"The kids—"

"Are fine," Jenny replied.

"Joey—"

Shaking her head, Jenny said, "Didn't call."

"Okay, I'm all out of guesses."

After a brief hesitation, Jenny shook her head. "You have enough problems right now, and I'm . . . just not ready to talk about it."

"All right. But when you are, I'm here."

Jenny looked at Megan briefly. Glimmers of unshed tears showed in the young woman's eyes. "I appreciate that. Really, I do. It's just that . . . this is something really old. And private." She held up her cup. "Let's eat, okay? I mean, I did go to all the trouble to make it."

"Okay." Despite her flagging reserves and screaming need to fix something and make it right because she felt all she'd accomplished during this day was a long string of mistakes, Megan calmed herself and turned her attention to the soup and sandwich. *She doesn't need a counselor now. She just needs a friend. And so do you.*

They ate in companionable silence, interrupted only by Jenny's brief departure to the vending machine to buy fruit juices. With the odd combination of soup, sandwich, and juice, Megan felt like she was having a meal with Joey and Chris. All that was missing were the cartoons on TV.

And home, she reminded herself.

She finished the soup and had a second helping, not just to make Jenny feel good, but because the company and the warm broth made her hungry and felt healing. After they'd completed the meal, Megan and Jenny threw the trash away. Even during the short walk across the room to the trash cans, one of the MPs went with them.

Jenny sent the MP a scathing look, then said to Megan, "These guys really take their job seriously. You'd think you were on the Top Ten Most Wanted list or something."

"It's a serious situation," Megan replied as they resumed their seats.

"Look," Jenny said with an edge to her words, "don't buy into the whole guilt trip they're handing out here. What happened to Leslie, it's bad. I'll agree with that. But she's the one who lost it. Not you. You walked into that house unarmed when a small army of MPs was ready to go in with guns blazing. You did what you could, and you're going to feel a little guilty that you didn't make it all better, but you tried."

The young woman's insight surprised Megan. *You taught yourself the recipe for chicken noodle soup from a book in the library, but where did you learn such wisdom?*

Megan remembered the talk Jenny had given her the morning after Chris had disappeared, how she had brought up the book she'd read about the Rapture and the Tribulation. Jenny had pointed out that God had allowed Megan to save Gerry Fletcher just long enough that he didn't reach the other end of the four-story plummet he'd started.

"Thank you," Megan said.

Jenny crossed her arms and looked a little embarrassed. "No big deal. I just don't want to see you tearing yourself up over this. The kids need you."

"I know."

"But they need something more, too, Megan." Jenny's tone got a little harder. "Television and playing all-night Monopoly is only going to take them so far. At some point, if they don't have more going on soon, they're going to freak out."

"I'm listening." Megan was surprised to see the strong side of Jenny McGrath come out when she was obviously in some kind of personal turmoil herself.

"They need to know what's happening," Jenny said, looking straight at Megan. "They need to know what they're supposed to do. A plan. That's what they need most of all."

"We're working on surviving," Megan said. "That's a plan."

"*No.*" Jenny's voice shook with emotion. A tear slid down her cheek. She started to wipe it away, then stopped herself. She took a short, quick breath, and her face relaxed. Not another tear fell, and the first one spread so thin it couldn't be seen anymore.

Megan knew the young woman's control was incredible, but she had no idea how Jenny had learned to exercise it.

"Survival," Jenny said in a calm and forceful voice, "isn't good enough. Thinking about surviving something—that gets you through days. Maybe years if you really work at it and lie to yourself and tell yourself that's all there is every day. But just thinking about surviving doesn't get you through life."

Where did you learn that?

"If you're going to save the kids here at this base," Jenny said, "you're going to have to help them understand the truth of what really happened three days ago. And you're going to have to let them know what they're supposed to do about it."

Megan couldn't speak. The last time she and Jenny had had a conversation like this, they'd been in the privacy of her home and talking over a breakfast of bagels. It was one thing to discuss religion and belief in the sanctity of her home, but to do so while being guarded by the two MPs was disconcerting. She wasn't strong enough for that. Even Bill Townsend had sensed that and never made her feel uncomfortable.

"I'm talking about the Rapture." Jenny definitely wasn't going to back off. "I tried talking to some of those kids today, to let them know what was going on. I even tried to get them to read the book I read. But maybe I didn't explain it right."

"Maybe they're not ready," Megan suggested.

"Megan, they . . . have . . . no . . . choice." Jenny punctuated her words with her hand, like she was pushing each word into place between them. "The Tribulation lasts seven years. And if something happens to those kids before they learn what they're supposed to do—" She let the rest of it hang.

Then they go to hell? Is that what happens, God? Would You really let that happen to them? The fear burned bright and hard inside Megan because she knew Jenny was right. But she didn't know what she was going to do about it. She bowed her head, breaking eye contact with Jenny. *God, I know we're not supposed to ask for signs, but if You could see Your way clear—*

"Mrs. Gander."

Hearing her name startled Megan. She glanced up and saw Dr. Lyons, the surgeon who had taken Leslie Hollister when she'd arrived in the emergency room. Lyons was a career military doctor, ramrod straight, and in his early fifties. During her time at the post, Megan had gotten to know him and his wife through her work and the occasional social function that accompanied it. Dr. and Mrs. Lyons were good people. He wore green scrubs and looked haggard.

Megan stood and went to Lyons. She tried to ask the question, but she couldn't make any words come through her constricted throat.

Lyons smiled tiredly at her and took her hand. "Leslie Hollister made it through surgery, Mrs. Gander. She's a strong girl. A fighter. She just wasn't ready to leave us yet."

Tears filled Megan's eyes. Before she knew it, Jenny was in her arms, hugging her and holding her tight, and for just a moment everything seemed all right.

❋   ❋   ❋

Sunshine Hills Cemetery
Outside Marbury, Alabama
Local Time 0418 Hours

Delroy woke lying facedown in the mud a few feet from his son's grave. Small trickles of water ran past him, only inches from his face. Rain pummeled his back, constant and relentless. After everything he'd suffered through, he hadn't had the strength to leave the grave-yard.

And where would he have gone? He didn't know. Getting here had been his only mission.

He didn't know when he'd fallen asleep, just as he didn't know what had awakened him now. The fecund stink of rotting vegetation filled the small, enclosed area of the makeshift tent he'd made from his rain slicker.

After he'd made his decision not to open Terrence's grave, he'd re-mained awake as long as he could and awaited the thing's return. He had no doubt that it would put in another appearance. The creature was bound to him; it wouldn't go away until it got what it came for.

And Chaplain Delroy Harte was very certain that what the thing was after was his soul. As trite as that sounded, he believed that with every fiber of his being.

You can fear and believe in a hellish creature that torments and perse-cutes, he berated himself, *and you can't let yourself believe in God's mercy. That didn't seem possible, but there it was.*

At the moment, though, Delroy felt there had been little in the way of God's mercy to believe in. Unfinished business had drawn Delroy from his ship during the fiercest trouble the crew had ever known, and had left him up to his thighs in his son's open grave.

God, help me to understand, he prayed, *because I can't see the mercy in that.*

During the time before he'd fallen asleep under the slicker, Delroy had admitted that maybe he hadn't returned home at God's behest. He was more convinced now that in his weakness Satan, not God, had drawn him here. For a time, thinking like that had helped. If he could believe that Satan had led him here, that Satan could take an in-terest in his life, wasn't it possible to believe that God did, too?

In the end, he'd had to admit that line of thinking was arrogant and decidedly wrong. He wasn't Job for God and the devil to fight over. And it was horrible to contemplate that the only way he could believe in God was to first believe that some devilish *thing* was out to get him.

High-intensity white light blazed onto the ground around Delroy. The light cut into the darkness under the slicker.

Cautiously, Delroy raised his head, exposing his face to the muddy rain that spattered against the ground beyond the slicker's edge. He felt certain the creature had finally gotten over its vanishing act and come back to torture him more. Despite what it said, Delroy knew he wasn't going to open his son's grave. Whatever was in that casket, whatever wasn't in that casket, Terrence wasn't here anymore.

A pair of black rubber rain boots with yellow piping followed the light. The light reflected against the shiny black surfaces.

"Hey," a deep voice said. "Come on up outta that mud."

Delroy didn't want to push up from the mud, though. When he'd first lain on the ground, the cold had seeped into his flesh. Now it felt like his body had made peace with the mud, and they shared his warmth between them.

"Get up outta there," the voice said again. "You're gonna catch your death laying there like that."

Delroy ignored the man, thankful that it wasn't the creature, and closed his eyes. He didn't know why he'd woken up. There was no reason to. And catching his death in the cemetery? It was a perfect place for it.

The light shifted; someone grabbed Delroy's left arm and flipped him over, exposing him to the cold rain. Only then did he realize how numb his body was. His teeth started chattering almost at once. His arms shook as he reached for the edges of the slicker to draw it around him again. After one try, he discovered that he was too weak to roll back over.

"C'mon. Get up outta there. Get on your feet."

Delroy squinted his eyes tight against the harsh light but still felt it stabbing into his brain.

The man holding the halogen light nudged Delroy with one of the rubber boots. "Can you get up?"

"I don't think so." Delroy struggled to stop his chattering teeth but couldn't.

The man sighed in tired frustration. "I'm gonna give you a hand."

"No." Resentment at the man's intrusion bubbled inside Delroy. He'd placed his life in God's hands by lying here on the cold ground.

If there was a God, if He was really interested in saving Chaplain Delroy Harte, then let Him do it. That wasn't for some stranger to do.

"You lay here much longer, you ain't gonna be here come morning," the man promised.

Suits me fine, Delroy thought, but he immediately felt guilty for thinking that.

The light shifted again, dragging up the man's thickset body. It settled on a badge revealed when the man lifted his raincoat out of the way.

"I'm a sheriff's deputy, mister," he said in a flat, no-nonsense tone. "You're getting up offa that ground. Whether you do it under your own steam or I hook onto you with a set of handcuffs and drag you feetfirst, you're coming with me."

"It would be easier to leave me here," Delroy said, trying to point out the unwise investment. "I'm not worth your trouble."

"Say, are you drunk?" the deputy demanded.

Delroy had to work to answer. He was so cold and numb his body didn't want to respond, and his head felt so thick and full that he could hardly think. "No. Not drunk." *Just bereft of belief. Abandoned by God. Punished because I wasn't perfect.*

"Well, I can't leave you here." The deputy squatted, grabbed Delroy by the back of his shirt and slicker, and muscled Delroy to his feet in an amazing display of strength. "Man, you are a big 'un, aren't you?"

Delroy didn't say anything. He felt like he was in a dream—*no, a nightmare*—and couldn't get out.

Once he had Delroy standing, the deputy tried to get him moving. Only Delroy's legs were too numb to work. He keeled over.

"Whoops," the deputy said, moving around quickly to catch Delroy across his shoulder so he folded at the waist. Even from that brief moment of being vertical, Delroy knew that he was a head taller than the deputy, but the man was broad and hefty, with shoulders an axe handle wide.

With surprising strength, the deputy shifted Delroy's considerable weight across his shoulders, then stood again and started walking. His rain boots sank deeply into the mud and made sucking noises when they lifted as he carried Delroy through the graveyard.

A car with a light bar and a whip antenna was parked a short distance away. The lights speared into the darkness, turning the rain gray and showing the downpour. SHERIFF'S DEPARTMENT stood out on the door over a seal that Delroy couldn't make out.

The deputy put his long-handled flashlight on top of the car, opened the door, and levered Delroy onto the rear seat. Delroy sprawled across it. The heat from the car's heater blew over him, waking throbbing needles of pain all over his body where the cold had soaked in bone deep.

Standing in the doorway of the car with the interior light showing on him, the deputy peered down at Delroy with irritation written on his beefy face. He was in his late fifties, a solid, husky man used to hard work. He had big hands and a neatly clipped mustache and round-lensed glasses.

"Haul your feet in," the deputy said.

Delroy did, but the effort lacked strength because now that he was out of the cold he was shaking all over.

"Get outta that slicker. I got a blanket in the back."

At first, Delroy didn't move.

"Get it off," the deputy said in a rougher, louder voice. "I come in there and have to skin you myself, I'm not gonna be happy about it."

Too tired to argue or resist anymore, Delroy starting shrugging out of the slicker.

The deputy stepped to the rear of the car as Delroy forced himself into a sitting position and continued pulling the slicker off. He couldn't get it off himself, but the deputy helped him when he returned with an olive army blanket.

"I'm going to get you to the hospital, get you checked out," the deputy said.

"I'm fine," Delroy said, shivering beneath the blanket.

"Mister, you laying out in a cemetery in a March rainstorm in the middle of the night, why if you check out fine physically, I'm gonna have your head examined, too." The deputy closed the door.

Seated now, letting the cushions take his weight, Delroy looked back at Terrence's grave. A mild burst of lightning strobed the sky and lit the grounds briefly. The fresh mound of earth that covered his son's grave stood out in stark relief. He'd covered the grave site back up before giving into the soul-draining fatigue that filled him.

The deputy slid in behind the steering wheel and knocked the mud off his boots before pulling his feet inside. A wire mesh screen separated the back of the car from the front. Switching on the overhead light, the deputy opened Delroy's wallet and flipped through it.

Delroy hadn't even noticed when the deputy had taken his wallet. Now, he didn't care.

A look of surprise showed on the deputy's face as he glanced over his shoulder through the wire mesh. "You a navy man?"

"Aye."

"What are doing here?"

Delroy didn't want to answer, just wanted to be alone. But he couldn't find it in himself to be rude to the man. "My son's buried in this graveyard. My father before him."

The deputy studied him. His eyes were pale blue and quick as a fox's. "That grave I found you by. Somebody dug that up."

"I did."

"Why?"

"Because I felt I needed to."

"Terrence Harte. That would be your son?"

Delroy knew then that the man had an eye for detail if he read the gravestones while getting him to his feet. "Aye."

The deputy hesitated, peering over his glasses with a steely gaze that softened a little. "How long since your boy passed?"

"Five years."

"It's a hard thing, losing a son," the deputy said.

Delroy didn't say anything.

"Lost one of my boys nine years ago." The deputy folded Delroy's wallet back up and dropped it onto the passenger seat beside him. "Was a drunk driver killed him. Crossed the white line. My boy never had a chance. Laid in a coma for seven months till we finally give up hope, and the hospital pulled the plug."

"I'm sorry to hear that." The words came automatically, but the emotion behind them was distant. Somewhere inside his dead heart, Delroy felt certain he did feel sympathetic about the man's pain and loss.

The deputy nodded. His eyes remained hard, but they were a little less suspicious now. "I gotta ask you something."

Delroy looked at him.

"You take anything out of that grave?" The deputy held up a hand. "Don't you bother lying to me either, because when I get you to the hospital, I'm gonna search your clothes. You took something, I'm gonna find it."

"No," Delroy said. "I didn't take anything."

"Good." The deputy let out a sigh. "You didn't take anything. That'll make things a little easier." He turned his attention back to the two-way radio and called in to dispatch, letting that person know he was en route to the hospital.

Delroy lay back in the rear seat of the cruiser and felt helpless. He hadn't lain out in the cold to die, as the deputy seemed to think, but he wouldn't have minded if that had happened either. He just hadn't figured out what he was supposed to do next.

A moment later, the deputy put the transmission in drive and headed toward the cemetery's entrance. Mud slung from the tires thumped against the undercarriage as the cruiser rocked over the uneven ground. Before the vehicle reached the highway, Delroy fell into a yawning black pit and slept.

✵   ✵   ✵

OneWorld NewsNet Corporate Offices
Bucharest, Romania
Local Time 1124 Hours

When Danielle Vinchenzo's call came through, Radu Stolojan stood at the silver tea service in his office preparing a cup. He gazed out over Bucharest with a feeling of contentment. The world was in turmoil, and that was exactly as it should be at the moment. Everything was going according to plan.

He returned to his desk and punched the speaker function. Few people had his personal number.

"Stolojan," he said.

"It's Danielle Vinchenzo."

Stolojan sat at his immense desk and tried to put a brighter note in his voice. "Yes, Danielle. You are well, I take it?"

"So far," the woman answered. "Things here are still hectic."

Glancing to his left, Stolojan studied the wall of monitors that ran news feeds from OneWorld as well as from FOX News and CNN. He knew the placement of each as well as he knew the back of his own hand.

Although he wasn't the director of OneWorld NewsNet, he was the power behind the throne. As Niccolò Machiavelli had written in his book, *The Prince*, a smart monarch surrounded himself with people willing to do the heinous things the monarch could not himself afford to do.

Stolojan was that man. At least he was one of them. He took enormous pride in that, as well as in the lucrative perks he received from his work. Nothing took place in the building, in the city, or in any of the around-the-world operations the news service was involved in that he didn't know about.

He studied the monitor that showed the latest footage from Sanliurfa, noting the icon in the lower right of the screen. Although they kept cycling scenes of the early morning attack on the city, Danielle and her crew had added footage of the search-and-rescue and recovery efforts now taking place in the war-torn streets.

"I see that." Stolojan took a biscuit from the silver platter on his desk. They were fresh baked and brought to his office precisely at eleven-fifteen every morning. He broke the biscuit open and inhaled the delightful fragrance. "I have reports that there were a number of casualties."

"There were."

Stolojan smiled. Large numbers of casualties were good for news. So far, the OneWorld NewsNet team was the only one getting live video broadcasts out of the city with any degree of success. That was also as things had been planned.

"Unfortunately," Stolojan said, "many of those casualties are unconfirmed."

"I haven't gotten an interview with Captain Remington yet," Danielle said a little defensively.

"By choice?" Stolojan felt irritated. Danielle had a freer agenda than most of the people working for OneWorld, but she wasn't as independent as she sometimes thought she was.

"The man is busy." Danielle's tone carried frustration.

Stolojan's irritation bloomed into full-blown anger. One of these days he would break her. He looked forward to that day, but knew that until then she was still useful. Holding the biscuit open, he took a knife and slathered creamy butter and orange marmalade onto the bread with delight. He had a child's sweet tooth.

"Get the interview," Stolojan ordered.

"I'm working on it."

"Captain Remington is hungry for media exposure." Stolojan eyed the biscuit appreciatively.

When he was young, still a boy, he'd run through Bucharest's streets and been treated with no more regard than a rodent. He'd been homeless, an unwanted child born to a couple who already had the two children allowed by the state. During those years, birth control was banned, as were any more than two children. Those unwanted children fought and died in alleys throughout the city, whether from beatings from police or other children, or from starvation or sickness.

Stolojan's employer had taken him from all of that. He'd been given the job at OneWorld, and there was nothing he would not do to make certain he stayed in Nicolae Carpathia's good graces.

"Remington loves the camera," Danielle agreed. "But he's not the guy most of the world wants to see."

Stolojan frowned. "Ah, yes, your sergeant. Goose Gander."

"He's not my sergeant," Danielle protested. "But he is the guy people want to see and hear when this story is covered."

Unfortunately, the media ratings that ran constantly on OneWorld's news broadcasts reinforced Danielle's assessment of her pet project. The share of the market the Turkish-Syrian war currently cornered was driven, in a significant part, by the first sergeant's presence. He was an American hero, and much of the American, as well as the Western, audience had embraced him. OneWorld had received a number of e-mails wanting to know more about Gander.

"In light of everything else going on in the world at this moment, the story in Sanliurfa is slight." Stolojan enjoyed the idea of deflating the woman's ego. He bit into the biscuit and relished the warm, sweet taste.

"Then why have me here?" Danielle asked. "For a story so . . . *slight?*"

Displeased, Stolojan put his biscuit down. Both of them knew that her presence in Sanliurfa was because she happened to be there when the war broke out. However, her ability to capture the attention of the viewers—especially the American viewers—was significant at this juncture. So was Sergeant Gander, although he wasn't the primary target they were after.

Nicolae Carpathia had several interests vested in the Middle Eastern war taking shape between Turkey and Syria.

"I want the interview confirming the casualties," Stolojan said, putting a little more force into his voice so they would both understand who was in charge. "I want it with Captain Remington."

"You'll get it."

"I know you didn't call to tell me that," Stolojan said. "Was there something you needed?"

Danielle hesitated. "I called for Lizuca. I keep getting her answering machine."

"She went home." Stolojan remembered the picture of the CIA man, Alexander Cody, that Lizuca had searched for.

"That's unusual."

"Why?"

"She told me she would help me with some research I was doing. She's never walked away from an assignment I asked her to take care of for me before."

"I told her not to waste her time pursuing the information you wanted."

"Waste her time?" Danielle's voice rose in disbelief and anger. "Mr. Stolojan, there is a CIA team operating in this city that is at odds with the U.S. Rangers for some reason. I've seen them, and I want to identify them. Given the present state of affairs here, I'd think that would be of some importance."

"Your mission there is to relay the news, Ms. Vinchenzo," Stolojan replied in an icy voice. "Not make the news."

"A CIA team—"

"Is of no interest to the news stories we're currently covering there," Stolojan said. "The people want coverage of the war. The Western world wants to see how the United States military is handling things, just as they did in Iraq. Our presence there with the stories they want is improving our market share in those areas. We are going to give them coverage of the war. Not stories about the CIA, who are probably there in an intelligence support capacity." He paused. "Are we clear on that?"

"Crystal." Danielle's voice was cold, distant.

"Good." Stolojan grinned, enjoying his triumph. He loved squashing the plans of others. The sense of power he got when he was doing so gave him a feeling of exhilaration that was unmatched by anything else in his life. "Then I'll expect that interview about the casualties taken there soon?"

"Soon."

"Very good, Ms. Vinchenzo. Did you need anything else?"

"No."

"Good day." Stolojan broke the phone connection and returned his attention to the plate of biscuits. He glanced at the wall of monitors, spending more of his time spying on the building's employees than watching the news. Over the years, he'd learned that controlling the news was a simple matter. Carpathia had become a master of it, and it was that skill that had brought him the presidency of Romania only a few days ago.

Those same skills now had gotten Carpathia an invitation to New York City to speak to the United Nations. OneWorld NewsNet continued to farm out footage of interviews with Carpathia, of his ascension to the Romanian presidency as well as his news conferences regarding his decision to go to the United States in these confused times. Other national news agencies had access to the interviews Carpathia would grant while in New York City and to his first address to the United Nations.

But the actions of OneWorld's employees interested Stolojan most. He exercised his control over them relentlessly. In Romania's struggling economy, working at OneWorld had quite literally changed their lives and the lives of their families.

Only Danielle Vinchenzo remained beyond Stolojan's reach.

But hopefully not for long. Stolojan grinned in anticipation and reached for another biscuit. She would make a mistake or serve past her usefulness. Then she would be his. Stolojan had already been promised.

OneWorld NewsNet Mobile Platform
Sanliurfa, Turkey
Local Time 1129 Hours

Weary and worn, Danielle gazed around the RV news center. The past few hours had brought precious little in the way of answers. However, they had gigabytes of brutal and bloody imagery from the attacks. The death toll was going to be high—again—when the final numbers came in.

If those numbers ever did, Danielle thought with a chill. No one knew for sure how many citizens of Sanliurfa remained within the city's walls. Many had fled in the first wave during the SCUD attacks, and others had disappeared over the ensuing days. Still more had already formed another mass, ready to flee at daybreak.

Captain Remington hadn't returned her message about conducting a live interview. Maybe he was awaiting clearance from the Joint Chiefs, but Danielle believed that the Ranger captain was still caught up in whatever was going on with the CIA team in Sanliurfa.

She clicked her digital camera to life and brought the CIA man's picture onto the screen again. She remembered him from the time she had seen him in Bucharest. *Who are you?*

The image remained silent.

Irritable and cranky, Danielle switched off the camera and gazed up at the feeds other news agencies pumped out. Local television stations in the area picked up those feeds, but they weren't able to hit the at-home audiences in the United States the way they hoped. Their phone communications appeared to remain intact, but they couldn't get video feeds out on the stories they covered.

Danielle felt badly for the other reporters. During brief lunches or meetings she'd had with them, the occasional debriefings held by Captain Remington and his Turkish counterpart, Captain Mkchian, all of the reporters had lamented the fact that they didn't have access to the rest of the world like OneWorld NewsNet did.

Stolojan's smarmy voice still echoed in Danielle's mind, setting off land mines of anger and frustration. When she'd taken the job with OneWorld NewsNet a few days ago, she hadn't considered that she might get a news producer who was so narrow-minded. After the years she'd put into the business, though, she knew she should have known better.

Impatient, Danielle stood suddenly, drawing the attention of the people working the computers and breaking down the footage and stories she and her team had turned in last night and so far this morning.

"I've got to stretch my legs," Danielle said.

"You should get some sleep," Costin Bogasieru advised, barely taking the time to glance away from the two monitors he scanned. His fingers never hesitated on the keyboard as he changed lighting, color, and film speed. Pieces of camera shots filled the monitor as he worked them into news bites for the hourly updates. He was in his early thirties but already had the practical mind-set of a much older man, though he remained on the cutting edge of computer systems.

"I can't sleep," Danielle said. Her mind was too busy, or maybe she was just too tired. She couldn't remember how long she had been up.

"Warm milk," Bogasieru suggested.

"No." Danielle glanced at the other end of the room.

Cezar slept in a fetal position on a Murphy bed. Three empty beer bottles sat next to the bed. His camera was in his arms and his belt of batteries was connected to the charger. Despite his drinking, he never seemed to get drunk, and any buzz he got disappeared the minute he went to work.

"I'll be back soon," Danielle said.

"Be careful. Don't forget your helmet."

Danielle scooped the Kevlar helmet from the folding chair by the wall, shrugged into her bulletproof vest, grabbed her camera case, and let herself out. She heard the RV's electronic locks *snick* into place behind her.

She walked through the rubble that filled the courtyard where the driver had parked the Adventurer. A building fronted the courtyard on the south side, with a solid mass of trees to the north and more trees that flanked the entrance and exit to the parking area. Four other vehicles, all of them wrecked and burned to the point of being only metal husks, occupied the courtyard. Thankfully, there were no bodies.

She lifted her camera from its case and took photos. The effort was a habit, a shorthand form of note taking. A picture was worth a thousand words, but a TV reporter had far fewer than that in a sound bite, so she wanted reference material to work from.

As Danielle walked, she gazed around. UH-1H Huey helicopters made the rounds with litters hanging over their sides. From the radio communications she'd monitored while in the RV, she knew the search-and-rescue teams were still finding and removing wounded soldiers and civilians. The Hueys ferried wounded to the military hospitals, or took emergency triage personnel to treat wounded on-site if those casualties needed to be stabilized before being moved.

Streamers of black smoke spiraled through the air and clouds of harsh smoke drifted through the city, bringing biting pain to throats and nasal passages. Several fires still raged, adding to the casualty lists and to the property damage.

In the full light of day, Sanliurfa lay scattered and broken. If she hadn't already been numbed by everything she'd seen over the past few days, Danielle felt certain she would have broken down and wept despite the professional distance she tried to maintain.

Sanliurfa was a historical city, one of the oldest around. Danielle knew from the background piece she'd done on the city soon after the retreating military forces had settled in Sanliurfa, that evidence of human habitation existed more than two thousand years B.C. Christianity had its roots there, and was followed by the Moslem beliefs and rulers that had constructed the architecture that still stood in so many places.

The city had worn many names throughout its life span: Edessa, Urfa, and finally in 1923—after the Ottoman Empire succumbed to the annals of history—Sanliurfa. Wars had torn the land all its life. Border disputes and issues over water rights regarding the Euphrates River—known as the Firat locally—remained high on the list of reasons armies fought or stayed prepared for war. Christian crusaders had traveled thousands of miles to sack the city in 1098, and it took fifty years for the Turks to take it back.

Medieval architecture stood shoulder to shoulder with modern buildings, hotels, and apartments. But the bazaars, the eight great marketplaces that still thrived on the agricultural business where people of several cities came to buy, sell, and trade vegetables, fruits, and meats as well as barter for handcrafts that included clothing, furniture, and dishes, had existed during all of that time.

Trade had been Sanliurfa's lifeblood, no matter what name the city wore. But that was all gone now. Danielle had seen two of the great marketplaces in tatters. The Syrian pilots had deliberately targeted those, taking the chance that many of the populace would gather there as normal to swap news and bargain for the things they needed while selling the things they didn't. The tactic had worked. Dozens of dead and hundreds more injured had resulted from the attacks.

Outside the courtyard area, Danielle walked south, following the natural boundary of the block. Even in the downtown area where she was, most buildings stood no more than two or three stories tall. None of them had windows. The glass had either been shattered during the first attacks or had been broken out later by soldiers or occupants so they couldn't turn into deadly shrapnel during the next attack.

An earthmover, borrowed from a Sanliurfa construction business, dug a great gaping hole in the park across the street. The claw scrabbled back and forth with loud clanks that echoed between the buildings. A line of trucks bearing the dead that had been gathered so far waited to dump the bodies into the mass grave.

Other squads dug more mass graves around the city.

The heat, Danielle knew from the reports she'd given, spread disease from rotting corpses quickly. If the military teams hadn't been ordered to delay Syrian occupation of the city and were on their way out, they probably wouldn't have bothered with the dead.

Whenever possible, American dead were buried apart from the Turkish people and military as well as the U.N. forces. If things went well and the Syrians were forced back into their country, American military would return to the city and claim their dead. Forensics would allow them to ship the bodies home to families to inter at Arlington or in family burial grounds.

For a moment, Danielle stopped and watched the mass burial. Several Turkish families clung to the sides of the military trucks. Soldiers gently but forcibly removed some of them who were overcome with emotion at their losses or simply wanted to know if their family members were among the dead.

It was horrible, and Danielle faulted herself because she was able to keep her distance from those involved. Finally, unable to bear the impersonal sounds of the earthmover as the scoop carved the grave, Danielle turned away. Farther down the street, she saw a man loading a small car. Evidently he had lost faith in the military to hold their positions.

A woman who was probably his wife came forward. She cried openly, one knotted fist in her mouth. She carried a child's car seat. Her husband joined her. He looked at the car seat and shook his head. Even though Danielle couldn't hear their voices over the sounds of the earthmover and the truck engines, she knew the couple was arguing.

The man tried to take the car seat from the woman. She held on to it desperately and shook her head. Tears streamed from her eyes and pain wrinkled her face like a prune.

Taking the car seat, the man spoke softly. The woman shook her head, tucking her chin against her chest and not meeting his gaze. He spoke again, more harshly this time because the tendons stood out on his neck.

For a moment Danielle thought the argument was only over the fact that there wasn't room in the tightly packed car for the seat. Suddenly she noticed that there was no baby or small child in evidence. Then she realized why there was no child: all the children were gone, taken away by whatever forces had made them vanish.

Danielle took a picture of the couple arguing over the child's seat. The scene was intimate and personal, but Danielle knew the same confusion had to be felt around the globe.

First Sergeant Gander's son had disappeared, too. Danielle had learned that Goose had a son through the bio information Lizuca was able to get from someone in Waycross, Georgia, Goose's hometown. Danielle hadn't been able to bring up his son's disappearance the few times she'd talked with the sergeant, and she didn't think he would have talked about his boy if she had.

She put her camera away again and kept moving. Walking through the smoke that clogged the streets, seeing all the debris from the broken buildings and the shattered trees and burned vehicles, she missed the RV. Inside the Adventurer, she felt removed from the threat and the agonizing aftermath of the attack.

Before she knew it, tears ran down her face as she thought about the young couple and the car seat and the mass grave surrounded by all the upset family members and friends. And First Sergeant Goose Gander who had lost a son and seemed at odds with his superior officer over the matter of the CIA team.

She'd noted that in the hallway. She didn't miss much. From everything she'd read about the 75th, Captain Remington and First Sergeant Gander had served successfully together for years. Maybe they had their differences of opinions during downtime or when they were on a routine peacekeeping mission, but Danielle didn't buy the possibility that the pressure of the war zone had put them at odds.

The only catalyst she could point to was the CIA man she couldn't identify. Yet. But she was willing to bet she could change that.

She took her sat-phone from her chest pouch and punched in the number. Military vehicles and civilian transport rolled by in the street, crunching through debris. In addition to the number she had for Lizuca Carutasu at OneWorld NewsNet, she also had the young woman's home number.

After getting the job at OneWorld, the first thing Lizuca had done was put in a phone. Her mother had protested the expense, the young woman had told Danielle, and the stories of how her mother had tried over the past years to manage her money had made Danielle laugh. Mrs. Carutasu's efforts reminded Danielle a lot of her own mother's micromanaging attempts when she'd first moved out on her own.

The phone rang four times before it was answered.

Danielle ducked into an alley and turned toward the wall so the street noise wouldn't sound so loud.

Mrs. Carutasu answered in Romanian.

Not having knowledge of the language other than to say hello and good-bye, Danielle said in English, "Hello, Mrs. Carutasu. This is Danielle Vinchenzo."

"Ah, hello. Hello." The woman's English was limited, so even a polite conversation was difficult. "Danielle Vinchenzo. Yes."

"Yes. Is Lizuca home?"

"No," the old woman said. "Lizuca not home. She should be sleeping. Is time for bed. She work very hard."

"I know," Danielle said. "I apologize. If it wasn't important I wouldn't have called."

"Oh, no," the woman disagreed. "You call. You call."

"I know I called." Danielle glanced out at the street. "I need to speak with Lizuca."

"Lizuca no here. She say she working. Say, tell Danielle . . . working. She know you call, yes."

"Yes."

"She say, tell working on *peek*-ture. Call you when she done. Then sleep, yes?"

The news heartened Danielle. Over the past few days she and Lizuca had managed to develop a rapport and get a few things past

Stolojan, including Lizuca's overtime, which came out of Danielle's budget. It didn't surprise her now that Lizuca would undertake to work on the picture on her own time.

Of course, Danielle didn't intend for the young woman not to get paid for her trouble. She knew from conversations with Lizuca that she was sole support for a number of people in addition to her mother.

"Thank you, Mrs. Carutasu," Danielle said.

"Okay. Good-bye." The phone hung up with an abrupt click.

Danielle put the sat-phone away in her vest. She took a deep breath and tried not to choke on the trace elements of chemicals in the dry air. She felt better. If Lizuca caught a break, Danielle knew she'd be in the middle of whatever game the CIA team was playing in Sanliurfa.

❄ ❄ ❄

All Saints Hospital
Marbury, Alabama
Local Time 0743 Hours

"Well, there you are."

Blearily, Delroy opened his eyes in the dimness of the hospital waiting room. Although a line of people had been at the hospital, most of them dealing with anxiety attacks or chronic medical problems such as asthma and weak hearts aggravated by the confusion and panic of the last few days, he'd finally been examined, judged healthy—although perhaps not mentally sound—and sent on his way. The hospital beds were full of accident victims and people needing sedation till they came to grips with everything that had happened.

Unfortunately, he had nowhere to go and all Delroy had to wear was the backless pink hospital gown, covered by a lime green bathrobe intended for a much smaller man. They had no slippers his size. Sitting in the waiting room, trying to figure out his next move, he'd drawn a lot of suspicious stares. The fact that his personal items—his wallet, his rings, and his watch—were in a clear plastic bag in his lap didn't help matters.

Turning his head at the sound of the booming voice and the blunt declaration, Delroy spotted the deputy who had brought him to the hospital standing a short distance away. He wasn't wearing his raincoat now, though he still wore boots that had been mostly wiped clean of mud. The sheriff's badge on his chest stood out and attracted the attention of the people in the waiting room.

The deputy came closer, eyeing Delroy skeptically. "They tell me you're gonna live."

"I am," Delroy admitted.

"Must be a lotta tough packed in all that tall."

Personally, Delroy didn't feel all that tough. He felt cold and weak. A headache slammed ceaselessly at his temples, and his eyes and nose burned.

After the triage nurses had started Delroy on the paperwork, the deputy had left. That had made Delroy feel somewhat relieved. He wasn't sure if he could be arrested for trying to dig up Terrence's grave, but if the deputy wasn't around to arrest him that was a good thing.

Only now the man was back, not ten minutes after the doctor had pronounced Delroy fit enough and sent him to the waiting room. All it would have taken was a brief phone call to let the deputy know Delroy had been released and outfitted in a bathrobe. His wet clothing sat in a plastic bag next to his chair.

Delroy hesitated. "Am I in some kind of trouble?"

The deputy rubbed his chin thoughtfully as if giving the question real consideration. "A man sleeping in a graveyard in a rainstorm. When he ain't drunk—I know that 'cause I asked the doc about your tox screen, by the way—I figure that man must be in some kind of trouble."

"I wasn't drinking," Delroy said.

"My first assumption was that you'd gotten out there and tied one on," the deputy admitted. "These here times, why they've been purely tryin' on everybody. Seen a lotta good folks these past few days trying to find some way to just get through it all. Drinking seems to be high on the list of some of 'em." He rubbed his hands together and shrugged. "Imagine my surprise when you hadn't been on a bender." He paused. "But you have been in a fight." He sucked on his lower lip, and sharp accusation gleamed in his eyes. "Yes, sir, you have been in a fight."

Caution filled Delroy. The deputy's demeanor was deceiving; all down-home, good old boy one minute, and steel-trap mind the next.

"The reason I know you've been in a fight," the officer continued, "is your face and your hands. Your face, all bruised up like it is, lets me know somebody whomped you pretty good."

Delroy let that pass without comment. The deputy had delivered the statement baldly in an effort to elicit response.

"But your hands—" The deputy crossed over to Delroy and picked up his hands in both of his. Although the deputy was shorter, his hands were as long and a little broader and thicker than Delroy's. The man could have filled gallon paint buckets with those hands. "Yes, sir, your hands tell me you give out about as good as you got."

Looking down at his hands, Delroy saw the split skin and abrasions over his knuckles, and the deep bruising and swelling that accompanied those injuries. As a chaplain and counselor, he'd been trained to look for signs just like those when he suspected men aboard ship had been fighting.

"I was attacked," Delroy said.

The deputy released his hands. "In the graveyard?"

"Aye. Something—" Delroy caught his mistake immediately— "some*one* attacked me."

"You know this someone?"

"No," Delroy answered, and the lie wasn't completely a lie. He thought he knew *what* the creature was, but he had no name for it.

"One or more attackers?"

"One."

The deputy squinted and made an obvious show of sizing Delroy up. "You're a big man. I'd want to think twice about jumping you even in the dark if I was alone. Take a pretty big fella to fight you chest to chest and belt buckle to belt buckle."

"I don't know what to tell you."

"I saw your hands when I checked you into the hospital," the deputy said. "Had a couple things to do here in town, so I went back out to the cemetery. Saw a tore-up piece of ground where it looked like two bulls had been fighting; it hadn't quite washed away in the rain. That was near your son's grave."

Delroy nodded. "That was where it happened."

"I really went out there expecting to find a body. Surprised me when there wasn't one."

"Whoever did it walked away." *Or vanished*, Delroy silently amended.

"You don't know who did it?"

"No."

"You see that person again, you think you'd recognize him?"

"No." And that was the truth. Every time Delroy saw the creature it looked a little different. He also knew it could look human if it wanted to. In fact, he suddenly realized that the creature could look like a deputy sheriff if it wanted to.

"Too bad. I hate unanswered questions. They tend to stick in my mind and I worry at 'em like a dog with a bone. One thing I found out, though: most questions usually solve themselves sooner or later. You just gotta keep your eyes open to see it happen."

Delroy pulled his bathrobe a little tighter and wished that the hospital had provided him shoes. His own were as soaked as his clothes. Despite being dry now, he still felt cold.

The deputy grinned and indicated the bathrobe. "How you like the hospitality?"

"I don't have any clothes," Delroy said, "except for the wet ones." He kicked the bag containing the sodden mess at the side of his chair. "I've been thinking about putting these back on, but I was hoping to find a laundry nearby. I guess I left my duffel."

"I've got your duffel out in my cruiser," the deputy said. "I saw it and took it with me. Figured you wasn't going but to one place after the doc cleared you: the Crossbar Hotel. I give you your clothes earlier, why you mighta gotten all dressed up and cut outta here before I had a chance to figure out what was what."

Delroy didn't know how he felt about that. In all his life, he'd never been arrested. "Am I going to be arrested?"

The question upped the interest of many of the nearby onlookers. A few of them started whispering to each other, their attention diverted from the televisions in two corners of the room.

"Nah," the deputy replied, shaking his head. "I'm not gonna arrest you. Just wanted to make sure you were all right, return your duffel to you, see if you'd come clean about the fight, and see what your plans were."

"Plans?" Delroy frowned. He hadn't made any plans past reaching the cemetery.

"Yeah," the deputy said. "What you plan on doing after you suit up in some of those clothes I'm gonna bring you?"

"I—" Delroy hesitated and decided to go with the truth. "I don't have any plans."

The deputy looked squarely at Delroy and nodded. "Kind of figured that. Lying in the graveyard like you was, you didn't look like a man that had planned his every move. You got anybody here in town you know?"

Delroy immediately thought of Glenda. But he didn't know if his wife—or ex-wife, as the case might be—was still in Marbury. She might have been taken in the Rapture.

No, not might *have been,* Delroy told himself. *She's gone. She's up there. She's up there right now with Terrence.* He hoped that he was right, and was instantly ashamed that he didn't simply believe that.

"No," Delroy said. "Nobody."

The deputy thought for a moment, took his glasses off, cleaned them, and put them back on. "The floor nurse said she recognized your name."

Delroy didn't say anything. Knowing that people might know who he was didn't sit well. The ones who knew him also knew that he'd quit coming back home after Terrence was killed and had more or less abandoned his family. He felt shamed about that.

"She told me your daddy used to be a preacher around here," the deputy said. "You bein' a chaplain and all, well I guess you followed in his footsteps."

"On my best day," Delroy stated, "I was never the man or the preacher that my father was." He knew that was true.

The deputy nodded and looked like he didn't know what to say.

"I've got money, Deputy," Delroy said. "Once you get me my clothes, I'll get out of here and find a hotel." After that, he had no clue about what to do.

"Thought you might do something else before you did that," the officer said.

"What's that?"

"Buy me breakfast," the deputy said. "After all, I saved your life out there. Should be worth at least a stake in a breakfast. I figure you gotta be hungry and you probably don't know the best place to eat at in Marbury if you ain't been here for a while. It's Hazel's, of course. Probably was around even back in your day."

"Yes, it was," Delroy admitted, surprised at how comforting that information was. His father had taken him there as a boy, and he'd gone there on Saturday mornings with Glenda when he was on leave before they did their weekly shopping down at the farmer's market and Werther's IGA.

"Well, then," the deputy said, "I gotta admit if you knew about Hazel's then, you'd have probably found it on your own. But if you weren't buying me breakfast, why then you'd have been without company, wouldn't you?"

Delroy didn't feel like company, but he didn't feel right about rejecting the deputy's offer.

"Don't go and be thinking about it so much," the officer said with an honest smile. "I'm a cheap date. You can afford me."

Despite the sadness and melancholy that weighed within him,

Delroy couldn't help but feel a little amused at the big man. "What's your name, Deputy? I didn't get the chance to go through your wallet."

"Oh, it wouldn'ta done you any good," the deputy replied. "My wife goes through it regular enough for the both of you." He stuck out a big, freckled hand. "Name's Purcell. Walter Purcell."

Delroy took the man's hand and felt the man's strength again. "All right then, Walter, I'll treat you to breakfast."

"Well, you should," Walter said. "Getting off pretty cheap for having your life saved." He sounded tough and serious, but he winked. "Well, what're you standing around for?"

Delroy gestured at the bathrobe. "My clothes."

"Hazel won't mind the bathrobe," Walter assured him. Then held his hands up. "I'm just joshing you. I'll be right back with your duffel." He turned and was gone.

Delroy watched the deputy go, wondering what he was letting himself in for by agreeing to have breakfast with the man. If Deputy Purcell hadn't insisted on breakfast, Delroy knew he wouldn't have eaten. He was also certain Walter knew that.

❀   ❀   ❀

OneWorld NewsNet Corporate Offices
Bucharest, Romania
Local Time 1251 Hours

In Radu Stolojan's office, the computer twittered.

The sound drew the producer's attention at once. Only one person had access to the videophone capabilities of the computer. He leaned forward and tapped his security code to answer the call.

The screen opened in a rushed swirling oval, revealing Nicolae Carpathia standing before a full-length mirror in an expensive hotel room. The Romanian president adjusted his tie.

"Good afternoon, Radu," Carpathia said in his calm baritone.

"Good morning, President Carpathia." Stolojan knew it was still early in New York City.

Carpathia turned toward the PC cam and smiled. "You can call me Nicolae. We are friends, after all."

"I know," Stolojan said. But he would never, in all his life, call the Romanian president anything but Mr. Carpathia. "I trust you had a safe flight."

"Yes. Things are going very well here. I have been invited to speak to the General Assembly of the United Nations this afternoon."

"I'll make sure OneWorld reporters are in the audience." Stolojan had been informed that was the plan, but this was the first word of confirmation.

"Thank you, Radu, but no special effort will be required. The press and publicity have already been taken care of." Carpathia took a moment and reconsidered. "Of course, we should have at least a few of our people here."

"They will be."

"But that is not why I called you."

Fear thrummed through Stolojan. In an eye blink Nicolae Carpathia had plucked him as a youth from the squalor and degradation of the alleys, raising and transforming him into a man of means. In even less time, Stolojan knew that Carpathia could crush him, break him down to nothing. And that would only be if Carpathia bothered to let him live.

"It appears," Carpathia said, "that we have another problem."

Stolojan swallowed hard. The taste of sour bile filled his mouth.

"Someone is apparently trying to access Alexander Cody's files at the offices there," Carpathia said.

Stolojan's first impulse was to ask Carpathia if he was certain. How could anyone know more about the operation going on inside the OneWorld building than he did? After all, he had all the security cameras and computer firewalls in place.

With a sick, sinking feeling, Stolojan knew that the only way Carpathia could have known was by having his own set of spies within the OneWorld NewsNet offices. Someone to watch the watchers.

"I believe you know who it might be," Carpathia went on with calm confidence.

"Lizuca Carutasu," Stolojan answered. There was no doubt in his mind, but he wished desperately to know how Carpathia knew that.

"Please check." Carpathia waited patiently.

Stolojan opened another window on the computer monitor and checked for off-site transmissions linked to the video archives that Lizuca accessed. He hadn't designed the software that allowed him to track the query back to its source, but he knew how to use it.

He also realized that if Carpathia had the capability to know that the archive files were being accessed from an outside source, he could have ordered the search done by whoever had given him the information. Stolojan took solace in that. If Carpathia meant him any ill will, he would have pointed out the mistake and the fact that he had taken care of it himself.

Only seconds later, the address of the IP searching through the video archives appeared on the computer screen. It was listed as Bites and Bytes, a cybercafé where computers, time, and access to the Internet could be rented for an hourly fee.

Stolojan opened another window and pulled up employee files. He read Lizuca Carutasu's address and found that the cybercafé was only blocks from the apartment where she lived with her mother and sisters.

"I can't confirm that it's her," Stolojan said. "But she lives near there and she is off."

"Then you should get someone over there," Carpathia suggested.

"Yes, sir." Working in the open window, Stolojan accessed employee files and took out a current picture of Lizuca Carutasu. He attached it to another file, then hesitated. "How do you want this handled, President Carpathia?"

The calm expression remained on Carpathia's handsome face. "For the moment, Alexander Cody is an important resource to me. Through him I have a more direct access to Captain Remington and the soldiers he controls. I do not want Agent Cody compromised in any way. Nor will I suffer betrayal."

"I understand." Stolojan entered an e-mail address and sent the message. He didn't know the name of the man who would receive the message, but he knew the results. Over the years, Stolojan had used the man twice before, and both times he had sent wreaths to the funerals from the corporation's petty cash. "There is a problem, though."

"Yes."

"I believe Miss Carutasu is working at Danielle Vinchenzo's request."

"She gave Miss Carutasu the picture."

Stolojan nodded.

"Why was I not informed?"

"I believed I had handled it by telling Miss Carutasu not to investigate the picture and by sending her home."

Carpathia thought for a moment. "Evidently Danielle saw Agent Cody in Sanliurfa."

Stolojan didn't know everything that Carpathia had going on in the Turkish city now under siege by the Syrians, but he knew that Cody was there and Captain Remington of the American Rangers was there.

Stolojan also knew that Carpathia had given use of the OneWorld NewsNet satellites to Remington during the border clash four days ago. And that preparations were being made now to offer them again.

"I will have to rethink the Danielle Vinchenzo situation, Radu," Carpathia said. "Until then, keep me posted on this assignment."

"I will."

Carpathia said good-bye, then ended the connection.

Stolojan watched as the open window on the monitor screen collapsed. He sat back in his chair and trembled. Few people knew that Nicolae Carpathia had a dark side to him. Over the years while working as first his aide, then as producer for the news service, Stolojan had seen it. People died when Carpathia wished them dead, and usually he had to do no more than mention it.

But no one, Stolojan felt certain, even those who had seen that dark side, knew exactly how bad things could get. They would, though, and Stolojan wanted to make sure he stayed in Carpathia's good graces.

✹   ✹   ✹

Bites and Bytes Cybercafé
Bucharest, Romania
Local Time 1303 Hours

Sitting hunched over one of the small tables that filled the specialty café, Lizuca Carutasu tore off small bites of her grilled-Gouda-and-broccoli-on-raisin-bread sandwich. She munched contentedly and sipped her raspberry tea.

The sandwich, like the computer time, was an extravagance. The cybercafé's food prices were high, but most people in Bucharest did not own computers. A lot of them did, however, own curiosity about the Internet and were willing to pay for the chance to learn about it.

All of the tables were taken. Lizuca had experienced a two-hour wait before one of the computers freed up. The décor was simple: garish neon lights twisted into a circuitry pattern and posters of American movies featuring cutting-edge computer technology. *The Matrix* shared space with *Johnny Mnemonic* and all three Terminator movies. Models of spacecraft, past and present, hung from the ceiling from thin monofilaments.

Before she'd gotten the job at OneWorld NewsNet, Lizuca had saved her tips from serving and some of each paycheck as a maid in one of the big chain hotels to spend time on the computers. She'd known she was preparing herself for another job and that it would take the skills she learned while surfing the Internet to get that job. But she'd also known that her mother would have scolded her for being so foolish with her money all the same. There were too many mouths to feed, and the computer time would have been viewed as a waste.

At the time, Lizuca had felt guilty about her once-a-week indulgence. She'd only allowed herself two hours a week. Any more than that and the guilt would have been too much to bear.

She watched the search function she was using as it crawled through OneWorld NewsNet's video and stills archives. If Danielle thought that a picture or information about the man in the photograph she'd sent might exist there, Lizuca was willing to bet that it did.

She took another small bite of the sandwich, relishing the smoky taste of the grilled Gouda cheese. She tried not to feel guilty, but she did. Not only could she not afford to eat like this, she couldn't afford the high calories either. Her mother would be all over her about her spending habits as well as her chances of some day attracting a husband.

Lizuca wanted to go to the United States. She'd seen so much of the country in the films she watched. She thought that it must be wonderful to live there, to have so many opportunities for a career, for friends, and—yes—for a husband. Personally, she preferred the lean-hipped young men in the American jeans commercials.

Working with Danielle Vinchenzo, Lizuca felt certain, would provide her with that chance. That was why she was willing to undertake the risks she was now taking.

The program she used now was a variant on a hacker's packet sniffer. The utility was like a bloodhound, searching for bytes that corresponded with the bytes in the digital picture from Danielle.

Staring at the screen, Lizuca suddenly became aware of a figure standing just over her shoulder. Reflected in the computer monitor's screen, the man wore a black hoodie and wind pants. He kept his hands tucked in the front pocket of the hoodie.

Fear rattled through Lizuca, freezing her in place like a mouse in an owl's gaze. She didn't know what had brought the fear on, but the feeling was a primeval thing that wouldn't be denied.

Wraparound sunglasses hid the man's eyes under the shadow of the hoodie, but his lower face was revealed enough so that she was certain he was handsome and that he was someone she had never met before.

"Lizuca Carutasu," he said softly.

Unable to speak, Lizuca turned to face him. Her heart hammered in her chest. What was it about the man that made her so afraid? She didn't know.

Casually, he took his left hand from the hoodie pocket and flipped his hand over. Lizuca saw a picture inside a plastic pocket protector wrapped around his wrist. It was a copy of the one she wore on her OneWorld NewsNet ID every day. There was only one place he could have gotten that picture.

Adrenaline flooded Lizuca's body even before the man drew the silenced pistol from his hoodie with his other hand. She stood and shoved herself out into the aisle between the tables, knocking over drinks and spilling food trays as she went.

Turning the corner at the end of the counter, Lizuca aimed herself at the door to the kitchen area, thinking she might at least have a chance if she could only make it to the alley.

The other café patrons must have noticed the man with the pistol then because they all yelled and screamed and started to scatter as he ran after her in a long, easy stride. He moved confidently, casually, like chasing someone down to kill was something he did every day.

The exit door had a shiny metal surface, so Lizuca saw herself running toward it. She also saw the elongated form of the man standing behind her, drawing the silencer-equipped pistol up smooth and steady. She reached for the door, mewling in fear.

Then something slammed into the back of her neck. Bright red blood sprinkled the metal surface of the door. She couldn't breathe and her legs turned leaden. She managed one more step, then a blow caught her in the back of the head and hurled her face first into the door. Surprisingly, she felt no pain, but she had no strength left either.

Two more blows struck her as she slid toward the floor. She was gone before her body hit the tiles.

United States 75th Army Rangers Temporary Post
Sanliurfa, Turkey
Local Time 1324 Hours

The fire raged out of control, twisting through the guts of the building near Sanliurfa's downtown sector. Flames licked outside broken windows like the tongues of maddened and hungry beasts knowing they were on the verge of breaking out of the cage that held them. Black smoke stained the sky, looking like loose stitches in a blue funeral shroud.

As the private driving the Hummer rolled the vehicle to a stop, Goose gazed up at the four-story structure and tried not to think about what it must be like for the people trapped inside the building. He clambered out of the Hummer, favoring his injured knee, and shouldered the M-4A1 automatically.

The day had turned hot after the cool of the night. Perspiration beneath the Kevlar-lined helmet crawled through Goose's hair and threaded down his neck. His BDU was sodden and caked with dirt.

"Corporal," Goose called out.

The corporal turned and looked at Goose. Wide-eyed in youth and green in experience, the young man looked hesitant. "First Sergeant, I'm Corporal Robinson."

Goose limped over to the group of soldiers standing at the front of the building. "What's the sit-rep?"

"First Sergeant, there are wounded trapped inside on the top floor. Could be the third floor as well. We don't know."

"Who?"

"Some civilians. Maybe a couple soldiers. Maybe a couple of our guys."

"How do you know that?" Goose scanned the windows and felt helpless. Anyone who was currently in the building obviously didn't stand much of a chance.

The lower floor consisted of shops. Fragments of the front plate-glass window advertised the existence of a restaurant in English, Turkish, and French. The three upper floors looked like offices, but now all of them were a heaped jumble of broken rock and mortar.

"We've been in touch with those people, First Sergeant." Corporal Robinson tapped his helmet. "Picked it up as radio bleed-over. Had my communications guy run it down because we thought we heard voices." He paused. "They weren't talking English. Not at first."

"What were they speaking?"

"I don't know, First Sergeant. But they're talking English now." The corporal verified the signal frequency.

Goose changed the frequency on his headset. He felt bone tired, then realized he was way past that because he was starting to get the false second wind that, for him, was the true sign of approaching exhaustion.

" . . . got to help us," a man with a heavy accent pleaded. "God, grant us mercy, you can't just leave us in here to die. Something has fallen against the door. We cannot get out. We're trapped. We—" The voice ended in a choking sob that Goose attributed to the smoke that filled the building.

Somewhere in the background of the radio transmission a girl screamed.

"I beg you," the man continued. "My wife and children are in here with me. Please. You can't just ignore our pleas."

Goose switched the frequency off. He didn't need to listen. He stared at the building grimly.

"First Sergeant," the corporal said.

"Did you send for a fire-rescue team?" Goose asked.

"Yes. They said they're on their way."

"When?"

"Couldn't have been more than a minute before I radioed you."

Goose had been in between, moving from one spot of havoc and disaster to the next when the call came in. He came to this site because lives were at stake. "Have your com get hold of them and tell them that I'm here and we need them now."

Robinson spoke rapidly.

"Have com stay in touch with the guy on the radio inside the building," Goose said. "Find out if he's familiar with the building. We may need some directions." He thought the op through, his mind sluggish with too much happening too fast. An idea occurred to him, but he waited until the corporal stopped speaking. "Where did the guy inside get a radio?"

"It's a shortwave set."

"Can we isolate where the signal is coming from?"

"Already tried that, First Sergeant. Need another receiving unit to make that happen. We're on a specialized frequency being broadcast out of Command. The triangulation isn't possible through the headset units." The corporal hesitated. "Not quick enough, anyway. If we had a full sat array we could work out of, that would be a different story." He pointed his chin back over Goose's shoulder. "Rescue unit's here."

Turning, Goose spotted the military fire-suppression truck rounding the corner and heading for the building. Soldiers in Nomex coveralls clung to the sides. The 75th had come prepared for their bit in helping guard the Turkish-Syrian border.

A lanky corporal crawled out of the passenger side before the big truck jerked to a complete stop. He waved and yelled to his squad, getting them up and moving. They pulled hoses from the rig and started making connections.

"First Sergeant," the rescue squad leader greeted. He looked worn and haggard. A second-degree burn covered the left side of his face. Clear blisters bubbled up from the reddened skin. His eyebrows and eyelashes were burned off. "I'm Corporal Timmons."

"Corporal," Goose replied, studying the burn, "are you sure you're up to this?"

Timmons met Goose's look with one of his own. "Yes, First Sergeant. We've just had a tough night of it. Don't let the look fool you. We look ragged but we're not running ragged. We're still up and we're still able." He glanced at the building. "What have you got for us?"

"Late detonation of a tank or a mortar round," Robinson answered. "Went off less than five minutes ago. I called as soon as we confirmed the fire. I held my men back because most of them aren't trained in that kind of SAR."

Goose knew Robinson had done the right thing under the circumstances. Search and rescue was a specialized field. That was especially true in a building in the middle of an active war zone.

"That delay didn't cause all that damage," Timmons responded.

"Negative," Robinson responded. "That building was hit several times during the initial attack this morning."

"Been a long time since then."

"I know. The man we're in contact with said that he and his family live there. They stayed in the basement during the attack and didn't come back up until they thought it was safe."

"Safe?" Timmons said in disbelief.

"They were getting out and had just finished packing when the round went off about five minutes ago. They know other people were killed. They listened to some of them die."

"And they didn't notice an artillery round sitting there waiting to go off?" Timmons shook his head.

"Civilians," Robinson explained. "These people weren't trained for what's happened to them in the last few days. Or for what's going to happen to them next."

Goose felt antsy and ready to get on with it, but he knew Timmons needed the answers to the questions he was asking. He was also aware that the families might only have minutes left before fire or smoke inhalation took them. Or before another unexploded shell went off. Staying active helped him keep his mind off the rift growing between Cal Remington and himself, and off the loss of Chris.

"If there was one round in there," Timmons said, "there might be more."

For a moment Goose thought the man might be looking for a way to deny the rescue.

"But if it wasn't dangerous," Timmons said with a painful grin, "everybody'd want to work SAR." He took an oxygen tank and mask from one of his crew and pulled them on with practiced skill, then told them the frequency his team would operate on while inside the burning structure. "We can't save the building, First Sergeant. We're all but out of water. But we'll get those people out of there."

"Good luck," Goose said.

The fire-rescue corporal gave Goose a thumbs-up and headed into the building carrying a fire axe.

The experts were in charge here now. All Goose could do was wait. Not wanting to think about the fiery paths the men trod inside the burning wreck or the family they might not reach in time, Goose looked for some quick distraction.

He tuned his headset to the general frequency and listened to the reports pouring into Command. Ranger recon teams worked to update the city's damage and losses sector by sector, combining their resources with those of the Turkish and U.N. forces.

The death toll and property loss were staggering. Reporters covered a lot of the action, but even the violence that had once again swept over Sanliurfa was eclipsed by the globalwide disappearances.

One of the newest stories getting a lot of play on the news was about a United Nations address by Romanian President Nicolae Carpathia. He was the same man who had cut off U.S. military access to his communications satellite while keeping OneWorld NewsNet in place in the city.

Goose had dismissed the stories. Carpathia was a politician; he was just seizing headlines the way politicians did to carry out their own agenda. All that remained was to see what his agenda was.

Although several of the reporters seemed to think the U.N. address was a big deal due to the present circumstances around the world, Goose had listened politely when it was mentioned, then gotten on with his recon details. Whatever Carpathia was doing, it couldn't touch him. He still didn't even know if he was getting out of his present assignment alive.

Or with a career intact.

Goose told himself that he was overreacting to the confrontation with Remington. But at the same time, subconsciously, he knew he was afraid that the captain was going to step over a line. Cal Remington wasn't a man who graciously lost an argument or a battle. Whatever steps the captain took against the CIA, if there were repercussions, they would definitely spill over onto his first sergeant.

Clicking back into the rescue frequency, Goose listened as Timmons and his team relayed what they encountered. Robinson's com gave them information he was able to get from the trapped family. They were on the fourth floor in the southeast corner.

"Lotta glad-to-see-yas, Search Twenty-Two," the com operator said. "Guy also tells me there may be people in the basement who didn't get clear."

"We'll check it out," Robinson said in a steady, confident voice. "Get me directions to the basement."

Goose shifted his weight in an attempt to ease some of the throbbing in his knee. He took his canteen from his hip and drank. In the heat, a soldier was supposed to drink whenever he could, as long as water rations were good, to remain hydrated. Those were standing orders.

"Com," one of Timmons's SAR men radioed back, "affirmative on the basement-door find. Got a heap of debris blocking the way."

"Six, this is One," Timmons said over the com. "Did you get the fire contained in that area?"

"Affirmative, One. We've got the fire here contained, but it's still raining down on us." The man's voice sounded strained and alien through the oxygen mask.

"We passed up the ignition point on the second floor, Six," Robinson replied. "You guys are under the hot spot. Keep an eye on the roof. It could all come down on you."

Goose watched the building burn and hated the useless feeling he had simply standing here. He needed to be helping, to be doing something to bring life out of death. He couldn't remember how many dead bodies he'd looked at so far, but he knew he'd never forget their faces. A number of teens, citizens of the city as well as sons and daughters of vacationers, had been among the dead. Thank God there were no children.

And that one small realization, that the children had been spared this massacre, rocked Goose. God loved children. Bill Townsend had always told him that. After Chris had been born, news about kids getting killed or hurt had hit Goose differently, on a more personal level. When one of the soldiers in his unit had lost a son to cancer, Goose had struggled to accept the death. In his mind, that could have been Chris. Children weren't supposed to die, but they did. The world was filled with monsters, accidents, and diseases.

And he had brought a child into that war zone.

When Goose had turned overprotective, Megan asked Bill what she should do. Bill had interceded and talked to Goose about God then. Goose had listened, tried to understand that children who died were admitted to heaven unconditionally.

The thought of losing Chris had gradually waned. Hearing Bill's convictions helped Goose, as his advice and counsel always had. Goose missed his friend now. Everything that was going on would have been a little easier, a little more understandable, if Bill hadn't . . . left.

That one word stirred up anger in Goose that he really didn't want, need, or mean. Bill *had* left. Whether or not he intended to, whether or not he had been given a choice, he'd left.

"Tango Fourteen Leader, this is Nine," a man's excited voice called over the headset.

"You've got Tango Fourteen Leader," Robinson said, automatically turning to where he had posted his squad member.

"I got movement up on the rooftops," the soldier said. "To the west, across from the target building."

Immediately, Goose turned to the west, raising his hand to shade his eyes from the sun. He spotted a man rising from the rooftop and fitting a long tube to his shoulder.

Recognizing the RPG-7 rocket launcher from years of experience with them, Goose shouted, "Get down! That's a hostile!"

A puff of smoke jetted from the back of the RPG-7. Less than a heartbeat later, the missile struck the building and the payload exploded. By that time, another figure popped up on another rooftop and fired another rocket.

Feeling helpless, knowing the combined might of the Rangers, marines, U.N. forces, and Turkish army hadn't been able to keep out small but determined detachments of enemies, Goose watched as the second rocket struck the target. Further weakened, the building sagged and started collapsing in on itself.

※　※　※

OneWorld NewsNet Mobile Platform
Sanliurfa, Turkey
Local Time 1329 Hours

Danielle worked standing up, getting her thoughts down on a yellow legal pad. When things got too crazy or she got too tired to think straight, she worked with paper and a pencil.

Cezar rummaged through the refrigerator and complained about the lack of choices. "You know," he said, finally selecting frozen pizza and moving toward the microwave, "there are restaurants open. Good restaurants with good food."

There were, Danielle knew. She'd done interviews with some of the people who had stayed behind to run their businesses. The few who had stayed told her that if they left their businesses, the family would lose everything. It was better, they said, to stay and believe in the Turkish army and their friends, the Americans, and to pray that they could turn the Syrian war machines back as they had been doing.

"Those restaurants," Gorca said from the corner, where he worked on one of the stalk microphones Danielle used when she needed both hands free, "are run by madmen."

"The hopefuls," Cezar argued. "They know the city will be held."

From everything she'd seen, Danielle didn't believe that for a minute. Sanliurfa was doomed to become a way station on the Syrian army's march into the country. It wasn't going to be a scenic one, though.

"Would you really want to eat anything a madman has prepared?" Gorca challenged. He was irritable because Cezar had slept and he hadn't been able to. Gorca had bemoaned that fact while watching the younger man sleep earlier, and Danielle had echoed the sentiments. Cezar's ability to sleep and forget about the war bordered on the inhuman.

"Now—" Cezar held up the microwaved pizza, slipping it from hand to hand to combat the heat—"I am eating this cardboard confection, you know. I tell you, frozen pizza—now *that* is a madman's creation. They should be made fresh, piled high with—"

"Miss Vinchenzo," Bogasieru called from the bank of monitors.

Shifting, grateful for the distraction because listening to Cezar and Gorca argue over anything—which they did frequently, especially over *Star Trek* episodes—tended to give her headaches, Danielle joined Bogasieru.

"You asked me to keep you apprised of any news concerning First Sergeant Gander," Bogasieru said.

Since the first sergeant is pretty much the anchor I'm doing these stories around, yeah. But Danielle didn't say that. She peered at the monitors. At present, OneWorld NewsNet was recycling pieces that had been edited down for brevity. She wasn't supposed to go live again for a couple hours, when Remington had condescended to give the media a brief interview.

"Where is he?" she asked.

Bogasieru pointed to one of the screens on the lower right. "Here."

As Danielle watched, she spotted the first sergeant kneeling beside a Hummer and bringing his assault rifle to his shoulder. In front of him, an explosion struck a burning building, igniting a dust cloud and sending large chunks of debris flying. The building buckled, caving in like a fighter past his prime who'd taken one punch too many.

"Where is that?" Danielle asked.

Bogasieru didn't answer, just tapped on his keyboard. The monitor beside the one showing the attack suddenly opened on a gridded map of the city.

"We have been tracing the actions of the other media groups in the city," Bogasieru said, "using the satellite array. I'll know the location in just a moment."

Yellow horizontal and vertical lines started coming together on the monitor. The gridded map of Sanliurfa magnified as the double sets of lines closed.

Danielle's sat-phone rang. Thinking it was Stolojan calling to make sure she was on the story, she scooped the phone from her hip and said, "I'm on it."

"Hello?"

The feminine voice startled Danielle, but she watched the action on the screen as the Rangers went into action. First Sergeant Gander returned fire from cover of the Hummer.

"Who is this?" Danielle asked.

"My name is Simona. I am sister to Lizuca."

From the distraught tone in the young woman's voice, Danielle knew something was wrong.

"Forgive my call," Simona said. "I got your number from my mother, yes? She could no make the phone call. Not after what happened to Lizuca."

A chill ghosted through Danielle. "What happened to Lizuca?"

The young woman's voice broke and she cried. When she spoke, her voice got higher and higher till it was squeaking at the end. "Poor Lizuca. My poor sister. She is *murder!*"

The announcement froze Danielle's brain. She thought she couldn't have heard what she'd just heard. "What happened?"

Simona cried for a time.

Danielle watched the attack on the monitor, her attention torn and the need to do something almost overwhelming.

"Lizuca," Simona said in a halting voice, "she is go to café, yes? To get computer information for you as she say. While she there, a man, he come up to her." She cried softly, and Danielle heard the keening of an older woman in the background. "This man, he say her name; then he shoot her."

Stunned, Danielle didn't know what to say. Tears welled up in her eyes.

"I must go now," Simona said. "We have many things to do to prepare for my sister funeral, yes?"

A thousand questions hammered at Danielle's brain. "What happened to the man who shot Lizuca?"

"He get away. He have gun. No one stop him."

"Was he identified?"

Lizuca's mother called out. The only thing Danielle recognized was Simona's name.

Simona answered rapidly in her native language. "I must go, Miss Vinchenzo, yes?" Simona said. "My mother, she needs me."

"Of course," Danielle said. "Did they identify the man who shot Lizuca?"

"No. That man, he get away. No catch. No identify. No find. The police, they still looking. I must go take care of my mother."

"If there's anything I can do," Danielle offered.

"Pray for us," Simona suggested.

The phone clicked dead in Danielle's ear.

Bogasieru looked up at her. "I have the location." He handed her a computer printout with directions to the building where the Rangers were under attack.

Danielle took yellow, lined paper, then wrote Lizuca Carutasu's name on a section of it. She gave the paper to Bogasieru.

"This woman was just murdered in Bucharest at a café," Danielle said. "I want you to find out as much information about the shooting as you can."

Bogasieru frowned at the piece of paper. "Bucharest is not part of our assignment, Miss Vinchenzo."

Danielle held on to her anger and pain as she shrugged into her gear. She looked at the man. "Find. Out."

Bogasieru held her gaze for only a moment. Then he dropped his eyes. "Of course." He swiveled back to the computers.

Looking at Cezar and Gorca, who had already grabbed their gear and didn't look happy as they stared at the monitor over Bogasieru's shoulder, Danielle said, "Let's roll."

"I'm driving," Cezar said.

"No," Gorca said with quiet but firm authority. "I will drive."

By the time they got outside to the Jeep carrying OneWorld NewsNet identification plastered all over it and flying from a twenty-foot whip antenna, Danielle had already slid behind the steering wheel. Cezar hurried around to the passenger side while Gorca hoisted himself onto the rear deck with deep resignation.

Danielle reached under the seat for the keys and turned the engine over. As she drove, she tried to sort through her thoughts and her guilt. It wasn't working.

What was that unidentified CIA section chief hiding that called for the murder of a young woman in Bucharest? What did OneWorld NewsNet have in its corporate files that the CIA agent would be willing to kill over?

She didn't know, but she was determined to find out. Whatever the information was, Lizuca Carutasu had gotten killed because she'd tried to find out who the CIA man was.

And Danielle knew she had put the young woman in harm's way. Licuza's death was her fault.

❋   ❋   ❋

United States 75th Army Rangers Temporary Post
Sanliurfa, Turkey
Local Time 1335 Hours

"Air support," Goose called over the headset as he stripped an empty magazine from his M-4A1 and shoved a fresh one home. "This is Phoenix Leader. Do you copy?"

"Affirmative, Phoenix Leader," the crisp voice responded. "We are en route to your twenty."

Shoving himself back up behind the Hummer, Goose pulled his assault rifle to his shoulder and took aim at one of the three buildings their attackers held. He pulled the trigger, spacing three-round bursts across the rooftop, chewing through the thirty-round magazine in seconds.

So far, they hadn't identified their attackers. They wore street clothes and burnooses, but so did a lot of Sanliurfa's citizens and some of the city's visitors. But they came equipped with rocket launchers and assault rifles.

During the morning, at other spots throughout the city, the military forces had been attacked by Syrian soldiers caught behind the lines as well as PKK members and other terrorists who had elected to serve whatever convictions drove them. As paranoid as the soldiers defending the city were, the strategy was probably to get the armies firing at shadows. With the division of Turkish, American, and European soldiers, a few cases of friendly fire because of itchy trigger fingers could go a long way to breaking up the partnership they'd been forced to undertake.

Goose knew the Turkish military was still having problems with the Rangers running the joint op. The U.N. forces had their problems, too, but the United States Army still maintained the largest and most heavily equipped firepower and tech in the world. The general consensus was to let the U.S. try to get all of their soldiers home.

The downside was that the U.S. was going to be blamed for every death that occurred in Sanliurfa, and the nation's critics were going to have a field day. If a U.S. soldier fell, it would be because the U.S. military had poor planning. If a U.N. or Turkish soldier fell, the loss would be attributed to a lack of coordination or because the U.S. military was following personal interest. Every citizen who died would be because the U.S. chose to insert itself into every international confrontation that came along.

The Whiskey Cobra gunship soared through the air, looking like a deadly dragonfly. But a dragonfly never came equipped with 20mm cannon, LAU-68 rocket pods, Hellfire antitank missiles, antipersonnel bombs, and a 30mm chain gun mounted underneath the carriage.

Beside Goose, Corporal Robinson smiled and said, "Those attackers are definitely in a world of hurt. They just don't know it yet."

Goose silently agreed. He shoved a fresh magazine home and glanced toward the burning building. Six warheads had slammed into the structure during the last minute and a half. The Rangers had succeeded in keeping some of their attackers pinned down. Teams were already approaching the buildings where the hostiles had taken up positions on the rooftops as well as inside the rooms.

"This is Search Twenty-Two," a young man called over the headset. He sounded slightly panicked. "This is Search Twenty-Two."

"Tango Fourteen Leader reads you, Search Twenty-Two," Robinson responded.

"My team is down. My corporal is down. We've got wounded, and we're part of them now."

"Understood," Robinson said, looking back over the bullet-riddled Hummer. "Tango Fourteen is coming to assist."

The marine aircraft maneuvered as if by magic, approaching at speed then hovering in place like a freeze frame on a DVD player. The 30mm chain gun opened up at once, hammering rounds across the rooftops and through stone walls, chewing holes through in rapid succession. The wicked and deadly fire made Swiss cheese of the buildings. The basso booming of the rounds detonating filled the air.

"Tango Fourteen, this brief intermission has been brought to you courtesy of the United States Marine Corps," the helicopter pilot said. "You're now free to move around your war zone."

"Affirmative, Rattler," Goose radioed back. "Thanks for the assist."

"Take care of your team, Phoenix Leader. We're gonna fly standby till you get your op clean and green. We'll control the horizontal and the vertical."

Goose ran toward the burning building, dividing the rescue team up into squads as he moved. The structure had three points of egress on the first floor. They used them all, swarming up the two stairwells at either end and going downstairs. The pile of debris still blocked the doors leading to the basement, where a dozen people had taken refuge.

The rocket blasts had scattered and damaged the SAR team, and the time allowed by the attack had enabled the fire more time to feed. The oppressive heat filled the building and twisted the black smoke before the acrid clouds found their way out.

Goose stayed low to the ground as he moved, but the position put increased strain on his bad knee. He willed himself to keep going in spite of the cold sweat that ran down his face and back.

The com op called out the locations in the burning structure, adding to and changing the intel as the teams worked through the scene.

Goose tripped over a dead body in the third-floor hall and sprawled. Close up, even though his eyes teared constantly, he saw that the corpse was one of the SAR team. A rocket blast had torn him nearly in half.

Help those you can help, Goose reminded himself. *You can't do anything for this boy.* He pushed his feelings into a nice, tight box, then set about stripping the SAR member's oxygen tank from his body. The oxygen helped, as did the mask, although he couldn't see any better than he had before.

Only a few steps ahead, Goose found the door that the dead soldier had reported hearing voices and banging behind. A burning section of the ceiling lay in the hallway and blocked the open door with a wall of fire that splashed across the ceiling like an upside-down waterfall.

"There's an old woman in here," a man called. "I can't get her out, and I can't move the blockage. I don't have any tools. Every time I tried to shift it, more of the ceiling came down."

Goose removed his mask so he could be heard better, but regretted it at once as the acrid smoke burned his eyes, throat, and sinus passages. "It's okay," Goose said. "I'm going to get you out." He turned his attention to the blockage and replaced the oxygen mask.

Glancing back at the dead SAR soldier, Goose spotted the fireman's axe halfway hidden under the body. He took the axe, positioned himself, and swung at the blockage as if he were back on his daddy's small farm.

The keen blade chopped into the ceiling section with sharp *thunks* that quivered up Goose's arms. Embers swirled all around him, stinging his arms, his chest, and his ears where the mask didn't cover them.

In seconds, he'd chopped the longest boards in two; then he used the axe to lever the bulk of the debris from the door. Only a few small flames danced on the floor, clinging to the carpet and the wood below. He stomped them out as a figure approached him through the smoke.

"Thanks for your help," the guy said. "I think I could have jumped out the window and made it. I might have broken a leg or two, but I would have survived. I couldn't leave the lady in this room. I knew she was an invalid so I came back for her, but I couldn't get her—"

Staring through the smoke, Goose stared in surprise at the man.

Looking much the worse for wear in smoke-stained clothing, sporting first- and second-degree burns, Icarus stared back at Goose with equal surprise. "You," Icarus said.

"Me," Goose agreed. "Fate seems to have a way of bringing us together."

"It's not fate, Sergeant," Icarus said, glancing over his shoulder at the open window. "I can explain—"

Another rescue worker stepped into the hallway behind Goose, emerging from the smoke.

Before Icarus could move, Goose powered a short right into the man's jaw, rolling all his weight and muscle into the blow. Icarus flew backward and, like his chosen namesake, dropped to the earth. He didn't move.

Goose stepped into the room. An old woman lay on the floor where the air was cleanest. She stared up at him with rheumy eyes and coughed fitfully.

The soldier stepped in behind Goose. He looked at the unconscious man on the floor, then at Goose. "You hit him," the soldier accused. He looked wide-eyed and innocent behind the oxygen mask.

Goose nodded. "He was panicking, Private." He put steel in his voice, showing his rank by tone alone. "Had to quiet him down so we could get him out of here."

"I understand."

"Good," Goose said. "See if you can help the lady. I'll get this one."

The soldier stepped over to the old woman, talked to her briefly, then picked her up in his arms and carried her out of the room.

Bending down, Goose pulled Icarus's deadweight over his shoulder. His knee popped and pain swelled like a balloon inside the joint. He regretted his decision to knock Icarus out at once. Getting back down the stairs was going to hurt.

But the guy wasn't going to pull a vanishing act again. This time they were going to talk.

United States of America
Fort Benning, Georgia
Local Time 0856 Hours

Megan sat in an uncomfortable straight-backed chair in the waiting room to Chaplain Augustus Trimble's office. Trimble was the ranking chaplain at the base, handpicked by General Amos Braddock for the position.

The waiting room was neat and immaculate. A floor-to-ceiling bookcase of pamphlets and Bibles and books occupied one wall. The room was quiet and contained. The heavy wood desk looked like it had been carved from a giant redwood tree and was as imposing as a battleship.

In the hallway, the din of the Joint Services Counseling Center remained constant. Men and women filled with desperate need or panic talked to personnel, pleading for help and understanding. The voices entered the room as a steady undercurrent of noise. All of those people sought help or hope in the face of the current dilemma.

Joint Services saw to financial and medical needs of military personnel and their families, providing planning and counseling and correction when necessary. They also liaised with local-government and law-enforcement bodies in the event of criminal or civil litigation involving members of the post.

But the chaplain's office was there to attend to the post's spiritual needs as well.

Sitting there as she had been for some time, listening to the people talking to the overworked receptionists manning the in-take tables, Megan felt guilty and nervous. She felt guilty because she wasn't work-

ing with the other counselors to take care of the teens left in their care.
The nervousness came from the fact that she was about to approach
Chaplain Trimble on a loaded issue. She had even more guilt because
she felt nervous about even bringing the topic up. She didn't have the
right to question the man's methods, his professionalism, or his faith.

Yet she was prepared to do all of that.

Jenny's talk in the hospital last evening had weighed heavily on
Megan's mind the rest of the night. Despite the good news that Leslie
Hollister was out of immediate danger and was, potentially, on her
way to a full recovery, Megan hadn't rested well. Though the Gander
house was stacked with teens and she was currently sharing her bedroom with some of the girls, Megan felt the absence of her family.

After lying awake for an hour after an imposed curfew, she'd gotten up and retreated to the patio and sat outside with the portable,
battery-powered TV the family used on camping trips. She'd watched
the news, learning little more about the situation in Sanliurfa, Turkey,
where Goose was posted. In the end, her thoughts constantly whirling, she'd found the book about the end times that Jenny had read
and talked about.

Sipping the leftover chicken noodle soup to combat the early
morning chill, Megan had started reading until she finally couldn't
keep her eyes open any longer. She'd gotten three hours sleep, and
she'd dreamed constantly that the teens she was watching over were
lost to the darkness because they didn't know what they were supposed to do now that the world had changed.

When she'd finally sat up in bed, rubbing her eyes and awake at
last, Megan had felt certain she knew what she was supposed to do.
She'd called Joint Services in the hopes of talking to one of the chap-
lains. She'd been surprised when Chaplain Trimble's personal assistant fielded the call and told her that Trimble himself would see her.

Megan had taken the invitation as a good sign. Now, however, after being kept waiting for so long, she was beginning to wonder. Her
cell phone rang and she answered it. "Hello."

"Mrs. Gander?" The voice at the other end of the connection belonged to a young lieutenant named Doug Benbow. Benbow was currently assigned as her legal representative regarding charges of
dereliction of duty in the Gerry Fletcher matter.

"Yes, Lieutenant," Megan replied.

"I thought we had a meeting this morning."

Another wave of guilt washed over Megan. "I'm sorry. We did
have a meeting. I forgot."

"Yes, ma'am," Benbow said politely. "After the night you had last night, I can see how that would happen."

Megan felt uncomfortable. She wasn't prone to forgetting things. Usually she was very organized. "I take it you heard about Leslie Hollister."

Benbow hesitated, then either felt that honesty was the best policy or that he was a weak liar even if he had good intentions. "Yes, ma'am. And I have to tell you, this isn't going to help our situation."

The Boyd Fletcher situation, Megan thought. Boyd Fletcher was the father of Gerry Fletcher, the boy Megan had tried to save from falling from a rooftop the night of the disappearances. Boyd Fletcher had brought the charges forward to the provost marshal's office, and Provost Marshal Frank Marion had filed the documentation against Megan.

"Ma'am," Benbow said, "we had discussed the hope of you maintaining a low profile. At least until we get the hearing out of the way."

"Yes, we did, Lieutenant." Frustration chafed at Megan. "I hadn't planned on Leslie Hollister ending up in the hospital last night either."

Benbow sighed. "Yes, ma'am. I know that. I'm sorry. That's not how I meant that to come out."

Chaplain Trimble's receptionist answered her phone, then looked up at Megan. She covered the mouthpiece. "The chaplain will see you now."

"Thank you," Megan responded, covering her own mouthpiece.

The receptionist was sixty if she was a day, matronly with an edgy professionalism and a no-nonsense approach to doing business. Since she'd stepped into the room, Megan hadn't felt an ounce of warmth from the woman.

"I've got to go, Lieutenant," Megan said.

"Mrs. Gander, we really need to talk. There are some things you need to know. There have been some . . . changes in how our situation is working out." The lieutenant's tone was ominous, and he clearly didn't sound happy.

A look of cold irritation filled the receptionist's gaze. She tapped her pencil and glanced at her watch. "Mrs. Gander, Chaplain Trimble is a busy man. He had me reschedule his entire morning to work you in, and—in light of everything that's going on at this post—" She made it clear that Megan should feel personally responsible for those problems as well—"I would think that you would show a little more consideration of the chaplain's generosity."

"I'm at Joint Services," Megan said. "I won't be long. Meet me here and we can work out details for when we can talk again."

"What are you doing at Joint Services?"

Megan knew she couldn't tell Benbow what she was planning. "I've got a meeting with Chaplain Trimble. I've got to go now. He's waiting."

"Trimble? He's one of General Braddock's favorite officers. They play golf together." Benbow sounded worried. "Look, just find out why he called the meeting—"

"I called the meeting," Megan said.

"Why?"

Megan gathered her attaché case and stood, trying to ignore the withering stare the receptionist was giving her. "I've got to go."

"All right. Tell me later. For the moment I need you to keep your head. Low profile, Mrs. Gander. Just keep thinking, low profile."

Megan said good-bye and closed the phone. She approached the door bearing large lettering:

MAJOR AUGUSTUS R. TRIMBLE
CHAPLAIN
UNITED STATES ARMY

How do you tell a chaplain how to do his job? Megan asked herself nervously. Then she opened the door and went inside. *Low profile. Just keep thinking low profile.*

✿ ✿ ✿

United States 75th Army Rangers Temporary Post
Sanliurfa, Turkey
Local Time 1359 Hours

As she watched the collapse of the burning building where First Sergeant Goose Gander had been fired upon by what turned out to be a group of PKK terrorists intent on carrying out their jihad against the Turks by way of killing American Rangers, Danielle's mind raced.

She'd already done a bit for the news, but the attack was almost miniscule in light of everything else that had happened in the city in the past few hours. Normally a bunch of people dying guaranteed airtime, but not this confrontation. After all, the PKK were only a handful of terrorists who had intended to take advantage of the confusion in the city to strike against their perceived enemies. With the past news stories, it would take an attack by the Syrian government to punch a hole in the news.

Three Rangers were dead and six more wounded. Efforts were still being made to count the civilian dead in the building, but no one expected to complete that because the fire had already rendered the building off-limits. By the time the flames were out, only a pile of smoldering rubble would be left.

Most of the PKK terrorists were dead, killed by an attack helicopter that still beat the air overhead while holding in a defensive pattern. A few had fled, but the military searched for them now.

Danielle had tried for an interview with Goose but hadn't been able to penetrate the cordon established by the Rangers. She'd wanted a couple sound bites with First Sergeant Gander, just enough to keep the points up on the ratings. Several viewers identified with the sergeant, commenting on the degree of professionalism he'd shown through the battles as well as the personal loss he'd had in his five-year-old son.

She'd seen Goose a few times. Primarily he seemed occupied with an unconscious man he'd carried out of the building and put in the back of a cargo truck that hauled supplies.

That piqued Danielle's interest because the other people who had been rescued from the building had been transported in medical vehicles displaying appropriate markings. In all the confusion, no one else seemed to notice that the man the first sergeant had carried out hadn't gone with them.

Maybe I'm just being paranoid, Danielle told herself. But then she spotted one of the CIA agents Captain Remington had confronted that morning. She didn't know how long he'd been there. *Or maybe I'm not being paranoid enough.*

The CIA agent lounged in the shade of a building and drank from a sports bottle. He wore khakis and a white shirt. His wraparound sunglasses masked his face. He blended in with the media people, but he wasn't one of them.

Danielle thought about Lizuca again, about the way she had been killed. She'd finally gotten the whole story from another employee she knew in the OneWorld NewsNet offices.

Stolojan hadn't returned any of her phone calls. His assistant said that he was "unavailable," but Danielle knew that Stolojan was only "unavailable" when he wanted to be.

So why was he avoiding her?

Unless he was worried that whatever had happened to Lizuca might spill over into the OneWorld NewsNet organization.

That gave Danielle something else to think about. If Lizuca was considered a threat that required assassination, what kept Danielle safe out in the middle of a war zone? The question erased any illusion of safety she had.

Lizuca had died trying to get information from OneWorld NewsNet's data banks. Didn't that prove something was there?

The question lent Danielle some enthusiasm and a reprieve from the guilt she felt over the young woman's death. She hadn't known that having Lizuca check on the identity of the CIA man would trigger repercussions at all, much less the girl's murder. If she'd known, would it have stopped her? She thought so, though she knew that, given her nose for news, it wouldn't have kept her from looking for answers, only from involving Lizuca.

She turned abruptly, watching as Cezar and Gorca started out from under the shade of an awning in front of an empty computer store. She waved them back and said, "Bathroom."

Cezar waved at her and lit a cigarette. "Take your time. Looks like we will be doing nothing here."

Danielle walked through the crowd of reporters until she was out of sight of her coworkers and the CIA man. *"Paranoia might not be easy to carry around, but it'll help keep you alive."* Hugh Taylor, the journalist who'd trained her to be an investigative reporter, had told her on day one. He'd repeated it every day of her internship, as if it were a litany, a magical spell that would keep safe the person who said it.

She found a group of reporters she knew from international stories she'd covered before pulling the Turkish-Syrian dispute that wasn't supposed to get as volatile as it had. Sid Wright was with the British Broadcasting Corporation and had been for the last seventeen years. He was an old hand with wars and the nations that made them. He was of medium height, wide-shouldered but dapper, and wore a hat to shade his face. FosterGrant sunglasses covered his eyes. His hair had more gray in it than brown these days, but he was still one of the best delivery guys working international news.

"Hey, Sid," Danielle called.

The British newsman excused himself from his cronies and approached her. "Not going live with a piece of this, Danielle?"

"I managed a sound bite and a couple slugs for the evening broadcast in the States," Danielle answered. "I'm also doing some framing for a small piece that might be used later."

"Unless something more exciting presents itself."

"Got it in one."

Wright glanced up at the helicopter hovering in the smoke-streaked sky. "Something tells me that's going to happen soon enough, love." He reached into his pocket and brought out a pack of Players and a Dunhill lighter. "So what brings you over here? Feeling like mixing with the rabble?"

"Actually," Danielle said, "I'd like to ask a favor."

Interest flickered on Wright's face for a moment. "The princess comes begging to her poor cousin? And what would that favor be?"

"I want to use one of your computers with Internet access."

"And OneWorld doesn't have enough of them? Or maybe they don't have the color you fancy? I thought Nicolae Carpathia and his little media empire owned a sizeable section of cyber reality."

"I want some privacy. That's something I don't think you get much of with OneWorld." Danielle felt bad about positioning her current employer in a suspicious light, but she had to push her personal feelings out of it. Lizuca had been killed and she had to find out how much culpability she had in the young woman's death. One way or another, she knew the information that the CIA man was being researched through OneWorld's digital archives had come through the media corporation.

"Ah, but OneWorld does pay the money, don't they, love? And they have all the toys." Wright sighed. "And with all the worldwide access OneWorld NewsNet has while the rest of us are standing out in the cold, why, you'd think the CEO made a deal with the devil himself."

"I just caught a break," Danielle said, trying to mollify Sid's wounded ego that she, only a little more than half his age, had netted such a plum job. "I happened to be in the right place at the right time."

"The way I heard it," Wright said, "they went looking for you. Had a corporate headhunter come down and raid you from FOX News."

"What about the computer?" Danielle pressed. "Is it possible or not?"

"Oh, it's possible, love. Anything is. For ourselves, we seem to be able to get e-mail in and out just fine for the time being. Just can't get the news out much past the immediate area. All I've got is a dial-up, I'm afraid. E-mail can be dreadfully slow depending on the size of the document you want to send or receive."

That news didn't make Danielle happy. "I'm going to need the computer for an hour or so." Sending the digital picture of the CIA man through a dial-up connection would take at least that long.

Wright led the way to a battered Land Rover sitting in a rubble-strewn alley. He pulled a notebook computer and a cell phone from the passenger seat, connected the two items, and punched in a phone number. Lifting the sunglasses, he looked at her as the computer booted up and logged on to the Internet server. "With you going outside your own resources this way, I have to ask why."

"I'm an investigative reporter," Danielle said. "Paranoia is part of my nature."

"Is it now?" Wright's light hazel eyes studied her. He wasn't an easy man to fool or to see through when he chose to hold secrets of his own. "Would this have anything to do with the young woman employee of OneWorld NewsNet who was killed in Bucharest only recently?"

Danielle eyed the British reporter levelly, kept her immediate emotions in check, then lied through her teeth. "I don't know anything about that."

Wright waited a beat, then nodded. "Uh-huh. I see. Well, then, love, if you need anything, let me know." He put his sunglasses back in place and walked away.

"Well, if I find out anything, I'll let you know." Feeling bad—a little anyway—about lying to Wright, Danielle focused on her task. If information wasn't coming from OneWorld NewsNet, then having someone outside the system go to it would be the best choice. That someone would be Mystic, a hacker so out there that most people thought he was a myth.

During an investigative piece regarding corporate espionage four years ago, Danielle had tracked down the person who called himself—or herself—Mystic. During the two months on the investigation, Danielle had come close to unmasking the person. In the end, though, Mystic had proven impossible to ferret out. He or she was a ghost in the system. And it was possible that Mystic was more than one person, according to some of the rumors.

Still, the mysterious person had been sufficiently impressed by Danielle's tenaciousness that Mystic had set up a connection through a message drop that she could use to contact him or her. Danielle suspected the connection was the person's means of taunting her for not finding out their identity. Or possibly some young teenager had developed a crush on her.

Over the past four years, Danielle had used Mystic's resources on

three assignments when she couldn't turn up information she
needed. Every time, Mystic had proven equal to the task. However,
the risk remained that Mystic would eventually get tracked down by
one of the corporations or governments that were targeted and would
meet a violent end.

Being in Mystic's database of regular contacts at that point was
definitely something of a risk. Danielle had been highly cognizant of
that risk each time before when she had asked for help.

When her borrowed computer was logged onto the Internet, she
accessed Mystic's mail drop. She typed out a message using the unflat-
tering Muckraker ID he had provided her.

Muckraker:>HEY. ARE YOU AROUND?

Mystic:>I'M ALWAYS AROUND. LONG TIME, NO HEAR.

Danielle knew Mystic would be sniffing around the entire connection, making certain there were no viruses or traps attached to them.

She typed:>BEEN BUSY. YOU?

Mystic:>EXPLORING THE BLUE NOWHERE.

The blue nowhere was cyberspace, named that by a number of
hackers.

Muckraker:>FIND ANYTHING INTERESTING?

Mystic:>LOL. LOTS. WANT ME TO CHECK INTO ANYTHING
ELSE INTERESTING?

Danielle decided to go with a semi-flirtatious response:>CAN'T A
GIRL JUST CHECK IN TO SAY HI?

Mystic:>SURE. BUT YOU'RE NOT THAT GIRL. YOU'RE ALL
BUSINESS, DANIELLE. NO FUN. BEEN WATCHING YOU ON TV.

Danielle felt slow-witted. Mystic was a resource she'd left untapped
during her investigation into the worldwide vanishings. *Dodging bullets
and advancing Syrian tanks will do that to you,* she told herself.

She typed:>DO YOU KNOW ANYTHING ABOUT THE DISAP-
PEARANCES?

The cursor blinked for a short time. It was an uncomfortable silence, and for a moment Danielle thought she had lost the connection or offended the hacker in some way.

Mystic:>NO.

That was the answer. Just a simple no. But it spoke volumes.

Muckraker:>I THOUGHT SOMEONE LIKE YOU WOULD BE IN-
TERESTED IN A GLOBAL PHENOMENON.

Mystic:>I AM. JUST NOTHING OUT THERE TO FIND. LOTS OF
CONJECTURE, SUPPOSITION, AND HORSE POOP.

Muckraker:>I'M GETTING THE SAME THING AT THIS END.

Mystic:>WAS THAT WHAT YOU E-MAILED ME ABOUT?

Me, not *us*. Danielle filed that away. Using *I* might have been a re-
flexive use, but *me* in the context it was used might be more subjec-
tive.

Muckraker:>I WANT A BACKGROUND CHECK DONE.

Mystic's response was immediate, the letters taking shape with
staccato regularity:>MUNDANE. NOT INTERESTED. YOU CAN DO
YOUR OWN SCUT WORK.

Danielle couldn't believe the response. She'd thought asking the
favor was a slam dunk because Mystic liked flirting with her.

Muckraker:>IS THAT ANY WAY TO TREAT A GIRL?

Mystic:>BLUE NOWHERE'S A BIG PLACE. LOTS OF PLACES TO
PLAY. DON'T WANNA LOSE ANY TIME.

Danielle thought quickly, seeking any leverage she might have.
Mystic didn't owe her any favors. In the past she'd felt like an oddity
for whoever was at the other end of the computer link, a passing interest.

Then she typed:>THIS GIG COMES WITH A BODY COUNT.
PROBABLY NOT SAFE ANYWAY. TTFN.

TTFN stood for *ta-ta-for-now,* a cute sign-off a lot of Internet cruis-
ers used. She waited, feeling crass at how she was using Lizuca's death
as bait.

A moment later, symbols appeared on the screen from Mystic:>???

Muckraker:>I HAD A FRIEND CHECK ON THE PICTURE I WANT
TO SEND YOU. SHE WAS KILLED ABOUT AN HOUR AGO IN A
CYBERCAFÉ IN BUCHAREST.

Mystic:>WHO KILLED HER?

Muckraker:>I DON'T KNOW.

Mystic:>YOU'RE HOLDING OUT ON ME. I CAN TELL.

Okay, you've got her or him or them interested. Time to set the hook.

Danielle typed:>THERE'S A CIA CONNECTION. THAT'S WHAT I
NEED YOU TO LOOK INTO.

Mystic:>GOTTA LOVE THE SPY GUYS. IT'S GREAT TO BUST
THEIR CHOPS. THEY GOOD GUYS OR BAD GUYS?

Danielle knew that there existed a certain moral ambiguity among
hackers, but they held true to their own codes. And most of them
championed underdogs.

Muckraker:>SHE WAS A FRIEND OF MINE. SHE WAS A GOOD
PERSON.

Mystic:>ERGO, THEY ARE THE BAD GUYS BY DEFAULT.

Muckraker:>I THINK IT'S MORE THAN JUST BY DEFAULT.

Mystic:>YOU SAID YOU HAD A PICTURE?

Muckraker:>YES.

Mystic:>SEND IT. I'LL FIND YOUR GUY.

Danielle hesitated before typing:>I THINK ONEWORLD NEWS-NET HAS INFORMATION ON THE GUY.

Mystic:>WHAT MAKES YOU SAY THAT?

Muckraker:>MY FRIEND WORKED FOR THEM.

The cursor blinked for a time. Mystic:>OKAY. I'LL POKE AROUND THERE.

Muckraker:>BE CAREFUL.

There was a brief lag in the response.

Mystic:>YOU TOO. I GET BUSTED, WHICH I TRULY CAN'T SEE HAPPENING BECAUSE I AM THAT GOOD, THEY'RE GONNA START LOOKING AROUND. EVEN IF THEY DETECT ME, THEY CAN'T FIND ME. BUT YOUR HEAD WILL BE THE FIRST ONE ON THE CHOPPING BLOCK. THIS IS YOUR LAST CHANCE TO GET OUT.

Danielle thought about that, but she couldn't back away. Not until she confirmed that Lizuca's death was connected to the CIA man's picture.

Muckraker:>NO. I'M IN.

Mystic:>GOTTA SAY I'M A LITTLE CONCERNED FOR YOU, BUT I'M GLAD YOU'RE STICKING. YOU'VE MADE ME CURIOUS AND FEEL CHALLENGED. SEND ME THE PIC. I'LL LET YOU KNOW.

Muckraker:>THANKS. WHEN SHOULD I EXPECT RESULTS?

Mystic:>OR WHEN SHOULD YOU START THINKING MAYBE THEY GOT ME?

Danielle hated to appear so blunt, but naked words were a downside to e-mail.

Muckraker:>YES.

Mystic:>ROTF.

Rolling on the floor, Danielle translated the e-mail jargon. *Terrific.*

Muckraker:>THIS ISN'T EXACLY A LAUGHING MATTER.

Mystic:>TRUE. NOT FOR YOUR FRIEND. BUT I FEEL JAZZED. GOING WHERE NO ONE HAS GONE BEFORE. THAT KIND OF THING. I'LL CONTACT YOU IN THREE OR FOUR HOURS.

Muckraker:>OKAY.

Mystic:>IF I GO BEYOND THAT WINDOW, THEY PROBABLY THREW A NET OVER ME AND PUT THE BODY IN A WOOD CHIPPER.

Danielle didn't respond, thinking of the hard way Lizuca had died.

Mystic:>SORRY. WASN'T THINKING. YOU LOST A FRIEND. GIMME THE PIC AND LET'S SEE IF WE CAN FERRET OUT SOME GET-BACK AGAINST WHOEVER DID IT.

Muckraker:>I'LL BE LOOKING FORWARD TO HEARING FROM YOU.

Danielle attached the picture of the CIA agent and pressed the Enter button. The menu box told her uploading the picture would take eighteen minutes. She sat and waited, watching the building continue to burn and thinking about the man First Sergeant Gander had taken charge of.

There were a lot of mysterious goings-on. Danielle could hardly wait to find out what the real story was.

❊   ❊   ❊

United States of America
Fort Benning, Georgia
Local Time 0907 Hours

Major Augustus R. Trimble rose from behind his massive desk as Megan entered his private office in the Joint Services building. He waved her toward an oxblood leather chair in front of the desk.

The office was large, bigger than most Megan had seen at the post. That was a sure sign that the base commander, General Amos Braddock, liked the chaplain.

Shelves containing books covered two of the room's walls. The other two walls were covered with pictures of Trimble with various political figures, including four past presidents as well as President Fitzhugh. Chaplain Trimble was obviously a man who liked to hang out his political connections for others to see. Only a handful of documents detailing his secular training held any space.

"Good morning, Mrs. Gander. Please, have a seat." Trimble was in his early sixties and overweight. His army uniform was tailored to be gracious to the twenty pounds he carried that exceeded army regs. A few strands of silver hair stuck stubbornly to his pink scalp. His face was round and his cheeks showed signs of turning bulldoggish. Oval glasses sat at the end of his narrow nose and emphasized how close set his eyes were.

"Thank you." Megan sat then noticed how Trimble gazed at her jeans a second too long. His dissatisfaction with her choice of dress was obvious. "Forgive the jeans," she said. "I know this isn't exactly professional attire, but a lot of the work I'm doing right now is hard physical labor."

She had volunteered the teens to help with transporting and passing out supplies to the general population of the post. Giving them something useful to do in addition to their counseling and grief sessions was part of the overall mental wellness plan Megan and the other counselors had come up with.

More than that, dressing in jeans and loose pullovers helped the teens relate better to her. Right now, the post was filled with guys in uniforms and short attitudes telling everyone what to do and when to do it. Those orders were directed especially at teens because they didn't have assigned duties and they tended to hang out in the middle of operations to find out more about what was going on. More now than ever, the teens felt ostracized amid all the military comings and goings.

Trimble held up a hand. "I'm not your supervisor, Mrs. Gander, and we're not here to talk about fashion."

Megan felt a little better.

"Although," Trimble went on, "I would like to point out that a uniform, or a professional appearance, is put on for a reason. When you lead people, you need to look like a leader. Not like one of those who need leading."

Megan bit back an angry retort. Chauvinism tended to thrive in certain pockets of the military. There was an upside to it. A lot of guys opened doors for her. The downside was that some military men felt like women were an afterthought to the overall effort.

"Sometimes," Megan stated in an even voice, "it's easier to lead people from within their midst rather than standing on the outside of a group. That way they don't tend to view you as an outsider. The men you lead wear uniforms. The kids I'm helping don't."

Trimble frowned and leaned back in his chair. He put his hands together over his ample stomach. "I'm glad we were able to have this meeting this morning, Mrs. Gander."

A wall of ice seemed to close around Megan, and she was suddenly not glad about the meeting at all. She waited, letting him take the lead. She wanted to see where he was headed.

"After the incident involving Holly—" Trimble rifled through a yellow legal pad on his desk.

"Hollister," Megan said in as neutral a voice as she could manage. "Leslie Hollister."

Trimble looked up at her over his glasses, then let the papers fall back to the pad, settling in his chair again. "After the *unfortunate* incident involving young Leslie Hollister last night, especially given the intricacies of your involvement, I was planning on speaking with you anyway."

Megan could feel her temper straining against the tight hold she was keeping on it. She wasn't rested and she already felt guilty. The handling she'd received during the investigation by the provost marshal's office, and then being kept under guard by MPs at the hospital, hadn't exactly been positive experiences.

"Why were you planning on talking to me?" Megan asked.

Trimble blinked. He put his hands together, rested his elbows on the desk and leaned forward. The move was an attempt to threaten to invade Megan's personal space, and she knew it.

Stubbornly, liking the chaplain less and less with each passing moment, Megan held her ground. Having her personal space invaded was hard on her. She liked having her boundaries. But that invasion technique was one of the first things people in command were taught. She had seen Goose do it with recalcitrant soldiers, but he had never done anything like that to her or the kids. However, when she had conferences with parents of troubled teens, the maneuver was one of the first things men tried to pull during a heated confrontation.

"As a friend and colleague, I would hope," Trimble said.

Hope all you want, Megan thought, *but I can't see it happening.* But she kept from saying that. She needed him to be on her side at least long enough to understand what she was going to say.

"You've had a rotten few days," Trimble said. "I understand you had a daughter who is one of those missing."

Megan forced the answer out. "A son, actually. Chris."

"Of course. Pardon me. There's just been so much going on." Evidently realizing that his space invasion wasn't going to work, Trimble leaned back in his seat again. "In addition to your own personal worries about your family, there was the debacle with the Fletcher boy—"

"Gerry," Megan said, wanting the man to at least know the names of the people he wanted to use against her.

Trimble picked up a pencil and tapped it irritably against the legal pad. "His father—"

"Private First Class Boyd Fletcher."

"—has chosen to pursue charges for dereliction of duty because you didn't inform his wife or him that the boy was in the hospital."

"Boyd Fletcher was the *reason* his son was in the hospital. He physically abused Gerry on a number of occasions. He'd done it before, and he did it that night."

Trimble frowned. "And how do you know this, Mrs. Gander?"

"Gerry told me."

"Before he disappeared?"

"Yes. That night."

Trimble sighed. "The problem is that Gerry Fletcher is no longer available to witness to that. He has disappeared. As has Helen Cordell, whom you contend could have supported your claims against Boyd Fletcher."

"Helen called me in to handle Gerry. She knew he was one of the kids I counseled on a regular basis."

"Well, Boyd Fletcher tells a completely different story. A plausible one, I might add." Shifting in the chair, Trimble placed the pencil precisely on the pad. "I'm afraid we're going nowhere with this conversation."

"This isn't the conversation I came here to have," Megan replied.

"Then why did you come, Mrs. Gander?"

"I need your help."

Trimble's eyebrows rose in surprise. "We appear to be at an impasse here, because—quite frankly—I see merit in the accusation Private Fletcher and his wife are making about you and their son."

"I want to talk about a different matter," Megan said. "Before we end up with more problems."

"More problems? We've got a hostile city right outside our gate, hundreds of soldiers missing from this post, and confusion raining down from the White House. How could we possibly have even more problems?"

"There are dozens of scared kids at this post, Chaplain."

Trimble cut in smoothly. "I'm well aware of that. There are also a number of concerned adults."

Megan thought for a moment, then decided on a different tactic. She needed Trimble on her side. He had the authority to put some kind of plan together. He could help put things back together. If she couldn't negotiate him past his negative feelings toward her, she needed to at least sidestep them.

"Why do you think all those people vanished?" Megan asked.

After a brief, telling hesitation, Trimble said, "I don't know. And I don't think anyone else does yet. Obviously there's some kind of new superweapon that we've not seen the likes of in play."

"Why couldn't it be something else? Something that we've known was coming but that we are now afraid or reluctant to admit has happened. Or we're in denial about it."

Trimble shook his head. "Mrs. Gander, I have no earthly idea what you're talking about, nor do I have time to waste trying to get you to simply say what is on your mind. I suggest that—"

Megan reached into her briefcase as Trimble spoke. She took out the book on the end times that Bill had left at her house and Jenny had read.

"I'm talking about the Rapture," Megan said, putting the book on his desk. "I'm talking about the end of the world as we know it. And that's exactly what has happened here."

Trimble eyed the book but made no move to reach for it.

"I'm sorry," Megan said, realizing the mistake she might have inadvertently made. "I don't know your faith. Maybe you don't—"

"Oh, come on, Mrs. Gander. I'm a military chaplain. I have a doctorate in divinity from Harvard. Of course I am a Christian," Trimble declared. "Born and bred. I know all about the Rapture. I've written theses on the subject. I daresay I can guarantee that I know more about the subject than you do after reading a book and being inspired by the events of the last few days." With a forefinger, he pushed the book back toward her. "I'm also quite familiar with this book."

"You don't believe that the church will be raptured before the time of the Tribulation?"

"Of course I do." Trimble settled back in his chair. "Father Kearny and Rabbi Smalls may be of a different opinion in the matter, seeing as how the Catholic and Jewish beliefs don't reconcile a rapture with the Tribulation in their versions of God's Word. I believe there will be the Rapture. But this is not it."

"Given everything that's happened, how can you say that?"

Trimble frowned. "If the Rapture had occurred, Mrs. Gander, let me assure you that I would have known."

Then the unspoken truth in Trimble's reasoning became crystal clear in Megan's mind, as if someone had suddenly opened the curtains to let the sun in. And Megan felt she knew where that sudden understanding had come from. All at once, she didn't feel quite so intimidated by this man.

"You don't believe the Rapture occurred because you're still here," she said.

A scowled turned the corners of Trimble's mouth down and darkened his eyes. "Be careful what you say, Mrs. Gander."

Megan thought furiously. "Did you know many of the people who disappeared?"

"Several of them, as a matter of fact."

"What kind of people were they?"

"Mrs. Gander—"

"Are you afraid to answer the question, Chaplain?" Megan knew she'd skated perilously close to the edge. She'd already raised Trimble's ire. She knew she might just take him past his breaking point. But the truths tumbling from her mouth felt like they were coming from somewhere outside of herself. It was like someone—or Someone—was putting words in her mouth and she had to say them.

Trimble didn't speak.

"My friends who disappeared," Megan said, "were all Christians. Devout, loving Christians who held God close in their hearts all the time. They were people who believed in God, who believed that Jesus would be back for them, and who had none of the faith conflicts that I carry with me." She paused. "My devoutly Christian friends, the ones who trusted God to guide their lives, are gone. And the children, of course—the innocents. Whenever I talk to others about relatives and friends they've lost, I keep getting the same descriptions. The missing are innocents and people who believed. People who *really* believed." She pinned the chaplain with her gaze. "Have *you* heard of anyone being taken who didn't meet that description?"

"Mrs. Gander, I don't think you—"

"That was a yes-or-no question," Megan said. Again, it was as though someone else were talking through her. A feeling of righteousness pervaded her. For the moment she felt entirely vindicated in her approach to this man and in the tenacity with which she clung to it.

"What do you want from me, Mrs. Gander?"

"I want you to teach the children," Megan said.

Her answer surprised Trimble so much that he was quiet for a time. "Teach them what?"

"About the Rapture and the Tribulation," Megan replied. "I want you to tell them about the rise of the Antichrist and about the seven years—of course, it's a few days less than that now—that will pass before Jesus returns to gather those who have reconciled their belief in Him. They need to know what's going to happen, how they're supposed to survive, and what they're supposed to do to serve God."

Trimble heaved a great sigh. "Do you know what would happen if I were to announce publicly that the Rapture had occurred?"

"Yes, I do. People would have some of the answers they need to make plans for the future. And they'd have a motive to discover the rest of those answers."

"Really? You think that's what would happen?"

"Yes."

Leaning forward again, Trimble placed his elbows on the desk and fitted his hands together in front of him. He spoke in a low voice. "Mrs. Gander, the Rapture *has* occurred."

Despite the chaplain's compliance, Megan was wary. The man's eyes were hard as flint.

"The Rapture has occurred," Trimble repeated. "Your son was taken from you by God. He's up in heaven now. And you're not."

Before she knew it, Megan was crying. The man was right. Tears ran down her face. Her lips quivered and her jaw shook. She tried to control the pain that coiled inside her. She felt all alone now, shorn of the Presence that had so recently seemed to fill her. She had been left behind. God had found her wanting.

"Don't you feel better knowing that, Mrs. Gander?" Trimble asked in a voice that made a travesty of any real sympathy on his part.

Megan didn't know what to say.

"Come on now, Mrs. Gander. As you told me, that's a simple yes-or-no question. Don't you feel better knowing that God took your son away from you and lifted him on high to heaven? That you failed Him somehow and got stranded here to face the Tribulation?

No, Megan admitted to herself. It was all she could do to keep from screaming that answer. The emotions she'd had bottled up inside threatened to break loose.

"What's wrong, Mrs. Gander?" Trimble asked. He was relentless in his attack. "Isn't that what you wanted to hear? Isn't that what you want me to tell all those children who have lost parents and younger siblings? Isn't that what you're asking me to tell other parents like yourself, parents who have suffered losses? Isn't that going to make everything all better for them?"

Megan closed her eyes to the man's cruel face. She wished she could block out his words as well as the sight of him.

"You want to know what will happen if I start telling people that?" Trimble asked. "Aside from the fact that I'll be relieved of my command pending a psychological evaluation?"

Megan wrapped her arms around herself and felt hopeless.

"People," Trimble stated in a calm, matter-of-fact tone, "will turn away from God in droves. Whatever chance I or any other man of

God would have had of instructing them in the salvation of their souls would be exhausted. Quite possibly forever."

Trembling, her hand to her mouth because she was afraid she was going to throw up, Megan forced her eyes open to meet the chaplain's harsh gaze. Tears blurred her vision.

"One of the first things those people are going to feel," Trimble said, "is betrayal. 'Why did God leave me behind?' they'll want to know. 'Wasn't I good enough for God?' Or, 'Why did God have to take my child?' or 'my spouse, or my parents, or my friend?'"

Megan grew scared and the pain in her heart threatened to consume her. She hadn't expected Chaplain Trimble to attack her with the truth, to pound her using the exact words she'd hoped he would say.

"Your son is gone, Mrs. Gander. If the Rapture truly has happened, you have no chance of seeing him again. Not as the child you knew. He will be changed in the eyes of the Lord. He will be in his new body. He will no longer truly be your son." Trimble was quiet for a moment. "That's what you're asking me to tell those kids you're so worried about." He paused. "I won't do that."

Megan struggled for control. She didn't know how everything could have skidded so far out of her control. She didn't know how she could lose everything. Or even why she was picked to lose it all. She hadn't been a bad person. She didn't deserve to still be here.

"I don't mean to sound rude or callous, Mrs. Gander," Trimble said, picking up his pencil and turning his attention to the legal pad on his desk. "It's just that I'm a very busy man. I made time to see you this morning because I thought I could help you. Obviously your problems are beyond my ability to deal with. I suggest you seek emotional help to learn to cope with everything you're going through." He paused. "The mistakes you made in the Fletcher and Hollister cases are indicative of how far you've let your grasp of your abilities become eroded." He flicked his eyes up to meet hers. "I just want you to know that I'm going to recommend that you be temporarily relieved of your job assignment. Until you get yourself together. I really feel you need some time to work on your own problems. I hope one day you'll thank me for that." He glanced down again at his desk, making notations on the legal pad. "Please find your own way out."

Dismissed, not knowing what else to do, Megan stood on legs that trembled so badly she knew they weren't going to hold her. Finally, without a word, she turned and walked away from the big desk.

She paused at the door and took a deep breath in an effort to calm herself. *God, please help me know what to do. Give me the wisdom and the strength to do whatever it is. I've got nothing left. No energy, no hope. All I've got are these tears. I give myself to You because I no longer know what I'm supposed to do. You are my Savior. Help me. Whatever You need from me is Yours.*

Megan had her hand on the doorknob when a calm suddenly fell upon her. She felt the Spirit of the Lord fill her. The difference in her was like the difference between a summer day and a winter night. The pain in her heart healed and her weak knees strengthened. She was not alone in facing Trimble. She knew she'd never be all alone again.

And in that moment she experienced a clearer understanding of what had just happened. Not only that, she knew what God wanted her to do. And she would do it. She let go of the knob and walked back to Trimble's desk.

Surprise twisted Trimble's features as he looked up and saw her coming toward him.

"No," Megan said defiantly. She wiped her tears. She no longer felt the need to cry. "You tried to make this all about me, Chaplain Trimble. You don't even care about the other people I want to help. But I know why. And so does the God you profess to believe in. Your answer came from all the fear inside *you.*"

"How dare you!" Trimble exclaimed. "How dare you say that to me?"

"When you said other people would wonder why they were left behind," Megan said, "you were referring to yourself. *You* want to know why you were left behind. *You* don't want to admit that the Rapture has happened. *You* are the one in denial. I wasn't taken, but I'm not alone in this room. You weren't taken either. And you just can't handle it."

Trimble looked apoplectic. "Mrs. Gander—"

"Don't speak," Megan told him. "Don't you *dare* interrupt me until I'm through, not after what you did to me just now. I failed God, yes. I could never let Him into my heart, not the way I should have. I was too proud, too sure of myself, too afraid. But I know I failed Him. And I know that the way back to Jesus is as simple as asking Him into my heart and life. And then listening to Him once I've asked Him to enter. I opened that door. Have you? "

Trimble opened his mouth then closed it.

"You used my son's loss against me," Megan said. Once again words tumbled from her mouth like gifts from God. "You threatened me with the idea that I would never see him again. His name is Chris,

Chaplain Trimble. Chris Gander. And I *know* I will meet him again. He's there in heaven now, waiting for me, and I *will* find out all I need to know to get my faith where it needs to be. I will find God's plan for my soul. God keeps His promises. I've prayed for His grace to save me. I won't be left behind again. Will you?"

Trimble stood, towering over her.

Megan leaned across the desk and invaded the chaplain's personal space, making the man back into the bookcase behind him. "I have an older son. He's no longer a baby. I watched him grow up, and I felt the loss of the small child that I held in my arms, that I fed and sang silly songs to, that I taught to brush his teeth and read and play basketball. Every day of his life, he changed. He's no longer the baby that I can remember so easily. He's a young man. And you know what?"

Trimble didn't say anything, held at bay by the conviction in her words.

"He's still my baby boy. No matter how much he's changed, he will always be my child. I love my son," Megan said. "I love *both* my sons, even though they're not the babies I was first given. And I believe I will know them always. In this life briefly, and in the next forever." She took a breath and stared him down. "You can make a difference, Chaplain Trimble. But it's up to you to decide to act. I believe that I was put here today to convince you of that."

"No," Trimble said. "The only thing you've convinced me of is how desperately you need help." He pressed the key on the intercom. "Margaret."

"Yes, Chaplain?"

"Have a security detail come to my office and remove Mrs. Gander."

"Of course, sir."

"You're making a mistake," Megan said. "You need to let God into your heart. The very fact that you're here proves it. And the way you've just treated me proves it even more. Remember Jesus saying, 'If any of you put a stumbling block before one of these little ones who believe in me, it would be better for you if a great millstone were hung around your neck and you were thrown in the sea'? You're tying that millstone around your neck right now. Please, think about what you're doing. Don't make another mistake."

"The only mistake I made was in thinking I would be able to help you."

"God help *you* then, Chaplain Trimble," Megan said, still almost heady from being filled with the Spirit, "because I don't think you can help yourself." She turned and headed to the door.

By the time Megan had the door open, two MPs were in the waiting room. Margaret silently pointed an accusing finger at Megan.

"I'm going," Megan told the two MPs.

"See that she leaves the building," Trimble said from behind her. "And make certain that she isn't allowed back in."

Megan walked and kept her head up. The MPs fell in beside her. They escorted her to the main exit. The people standing in lines out in the hallway fell silent and gazed curiously after her.

Lieutenant Doug Benbow was coming through the front doors. Spotting her, he stopped and waited outside with his hat in his hands.

Megan went through the doors, flanked by the MPs.

"Stand down," Benbow told the MPs.

"Sir," one of the MPs said, "we were given orders to escort Mrs. Gander out of the building."

"She's out of the building. Now back off."

The MPs hesitated as Megan came to a stop beside Benbow.

Benbow stepped forward, inserting himself between Megan and the military police. "Privates, do you see that bar on my collar?"

"Yes, sir," one of the MPs said.

"Then acknowledge it."

Both MPs snapped off salutes.

"And leave," Benbow ordered.

Reluctantly, the MPs turned and reentered the building. They took up positions just inside the doors and stared through the glass, looking like two well-trained attack dogs.

Benbow turned to Megan. "Now I have to admit, the last thing I expected to see when I got here is you accessorized with MP bookends. Again. Especially after last night."

Megan looked out at the sunshine, feeling more energy than she had any right to after the days she'd put in. Somehow, what had happened in that office had changed her forever. There was a lightness to her, a wellness she hadn't felt in a long time. She was ready to get back to doing what she knew she needed to do.

Trimble's referral, if the chaplain really followed through on the threat, would take days to get through channels. Even if he did carry out his threat, counseling services were severely strapped. Her supervisor wouldn't like the idea of losing someone when he needed every person he could get his hands on.

It would work out. She knew this because she knew God was with her. Somehow, this had all happened to let His plan for the world move forward. She knew it as surely as she knew her own name.

She started for the parking lot.

Falling into step beside her, Benbow said, "On the phone before you went into Chaplain Trimble's office, we did discuss the whole low-profile concept, right?"

"That didn't work out for me," Megan said.

"Judging by the evidence of those MPs," Benbow said, "that would be an understatement."

United States 75th Army Rangers Temporary Post
Sanliurfa, Turkey
Local Time 1412 Hours

Seated behind the wheel of the Hummer, Goose's back warmed uncomfortably from the weak afternoon sunlight piercing the fog of
dust and smoke hovering over the city from the debris thrown into
the air and the areas that still burned. The tang of chemicals and
charred rubber left a taste on even the shallowest breath he took
through the cloth mask that covered his lower face.

Under his armor and LCE, his BDUs were drenched with sweat.
His eyes burned from the chemicals and the lack of sleep. He sipped
from the canteen and turned to survey Icarus.

Icarus was lying on his stomach on the rear deck of the vehicle.
Green ordnance tape bound his hands behind his back and his feet
together. His clothing was ripped and stained with dirt and blood. At
least some of the blood was his.

Goose had stored the M-4A1 in front of the passenger seat out of
easy reach of his prisoner. He kept his M9 pistol on his knee. Shifting,
he capped the canteen and tossed the container into the passenger
seat.

A quick glance around the alley where he'd chosen to confront the
rogue CIA agent revealed that they were alone. At present, Captain
Remington had cut Goose loose, leaving the first sergeant to his own
devices. With his captive in hand and no one the wiser, he intended
to make use of the time.

A heap of broken rock and glass spread over a cargo truck blocked
one end of the alley. The other end opened onto a little-traveled street

off the main path the military teams used to ferry wounded, dead, and supplies.

Goose looked at his prisoner. "You can stop faking. I know you're awake. I saw your breathing pattern change five minutes ago. Lying there like that is just going to waste the time you have to talk to me."

Icarus kept his eyes closed a little longer. Dried blood formed a comma from the corner of his mouth to his chin, then darted down his neck like an exclamation point. The blood had come from the damage Goose had delivered with his punch.

When he opened his eyes, Icarus said, "You punch like a mule, First Sergeant. For a while there I thought you'd broken my jaw."

Goose barely marshaled the fury that resided within him. Icarus was the reason Goose had fallen into disfavor with Remington, and he was the reason the captain was risking his career warring with Alexander Cody's CIA team instead of focusing on the holding effort going on in Sanliurfa.

"I can't say that would have been an altogether bad thing," Goose said.

Icarus worked his jaw. "Well, I wouldn't have enjoyed the experience." He shifted a little. "You have me tied up?"

"Yeah. Ordnance tape. Works about as well as handcuffs. Unless you have a knife to cut through it."

"Which I don't," Icarus said.

"No," Goose said. "You don't. I made sure of it." He'd found two knives on the man: one scabbarded on the inside of his left arm and one in his right boot.

"I'm thirsty."

"I don't care," Goose said. "A few days ago, you confronted me in a bar. You were wearing a bomb, which you said you would set off if I attempted to restrain you. I'm not inclined at this juncture to cut you any slack."

"I wouldn't have exploded the bomb."

"I don't know that."

"It was just a threat," Icarus said in a dry voice. He broke into a fit of coughing. "I just needed to get your attention."

"You got it then," Goose promised. "You've still got it." He worked to keep his tone harsh and aggressive. He felt badly about tying the man up and leaving him in what had to be an uncomfortable state.

"Could I have some water?"

"After we talk. You want water, you'll earn water."

Icarus squirmed. At first Goose thought the man was trying to free himself from his bonds; then he saw that Icarus was only trying to turn so he could better face him.

Icarus's eyes darted around the interior of the Hummer. "We're the only ones here?" he asked.

"Yeah."

"Why?"

Goose hesitated, letting the silence draw out till it became threatening. In the distance, truck engines whined and men shouted.

"I wanted to talk to you," Goose said.

"What do you want to know?"

"Everything."

Icarus laughed, but there was no mirth in the effort. Instead, he sounded bitter. "I can't tell you everything, First Sergeant. If I did, I'd have to kill you."

"That," Goose said, "would be a mistake to try."

Icarus looked at him. "Do you know why I approached you in the bar? Why I helped you with those wounded men this morning during the attack?"

Goose waited. Men who were at a disadvantage had a tendency to talk during gaps of silence.

"Because I saw something in you that I thought I could trust," Icarus said.

Goose still said nothing.

"I need someone I can talk to." Icarus's statement was plain, without inflection, but his reddened eyes looked haunted. "But you have to know that the minute I say what I have to say, your life will be forever changed."

The solemnity with which the man announced his claim created a chill in Goose's stomach.

"Have you met the CIA agents yet?" Icarus asked. "They were watching you."

"We've met," Goose said.

"You've talked to Special Agent-in-Charge Alexander Cody?"

"Yeah." Goose decided to throw his prisoner a bone. "We didn't exactly get along."

A pained smile twisted Icarus's lips. "Even under the best circumstances, Cody isn't a good man. These circumstances we're under right now? These are as bad as they can be."

Goose waited.

"Why didn't you turn me over to them?" Icarus asked.

"I may still."

Icarus nodded. "If you do, they will kill me." He paused. "You know that, don't you?"

"No."

"They will."

"Maybe they've got reason," Goose said. "I'm not overly fond of you after the bomb threat."

Icarus gazed at the canteen lying in the passenger seat. "Haven't we talked enough yet?"

Without a word, Goose picked up the canteen, opened it, and poured water into Icarus's mouth. The man drank greedily, then had a coughing fit and spewed water over the rear deck.

"Sorry," Icarus apologized.

That small thing, an unconscious social amenity, made Goose feel horrible about what he was doing. Still, he steeled himself. *This guy knows what happened to Chris and the others who disappeared. You can't cut him any slack. You need answers.*

Goose capped the canteen and put it away again. "Why does Cody want to kill you?"

"Because I know too much. I learned more than they ever expected me to. I wasn't supposed to live after they blew my cover to the PKK."

The announcement caught Goose by surprise. "The CIA blew your cover to the terrorists?"

Icarus grinned. "Yes." He shook his head in wonder, then sighed in exasperation. "You don't know anything about what you've gotten involved with, do you, First Sergeant?"

"Cody talked with Captain Remington," Goose said. "Cody persuaded the captain to send me and my team after you."

"Only because the PKK didn't kill me instantly. That's what Cody was hoping for, you see. I did the job they sent me into the terrorist cells to do, but they hadn't counted on my finding out the things *they* were doing. Once my cover was blown, Cody and his team couldn't allow me to end up in Syrian hands. If you'd turned me over to them, Cody would have killed me and buried me as soon as we were out of sight."

"All I hear right now is a lot of lip service. Make me a believer."

Icarus grinned. "It's ironic that you should say that, First Sergeant, because making believers is what this is all about." He paused. "How much time do you think we have?"

"I don't know," Goose said.

"Your captain doesn't know you have me, does he?"

"Not yet."

"You and Remington are supposed to be close."

"We are," Goose said and felt guilty instantly. "Cal Remington is like a brother to me."

"You must not have any brothers."

The man's words bit into Goose. After he'd been born, his mother hadn't been able to have any more children. Only a few years later, she'd died from a degenerative heart condition that wasn't discovered till she was already gone. He and his father had struggled through alone.

"I'm sorry," Icarus said. "I can see I touched a nerve."

"Get to it," Goose growled.

"Why doesn't the captain know I'm here?"

Goose hesitated. "Because we've got different agendas."

"Are you going to turn me over to Remington after we finish talking?"

Goose didn't answer.

Icarus rolled over and lay more or less on his back, partially propped up by his bound wrists. "I need to know, First Sergeant."

"I don't know what I'm going to do."

"Then holding me here, finding out what I'm worth, isn't about career advancement?"

Goose struggled, trying to figure how best to answer the question. A quiet calm descended over him, like during those times he'd talked with Bill Townsend. *You've got nothing to lose with the truth.*

"I've got a son," Goose said. "His name is Chris. He's five years old."

Icarus's eyes locked on Goose's. "Chris has disappeared."

The pain Goose felt nearly swelled his throat shut. "Yes," he said hoarsely.

"And you thought I might know something about that."

Goose felt a single tear run down his cheek. He didn't try to hide it, didn't try to brush it away. "I love my boy. I want him back."

"God help you find peace, First Sergeant," Icarus said. "I can't help you with that. No man on this planet can help you get your son back."

Anger returned to Goose full force. He felt shamed that he had revealed his weakness to his prisoner. He struggled to find words, to make his voice work again in spite of his tight throat.

Silence stretched between them for a long time, punctuated by the rumbling trucks in the distance and the noise of Goose's radio headset.

"If I could help you," Icarus said finally, "I would."

Without a word, Goose slipped his combat knife from his LCE and leaned across the seats. Icarus drew back from him. Roughly, not trusting his voice, Goose grabbed the man's shoulder and rolled him onto his stomach. Icarus kicked and flopped, evidently thinking he was about to have his throat slit. Instead, Goose cut the tape binding the man's wrists and his ankles. Freezing instantly, Icarus gazed up at Goose.

Slumping back into the front seat, feeling torn and worn completely out, shamed on several fronts, Goose returned his knife to his LCE.

Icarus massaged his wrists. "What are you doing?"

"Letting you go."

"Why?"

"Because I believe Cody and his people will kill you if I turn you over to them." Goose breathed out his pain and bored through his feelings to the dead center of himself—the part he sought when he needed to be cut off from all things mortal and weak. That dead space, without even a will to survive or hope for a tomorrow, was the most dangerous part of a professional soldier on a battlefield. Death became an abstract; losing, an illusion. Nothing touched him.

Icarus sat up. "Are you all right?"

"No. Go." Goose leaned his head back and closed his eyes. *Sleep,* he commanded himself. *You need it. Just sleep and do whatever you need to do next.*

"What do you think happened to your son?" Icarus asked.

"I don't want to talk about this," Goose said in a flat voice.

"I think you need to."

Slowly, feeling the distant nudge of irritation at the man's callous stupidity or death wish, Goose lifted his head and looked at Icarus. Goose lifted the M9 and pointed it at the man's face.

Icarus held his hands up.

The pistol felt like an anvil at the end of Goose's arm. Memories of Chris tangled in the roiling violence that demanded release from within him.

"Your son," Icarus said in a quiet voice, "is safe."

Goose willed himself to pull the trigger. He wanted to feel the buck of the pistol against his palm. A line would be crossed if he did, and he knew it. But something had to be done. He was stuck. He couldn't go on. He couldn't accept.

"Chris felt no pain," Icarus said. "God came and took your son up as He took all the other children."

"Go. Away." Goose kept the pistol centered.

"First Sergeant, I know there are people in your group who have talked about this. About the Rapture. I've heard Corporal Baker talk about it in his tent church."

Goose thought about the way Baker's little church had grown over the past few days. A lot of soldiers from the Rangers, the marines, the U.N., and the Turks had ended up there. When he wasn't on duty, Baker preached there constantly, offering guidance, support, and understanding of everything that had happened.

Icarus has been hiding out there, Goose realized. He knew the tent would have been a perfect spot. No one checked the soldiers gathered there. The sheer numbers and desperation of those who went there offered anonymity.

"Don't you believe in God?" Icarus said.

The question pushed at Goose on a physical level he'd never before experienced. He kept the pistol leveled. "I believe in God. And I hope you do, too, because you're four pounds of pressure away from becoming a footnote in history," Goose said. "Get away from me."

Icarus was quiet for a moment. "I can't."

"Then you're going to die."

"I was drawn to you, First Sergeant," Icarus said, "by something greater than myself. I know that now. There's a reason we've been put in each other's path."

"No."

"You found me today. When no one else has been able to. When I least expected it."

"Luck," Goose said. "All of it bad."

"You're not turning me in."

"I know. I already regret it. You're just lucky that I don't have it in me to care any more than I do." Goose knew that was true. He felt empty, totally bereft due to his pain over the loss of Chris. And now the absence of any hope he'd had of getting his son returned to him. "Get away from me or I swear I'm going to kill you."

"You're no killer. Not in cold blood."

"Maybe I am today."

"Then shoot me," Icarus invited.

For a long moment, Goose held the pistol on the other man. Then he dropped his arm, opened the door, and slid out of the Hummer into the merciless heat of the afternoon sun. He leathered the M9 and pulled the M-4A1 over his shoulder.

"First Sergeant," Icarus called after him.

Goose started walking, feeling the pain in his bad knee snap at him as if he'd stepped into a bear trap. He kept his eyes forward, willing himself not to think about anything. But he remembered in spite of himself.

He remembered feeling Chris's heart beat against his chest as his son slept with him in bed on lazy mornings, in a sleeping bag during camping trips, or on the couch when they'd both inadvertently caught a nap while watching superhero cartoons.

"First Sergeant."

Goose ignored Icarus. He wasn't going to think. He wasn't going to allow himself to care.

"You can't just walk away from this."

I can, Goose thought. Then he heard footsteps moving up rapidly behind him. Icarus's shadow joined his on the ground, squashed small by the midafternoon sun. In his peripheral vision Goose caught sight of the man's arm lifting; then he felt the weight of Icarus's hand on his shoulder.

The anger and pain Goose had tried to lock away burst loose. He turned on his left foot, felt his knee protest, and snapped his right hand out in a jab that caught Icarus on the side of the jaw.

Icarus staggered and nearly fell. Then, with a cry of inarticulate rage, the man threw himself at Goose.

Goose lifted his left arm and blocked Icarus's initial blow, set himself, feinted with a left, and followed up with a hard right that he'd intended to put squarely between Icarus's eyes.

Instead, Icarus stepped quickly to the left, brushed Goose's right arm away and down, and drove a roundhouse kick to Goose's ribs. Goose's breath left his lungs in a rush, and white-hot pain ignited within him. He stumbled back a step, favoring his weak knee.

Icarus came at him, stepping, kicking once in a faked attempt at Goose's crotch, then followed immediately with a front snap kick that caught Goose in the face. Stunned, Goose nearly fell, but caught himself, then saw Icarus launching another kick. Goose slipped to one side, roped his right arm under Icarus's extended right leg, and drove his left fist into his opponent's face.

Hammered down, Icarus hit the ground, but quickly twisted away from Goose. Still on his side, Icarus managed a sweep kick that knocked Goose off his feet. Goose tried to stand, but Icarus came up off the ground at the same time and threw himself forward again. They grappled on the debris-strewn ground.

That was Icarus's mistake. Goose had wrestled in junior high and high school. There wasn't a more dangerous fighter in the world than a wrestler gone to ground. Still, hours of battle and combat stress as well as days of living on the run and prior existing wounds and injuries made for a short fight.

Goose held Icarus in a choke hold when he felt the fight go out of the man. Goose's breath whistled in his own lungs as he released the man and shoved him away.

Icarus lay on the ground. He coughed and blew dust as he struggled to regain his breath.

Forcing himself to his feet, almost unable to bear the screaming pain in his knee, Goose stood swaying. After getting his feet solidly under him, he walked over to Icarus and grabbed the man's belt, lifting him from the ground.

"Stand," Goose ordered. He gasped, unable to speak at length.

Wobbly and weak, Icarus stood. His face was bloody and caked with dust. He peered warily at Goose.

"Get your . . . hands up." Goose lifted his own hands up and clapped them on his head. "Easier . . . to breathe. Opens . . . lungs." He worked on getting his own breathing back under control. The heat made the air thin and dry.

They stood uncertainly for a few minutes, staring at each other.

Pain pounded inside Goose's head. Two teeth were loose. Every breath stretched his bruised ribs.

Icarus's nose was broken and crooked. He spat blood at his own feet. Both his lips were puffy.

"That," Goose said after a time, "has got to be the stupidest thing I've ever seen a grown man do."

Icarus glared at him belligerently. "Are you ready to listen now? Or do we have to do this all over again?"

"You're crazy."

"I need to talk to you."

"We're through talking," Goose said. He spat blood as well, then wiped his swollen lip. He knew his face wasn't in much better shape than Icarus's.

"You wanted to talk to me earlier."

"You've already told me everything I need to know. You said you don't know how to get Chris back. I believe you."

"But that's not all I have to tell you."

Goose shook his head. "You want to talk about the Rapture?"

"That's what happened."

"That's what *some* people are saying is what happened."

"How can you doubt?" Icarus demanded. "You said you believed in God. Don't you see His hand in this?"

"It doesn't make sense. God wouldn't take my son. So it has to be something else. What I want to know is how can *you* believe?" Goose responded.

"Because believing—" Icarus halted for a moment—"believing *anything* else is impossible."

Goose was haunted by Bill Townsend's words. Before Goose had met and married Megan, Bill had talked to Goose about faith and the end times.

"It's all about believing, buddy," Bill had said while they'd worked on Goose's pickup truck. It had been a lazy Sunday afternoon, after Bill had persuaded Goose to go to church with him that morning. They'd scheduled the afternoon for changing oil and doing light mechanical work on their vehicles. "See, you've been around the world a few times now. Fought in more wars than most men have ever seen. And you've come away from all of them whole, Goose. Have you ever wondered how that happened?"

Goose had. During those years, he'd seen good men die in the Middle East, in Bosnia, in Africa, and again in the Middle East.

"Is it because you're a good soldier, Goose?" Bill had asked. "I know you don't think that covers everything you've gone through. Just lucky? Nah, luck runs out. It's something more, and that's what's scaring you now."

Just when Bill had come into his life, Goose had struggled with his own personal problems. Despite his successes in the military, his life was empty. He'd supposed part of it was because Cal Remington had been accepted for OCS and was wearing lieutenant's bars and moving in different circles.

"Once you eliminate luck and superstition, get over all those ideas that you're actually that good or are in any way responsible for your survival despite the odds against you," Bill had continued, "then you come down to the hardest decision you'll ever make in your life. At least, in this life. You have to start looking at faith, at the plain and simple fact that God has a plan for you and it's not your time to check out."

As good-naturedly as he could then, Goose had argued against faith. Thankfully, Bill hadn't taken offense.

"Some people are just more stubborn than others," Bill had said. "But you know what? No matter how long it takes, God will wear you down. You'll be shown enough life, enough struggle and conflict, that ultimately you'll see that faith is the only way to go."

Goose had argued more, pointing out that faith in something—or Someone—that couldn't be weighed or measured went against everything he knew from his time in the military.

"You're looking at it wrong, Goose. Faith isn't just harder because you can't weigh and measure it. Faith is also easier because you can't weigh and measure it. There's no criteria you have to meet, no recon you have to do, no SOP to follow in order to become a believer and put your faith in God. All you have to do is open your heart and acknowledge Him, let Him work through your life as He sees fit."

"I can't believe God did this." Only after the words had left his lips did Goose know that he'd spoken out loud.

"I know. I had the same problem. Sometimes I still do." Icarus wiped his bloody face with a sleeve.

"I've got to go." Goose bent down to pick up his helmet, which had fallen off during their fight.

"Hear me out," Icarus said. "Please." He looked desperate. "I might not get out of this city alive. If Cody's men find me, I'm dead. Someone else needs to know what is going on."

Goose stood, but he wanted nothing more than to get back to his unit.

"Please, First Sergeant."

A truck rumbled by on the street at the alley mouth.

Suddenly aware that they were standing out in the open, Goose motioned toward the shade on the west side of the alley. "There."

Moving painfully, Icarus walked to an uneven stone wall, then slumped to a sitting position.

Goose sat beside him. He freed his canteen, cracked it open, then handed it to Icarus. They both drank.

"I'm a spy, First Sergeant," Icarus said.

"You're CIA," Goose said. "I knew that."

Icarus shook his head. "More than that. I'm also Mossad."

That surprised Goose. The CIA agent Alexander Cody hadn't said anything about that. The Mossad was Israel's spy group, one of the best in the world, and one of the most ruthless.

"Cody found out?" Goose asked.

Icarus shook his head. "No. That's my secret. But it was important that I tell you."

"You're a double agent."

"A triple agent, actually. I was Mossad, pretending to be a CIA agent, pretending to be a PKK terrorist."

Goose digested that with difficulty.

"In my assignment for the CIA," Icarus said, "I was supposed to infiltrate the PKK and set up a computer network inside their systems that would allow the CIA better access into the terrorist organizations."

"Terrorist cells don't communicate with each other much," Goose said, remembering all the training he'd had in counterterrorist measures. "That's one of the things that makes them so dangerous."

"But they're making more and more contact with each other," Icarus said. "Terrorist organizations are made up of men. Men are fallible. The erosion of the terrorist cells is a natural occurrence with the advent of the Internet and other electronic communications. The program I secretly installed into the PKK cell's computer systems allowed the CIA to better monitor that cell's activities as well as others they contacted. The progression of the program spread with each contact. The program is an amazing piece of work."

"But you were also spying on the CIA," Goose reminded.

"Yes. The Mossad have been on the alert ever since Dr. Rosenzweig invented his fertilizer. Israel's increased capacity to produce and provide crops in the Middle East as well as parts of Europe has greatly impacted markets the United States has controlled for decades. The possibility of Dr. Rosenzweig's fertilizer formula getting into the hands of the world was even more problematic."

"Do you think the U.S. government would—"

"Do anything they could to control the distribution of Dr. Rosenzweig's formula?" Icarus nodded. "Yes, I do. So do the Mossad commanders I work for."

"Have you been in touch with the Mossad?" Goose wanted to know how complicated the situation brewing in Sanliurfa was.

"No."

"So you haven't been able to arrange exfiltration?"

"No. For all I know, they believe I'm dead. The means I had of contacting them is gone. I can't get a message out."

"Would they come if you did?"

"Possibly," Icarus said. "Or send a sweeper team in to eliminate me and whatever I might give up." He paused. "Just talking to you like this, I've put your life at risk if they ever find out. So it would be in your best interest to limit who you reveal this conversation to."

Goose nodded.

"The reason the Mossad was watching the CIA," Icarus went on, "was due to some intelligence work they were doing in Romania."

"Romania?"

"Yes. Over the last several years, there has been a push in the intelligence circles around the world. When these new networks could be traced, which wasn't often, they led back to Romania."

Goose thought about the way OneWorld NewsNet happened to be on hand when the Turkish military effort as well as the U.S. and U.N. needed them most.

"Romania," Goose said, "doesn't seem like it would be a hotbed of international spying. For one thing, what could they hope to gain?"

Icarus was silent for a time. "What about the world, First Sergeant? Would that be enough?"

"This is insane." Goose tried to wrap his mind around the idea but couldn't. "How could Romania hope to take over the world?"

"Not Romania," Icarus said. "One man . . . no . . . I mean one being."

Goose looked at the other man.

"The Rapture has happened, First Sergeant," Icarus said in a soft voice. "Your son was taken by God, as were all the other children and all those believers who knew He would come and trusted in Him and accepted Him."

Tears stung Goose's eyes as he thought of Chris again.

"Don't feel too sad for your son," Icarus advised. "He's safe. No evil can ever touch him. He was an innocent. You need to believe that." He paused. "The people you have to worry about now are those who were left behind. For the next seven years, they'll be subjected to trials and tribulations that will kill many of them and put others through the most fearful things that a human can endure."

"What are you talking about?"

"It's the time of the Tribulation, First Sergeant. The time of final decisions of whether to believe or not to believe."

Goose remembered the times Bill had mentioned the Tribulation. The events that followed the Rapture were supposed to be horrific, but that was all Goose really remembered. Wait . . . there was something about the four horsemen and seals and trumpets . . . but he couldn't remember much else.

"Talk to Corporal Baker," Icarus advised. "I was raised in the faith of my country. The concept of Christianity as Baker follows it remains new to me. I am trying to learn, though."

"This can't be possible," Goose objected.

"Talk to him. He will be able to explain it better."

"You said the CIA alerted the PKK that you were a spy?"

"Yes."

"Why?"

"Because I'd discovered the other spyware program in the terrorist networks," Icarus said. "I wasn't supposed to do that."

"Other spyware program?"

"Yes. The one put there by the being in Romania."

"You keep referring to the person as a *being*."

Icarus worked his jaw gently. "Yes. That is what he is. While researching the CIA records, I found out that Section Chief Alexander Cody has had extensive dealings with that being."

"So Cody—"

"Isn't pursuing a wayward CIA agent." Icarus smiled. "He wants to kill me before I can reveal what he's been doing. Though if you told him I was a Mossad agent and he could find the information he needed to make that stick, he'd have all the excuse he needed to get away with my murder."

Goose struggled with all the concepts that were being dumped on him in addition to the loss of Chris. It was overwhelming.

"First Sergeant."

Goose shook his head. "I can't buy what you're telling me."

"It's the truth."

"If I believe it, I also have to believe that I'll never see my son again. I can't do that." Goose felt selfish as soon as he admitted that.

"Not true," Icarus said. "You just won't see him again in this life. Chris is with God, and he's waiting for the time when you'll be reunited. All you have to do is listen to the God you believe in before it is too late. He has a plan for you."

Goose thought of what he'd been through in the past few days. Tears welled in Goose's eyes. He pulled his knees up and buried his face against his forearms. *It's too much, God. You're asking too much. You can't expect me to give this much.*

"First Sergeant," Icarus said. "Goose."

Goose ignored him.

"Chris isn't hurting," Icarus said. "Everything I've talked to Corporal Baker about tells me that your son is in no pain. He's with God. He is happy. He knows that you will make the right decisions. He can wait, just as you must learn to. Isn't that what you would want for him? That he is happy and safe?"

A long time passed. Icarus sat beside Goose without speaking.

Gradually, Goose was able to push the pain and confusion away. He knew that Megan was getting through the situation back in Fort Benning, and that it was bad back there, too.

Icarus had a point. Chris wasn't in the middle of the mess at Benning. But Goose needed his son. He needed him, and he missed him with an ache that just wouldn't go away.

He had to be strong. For his men. For Chris. And for Megan. She had to know the things he had learned. Together, as they'd always done, they'd grow in their hope.

And in our faith, Goose thought. *God, please help me with my faith. I'm looking for You. I just can't seem to find my way to You right now.* Even as he prayed, though, part of him still felt foolish. But he did at least feel like he knew where to start asking questions.

After a time, he lifted his head. "So who is it?" Goose asked.

Icarus gave him a questioning look.

"The *being* in Romania," Goose said. "Who is it?"

Icarus hesitated. "A man named Nicolae Carpathia. Maybe you've heard of him."

"Yeah," Goose said. "I've heard of him."

"Are you aware that Carpathia is in New York City right now?"

Goose had heard some of the news talk going on around the reporters. They said Carpathia was a big deal. And Goose knew why Carpathia had pulled the satellite support for the struggling troops in Sanliurfa—so he wouldn't appear to be taking sides.

"Carpathia is going to address the United Nations," Icarus said.

"Yeah. So?"

"He has plans—many plans. I'm not privy to them, so I don't know why he is there. But I do know this. In Revelation in the Christian Bible, a man of power rises after the Rapture and manages to unite what is left of the world. The surviving population believes him at first to be a savior, but he isn't. He is there to subjugate and confuse those who have lived through the Rapture but still haven't found their faith. That is what Nicolae Carpathia will eventually do. It is what he *must* do."

"The Antichrist?" Goose asked, stunned. "You're saying Nicolae Carpathia is the Antichrist?"

Icarus looked at him for a moment then nodded. "Yes. That is exactly what I am saying."

"Who else knows this?"

"I've told only you—" Icarus hesitated—"but I can't be the only one who knows. There are others who have been looking for this thing to happen longer than you or I have been alive. Not everyone will be caught off guard. There is hope. Men like Corporal Baker will also rise and be heard, and their voices will sway those who need to be saved."

"You make it sound like we're at war. And not just with the Syrians."

"Make no mistake, Goose," Icarus said. "We *are* at war. All of us. With an enemy greater than any we have ever faced. And the stakes are our immortal souls."

"What are we supposed to do?"

"What every other warrior in battle does: we survive, and we pray that God strengthens us so we can make a difference. We pray for God to save our souls and show us the way."

Goose lowered his head for an instant, unable to believe what he was hearing. *God*, he prayed, *please guide me now. I need Your help. I've lost my way in this terrible place. What do I do?* For Icarus's words, as crazy as they seemed, had the ring of truth behind them.

For just an instant, the peace of God's presence filled Goose. Then he thought of Chris, lost to him forever. It hurt too much. If Icarus was right, Chris was lost to him as surely as if a war had killed him. Therefore, Icarus couldn't be right.

And when Goose looked up, Icarus was gone.

IN ONE CATACLYSMIC MOMENT
MILLIONS AROUND THE WORLD DISAPPEAR

Experience the suspense of the end times for yourself. The best-selling Left Behind series is now available in hardcover, softcover, and large-print editions.

1
LEFT BEHIND®
A novel of
the earth's last
days . . .

2
**TRIBULATION
FORCE**
The continuing
drama of those
left behind . . .

3
NICOLAE
The rise of
Antichrist . . .

4
**SOUL
HARVEST**
The world
takes sides . . .

5
APOLLYON
The Destroyer is
unleashed . . .

6
ASSASSINS
Assignment:
Jerusalem,
Target: Antichrist

7
**THE
INDWELLING**
The Beast takes
possession . . .

8
THE MARK
The Beast rules
the world . . .

9
DESECRATION
Antichrist takes
the throne . . .

10
**THE
REMNANT**
On the brink of
Armageddon . . .

11
ARMAGEDDON
The cosmic battle
of the ages . . .

12
**GLORIOUS
APPEARING**
The end of
days . . .

FOR THE MOST ACCURATE INFORMATION VISIT

www.leftbehind.com